A SMART ADDRESS

Six Dead and a Missing Cat

A. GILL-GRAY

First published in Great Britain in 2025 by
The Book Guild Ltd
Unit E2 Airfield Business Park,
Harrison Road, Market Harborough,
Leicestershire. LE16 7UL
Tel: 0116 2792299
www.bookguild.co.uk
Email: info@bookguild.co.uk

Copyright © 2025 A. Gill-Gray

The right of A. Gill-Gray to be identified as the author of this
work has been asserted by them in accordance with the
Copyright, Design and Patents Act 1988.

All rights reserved. No part of this publication may be
reproduced, transmitted, or stored in a retrieval system, in any form or by any means,
without permission in writing from the publisher, nor be otherwise circulated in
any form of binding or cover other than that in which it is published and without
a similar condition being imposed on the subsequent purchaser.

The manufacturer's authorised representative in the EU
for product safety is Authorised Rep Compliance Ltd,
71 Lower Baggot Street, Dublin D02 P593 Ireland (www.arccompliance.com)

This work is entirely fictitious and bears no resemblance to any persons living or dead.

Typeset in 11pt Minion Pro

Printed and bound in Great Britain by CMP UK

ISBN 978 1835742 433

British Library Cataloguing in Publication Data.
A catalogue record for this book is available from the British Library.

For my wife Lia – the best.

BODIES don't usually fall off roofs in the West End of Edinburgh. Yet that extraordinary occurrence happened on a warm August day in 2018.

The day began with a cloud-occluded sky and a spit of rain, but gradually brightened until reasonably strong sunshine – at least for Scotland's capital city – emerged in the late afternoon dappling the back gardens of Balmoral Square Mansions.

At this point it should be observed that the improved weather conditions were of no interest to the deceased. For Miss Arabella Pettygrew – a sixty-nine-year-old spinster known to her few acquaintances as Bella, though not in her hearing – had fallen from the top of her three-storey Victorian apartment building in the early hours of the morning.

The clamour of church bells drowned any signals of distress – screams of mortal agony or otherwise – that might have attended the event. In an ironic coincidence ordained by powers far beyond man's knowledge, the cathedral less than a hundred yards away was marking the feast day of the Transfiguration of Christ in the peeling of bells. Each of the mighty bronze bells was engraved with a name representing a heavenly or cardinal virtue: Justice. Fortitude. Humility. Faith. Temperance. Patience. Holy

Fear. Devotion. Hope. Peace. Charity. Only Prudence was missing from the litany. As investigators would later conclude, prudence was the one attribute the hapless victim had not shown.

Hurtling through the air at 120 miles per hour Miss Pettygrew's head initially glanced off a stone balcony smashing her face beyond recognition before impaling herself on the spike of a wrought-iron railing. The resulting impact ripped a fist-sized hole in her stomach causing some of the intestines to spill onto the pavement.

Unfortunately, the seagulls – a plague in the streets of modern-day Edinburgh – discovered Miss Pettygrew's body first and enjoyed what one might call their own feast day, making a meal out of the leaking corpse as it hung suspended from the railings. And all the while the sweet tintinnabulation echoed on the morning air as if to mock the macabre tableau.

A group of children playing football later in the private residents' gardens adorning the centre of the square found the scattered remains of what turned out to be a string of Miss Pettygrew's intestines, while a glistening eyeball, slick with blood, was discovered by a parking attendant on the roof of a light-blue Fiat 500.

DETECTIVE Inspector Richard Strawberry should have been a happy man. He had just piloted his electric bicycle through the glorious environs of Morningside and was sitting in a garden on a wonderful summer day. Furthermore, he had recently become involved in a relationship with Fiona McLuckie – the beautiful blonde rising star of Scottish curling. After a long, severe winter stuck in the dreich confines of Gayfield Square Police Station it was great to feel the heat on his skin in a genuine Scottish summer. Two weeks of temperatures in the mid-twenties until at least 7 p.m. Eating al fresco with his girlfriend in his small garden flat in Woodburn Terrace sans cardigan. Virtually unheard of in a country which is the natural constituency for anoraks, kagouls, and indeed all storm-proof clothing.

Yet here he was on a bench in Balmoral Square Mansions contemplating violent death and part of the small intestine of Arabella Pettygrew. He had read somewhere that the human intestine, if unravelled, stretches to more than twenty feet. The thought of that slick uncoiling induced a fleeting nausea. Not for the first time Strawberry wondered if he had embarked on the right career.

Charlie had been his motivation. The idea of finally

finding out about what had happened to Charlie on that terrible day so many years ago, the stomach-churning impact of which still made it feel like yesterday. What better way of solving a mystery that had haunted him since childhood than joining the police force. At the time of his graduation the police were pushing a campaign to recruit university entrants with the promise of quick career advancement. So he had taken the bait and done his stint at Tulliallan Police College emerging hardly at the top of the honour role, but somewhere in the middle and that had given him hope for a future career in uniform.

Now, however, he was having second thoughts. Possibly it was the fact that in ten years of policing he was no further forward in his personal quest than on day one. Charlie's disappearance was still a complete mystery in a case that had long since gone from cold to deep freeze status. Perhaps it was his lack of success in charge of the ongoing investigation Operation Treetops. Maybe it was an ominous sense of foreboding about this new mystery of a pensioner falling to her death in one of the most prestigious streets in Edinburgh. Or perhaps his good fortune in having a girlfriend like the ambitious and dazzling Fiona was making him reappraise his life.

The metallic screech of machine on metal jerked him from his reverie. Over the road a fireman was using a buzzsaw to cut through the railing, while two colleagues eased the corpse into a body bag. The sight of the iron arrowhead protruding from her stomach induced another wave of nausea for Strawberry as the firemen fought to zip up the bag.

No siren. No flashing light. No breaking speed limits.

No running stop signs. Emergency services are for the living. There would be no Lazarus-style resurrection for Arabella Pettygrew. The ambulance rolled quietly to the kerb. The paramedics – normally life-savers – were today in the less accustomed role of undertakers. Her grim remains were loaded aboard for the short journey to the morgue and the post-mortem.

Strawberry would know more the following morning when Angus McNiven, the police pathologist, deigned to finish his report.

Meantime, he was girding himself for the neighbours. The few who were still ambulatory had gathered at a discreet distance from the gruesome scene, speaking in hushed tones though not missing a single detail. They were no doubt harmless in their dotage. But Strawberry couldn't shake the metaphorical image of vultures preparing to feast on a carcass.

The other residents were indoors, either peeping from behind net curtains, or talking to neighbours on their answer to jungle drums – ancient black Bakelite phones. Most of them were north of geriatric and all of them were completely eccentric.

Balmoral Square Mansions had a certain reputation in Edinburgh. Like parts of the New Town, it was a highly privileged enclave of old money and fossilised views. It was a street of retired judges, clergymen, bankers and accountants. In a long-running debate, similar to the controversy over whether the famous links golfing community in East Lothian should be pronounced Gullane or Gillane, the name of their prestigious street stirred endless snobbish arguments among the residents.

More precisely it was the first word of the address. Was it pronounced Balmoral – the short utilitarian version – or *Baalmorale*? Most of the prominent long-standing residents favoured the latter arguing that you could not hurry a word with such royal associations. A regal name should be held on the tongue like a fine wine, its syllables elongated, savoured in the mouth and rolled out elegantly – a red-carpet word of such grandiosity as to be celebrated in a rich cacophony of vowels for those privileged few fortunate enough to reside at the address.

For Balmoral Square Mansions was the real McCoy. Nothing so vulgar or nouveau riche as Morningside or Stockbridge with their B-list Kensington-style yuppies, or the young, thrusting middle-class families decamped from London and the Home Counties. No, this was genuine dyed in the tartan and tweed Edinburgh where the first question was always 'What school did you go to?'. If the answer did not meet the required social criteria, there was no second question.

Entering Arabella Pettygrew's top-floor flat was a culture shock to Strawberry. The forensics team – looking like alien investigators in their white hooded coveralls and elasticated plastic shoe protectors – had already swept the flat searching for prints or suspicious body fluids. Nothing had been found. Nothing had been disturbed – and that was the understatement of the millennium.

Miss Havisham was the detective's first reaction as he surveyed the stacks of yellowing newspapers piled halfway up peeling wallpaper, cutlery and assorted china scattered on a clumsily varnished hall table, and a Ruth Rendell novel entitled *A Judgement in Stone*, lying on a rolled-up rug covered in plaster dust. He automatically picked up the book and placed it on the hall table.

Halfway down the hall an old cupola had simply been abandoned on the floor and when he looked at the ceiling he saw sagging plaster and damp watermarks with a bucket under a particularly damaged area.

Picking his way over loose floorboards, he discovered what he guessed was her lounge, if only because there was a black and white TV on a broken-down coffee table squeezed into a corner. There seemed to be no rhyme or reason to the way the flat was arranged.

Moving further into the interior he found a toilet, perfectly clean, but with another leaking ceiling, and a tired though orderly kitchen with bent and rusting horizontal bars running halfway up the outside of the window.

The most surprising room of all was at the rear of the property. It was floodlit with sun streaming through a large glass cupola. The floor of the room was also reinforced glass with a dizzying and disorienting view directly down to the landing on the stair below. But the room was completely bereft of furniture or any other sign of domestic comfort. Bare walls, bags of plaster and a set of ladders sufficed as its utilitarian decoration.

In contrast, Miss Pettygrew's bedroom – although still in need of a good paint job and featuring the ubiquitous watermarks on the ceiling – seemed an oasis of calm arrangement compared with the Narnia of chaos in every other room. Strawberry noticed it was the only room in the house with curtains.

A flash of black fur shot from under the bed evoking an involuntary gasp from the detective. Shit – a cat! Of course every old spinster had to have a cat and he should have anticipated something like this. He hadn't though and he could feel the effects immediately. His eyes were already itching and now his nose was running. The sneezing started as he rummaged in his pockets for the inhaler.

He began running to the door, coughing as he fled, searching frantically all the while for his precious inhaler as his breathing grew more ragged. He had to get away from the bloody cat before he had a full-blown asthma attack. He was outside on the landing and gasping for air when his fingers closed round the inhaler in an inside jacket pocket.

He was triggering the device and greedily puffing the medication when he heard the flat-footed sound of his colleagues on the roof. As his breathing calmed, he made a mental note to call the RSPCA. His condition wasn't the cat's fault, after all. Then he returned to concentrating on the grim reality of the investigation.

Angus Robertson – fresh out of Tulliallan having come second top in the honours roll – was the youngest detective Strawberry had ever seen. "Mark my words, that boy will go high," was Superintendent Bert Rothesay's verdict when assigning Robertson to Strawberry's team. Strawberry had no doubt of it. The smart wee bastard was already high. On the roof to be precise – and, if Strawberry was not mistaken, he could hear him coming down now.

"That ladder is dangerous, sir. Not for anyone of a vertiginous disposition," reported Robertson as he entered the apartment slightly breathless from his exertions.

Strawberry was still breathless for an entirely different reason he did not broadcast to his colleagues. He went on the offensive in a bid to cover his malady. "You mean it wouldn't be good for anyone who doesn't like heights, Robertson. I know we're in the police force, but do try to speak English in simple, comprehensible sentences."

"Yes, sir. Sorry, sir."

"Anyway, that's why I sent you up there. One look at that ladder going vertically up into a space you couldn't swing a cat in (he smiled to himself as he thought of Miss Pettygrew's now-orphaned moggie) in the pitch-black with a small trapdoor at the end, and I thought, this is a job for an honours-roll cadet whose dad was a former chief constable. Anyway, enough of this badinage – sorry, Robertson, I meant joking. Your report, please."

"Well, forensics couldn't find anything untoward – sorry – I mean suspicious. It's a flat roof and it's in pretty bad condition. Someone's tried to repair it with masking tape and not done a very good job."

"I can well imagine that, Robertson. One look at that ceiling in here gives the game away. The place is leaking like a sieve. Any trip hazards?"

"No, sir."

"Any blood, or other bodily fluids?"

"Nothing, sir. A clean bill of health from forensics."

"An unfortunate description, Robertson, given that Miss Pettygrew is currently lying in the morgue with an iron railing sticking out of her guts. All right, thank you. Get back to Gayfield and write your report." Strawberry sighed. "I'm going to start interviewing the neighbours."

MARJORIE Agincourt lived in the apartment two floors below the late Arabella Pettygrew. On the phone making the interview appointment – apparently a challenge for Mrs Agincourt's diary, despite the fact that she rarely left her home – Strawberry had been given an indication of what he might expect.

"I have no idea of how I can assist you, Inspector," she said in her most regal Jean Brodie tones – rich in self-regard and oblivious to the world beyond her privileged address. "It may be difficult for you to believe but – although we were neighbours for the best part of thirty years – I was never in her home – and while my beloved Hamish was alive we rarely socialised. I would describe Bella as a classic spinster and a bit of a hermit, certainly in her later years."

"Even so, it would be helpful to our inquiries if I could speak to you in person, either at the station, or your home." Strawberry heard the exasperated sigh at the end of the line.

"Station! Police station! I have never been in a police station in my life and I don't intend to start now. Full of women of ill repute. Vagrants. The flotsam and jetsam of society. What would Hamish think? No, a police station is out of the question. If you must interview me it will have to be at my home." With that Mrs Agincourt's black Bakelite receiver went down with a solid clunk terminating the conversation. Strawberry was thus prepared for a difficult encounter and so it proved.

Sitting in Marjorie Agincourt's drawing room – a space big enough to play five-a-side football – the detective marvelled at the secret world that lay behind the Victorian facade of so many of the capital's grand streets.

The crystal chandelier, tinkling gently as Strawberry had moved across the original parquet oak floor, would not have been out of place in a castle.

The walls were decorated in a series of large oil paintings depicting Scottish landscapes – glens at sunset, mountains at sunrise, or shrouded in a dawn mist. Other canvasses featured iconic symbols. The Forth Rail Bridge with the Flying Scotsman racing across belching a plume of white smoke high above the red iron stanchions. The statue of Bonnie Prince Charlie proudly standing in Glenfinnan at the mouth of Loch Shiel.

Pride of place went to the military paintings. The charge of the Scots Greys on their magnificent white horses at Waterloo, and a reproduction of some obscure African conflict featuring a thin line of crimson uniforms about to be overrun by Zulu warriors. But the most imposing image was the life-size portrait of a soldier in full uniform, ceremonial sword at his waist, holding a busby, and sporting a jet-black walrus moustache.

"I see you like my paintings. That's my Hamish in his pomp," trilled a voice somewhere in the vicinity of the distant bay window.

'Bizarre' was the word that leapt into Strawberry's head as he drew nearer and beheld Mrs Marjorie Agincourt.

Perched on a threadbare gold velvet chaise longue buttressed by a scatter of floral cushions, she looked like a faded maharajah. She was wearing a cream-coloured kaftan and a pink turban emblazoned with a badge depicting an elephant, beneath which were two crossed swords. It occurred to Strawberry that both Mrs Agincourt and her late husband, Hamish, shared a penchant for big hats.

Mrs Agincourt began tapping the floor with a silver-handled walking stick. From the indentations on the parquet surrounding her seat Strawberry deduced that (a) this was her favourite spot and (b) the tapping was an unconscious gesture in times of stress or irritation. Had he been a betting man his money would have been on the latter emotion.

"We were stationed in Asia. He was mentioned in despatches during the Malayan Emergency. Stopped a mob of dirty commies breaking into the British Embassy. Shot a couple of them and was wounded in the leg himself." Mrs Agincourt, small and stick-thin in her oriental clothing, seemed to grow a couple of inches at the recollection.

In an instant, like brooding thunderclouds, her mood darkened. "He made the rank of major before the bastards judged him medically unfit and retired him," she said, the sourness creeping into her voice. "Then we came back to sunny Edinburgh. Oh, he put a brave face on it. Immersed himself in the Garden Association, but he was never the same again, poor dear. Never got over the loss of his career. He was a soldier man and boy. Died three years ago. They said from cancer, but I think what really killed him was the weather in this damned city. The damp got into his bones."

Strawberry made what he hoped was a sympathetic face as he silently cursed not getting one of the constables along. Female empathy and all that. Brenda Gunn from lost and found would have been ideal. It was in the eyes. She had that forlorn golden Labrador look. Strawberry knew he didn't have the gender, or the eyes, for such maudlin occasions.

As suddenly as it had arisen Mrs Agincourt snapped out of her sentimental musings into acid sarcasm. "So what can I do for you, Mr Raspberry?"

"It's Strawberry, actually."

"Raspberry, strawberry, gooseberry. What kind of name is that, Detective? Are you a gooseberry, or perhaps you're a camp – a camp jamboree." At this Mrs Agincourt collapsed into a fit of the giggles stamping her cane on the floor while Strawberry looked on in bemusement. Then the penny dropped. Camp. She thought he was gay.

"Actually, I am going out with the most wonderful girl." *As if it's any of your business, you old crone*, he thought to himself.

"Oh yes and what is she – a Girl Guide? Does she like Scout jamborees too?" And she was off again, cackling like one of the witches in *Macbeth*.

Despite his best efforts, Strawberry found himself rising to the bait of this preposterous old hag. "Fiona McLuckie is an up and coming star in the world of Scottish curling. Perhaps you have heard of her, or seen her on television?"

"Never watch television. Opium of the brain-dead masses," sniffed Mrs Agincourt. "The wireless, Radio 4, that's where I get my information. Curling? Curling, you say. Is that even sport? Don't Red Indians play that game with people's heads?"

"Lacrosse," said Strawberry. "I think you might be referring to the possible origins of lacrosse played by Native Americans."

Strawberry moved on quickly before he was ensnared in another facile conversation. "At any rate, I am here on the serious matter of the unexplained death of your neighbour Miss Arabella Pettygrew. We believe she fell from the roof. Can you shed any light on her state of mind?"

"You mean, was she a loonie?" Marjorie emphasised the last word in a way unique to the Scots' tongue with the emphasis on the last syllable. "Did she kill herself? Is that the implication of your question, Mr Raspberry?"

Strawberry decided to ignore any further juvenile barbs. "Yes, it is, Mrs Agincourt."

"Bella was certainly eccentric (*pots and kettles* thought Strawberry) but I would never put her down as suicidal. No doubt she was on the roof doing her usual thing and simply fell."

"Her usual thing?"

"Why, yes. Aren't you supposed to be a detective?" Mrs Agincourt scoffed, but continued. "The woman was obsessed with the roof. Rain or shine, well, particularly rain (she whinnied at her joke) and she was up there taping the roof."

A sixty-nine-year-old woman climbing a fifteen-foot vertical ladder onto a roof two hundred feet above the ground. It was beyond reason, thought Strawberry. Mrs Agincourt seemed to divine his thoughts.

"Bella wasn't your average female pensioner, Inspector. I understand that she had been very sporting in her youth – climbing Scottish mountains with her *pappa*. She continued to be absurdly fit walking in the Braids, the Pentlands, Blackford Hills – all over the place – taking photos as she went with that ancient Box Brownie of hers." Mrs Agincourt whinnied again at the thought. "So the roof and heights presented no challenge to her and over the years she became obsessed with repairing it as the leaks increased."

"Why didn't she get the repairs done professionally? Enlist the support of neighbours in the stair? After all, the roof is a communal responsibility in an apartment building."

"With age and spinsterhood, Bella became ever more reclusive, Inspector. Perhaps she was ashamed of her apartment. I have no idea. Over the years she did engage different builders but they were far from reliable."

"I know the kind. Bodgit and Scarper," said Strawberry.

Mrs Agincourt looked at him blankly. "I don't think she engaged any company of that name."

"Well, thank you for your time. You have been very helpful."

"I doubt that, Mr Raspberry. Anyway, toodaloo."

Once more Strawberry trekked across the drawing room to the tinkling accompaniment of the crystal chandelier. He could not delay the inevitable any longer. It was clearly time for him to go onto the roof – and judging from this interview – throw himself off.

The minute he was gone, Marjorie Agincourt picked up the black Bakelite handset and dialled a number she knew without consulting her pocket book. "It's about Bella. We need to talk," she said, without the slightest trace of sarcasm in her voice.

THE blackness was all consuming. But Strawberry didn't dare search for his smartphone to illuminate proceedings. He needed both hands for the ascent of the ladder – even though they were sweating from the nervous energy of hauling himself up the rungs. "Come on, man, only fifteen feet, one step at a time," he muttered to himself as he tried to control his breathing.

He hated heights. He never went near cliff edges, or precipitous paths. He remembered having to climb the Scott Monument a few years ago after someone had launched themselves from the top, and hugging the inside railing for every one of the 287 steps.

"Must be nearly there," he breathed in the sepulchral darkness. Slowly releasing one hand, he reached tentatively upwards until his questing fingers found the trapdoor. He pushed. The door remained stubbornly shut, but he heard a metallic rasping sound. Christ, a lock or a bolt; which was it? "That smart wee bastard should have warned me," he said, cursing Robertson. Steadying himself on the rung, he reached again, fingers scrabbling along the surface of the door until he found a bolt. He pulled and the bolt eased back in one smooth movement, which made sense given the bloody number of times Arabella Pettygrew was up here, he thought.

Another shove and the door clanged open and daylight flooded in. Strawberry readied himself for one final effort and hauled himself onto the roof where he lay like a floundered fish gulping in the air for several minutes. He stood up gingerly, looking directly at the ground until the dizziness subsided before raising his gaze.

The roof was entirely flat stretching for about 100 feet with a large cupola in the middle. Black masking tape had been crudely applied to much of the surface – layer after layer – over the years in what must have been a vain attempt to halt the ingress of water. At the outer limit of what he judged was the front of the building there was a low parapet wall – a very low parapet wall! Shit! He was going to have to do this.

Bent double as if fighting a gale – though there was not a breath of wind – he edged towards the parapet. Then for the last few yards got on all fours and crawled. *Thank God no one can see this performance*, he thought. If he hadn't been on his hands and knees he might have missed the tiniest impression of a shoe. By the appearance of the ridges, it looked like a trainer with a distinct break where the front part of the tread was worn away. But then that decision would have to be for forensics. How could the clowns in Fettes Avenue have missed it? Someone was going to get a rocket the minute he got off this godforsaken roof. Summoning all his courage, he stood up shakily and made himself look out across the landscape.

There was the communal garden 200 feet below and beyond that the twin spires of one of the city's many churches and the grand streets, like so many places in Edinburgh, named after Victorian English monarchs, noblemen and grandees. Further out, the roofs of the New Town, where Robert Louis Stevenson had penned his famous adventure *Treasure Island* as he looked out over the Forth imagining pirates in Queensferry.

Beginning to hyperventilate at the stress induced by the height, he forced his mind to concentrate on pleasant thoughts – his girlfriend, Fiona, his pride in her curling prowess, the satisfaction of a clean and tidy flat – a place for everything and everything in its place.

As his breathing came under control, he was able to focus on the parapet wall. It was in better shape than the roof, but he saw one small section that might have been looser than the rest. It looked like one of the capstones was close to being dislodged.

He was going to have to do this. Taking deep, slow breaths, he girded himself to crawl the last few feet to the base of the parapet. Then gradually, inch by inch, he hauled himself up the wall chanting repeatedly, "Don't look down, do NOT look down."

As his head reached the top, his fingers touched the loose stone. Then his hand was grasping thin air as the stone fell from the roof to the pavement below. There was a terrible metallic crash then the deafening whoop of a car alarm.

As he scrambled on all fours across the roof to the trapdoor, he wondered if forensics had even bothered seriously investigating the roof.

THE banks of harsh sodium lights reflected a variety of wickedly sharp stainless-steel knives and saws hanging on the wall above an equally shiny industrial-sized sink and drainer.

The pitiless glare also revealed the corpse of Arabella Pettygrew in all its gory detail. She was lying face up (or what was left of her face) on the white marble table. The body was bone-white, apparently leached of all blood. Strawberry knew it would be rock-hard and ice-cold.

He remembered the last sight of his father in the funeral parlour. He had kissed his brow in final farewell. He would never forget the coldness of the skin and its granite hardness.

The police pathologist Angus McNiven was immune to such emotion. Bent over his charge, he barely grunted when Strawberry entered the room. Then decided to launch into a lecture for the detective's benefit.

"There are fourteen bones in the face and twenty-two in the skull. The back of the head survived relatively intact. But the deceased hit the balcony face-first resulting in twelve facial bones being broken. Only the maxilla bones remained intact, while the nasal bones were pulverised and most of the other bones were smashed beyond recognition, as you can see."

Strawberry saw only too well and gratefully accepted the face mask offered by McNiven's female assistant.

Seemingly oblivious to Strawberry's discomfort, McNiven continued his macabre litany of the injuries sustained. "The impact of the body hitting the iron railing caused immediate and massive trauma to the stomach – though she would undoubtedly have been dead before this juncture."

McNiven moved the body onto its front – the sound was a soft, wet slap like a large fish being moved on a fishmonger's slab. He pointed at an area behind the knee. "There is one inexplicable injury," he said. "You will observe there are faint, slightly inflamed weals on the back of both legs. It's very difficult to be certain but this would possibly indicate that the deceased has either come into contact with an object, or been struck by something."

Strawberry saw the marks, but found himself thinking instead about worms. A morass of slimy grey worms slithering and sliding and Miss Pettygrew sitting bolt upright on the pathologist's table and hauling an interminably long iron spike from her stomach in a sucking sound that seemed to go on forever.

The overhead lights suddenly felt much brighter. McNiven and his assistant appeared much bigger and louder and like some macabre mantra, the pathologist was repeating the same phrases over and over again: "facial bones smashed beyond recognition" and "immediate and massive trauma to the stomach". The ceiling, the marble slab, Arabella Pettygrew's bleached and bloodless corpse, the razor-sharp saw and stainless-steel knives, started to spin faster and faster – and Strawberry blacked out.

He came round slowly to find himself staring up at a large pair of breasts. "Brrrrr – brrrr – brrrr." Had he really just made that sound like a sexually obscene phone ring tone? Please, God – no! The only woman he knew with breasts like that was 'Brrrenda'. Had he actually spoken out loud the name of the female constable from lost and found in a moment of uncomprehending lust?

Then as his vision returned he saw with the most blessed relief that it was not his colleague with the sad puppy-dog eyes, but McNiven's assistant.

Recumbent on the morgue floor, inhaling the smell of the linoleum combined with an astringent floor cleaner, he promptly turned on his side and vomited.

THE Glaikit Twins' arrival in Balmoral Square Mansions was announced in a cloud of belching smoke from the rusting exhaust of their clapped-out Ford Transit.

The van's occupants, Bob and Ginger Duncan, had earned the nickname at secondary school for their extraordinary stupidity. Their father was a Geordie, but they had moved to Musselburgh – a small town on the outskirts of Edinburgh – when they were children.

Nor were they twins, but very physically different-sized brothers. Bob was small, dark and always looked in need of a good feed, while Ginger was the opposite extreme – a freckled giant with a paunch to match. Now middle-aged, the pair had been on the dole for over a year with the collapse of the building trade during the recession.

But today the roofers were in high spirits. They had the feeling their luck was turning as they parked and made their way along the street.

"It's been a while, Ginger," said Bob.

"Aye, a while. What has, Bob?"

Bob sighed in exasperation. "A while since we were in this fancy street. Remember the last job at No. 37? That was a good one. We made a killing there without raising a sweat. Kicked a few tiles loose. Broke a few more. Nicked the replacements from St Oliphant's roof. Then charged the old dear a thousand quid for half a day sunbathing on the roof. That's what I call a proper job – a result, Ginger."

"Aye, a result, right enough. Is that why we're here again, Bob? For another result at No. 37?"

"Not the same place, you daft bugger. That would be stupid. No, pastures new, Ginger. Number 15 – the Tweedies, remember? We did the quote last week, but we'll milk them for a bit more than that. Remember the apartment – a palace."

"Three bogs with showers and that velvet bog paper. Who can afford that?" There was wonder in Ginger's voice.

"Right you are, Ginger. Just let me do the talking."

"Fine. But remember, Bob, I'll need ma dinner."

Bob nodded indulgently and started singing 'Fog on the Tyne' as they sauntered to the job. Ginger joined in the chorus.

Three hours later they had accomplished the first part of their fraudulent modus operandi. The tiles on the Tweedies' roof had been kicked loose, while others had been broken. That feat of vandalism had taken fifteen minutes and they spent the rest of the time sitting around smoking.

Ginger's growling stomach insisted it was dinner-time, so they climbed back in the van for a break before completing part two of the scam – stealing tiles from the church roof later under cover of darkness.

A copy of Bob's favourite rag, the *Hoots Mon*, was on the dashboard. He had been in too much of a hurry to look at it this morning. But now, while Ginger was in the back wolfing down a second Greggs sausage roll, Bob picked up the paper.

DEATH PLUNGE HORROR screamed the front-page headline. Underneath, the story raced on in its usual breathless, sensational prose.

> *A 69-year-old woman plunged to her death yesterday from a roof in one of Edinburgh's most prestigious streets. The body – discovered in the early morning hours – was impaled on railings. Scavenging seagulls had already scattered various body parts by the time her grisly remains were discovered. Police remained tight-lipped about the horrifying scene in the city's fashionable West End. A police spokesman said: 'It's too early to comment on whether the incident is a tragic accident – or whether there are any suspicious circumstances. Our investigations are continuing.' The woman has not been named.*
>
> *Meanwhile, traffic warden Ravinder Singh made a macabre discovery on his rounds. He said: 'I was about to give penalty fine on car parked without ticket. I was taking mobile photo when noticing something on roof. It was eye. All bloody with string attached. Oh my days, so shock.*

Bob turned to his brother – a look of alarm on his face. "Ginger, you remember that warden who booked us last time we were here?"

Ginger spluttered pastry flakes and bits of grey meat that looked more like motorway infill than sausage as he replied. "Uh huh. Slapped it on our windscreen. Said he couldn't do anything once it was slapped on the windscreen. The bastard."

"Never mind that. What did he look like?"

"That's easy. Foreign. Asian bloke. Crap English. Should learn…"

Throwing the paper back on the dash, Bob was reversing the van in a screech of burning rubber before his brother could finish the sentence.

MARJORIE Agincourt was in her usual window seat in the drawing room: custodian of the street, scourge of litter-louts and kerbside furniture dumpers. Despite Olympic-class competition, she was also the greatest nosey parker in Balmoral Square Mansions.

Her principal irritation and number one target were those dog lovers – and there were many in the West End – who allowed their animals to defecate on the pavement without cleaning up the mess. It was not unknown for her to yell from her second-floor apartment – in the manner of earlier times when Edinburgh tenement dwellers emptied their waste shouting 'gardyloo' – "Baggy" at such offenders.

The second most heinous crime on her list were neighbours who, upon finding the communal skips full, simply left their bin bags on the street for the seagulls to tear apart. Donning a pair of old yellow washing-up gloves, she had gone through the abandoned bags on several occasions braving the stinking nappies, plastic milk bottles, and rancid half-eaten tins of baked beans in the search for any letter or document that would reveal the miscreant's name and address. If successful, she would pick up her black Bakelite telephone and report the offence to the environmental authorities. An interfering woman, though hardly stupid, Marjorie knew the council was unlikely to take any action. But reporting the misdemeanours made her feel so much better.

This morning, however, she had noticed something entirely different – though no less disturbing. Employing her husband's field glasses that lived permanently on a nearby coffee table (a personal gift from Montie following the Battle of El Alamein) Marjorie focused the powerful binoculars on the communal gardens in the middle of the square.

During the past few days she had begun to notice unusual activity. First, the regular team seemed to have been replaced by another company. Second, and much more disconcerting, was the fact that they didn't appear to have any idea about pruning the vegetation sympathetically. They seemed to be simply slashing the tops off the trees willy-nilly without any regard to the aesthetic pleasure the gardens gave to her and other residents lacking the benefit of their own private garden.

She suspected the hiring of such obviously amateur arborists was a cost-cutting move on the part of the council. But she had to have more evidence, so she readjusted the binoculars and zoomed in on one particularly frenzied individual hacking wildly with a chainsaw.

The figure in green overalls bearing the legend Happy Trails Tree Surgeons swam into vision so enlarged that he seemed to be in the drawing room with her. Slightly dizzy at the magnification, she swung the field glasses towards another figure in overalls standing in the middle of the parkland – and almost fell off her chair. The man was staring straight back at her through his own set of binoculars.

"**SILLY** old bint just about had a canary. That'll teach her," laughed Dougie Nichols, lowering his binoculars.

But it was a nervous laugh. As leader of the surveillance team he knew it was imperative that they remain undercover. Blowing that cover would wreck weeks of planning and ruin any possibility of a successful outcome for Operation Treetops.

In turn, it would be a major setback for his own police career – a prospect the ambitious Nichols could not contemplate.

As if reading his thoughts his deputy David Meikle chipped in. "Maybe we could scare the busybody off, boss. Send a uniform round."

Nichols tried to disguise his impatience at the gauche remark. He understood that Meikle was young and his heart was in the right place – even if his head wasn't.

"I'm afraid that's precisely the last thing we should do. Such a move would flag up a police presence to the people we're watching. At the very least they would take greater care. Worst case – it might even scare them off. Then we'd have to start all over again and lose all the investment and man-hours we've put into this investigation. We are close to a result now. I can feel it. So the best thing to do is keep our heads down until we have enough evidence to nick these people."

Privately though, Nichols was concerned about the dramatic turn of events with the death of Arabella Pettygrew. Could there be a connection with the incident and the case he was investigating? Or was it pure coincidence? The trouble was that Nichols did not believe in coincidence. No professional police officer with years of experience ever did. Ninety per cent of the time there was a link. The tragic accident, suicide, or murder of the old woman could not have happened at a worse time for his inquiry – and now that bastard Strawberry was all over it.

Nichols knew Strawberry of old. They had been contemporaries at Tulliallan, had graduated from the same class and joined the Lothian and Borders force (as it was then before the amalgamation) at the same time. They had never liked each other. Nichols was a plain-speaking, old-school policeman, while Strawberry was the new kind of liberal the force seemed to be attracting. Wishy-washy when action was called for, yet maddeningly on-point in the new regime of political correctness. And worst of all – Strawberry was in overall charge of Operation Treetops.

Nichols's musings were interrupted by a series of curses from the leafy canopy somewhere above him. "Fucking seagulls."

Nichols recognised the voice of PC Derek Murch and seconds later the frazzled figure emerged in a thrash of arms from his perch in the upper boughs of a tree. When the head of Murch finally appeared it was decorated with a splatter of white bird shit in his hair and running down his cheek.

"That's the third time this week, sir. Bloody vermin. Can't we shoot the buggers?"

Nichols tried to hide the grin – though Murch's colleagues, who had all suffered the same aerial bombardment, were guffawing at his misfortune.

"What's your plan?" asked Nichols. "Wander along to the firearms section and sign out a Glock? The quartermaster says, 'And what do you intend doing with the gun, PC Murch?' and you say: 'I just want to slaughter some seagulls who keep shitting on my head.' Why not go the whole hog and borrow a sub-machine gun from one of our guys at the airport? Setting aside the fact that they are a protected species, have you considered the possibility of collateral damage? What if we hit one of the residents in Balmoral Square Mansions? Don't you think that might give us a bigger problem than a splat of bird shit on your head?"

For a second Nichols visualised the image of the nosey parker with the binoculars lying in a pool of blood in her drawing room. At least that would be more effective than sending a uniform round. He shook his head to banish the thought. "No, I don't think that idea will fly, Murch. We'll simply have to grin and bear it."

"How about an air rifle then, sir?"

MARJORIE Agincourt was in a state of high agitation. She had been fretting all day about the shocking fright the man with the binoculars had given her.

What possible reason could he have for spying on her in her home? Was he a peeping Tom? Some kind of depraved beast who might creep up the stairs in the middle of the night, break into her apartment and inflict heaven knows what abomination against her person?

She shuddered at the thought and, in her mounting dread, gazed upon the painting of her dead husband. "Hamish – Hamish! My protector," she wailed. "If only you were here now, you would know what to do. Unsheathe your sword and cut off his thingummyjig if he dared enter my boudoir."

But Hamish was not here. She must steel herself, be brave and act.

That is what her husband had done in the Malayan Emergency. Without hesitation or any thought for his personal safety he had leapt to the defence of the realm, taken out his revolver and slaughtered the filthy communists threatening to invade the British Embassy.

That is what she must do. Her home was her embassy, her sanctuary. She did not possess a firearm, but somehow she must defend her honour against the savage in the garden. Even so, Marjorie wrung her hands at her desperate situation. Action now! Concentrate on the options.

She found herself staring at the chunky black Bakelite telephone. Her lifeline to the outside world. Option 1. Phone the police and that annoying Mr Raspberry. She couldn't bring herself to do it. Option 2. Phone Nigel Smail, the chairman of the Garden Association.

She had wanted to contact him all day after the sacrilege of what she had witnessed those people, who called themselves 'tree surgeons', do to her beloved trees.

She looked across the acres of her drawing room to the grandfather clock. The distance was so great she had to shuffle ten yards to read the time. "Forty-five hairs past a sleepy freckle," she mumbled in childhood memory of a nonsensical rhyme.

It was 8.45 p.m. Late for civilised communication, but this was an emergency. Also, like Raspberry, Nigel Smail was 'a camp'. That was common knowledge in Balmoral Square Mansions. Perhaps camps stayed up later than normal people? Clutching the receiver, she promised herself that she would hang up if Nigel's new 'bottom boy' answered. He did – and in her anxiety – she didn't.

"Jeremy Sheldrake," came the piercingly thin voice at the other end of the line. "Who is calling?"

"Let me speak to Mr Smail, please."

"Please state your name and I will see if he is available."

This was insufferable. Nigel was seventy if he was a day, and here she was kowtowing to his fifteen-year-old bottom boy for an audience.

"It's Marjorie. Tell Nigel it's Marjorie."

"Will he know you?"

Marjorie bit her tongue so hard she almost drew blood. "Marjorie Agincourt. I'm a neighbour on the Garden Association. I must speak to him. It's an emergency."

She heard the clunk of Nigel's black Bakelite phone go down, Sheldrake's piping voice summoning the master and then Nigel himself puffing towards the receiver.

"Madge. *Quelle surprise!* What can I do for you on this delightful summer evening?"

She hated being called Madge, which is why Nigel did it. Ignoring the taunt, Marjorie decided to come straight to the point.

"Nigel, I apologise for the lateness of my call, however, I am concerned. There's something odd going on in the garden. As you are chairman of the association I thought it best to contact you."

On the few occasions when Marjorie had conversed with Nigel Smail, she had found it difficult to get a word in edgeways as he loved the sound of his own voice.

This time there was silence on the end of the line. Finally, almost hesitantly, Nigel filled the static void. "Don't worry, we're never in bed until after ten. Please expand, my dear."

Trying to banish the carnal image of Nigel and a youth rolling around under the covers, Marjorie elaborated. "Have you noticed that our regular gardeners have disappeared and been replaced by a company called Happy Trails Tree Surgeons?"

Now in full flow Marjorie rushed on. "I tried to find them in the *Yellow Pages*, but there was no trace of any such name. My first concern is that they are perhaps amateurs hired by the council to save money because they appear to be hacking in truly barbaric fashion at the trees without any thought for their beauty or historic nature."

"I had noticed the change in personnel, Madge. As association chairman it is my job to see everything – you can be assured of that fact."

Marjorie noted that Nigel was back to his pompous self.

"Indeed the council wrote informing me that there would be a temporary alteration in the gardening arrangements. Unfortunately they did not furnish any further information as to the reason. So I am as much in the *foncé* as you. But you said that was your first concern. What is your second?"

Nigel might be a camp, but she had to admit that he didn't miss a trick.

"I had the most alarming experience. I was sitting in my window minding my own business, but obviously keenly interested in the devastation of our communal garden. For greater clarity, I used Hamish's field glasses (she could feel the blush coming up from her throat) to see…"

"Of course, I understand, Madge."

She could hear the smirk in his voice, but was too anxious about the incident and pressed on. "Yes, well, I identified the company name on one man's overalls. Then I switched the focus to another one and found him staring straight at me, in the privacy of my drawing room, with a pair of binoculars!"

Nigel couldn't help himself. "Sounds a trifle *pots et bouilloires*, Madge. Anyway, it does seem strange. I can't imagine what a horticulturist would be doing with binoculars. As chance would have it our next meeting of the Garden Association is tomorrow evening. It's the Cruduckers turn to host. I will add your concerns to the agenda."

MARJORIE was standing eye to glittering eye with the mounted head of a miniature crocodile on the wall of the Cruduckers' hallway. The reptilian jaws of the stuffed creature had almost dislodged her turban so packed was the corridor.

Marjorie had never seen a meeting of the Garden Association so crowded. There was standing room only in Fanny and Emile Cruducker's exotic basement and the hubbub was deafening. Most of the square's residents seemed to be there and involved in animated conversations with neighbours they would normally barely nod to in the street.

Then it dawned on her. This was the first time such an assembly had taken place since Arabella Pettygrew's death and her neighbours – aghast yet simultaneously swooning with excitement – were trawling over every grisly morsel of the event. Swopping stories, sharing revelations, expounding theories as to the cause of her dramatic demise. And where more appropriate to air such views than the Gormenghast-style surroundings of the Cruduckers' apartment.

Amid the pandemonium, Marjorie took the opportunity to look around. The eccentric American couple had lived most of their lives in the square, but they had travelled extensively. And, as is the mode of Americans who venture beyond their own borders, had collected all manner of paraphernalia. Their speciality appeared to be heads, ranging from the aforementioned baby crocodile head to what looked like a very real pygmy head sitting under a lamp in the corner of their dark red lounge. Another favourite in this emporium of gewgaws was a large collection of pots and pans hanging from the ceiling of a brightly lit yet chaotic kitchen.

The resounding crash of a gavel silenced the throng. Nigel Smail, seated at a table with the association secretary, Dorothea Hislop, called the meeting to order.

"Please, ladies and gentlemen. We have a very full agenda this evening and the only way to get through it is to have attention and orderliness.

"First, a few words in remembrance of one of our own. Arabella Pettygrew's untimely demise has been a terrible shock to us all. I did not know the lady well. She did not attend Garden Association meetings." At this, Nigel could not help a dismissive sniff. "But she lived among us for many years and I am sure I speak for us all in extending condolences to her family and friends."

Nigel cleared his throat in what was clearly aimed at being a full stop to the brief tribute. Then someone standing at the back of the room began reciting the Lord's Prayer, all heads automatically bowed, and another sixty seconds elapsed. Nigel – with no religion apart from a fussy pedantry – made a second attempt to gain the attention of the room. "Dorothea, would you be so kind as to read the minutes of the last meeting, please."

As Dorothea droned on, Fanny Cruducker's head

visibly drooped. Then she began snoring, a soft purr at first, but gradually building to the sonorous intensity of a small motor-bike. Emile nudged her gently with no effect upon, by this time, the escalating scale of Fanny's engine. Then he nudged her more forcibly causing a sudden loud snort, whereupon she shot bolt upright crying, "What's happened?"

Nigel ignored the commotion. He was well used to Fanny drifting off during committee meetings and suffered it with the knowledge that Americans were a very different race of beings.

"And now we come to item one on tonight's agenda," intoned Dorothea. "The non-payment of annual subscriptions for the upkeep of our beautiful garden." There was an audible intake of breath from the assembly. "As you all know, we sent out a letter to every resident recently naming the guilty parties. James McGregor and Roger Blackwood have not paid the annual subscription of £120 for the last two years. Indeed Mr McGregor attempted to cast a slur on our hard-working committee by claiming the fees were too high. He then distributed a malicious pamphlet accusing us of negligence and maladministration of the association's budget." The colour had risen in Dorothea's cheeks. "Those of you who attended the last meeting will recall the unanimous vote in favour of the committee. We now believe it is time, time long overdue I might add, to force those two individuals – McGregor and Blackwood (she almost spat the names) – to pay their dues.

"We are asking for the members' permission to seek legal remedy against the pair. All those in favour, please raise your hands." A forest of hands went up. The residents knew only too well the power of social opprobrium in Balmoral Square Mansions.

In common with other select addresses in the city, it was the equivalent of blackballing. There was never anything so overt or vulgar as verbal or physical abuse. Much more effective was the simple and universal act of giving the cold shoulder to any individual who dared question convention. All in the Cruduckers' drawing room that night shuddered at such a fate – except one man.

A deep voice boomed out from the back of the gathering. "What about the money for the garden party, Smail? What's that spent on, eh?" All heads swivelled, craning to identify the questioner. Nigel recognised the tones only too well. It was James McGregor himself. He must have sneaked in just before the beginning of the meeting. The man had the cheek of the Devil. Nigel drew himself up to his full magisterial height of five-foot-five before addressing the usurper who dared interrupt his meeting.

"Mr McGregor, you – and your associate Mr Blackwood – will soon be the ones answering questions. Legal questions in a solicitor's letter. Questions about evasion. Evading your duty to pay for the upkeep of our communal garden, unlike everyone else here who pays their dues, you shirk your financial obligations. But you will soon be brought to account for your antisocial behaviour."

The crowd murmured their approval. One wag even shouted, "Pay up, pay up." The chant was not taken up. Chanting was what football supporters did. Chanting was beneath the dignity of the residents of Balmoral Square Mansions. The silent treatment was more their forte.

McGregor continued unabashed. "Account? You talk about being brought to account, Smail. That is a very interesting word. It's the accounts – and the financial obligations – of you and your committee that interest me. They might also interest the residents here if they knew that the budget for the wine purchased for the last garden party was £1,500."

Nigel Smail smirked in triumph. "Everyone knows the wine budget, McGregor. It's all there printed and recorded in our accounts."

"Yes, it is. But what the people here don't know is that 150 bottles of Pinot Noir and Sauvignon Blanc were bought for the last garden party yet only 100 appeared at the event. What happened to the other fifty, Nigel? Are they in your private wine cellar for the exclusive use of you and your committee chums? Or perhaps they have been quaffed by you and your little boyfriend?"

Nigel turned the colour of his maroon corduroy trousers as the drawing room disintegrated into a discordant babble of voices. Shouts of "Shame", "Prove it" and "Show us the proof, McGregor" rose above the cacophony.

Seeing that Nigel had lost the power of speech, Dorothea attempted to restore order. "That is an outrageous and libellous accusation, Mr McGregor. You should withdraw it immediately or face the legal consequences."

Amid the fury, finger jabbing and faces contorted in anger, McGregor appeared to be the calmest person in the room. "I have said what I wanted to say. I will not withdraw my statement because it is true and I can prove it – though I will now withdraw myself." And with that McGregor left the room.

Still reeling from the accusation, Nigel had to be helped from the platform by his young friend Jeremy Sheldrake. Weaving unsteadily through the crowd to the exit, he appeared to be wandering mentally as he repeatedly mumbled "Calumny. Lies – all lies."

Dorothea – a small, plump Irish woman with overpowering BO, a moon face and a penchant for hand-knitted cardigans – was about to call the shambolic meeting to an end and the crowd were collecting their coats when Marjorie intervened.

"There remains one outstanding issue on the agenda, Dorothea. I phoned Nigel last night as a matter of urgency to report some very odd things happening in the garden."

"Surely this can wait," said Dorothea, somewhat impatiently. She was thinking about her two Labradors at home – Ebony and Ivory. It was already past their feeding time, after which they still needed to be walked in order to do their business. "Nigel is clearly in shock after these dreadful allegations. When he recovers, your concerns can be taken up then." The residents, more than ready to be off home, nodded in sympathy.

But Marjorie was determined to be heard.

"No, it can't wait, Dorothea. Not for those of us who love our communal garden and would never wish to see it destroyed."

The departing crowd started to waver with a number sitting down again. Marjorie pressed on quickly.

"As some of you might be aware there has been a

change to the company that tends to the garden. A change for the worst. The new people are cutting and slashing at the trees and bushes without any apparent regard for the design of the garden. Many of the trees have simply had their tops lopped off with chainsaws. It's like…" and here she employed a phrase she had heard recently on Radio 4's *Today* programme, "…'ground zero' out there. It's an act of outright vandalism that must be halted immediately."

"Ground zero. Tosh and nonsense. Your phrases are all to cock, Marjorie," piped up the instantly recognisable voice of 'The Lieutenant', aka Jock Witherspoon, long-time resident of the square and a former member of the Royal Highland Fusiliers. "Sounds more like scorched earth tactics. Ruskies did it to the Jerries in WW2. Burned barns to the ground, destroyed crops. Didn't leave a thing standing. Cut off the Huns' supply lines. Starved them to death."

"Oh come, come, Witherspoon," interrupted Peter Tweedie. "Balmoral Square Mansions is hardly Stalingrad. Any of that kind of Russian behaviour here would get short shrift."

There was a murmur of patriotic approval from those remaining.

Ignoring the intervention of 'The Lieutenant' and Peter Tweedie, Marjorie pressed on with her attack.

"It is the primary duty of the association committee to protect our wonderful communal garden." Looking around the room Marjorie saw an increasing number of heads nodding in agreement.

She decided to refrain from disclosing the incident with the binoculars. Privately she acknowledged such an admission might hinder her cause to the point where some less-charitable people might consider her a 'loonie'.

"In the absence of the chairman I call on you, Dorothea, as association secretary, to table a motion for a vote on contacting the council to sack the company Happy Trails Tree Surgeons and reinstate our old gardening company before any further desecration takes place."

"I will second that motion," said Fanny Cruducker, who now seemed to be fully awake.

Hearing the murmur of approval, Dorothea realised she had no option. The quicker they had the vote, the quicker she could get home to her dogs – and attend to the orders.

"All right. A show of hands, please. All those in favour of a complaint to the council?" Dorothea didn't need to go any further. The forest of raised arms illustrated perfectly how dear the communal garden was to the residents of Balmoral Square Mansions.

PC MEIKLE spotted the car first. It was his turn to brave the seagull shit and he was up a tree slaughtering the branches with the chainsaw when through a new gap in the foliage he spied the vehicle entering Balmoral Square Mansions. It glided to a halt in a parking bay thirty yards down the street beside the garden railing.

"Bentley's back, sir."

Nichols looked out beyond the railings at the vehicle. Silver, tinted one-way windows so those inside could look out, but curious individuals like him could not see inside. One hundred and fifty grand if it cost a penny. Plates he had never seen before: obviously foreign, but nothing he was familiar with. Here, in the same spot at the same time for the third day running. Pure coincidence, or something germane to their inquiries? At long last maybe the break they were looking for.

Nichols got on his mobile and quoted the registration. His request had to be processed through official police channels to the appropriate outside authority.

An hour later a sergeant in the control room at Gayfield Square returned his call.

"Apologies for the wait, Dougie, but your request finally had to go through the Foreign Office. They were at lunch when we called," said the sergeant. "You know how lackadaisical these Whitehall punkah wallahs are where anywhere north of Watford is concerned."

Nichols made a heroic effort to control his impatience at the long-winded explanation. "So, what's the score, Sergeant?"

"Not great, I'm afraid. It's a Nigerian plate registered to a woman named Savannah Bullion. Someone big in their embassy. Diplomatic immunity. Virtually untouchable as far as we're concerned. You can't go near her."

STRAWBERRY was on his bicycle again. The electric version had been his choice after an experimental run around Gladhouse Reservoir with a group of proper cyclists. Friends who had all the gear – racing bikes the cost of a small car, lunch-boxes bulging through Lycra, jaunty caps and specialist shoes. They backed up the expensive kit with epic cycle tours involving monstrous mileages up precipitous Spanish and French mountains.

In such company Strawberry had suffered a disastrous Sunday morning. It started happily enough. He found himself scooting along like Road Runner at the head of the pack with the electric bike whirring reassuringly into overdrive and carrying him up steep hills. But the battery had expired after twenty miles in the wilds of East Lothian when it should have lasted fifty. He was left pushing the machine, which felt like the weight of a Panzer tank, the last mile up Swanston Hill to the lights at Oxgangs. The experience had been salutary but Strawberry had persevered with other models and he was now a convert to this relatively new form of transport – at least in Edinburgh.

The bicycle allowed him the luxury of fresh air without too much effort – and the ability to think more clearly about his police work without the constant interruptions of riding in a police car.

The weather remained warm and welcoming as he cycled over Churchill, past Holy Corner and on to the coffee shop precinct of Bruntsfield.

He had the sudden urge for an ice lolly. A brand called Mivvy had been his favourite as a child. Manufactured by Lyons Maid and featuring an ice-cream centre, it came in a selection of coatings, but he especially enjoyed orange and strawberry. A newsagent on the corner of Montpelier Park next to the bank stocked something like them.

Dismounting from his bicycle he kicked the stand out and took the additional precaution of leaning the machine against a lamp post. It was after all brand new and had cost him a small fortune. It was the rush hour in Edinburgh and he found himself in a queue behind several commuters buying a newspaper, cigarettes or a chocolate bar as a breakfast substitute before catching a bus to work in the city centre.

The Pakistani owner of the newsagent was the only person serving and Strawberry waited patiently while a young woman dithered over which magazine to buy.

It was only due to a lull in the flow of traffic that Strawberry heard the sound – an all too familiar scraping noise of steel against pavement.

He threw down the *Hoots Mon* he had picked up and raced for the exit – just in time to see a young man mounting his bicycle and steering it into the traffic.

Strawberry began to sprint after the thief, who had rounded a bus and was now thirty yards away pedalling fast. The detective started to sweat almost immediately as his breathing degenerated to ragged gasps. Cursing his lack of fitness, he watched in despair as the man went straight through a red light and rose out of the saddle to propel the bicycle faster.

That motion was his big mistake. In doing so, he overbalanced, panicked, pulled on the front brake and went over the handlebars.

Strawberry arrived on the scene as the thief was attempting to get up. He grabbed the man by the collar and twisted his arm behind his back – much to the alarm of a group of passing schoolgirls. The thief screamed and sagged as though unconscious.

Strawberry found himself in the ridiculous position of having to defend his actions and recount the incident to a growing band of bystanders. Meantime, the girls continued to regard him with suspicion and coo over the thief.

The man looked about thirty. He had dirty blond hair above a badly sunburned forehead and there were sores around his lips and nose. Additionally, he had the odour of a dead goat. From his smell and the state of his clothes Strawberry reckoned he was rough sleeping. But beneath the dirt and the wounds he had soft, regular features and was handsome in a feminine sort of way. So Strawberry could understand the schoolgirls' concerns. But their sympathy stirred his ire, particularly as he knew the man was feigning unconsciousness. He realised there was no alternative but to do the last thing he wanted to do.

He produced his warrant card and announced in a none-too-steady voice – as he was still recovering from the chase – "I am a police officer. This man is under arrest for attempting to steal a bicycle."

After summoning a patrol car on his mobile and

handing the thief over, Strawberry continued on his journey.

He had been in a fine mood before the incident, anticipating the ice lolly, daydreaming about the perfect contours of Fiona's derriere, or the alphabetical neatness of his newly installed bookcase. But the theft had soured the morning returning him to the grim reality of his duties.

Today he must focus on the forthcoming interviews with the residents of Balmoral Square Mansions. If Marjorie Agincourt was anything to go by the process would be weary and time-consuming. Yet time was not on his side.

His boss, Superintendent Bert Rothesay, was already badgering him for results. Operation Treetops had been going for a week without any discernible breakthrough in terms of evidence. Although Nichols was in charge of the surveillance teams, Strawberry was in overall command and the buck stopped at him.

Now there was the additional interference of the residents' Garden Association. Strawberry had received a curt text from Rothesay warning him to wrap things up quickly as he was coming under pressure from the council asking 'awkward questions' about when their own workmen could return to their duties. The residents were on the warpath about the 'ground zero' approach to horticulture adopted by Happy Trails.

To make matters worse, questions had been posed by one of the more perceptive residents (nosey parker Marjorie Agincourt) about the provenance of the new gardeners.

Then there was the extra not inconsiderable

complication of Arabella Pettygrew taking a head-dive from the roof of her third-floor apartment.

As if there wasn't enough going on in the street, there was now a suspicious death to contend with.

Strawberry guessed that was the way of things. A place like the square was quiet forever and then suddenly a series of events shattered the civilised veneer. He likened it to waiting for a bus for forty-five minutes – and then three of them turned up at the same time.

Finally arriving in the square, a sweating and slightly dishevelled Strawberry chained his bicycle to the garden railings and removed his manbag from around his shoulders. It had been a gift from Fiona, purchased on a curling trip to Italy. Apparently fashion-conscious Italian men had been using manbags for years for their essentials in order to save the pockets of their designer suits from being ruined by keys and coins. The fashion was also catching on in London – a place full of 'metrosexual men', according to an article he had read in a men's magazine.

Strawberry thought he might be one of them. After all, he bought personal grooming products – skin creams and unguents. He bothered about dandruff. Went food shopping for Fiona when she was training – and actually enjoyed eating quinoa. He also took a genuine interest in fashion – both men's and women's. Flossed and recycled religiously – and now he possessed a brown leather manbag from Italy.

Such an item was still a dangerous purchase in certain parts of Scotland. For example in Fort William, from whence Fiona originated, wearing a manbag could very well lead to bloodshed in some of the less salubrious pubs.

It was perhaps more acceptable in the more liberal environs of Edinburgh – and Strawberry found it genuinely useful. Besides his keys, it contained his phone, notebook, inhaler and lip-balm as he suffered from chapped lips when cycling.

He was sure that many of his colleagues thought him gay – possibly viewing Fiona as a convenient smokescreen. But he was not gay. The sap most certainly rose in the loins of DI Richard Strawberry, especially on warm summer days like this.

He squirmed with embarrassment when he recalled his muddled state fantasising about Brenda Gunn as he recovered consciousness on the morgue floor. Flushing at the memory, he fished his notebook out of the manbag and consulted the list of residents who had to be interviewed. The Tweedies, Peter and Marcy, were first up.

They lived on the ground floor at No. 15. He pushed their intercom, which emitted a musical chime – an uncharacteristically vulgar sound in Balmoral Square Mansions. A middle-aged man in pink trousers, brown leather-tassled loafers (no socks) and a loose fitting blue and white striped shirt answered the door.

"Ah, the detective," he said with the air of a man who had just made a profound statement. Strawberry was ushered through the upstairs hall, decorated in a modern tartan theme, downstairs to an open-plan lounge, kitchen and dining room.

The large room looked out on an uphill garden through French windows. A well-maintained woman around the same age as the man was sitting reading a coffee-table magazine on a candy-striped settee. She rose as Strawberry entered the room extending a gold-braceleted arm.

"Marcy Tweedie. Unfortunate circumstances, but pleased to meet you, Inspector." She motioned for Strawberry to sit on the opposite settee and arranged her face in an accommodating smile. "Anything we can do to help. We are at your disposal, Officer."

"Nice basement," said Strawberry as he appraised the Poggenpohl kitchen and a crystal light above the island that probably cost the equivalent of his annual salary.

"Well, we call it a ground and garden apartment, Inspector. I always think 'basement' is, well, such a basic word." She uttered a small laugh at her clever wordplay.

"Absolutely, darling," chimed in her husband. "You know, Inspector, in the nineteenth century when these buildings were originally constructed and one family occupied them, the basement was the exclusive domain of the understairs staff. The clue is in the ceiling, Inspector. Can you guess?"

Strawberry was irritated already and the interview had not progressed beyond the so-called pleasantries. "Please put me out of my misery, Mr Tweedie," he said.

"Well," said Peter Tweedie, looking particularly pleased with himself, "the basement was the only part of the building without any ornate coving – the servants quarters, *voil*à!"

"The history of Edinburgh's privileged class is certainly fascinating, Mr Tweedie," said Strawberry. "One can only wonder what the SNP would make of it."

"Please, Inspector, don't get me on to politics. That ghastly woman Sturgeon. Bears a striking resemblance to wee Jimmy Krankie, don't you think? Yes, but she will have her revenge. The amount of taxes we pay on these houses is already skyrocketing. And what do we see for it, Inspector? Rubbish bins overflowing. Filthy litter-strewn streets. Our roads a patchwork of potholes constantly under repair with so many diversions one often has to travel miles in circles to get to one's own house. Our pavements major trip hazards for the old and infirm. While all our taxes go to the socialist republics of Glasgow and Dundee."

The character assassination of the First Minister aside, Strawberry reckoned it was time to get to the point.

"I am here to ask you about your neighbour. As you know, Arabella Pettygrew recently fell to her death from the roof of her apartment."

"A tragic affair," said Marcy, sniffing as she reached for a tissue.

Strawberry nodded. "Can either of you throw any light on the incident?"

"Miss Pettygrew kept herself to herself, Inspector," said Peter Tweedie. "Anyone in the street will tell you that. But was it an accident?"

"What do you mean, Mr Tweedie?"

"Well, I didn't get the impression that she was the type to kill herself. Old school. Stiff upper lip. Too British, if you know what I mean."

Seeing Strawberry's puzzled expression, Peter Tweedie explained. "From the little we knew or observed of Arabella Pettygrew, she was a fiercely independent person with a mind of her own. I believe she would have thought it an act of utter cowardice to commit suicide. I simply don't think her character and upbringing would have allowed her to do such a thing."

"So what do you think happened, Mr Tweedie?"

"I don't think she tripped and fell, Inspector. Everyone knew that Arabella was constantly on her roof trying to fix the leaks. She might have been a pensioner nearing seventy. But she was a fit woman and as sure-footed as a mountain goat. No, I think it was murder, Inspector. Someone pushed Arabella Pettygrew off the roof."

"Do you have anyone in mind, Mr Tweedie?"

He looked at his wife for confirmation. Marcy nodded. They had clearly talked about this before his arrival, Strawberry decided.

"We recently engaged two builders – brothers named Bob and Ginger Duncan – to repair the roof of our own building. Unfortunately our neighbour on the top floor has told us that water is still coming through her lounge ceiling."

"Cowboys perhaps, but you are surely not about to make a serious accusation based on that?" said Strawberry.

"Absolutely not, Inspector," said Peter Tweedie. "I have my suspicions about these men because I recently heard through the street grapevine that Arabella Pettygrew engaged them to do a job on her roof a year ago. She sent them packing with a flea in their ear when she discovered them vandalising the roof rather than repairing it."

SUMMER evenings were challenging for the Glaikit Twins. They were forced to wait for darkness in order to cover their clandestine activities.

It was 11 p.m. before the brothers dared to climb onto the roof of the church. Naturally they had to continually switch targets, though church roofs were particularly productive for their lack of security and the lodestone of lead on offer.

This time they had chosen a church just off Morningside Road. It had been the late Labour Party leader John Smith's place of worship and was on the same street where the last men to be hanged on a public gallows for theft in Scotland had met their grisly end. A plaque in the road marked the exact spot.

Neither Bob nor Ginger Duncan was aware of this grisly fact – and even if they had been, they would have taken no notice. Omens did not move them. They were men of severely practical mien.

Bob had gone up round the back of the church using a green plastic waste bin to hoist himself up the wall from where he attached a rope to the top of a drainpipe. Shinning up the pipe and then onto the roof, he hissed at Ginger to throw up the theft kit – a large chisel and three hessian sacks.

Ginger followed more slowly up the rope breathing

heavily and having to stop at several points. He finally made it with Bob having to haul him onto the platform. "You're peching like an old man, Ginger. Look at the gut on you. For God's sake, put it away."

Ginger dutifully pulled his T-shirt back down over his exposed paunch and climbed to his feet.

"They sausage rolls will be the death of you. Heart-attack food. You mark my words," declared Bob. "Now let's get a shift on. I'll chisel and you fill the sacks."

The brothers had filled one sack with contraband lead and were halfway to filling a second when the roof was suddenly bathed in white light and a deafening noise and blast of wind that grew in alarming intensity.

The helicopter was hovering forty feet above their heads, the velocity of its rotor blades threatening to blow them off the roof. Bob tried to look up but had to cover his eyes from the blinding glare. A piercing screech of electronic static rent the night air followed by a disembodied voice speaking through the loud hailer. "This is a police command. Freeze. Do not move. Stay exactly where you are. Officers on the ground are making their way onto the roof."

Bob shouted to Ginger, but his instructions were lost in the din made by the helicopter. For the first time in his living memory Ginger made a decision independent of his brother. He shambled to the edge of the roof, took a ragged breath, and then jumped.

Bob threw his hands in the air as though being held up at gun-point. He stayed that way, rigid with shock, until a policeman brought him down the drainpipe and handed him over to a colleague who handcuffed him.

He was just in time to see his brother being stretchered to an ambulance by two paramedics. "Is he okay?" Bob stammered.

"Hard to say," said the policeman. "It was about a twelve-foot drop, but he fell awkwardly. He was unconscious when we got to him."

"I told him to stand still," wailed Bob. "He couldn't hear me. Why did he jump for nicking a few bloody lead tiles?"

"It's not about the tiles," said the policeman. "We would hardly send a helicopter in for the theft of lead tiles now, would we?"

Bob Duncan stared uncomprehending at the policeman as his head was pushed down and he was put into the back of the patrol car.

"You've made the big time, buddy. You and your brother are in deep shit."

BOB Duncan was in a cell at St Leonard's Police Station by the time Strawberry arrived. He had already been processed at the desk, charged with theft and had his valuables, including his belt, removed and put in a polythene bag.

Strawberry observed him through the door grille. He was pacing around the cell clearly in a state of agitation. Now would be good, the detective decided, in the immediate aftermath of the trauma of the arrest when the suspect was exhausted and confused. Not later in daylight by which time he would have had several hours to collect his thoughts and plan his story.

"Take him to the interview room," he instructed the desk sergeant. "Is Gunn here yet?"

"She's waiting in the canteen, sir."

Strawberry made his way to the canteen. He had asked for her presence as a reassurance to Duncan. Not exactly good cop/bad cop because that was not Strawberry's method. He simply reckoned he would get more from the suspect if there was a sympathetic face in the room.

She was sitting alone nursing what passed for coffee but tasted like sump oil. At such an ungodly hour there was no one else in the canteen. The shift changed at 5 a.m. The cars would still be out looking for drunk drivers, or enforcing crowd control at A & E. Strawberry sat down on the unyielding dirty white plastic chair opposite her.

"Thank you for agreeing to help out, Gunn." She looked, what was the word, bashful.

"Not a problem, sir. Gets me out of lost and found for a while. It can get a bit predictable in there."

"I suppose so." Strawberry smiled. He meant his expression to be reassuring, but somehow the whole situation felt awkward. Even though she was his subordinate, he felt an explanation was due.

"I was in the vicinity of the stolen property room recently."

"You mean you were in it, or passing it, sir?"

"Point taken. Police speak. I don't know why I said that. It's a pet hate of mine. I gave young Angus Robertson a bollocking for it the other day and now here I am doing it. Next I'll be substituting 'now' for 'at this moment in time'." Strawberry laughed somewhat nervously. Gunn simply looked at him.

"Anyway, I couldn't help but overhear how you dealt with that guy who had lost his forty-two-inch plasma. Remember?"

Gunn paused, collecting her thoughts. "Oh right. That was in June. A month's an eternity in lost and found. Yes – a burglary it was. Two scallies broke into his flat in the middle of the night when he was sleeping. Stole the TV and his car keys. Trashed it next morning after a police chase. They were on another job."

"And you advised the guy to claim for a whole bunch of CDs that weren't in the car."

She flushed but looked defiantly at Strawberry.

"Insurance companies are fraudsters. Every officer in stolen property knows that. That poor sod was robbed twice that night. Once by the two scumbags from Apache Territory, and the second time by the shysters in suits who refused to pay out on his TV because he mistakenly sent them the wrong receipt – and then gave him a rock-bottom price on his trashed car."

Intelligent but feisty, better tread carefully here, thought Strawberry.

"You misunderstand me, Gunn. I suppose I have a reputation for playing by the book and I would usually not condone that kind of advice. But on that occasion I thought you did exactly the right thing. It showed, eh…" Strawberry found himself searching for the right word again. He was doing a lot of that in what was becoming a strange conversation with a junior officer. "It showed humanity, Gunn. I admire that."

Strawberry shifted uncomfortably in the hard plastic chair. He could feel his pants sticking to the seat. "That's why I have requested that you be seconded to my current investigation, Gunn. I think you have the sympathetic manner we need for what is a very tricky case."

She blushed and looked down at her coffee. When she raised her gaze again Strawberry noticed that one eye was slightly lazier than the other. Few faces are perfectly symmetrical. He had read that in one of his men's magazines. Only the most beautiful people – models – have perfect faces. Gunn wasn't a model, but she was interesting. Strawberry reckoned her lazy eye suited her.

When they entered the interview room Bob Duncan was already seated at the table. There was a cigarette in the corner of his mouth. He was fidgeting and staring at the large tape recorder on the desk. The duty sergeant was standing in a corner of the room.

"Thank you, Sergeant, we'll take it from here," said Strawberry. He sat down in the seat directly opposite Bob Duncan and indicated for Gunn to take the chair alongside him. He made the introductions and sat back giving Bob Duncan the opportunity to say something. Duncan stayed silent. *An old hand*, thought Strawberry. But he was very agitated – and that was an advantage in any criminal investigation.

"Old technology, Bob," said Strawberry, indicating the tape recorder. "God knows when Police Scotland will ever catch up, but I guess it will have to do."

Bob kept shtum, but his eyes followed the winding reel as Strawberry switched the recorder on.

"For the purposes of the tape my name is Detective Inspector Richard Strawberry. Also in the room is my colleague Constable Brenda Gunn. It is 3.25 a.m. on Wednesday 8 August, 2018 and we are interviewing Mr Bob Duncan as a possible suspect in the murder of Miss Arabella Pettygrew – a late resident of 12 Balmoral Square Mansions."

The cigarette fell from Bob Duncan's lips. He started speaking at machine-gun rate. "What's this about? You nicked me and my brother for stealing lead from a church roof. Fair enough. There was no mention of any old woman or a murder. I don't know anything about that."

Strawberry raised his hand in what appeared a peace offering. "Bob, at the moment you are here helping us with our inquiries. We will get to the lead at some stage, but that really is a very secondary concern for us right now. If you are straight with us we might be lenient on the lead."

"I didn't do any murder, Mr Strawberry. Neither Ginger or me is that kind of criminal. Nicking – okay – yes. But physical assault – murder – never!"

"All right, Bob, but you said – and I'm quoting you here. We can play back the tape if you don't believe me. You said, 'any old woman'. How did you know Arabella Pettygrew was an old woman, if you don't know anything about her?"

"She's a miss and with a name like Arabella – old-fashioned handle – she must be an old woman."

Bob was fingering his ear and he had broken eye contact with both officers.

Strawberry nudged Gunn under the table. She cleared her throat. Her big sympathetic eyes looked directly at Bob Duncan. "Come on now, Mr Duncan, it's clear to us that you have heard of Arabella Pettygrew. If you tell us what you know – all of it and truthfully without leaving anything out – as the Detective Inspector says we could go the route of a plea bargain."

That sounded a promise too far for Strawberry, but he decided to let her roll with it.

Bob Duncan was looking back at Brenda Gunn. He appeared almost hypnotized by the transparent honesty in the constable's hazel eyes. "Okay. I remember the old girl. We did do a job for her, but that was about eighteen months ago and we never seen her since. I swear."

"CCTV images from Balmoral Square Mansions show that you were actually in the street late last week. You parked your van. You and your brother were then clearly seen on video camera walking along the street and entering No. 15. Three hours later the camera picked you up again leaving No. 15 and returning to your van. Five minutes later you left the location in a hurry judging from the tyre marks in the parking bay, which of course have not been erased as we have had very little rain the past few weeks."

Bob's hand had moved from his ear to his chin, which he was rubbing earnestly.

"It's right. We were in the street. But we were on another job. It was for a Mr and Mrs Tweedie. They needed their roof repairing, so it was nothing to do with Arabella Pettygrew. We never seen the woman again since the job I told you about eighteen months ago."

"Going back to that job you did for Miss Pettygrew," said Strawberry. "We understand it ended badly. That she threw you off the job because she caught you vandalising the roof – not repairing it."

Bob Duncan shrugged. "Yeah, there was a disagreement. She come up on the roof." He shook his head in rueful memory. "Imagine it. An old woman like that moving about on that roof like a bloody billy goat. She was better at heights than Ginger and him half her age."

"So she caught you kicking tiles loose?" said Gunn.

"It's not as simple as that. Sometimes we have to loosen more tiles so we can get a stable base for re-laying a whole section. She just got the wrong end of the stick. That was all."

"Either way, she got the wrong end of the stick and she fired you," said Strawberry. "You harboured a grudge about being thrown off the job so you came back late one night a couple of weeks ago and returned the compliment by throwing her off the roof."

Bob Duncan pushed back from the table rocking on the rear legs of the chair. "Honest to God, Mr Strawberry, that just didn't happen! Okay, we tried to fiddle the old woman, make a bit more from the job. Ginger and me are crooks, but we would never harm anyone. We were never up on that roof again. We never killed her."

"Why then did you leave the scene in such a rush last week? That doesn't look like the action of innocent men to me," said Gunn.

"I just saw the paper in the van. Read the story about her falling off the roof. I panicked because I thought we would get stitched up for it. And I was right. Here we are, or here I am," wailed Bob Duncan. "Look, please, officers. I need to know about Ginger."

Strawberry spoke for the benefit of the machine. "This is Detective Inspector Richard Strawberry. I am pausing this interview at 4.15 a.m." He switched off the tape recorder and left the room with Brenda Gunn. He turned to her in the shabby corridor. "Apart from the plea bargain bit, that was pretty good, Gunn."

Gunn looked flustered and began to apologise. "No need, Gunn. But you owe me one and I need you to do something that could be unpleasant."

Five minutes later Strawberry eavesdropped outside the interview room as Brenda Gunn broke the news to Bob Duncan that his brother was dead.

He lengthened his stride down the corridor when the remaining Glaikit Twin started to sob.

BLESSINGS McKenzie had never before witnessed such an influx of recruits to train as bell ringers in her twenty years as provost of the cathedral. What was additionally curious was that all three of them were young men. In fact rather strapping individuals who looked as though they would be more at home on a rugby pitch than pursuing the hobby of campanology.

Still, they made a refreshing change from the staple fare – old and doddery people. Florrie Armstrong, who got in such a tangle with the ropes that she nearly strangled herself with her scarf on one occasion. Then there was 'The Lieutenant' who lost his false teeth, so intense was his effort the first time he tried ringing the bells.

Most of the recruits were men in cardigans threatening to expire as they puffed up the worn stone steps to the bell tower. Give them enough rope, reckoned Blessings McKenzie, and one of these days some pensioner was literally going to hang themselves.

So it was, how would she describe it – uplifting – yes, spiritually uplifting to welcome a new breed of bell ringer. And, truth be known, Blessings was quite partial to rugby types as evidenced by regular trips to Murrayfield in her youth.

Such inappropriate thoughts would cost her at least ten Hail Marys later in confessional. For – although she worked for the other side so to speak and the intervention of real life had destroyed much of her faith – like many of her countrymen, Blessings own religion was rooted in a staunchly conservative African Catholicism and as a remnant of childhood she had a nostalgic fondness for the confessional. She also believed her transgression had been worth it, or at least would have been if she ever managed to see the young men.

For a degree of mystery surrounded the new volunteers. They arrived punctually every day for the induction training on 'learning the ropes'. But then went straight to the bell tower where they remained incarcerated all day with the door always firmly locked behind them.

Blessings knew this because she had climbed the stairs under some pretext one day and tried the door.

Secondly, she had never seen Roger Lumsden, the cathedral's designated bell instructor, once since the day they had started.

Thirdly, and strangest of all, was that she had never heard any evidence of their training – the actual ringing of bells.

Admittedly, the trainees had a series of technical things to master before they were let loose, but they had been up there for a week now and not a tinkle had escaped the tower. She had attempted to beard the bishop on the subject, but he had brushed her questions aside declaring he was far too busy contemplating the forthcoming Sunday sermon to address idle tittle-tattle.

Even so, Blessings was determined to get to the bottom of the mystery and she resolved to hide overnight in one of the cathedral's many nooks and crannies in a bid to solve the conundrum.

"**NEW** orders from Strawberry high command," announced Dougie Nichols in a tone dripping with sarcasm. "All the trees opposite the target address are to be topped to a level where we can get a clear sighting of every bugger that enters or leaves – and that includes the postie, the pizza delivery boy, the meter reader, the Waitrose home-shopping guys. You name it."

The team groaned. They were mentally and physically exhausted from this operation. Sunburn. In a couple of cases sunstroke, which had to be a first in Edinburgh, with PCs Meikle and Murch puking their guts out and having to be put in a taxi.

Then there was the bird shit. So much it felt at times like they were on the Bass Rock instead of a civilised space in the middle of well-heeled Edinburgh. "Right, let the chainsaw massacre begin," ordered Nichols.

He retreated to the middle of the garden to allow himself to think above the whine of the blades. He watched as the treetops began to receive a severe haircut. He could smell the sharp tang from the freshly cut wood as the canopy of leaves collapsed. He had already heard about the Garden Association meeting and the call to reinstate the real gardening company. At some stage, and it would be very soon now, their cover would either be blown, or the weight of residents' opinion would be so overwhelming that they would be forced to retreat and rethink their strategy. He knew Strawberry as nominal head of the operation would get most of the flak – and although that would have given him great satisfaction, he was conflicted. The last thing he wanted was to be tainted by association with failure.

At best they had another week to wind up the operation and arrest the ringleaders. He fished out his walkie-talkie and made contact with the bell tower. "Give me some good news, Dreever. Something I can relay to high command."

On the other end of the line PC Dreever looked at his two colleagues on their perch in the stone tower. Their binoculars had been trained on the target since 8 a.m. and it was midday. Apart from a two-minute changeover every thirty minutes their vigilance had been absolute. He didn't need to ask them.

"Nothing, sir – except for the postman. We checked him out with their collection centre. Our description tallied exactly with theirs – tall, skinny, middle-aged guy with sandy-coloured comb-over."

"Bobby Charlton lives," muttered Nichols.

"What's that, sir?"

"Nothing, Dreever. Before your time. A sad joke – a bit like this operation really. Look, I know you guys are knackered, but let's keep focused. If we don't crack this soon we'll all be back to Gayfield with our tails between our legs."

"There is one thing, sir. I'm afraid it's bad news."

"Go on."

"Well, Holy Smokes gave us the nod this morning that

his provost is snooping around the bell tower. Suspicious about the lack of bell ringing, he says."

"Who the hell is Holy Smokes, Dreever?"

"Ugh, that's the bishop's nickname. Apparently it's an American slang exclamation meaning 'good heavens.'"

"Appropriate, but we better forget the nicknames. If politically-correct Mr Strawberry hears, you'll no doubt be up on a disciplinary."

A GLORIOUS Sunday morning and Fiona was in the lounge doing her stretches. A big international curling competition was coming up in Hong Kong and she had intensified her training for the event. She was practising the bending motion needed to launch the stone towards the jack. Her right arm extended. Her body low to the ground. Her bottom encased in a pair of taught pink shorts – a high, perfect moon obscuring the TV with Andrew Marr chuntering on in the background about Brexit.

Sitting in his favourite armchair, Strawberry didn't mind. The sight of his girlfriend's bottom was far more interesting than watching the wee Scottish politico with the big lugs – even if the room was in a bit of a state with her training gear strewn all over the place as well as a distinctive groove in his new engineered wooden floor from her repeated motion.

Earlier, while Fiona was still asleep, he had walked to the shops for the newspapers and the morning rolls. The fresh air was a relief after the dreadful night he had endured. Without warning the black dog of despair had suddenly descended. Mind whirring, unable to still the churning thoughts, he rose carefully. Fiona stirred, mumbled and threw an involuntary arm out in unconscious protest, before turning over to continue snoring. Strawberry made it to the bathroom just in time to get his head down the toilet bowl in the first of several brutal technicolour yawns. When the retching subsided to a final sour, watery evacuation, he slumped exhausted on the cold tiled floor, head thumping as he shivered at the mental demons that assailed him. Charlie's voice, destined to be forever that of the child he had loved, whispered the entreaty he had heard a thousand times. 'Where are you? I tried to wait. I'm waiting still. Please. Please find me.'

The migraine and the beseeching message had gradually subsided until they were both a dull memory fading as the sun came up on Blackford Hill highlighting the massed ranks of whins in bright yellow bloom. A group of early morning cyclists sped past his flat in Woodburn Terrace. He watched as they struggled up the steep incline of Braid Avenue. He imagined himself on his electric bicycle, sitting upright like the man on the Derny, and passing them with ease on the gradient. He would smile and doff his hat if he had one.

It was a relief to have the day off from his police duties and he had meant to make the most of it. A cycle around the Braids and on to the historic village of Swanston, where Robert Louis Stevenson had once had a cottage, would have been an ideal way of winding down and dispelling the ghosts of the previous evening.

But he didn't have time for that today. Taking advantage of the sunny spell, Fiona had announced the organisation of a barbecue to which she had invited her curling girlfriends as well as insisting that Strawberry invite some of his male work colleagues.

He recognised his girlfriend's romantic inclinations.

Like most young women she revelled in the role of matchmaker: putting strangers together in the hope of buying a hat. But that desire did not take into account the problem Strawberry had in enlisting the required men. He didn't really socialise at work preferring to keep a distance from most of the other officers. Although many officers in the police force stuck together even off duty in a kind of tribal us- against-them policy and were often wary of making close friends from civilian life, Strawberry was perfectly happy to leave the job at Gayfield Square. Dougie Nichols was definitely out. He could never invite his arch-rival to his flat. But he forced himself to ask Meikle and Murch and a couple of the male call handlers.

When he had mentioned the Scottish female curling team they had all accepted with alacrity. Fiona was mollified and that was the main thing. As she was busy training, he volunteered to do the shop and after coffee and a bacon roll, set out for Waitrose in Morningside Road.

The upmarket supermarket was *the* destination of choice certainly for anyone living in the most prosperous Morningside streets like Nile Grove, Albert Terrace and Hermitage Drive. But there were also the upwardly mobile, young, aspirational Morningsiders from Woodburn Terrace, Canaan Lane and Jordan Lane. Strawberry counted himself among those people.

As usual the place was packed with the silver-surfer brigade and yummy mummies with squadrons of infants in buggies and their siblings enrolled at expensive private schools. The deli and bakery sections were doing a roaring trade and the lines at the checkouts were being helped to pack by fresh-faced Cubs and Brownies with charity buckets hoping for donations.

After selecting the normal barbecue fare – sausages, hamburgers, buns and spicy sauces, plus a variety of expensive crisps, wine and craft beers – Strawberry headed for the biscuit section in the hunt for Fiona's lemon and ginger favourites. Unfortunately, informed the polite assistant, they were out of stock and would not be reordering. Switching targets to the freezer he chose three tubs of Häagen-Dazs pistachio Italian gelato – and vanilla for the men.

Joining the queue he glimpsed a well-known Westminster politician two ahead. In power he had been unmistakable with his bushy black monobrow a startling contrast to a head of snow-white hair. Despite an innate dislike of politicians – no matter what the stripe – Strawberry found himself observing the man discreetly. As he spoke to the checkout girl in his soft, lawyerly voice, he half turned to get a plastic bag and Strawberry got a shock. The man had dyed his eyebrows to match his hair colour. Maybe he thought that rendered him incognito. He needn't have worried, thought Strawberry. Most shoppers over a certain age would certainly have recognised him. But Morningside was a different world. A world so reserved and withdrawn that no one would have dreamed of invading the man's privacy by actually talking to him. George Clooney could have walked the aisles without being disturbed.

Finally making the front of the queue, the checkout girl gave Strawberry a merry "Hi ya" – the standard Edinburgh greeting from a particular class of person, especially females. Then he allowed a Brownie with pigtails and a charming gap-toothed grin to pack his shopping.

Back at the flat, Fiona had finished her routine and was busy in the kitchen preparing desserts. Strawberry sighed as he saw her clothes still scattered on the floor and began tidying up. Her messiness had irritated him when they moved in together, but he quickly realised that allowances had to be made when you lived with another person. After all, she had told him that his snoring often drove her crazy.

Murch was the first guest to arrive. A uniform can cover up a multitude of sins. Even transform a very ordinary looking man into something, if not desirable to the opposite sex, at least worth a look. There is a presence to a tunic and it is a well-known phenomenon that women prefer men in uniform. Unfortunately, out of uniform, Murch had about as much presence as a mole catcher.

Minus the hat, his close-cropped ginger hair was there for all to see in glorious technicolour. While the bill of a police hat could be pulled down to partially hide the eyes and exude a kind of exciting menace, Murch's face *sans* hat was a freckled, doughy affair testifying to a traditional Scottish diet. His clothes were equally unedifying. A voluminous red and white chequered shirt – Fiona quipped that if he sat down someone might mistake him for a table and put a plate on him – and a pair of jeans that were hanging in folds beneath his considerable arse.

Meikle turned up soon after riding over from Marchmont on a scooter – and a top-floor squat he shared with four equally junior colleagues.

The instant he sat down the oil on the bottom of one pant leg – presumably the one he used to kickstart his scooter – was deposited on the base of Strawberry's settee. He had to go into the kitchen and chew on his knuckles to stop from screaming.

In civvies, however, Meikle was a much more presentable character. He was tall and dark-haired and clearly worked out at the gym a lot from the way his biceps sprang from a tight-fitting T-shirt.

The pair drifted out to the barbecue and snagged a couple of beers from a bucket of ice. Much, in particular, looked in an almost ecstatic panic – as if anticipating the dancers from the Folies Bergère to come high-kicking through the back green at any moment. He started chattering inanely at Meikle, who maintained a cool demeanour enhanced by a pair of shades – though the sun had disappeared.

The two male civilian call handlers arrived next; the balding one was in a cheap suit, and the other was wearing a knitted tie and a beige linen jacket that looked like it had belonged to his dad. They hung around the kitchen being polite to Fiona – though quietly ogling her – before finally venturing outside to join the 'uniforms'.

Ten minutes later, when male conversation had all but died, a commotion at the front door, sounding like a pandemonium of parakeets, announced the arrival of the women.

Much looked as if he was going to faint. Did this guy ever get out wondered Strawberry? The two civilians stood stock still – beers halfway to their mouths – in silent mime. Even the chilled Meikle, who had moved his shades onto his head, snapped them back down over his eyes. And action!

From the moment the female curlers made their entrance, Strawberry knew there had been a terrible mistake – a social calamity he would never recover from, and one that would reverberate around the canteen to the strains of gleeful laughter for weeks to come at Gayfield Square.

The instant the women appeared, the expectations – whether hopeful, romantic, or libidinous – entertained by the men in the back green were dashed at the sight of the female curlers.

There were four women all right. They were international curlers, or rather (and this was a crucial caveat) they had been international curlers. They were the well-known, if slightly wrinkled, faces of the Scottish team who had brought glory to the country by winning the gold medal in the Winter Olympics in Salt Lake City circa 2002. Strawberry remembered watching it live along with most of the nation on a memorable Friday. He was thirty-five now. He had been eighteen at the time.

Downing the remnants of his beer in one gulp, Meikle was the first to make his excuses and leave. The other three men attempted brief and desultory conversation with the women, but their faces betrayed their disappointment and after fifteen minutes the only man left at the barbecue was Strawberry.

Later, as they tidied up and pre-washed the dishes in the kitchen (he insisted on rinsing prior to putting them in the dishwasher), Strawberry tentatively broached the subject.

"Fiona, I thought you had invited your teammates."

Fiona paused in wiping a tabletop – a look of bemusement on her face. "I did, Richard. I practise with Rhona and the girls all the time."

"Yes, but I don't think my colleagues, who are all young enough to be their sons by the way, expected to literally be meeting the golden girls at the barbecue."

Finally cottoning on, Fiona laughed. "Oh, I see what you mean. The veterans are my friends. I've learned so much from them I can't begin to tell you. Of course you are talking about the girls in the current Scottish team?"

"Exactly. The girls who are young. The ones who are the same age as you. The same age as the men I invited, Fiona."

"Heavens, Richard, I thought you knew. They are far too bitchy. I hate them. I would never invite them round socially."

MONDAY morning first thing and Strawberry was standing on the carpet of Superintendent Bert Rothesay's office. Not only was he physically on his boss's carpet but he was also figuratively speaking on the carpet.

Rothesay was writing when Strawberry entered his office and he continued, letting his subordinate sweat.

Strawberry hadn't worked long for Rothesay, but long enough to know the score. Coming up thirty years on the force, the superintendent was old school and tough as leather. They say you can't judge a book by its cover, but Rothesay gave the lie to that adage. The skin on his face was as coarse as tree bark. Much of it caused by his fondness for the bottle. He had the classic drinker's nose; a large red, veined, bulbous affair. His nickname was The Singing Detective – although he did not suffer from psoriasis and had never been heard to sing a note.

He finally put down his pen and looked at Strawberry, shaking his head mournfully. "This isn't going very well, is it?"

Despite swearing he would not succumb in this room, Strawberry shifted from one foot to the other. "Operation Treetops has been a challenging surveillance. That is true, but I believe we are due for a break."

Rothesay grunted. "Let's hope you're right. The council

leader is bending the chief constable's ear about this whole gardening issue. So I am getting a kicking – and now you are getting a kicking, Strawberry. That's the way it works." Rothesay paused to let the message sink in. "And now there's this suspicious death. Is there any connection with Treetops?"

"Still investigating that too, sir. We haven't made any link yet, though it does seem a strange coincidence. I'm not happy about coincidences. All we can say at the moment is that we are tending to the possibility that there was foul play involved in the death of Arabella Pettygrew. But I am still interviewing the neighbours and other persons of interest."

"I heard about the Glaikits. I remember nicking them when I was on the beat. Career thieves, but murder? I never thought them capable of murder."

"Nor do I, sir. I went through their sheet. They committed a lot of robberies, but never so much as laid a finger on anyone in the commission of these crimes. If anything, they were runners, not fighters. On a number of occasions over the years they have been discovered. Every time they chose flight as the option – and Ginger was big. He could have done someone serious damage."

Rothesay nodded in an expression of what might have been sorrow. "Aye, well, Ginger won't be doing anything to anybody any more."

"We released Bob Duncan on bail shortly after the news of his brother," said Strawberry. "He's still in the picture, but on the margins, I would say."

Rothesay sighed. "All right, Strawberry, we have to get this sewn up – particularly Operation Treetops. I'll give you to the end of this week. After that we'll have to retreat and think again. The council leader has a personal friend on this gardening committee. Apparently he's bending his ear every day, which means the chief's getting the same treatment from Chambers."

Strawberry had made the door and his hand was on the handle when Rothesay grunted again.

"Nearly forgot. There's a serial killer on the loose, Strawberry."

"Sir?"

"A Jonathan Livingston."

"What? We've ID'd him already?"

"No, you idiot. Jonathan Livingston Seagull. The book, Strawberry. Oh, never mind. It's seagulls: someone is killing them. Found two in the Grassmarket. Another couple in the Bridges. More in Princes Street Gardens and St Andrew's Square. The animal rights people are going nuts. As if that's not enough wee Jimmy Krankie – that's the *Furst Meanister* to you – has raised the issue in the Parliament. So get on it, Strawberry, it's a priority."

Strawberry was in the act of leaving and had the door half closed when a chilling thought occurred. "Sir, do we have any information on how the birds are being killed?"

The responding growl of The Singing Detective followed him into the corridor. "One of the PCs mentioned finding a pellet in one of the birds. Just get on with it, Strawberry."

STRAWBERRY'S mind was in turmoil as he took the steps downstairs two at a time. Pellets. Air rifles. PC Murch?

Dougie Nichols had reported the conversation about the bird shit and Murch's suggested solution, laughing while he told Strawberry. But there was nothing funny about the prospect of a rogue copper massacring a protected species.

Christ, as if he didn't have enough on his plate. Operation Treetops, the dead pensioner, a serial killer on the loose slaughtering birdlife, the animal rights brigade up in arms, questions in the Scottish Parliament. And to cap it all, Bert Rothesay on his case.

He had the dismaying sensation of being overwhelmed by events. As always, such anxiety went straight to his bowels. It was touching cloth by the time he rushed into the men's. He just made it into the first cubicle. Pants down. Thunderbirds are go. Blessed relief. Was there any better feeling in the entire universe – apart from sex with Fiona – than voiding one's bowels? He reached for the toilet roll – and found himself staring at brown cardboard on the holder. Still sitting on the bowl, he swivelled his head around the cubicle floor. Nothing. Not a tissue. Not a discarded newspaper. Not a scrap of paper anywhere to be seen. In his charge to evacuation he had ignored one vital rule. Always check the loo roll before opening the trapdoor.

Though there was nothing left to discharge, he could feel his stomach cramping with the stress of his predicament. Big breaths. Breathe in and out – slowly. Now, listen.

Strawberry listened as he had never listened before. Apart from the trickling sound of water from a tap that hadn't been repaired in months, there was silence.

He slid the lock, waited for a second, took another deep breath and – pants around his ankles – shuffled as fast as possible into the next cubicle. Door locked. Made it. Breathed out. Scanned the stall. No paper.

The next few minutes were among the most stressful of Strawberry's life – and that included close encounters with violent criminals.

Pants at his ankles, he shuffle-ran into all five cubicles without result. Finally, heart in mouth, trousers still at ankles, he launched himself on the longest and therefore most perilous journey to the sink and the paper towel dispenser. Empty! Dear God. This was really all about cuts to police budgets. Even so, if he ever got out of this situation, he would track down the cleaning staff and murder every one of them!

Strawberry managed to shuffle-run back to a cubicle just as the main door was opening. He slid the bolt and stood sweating listening to the sound at the urinal.

The man was pissing like a horse and the noise was going on forever. It finally stopped, a tap gushed and then the hand dryer rattled into geriatric life. Strawberry was girding himself for the most pathetic, embarrassing request of his thirty-year existence when a copy of the *Hoots Mon* sailed over the top of the cubicle. It was accompanied by the departing voice of Dougie Nichols. "Always remember to check before you drop anchor, Strawberry."

WHEN Dorothea Hislop arrived home after the Garden Association meeting she took her Labradors Ebony and Ivory out round the block to do their business. It had been a long day and she was really too tired to go any further. But she had taken the time to collect her black baggies before leaving the apartment. Unlike a number of rogue residents – and non-residents she termed 'dirty stop-offs' – Dorothea always tidied up her dogs' mess. She had vowed never to be on the receiving end of one of Marjorie Agincourt's notorious 'baggies' calls.

Apart from anything else, Dorothea was a careful person. She did not draw attention to herself. She travelled under the radar of the hum-drum activities of Balmoral Square Mansions. Her only reason for volunteering for the position of association secretary was to maintain respectability and pick up local gossip, which always spread like wildfire inside that group. Such information might be vital one day.

While the dogs sniffed at railings and cocked legs against lamp posts, Dorothea wondered how Nigel Smail was. Hopefully he had recovered from the dramatic contretemps and was tucked up in bed with a cocoa and his friend Jeremy Sheldrake.

Marjorie's intervention had been a surprise. Nigel

hadn't mentioned additional business but that was typical. He was forgetful and often preoccupied with the increasing number of residents, especially newcomers, who brazenly ignored paying their subscriptions – one or two for years on end! She knew the accounts were in a bad way and Nigel was stressing about the possibility of having to put the subscriptions up – a move that would not be welcomed even by his most loyal followers.

Her dogs suddenly started a terrible commotion and Dorothea looked up to see a large brown and white spotted mongrel rushing at them.

"Rommel! Rommel, come here, boy." Dorothea instantly recognised a languid Home Counties accent and her Irish hackles rose at the patrician sound. Emerging from the darkness at a casual stroll, the owner of the voice was an attractive blonde woman Dorothea guessed at being in her late thirties. She had never seen the woman before.

"Awfully sorry," said the woman as she continued to stroll towards the fracas caused by her animal. "Rommel's a rescue dog," she added by way of explanation for Rommel's behaviour as he tried to bite Ebony.

"Perhaps, but he needs to be under control," said Dorothea. "All this barking will wake the neighbours."

Undeterred, Rommel squatted and did his business – a considerable pile – in the middle of the pavement before trotting back to his owner. She attached the lead and began walking away leaving the steaming ordure *in situ*.

"Wait," called Dorothea. "Aren't you going to do anything about that?"

The woman continued walking, raising a hand in

a vague wave, either of farewell or dismissal. Dorothea firmly believed the latter as she was left staring at the back of the woman's head and what she supposed was a fashionable chignon held in place by a large comb.

Dorothea considered going after her and remonstrating, but such an episode would draw unwanted attention. Also, she had more pressing things to worry about.

When she returned home her fears were confirmed. She could hear the phone ringing as she put the key in the door. She got to it just in time knowing that only one person would be phoning at this time of night.

"Don't let the dogs out. It's not safe," came the anonymous metallic command from the other end of the line. At the end of the curt message the connection terminated leaving Dorothea listening to dead air and wondering what was going to happen to the orders now.

JEREMY Sheldrake answered the door. He was fully dressed, but waving a long cane feather duster.

Strawberry had witnessed feather dusters in risqué plays featuring French maids at the Edinburgh Fringe. He speculated as to whether he and his colleague Brenda Gunn had interrupted the foreplay to some kind of sex game.

Jeremy ushered the officers into the drawing room where they found Nigel Smail, thankfully also fully dressed, in what appeared to be the de rigueur uniform of pretentious middle-aged, middle-class men living in the street – maroon corduroy trousers, voluminous linen shirt (open at the neck) and brown leather-tassled loafers.

His face was soft and fleshy and he radiated a sense of entitlement still to be seen in certain select Edinburgh districts. Strawberry had assumed rather naively that in the twenty-first century this type of person – the dry, drab, carefully assessing, opinionated snob – had disappeared. He was clearly mistaken as amply illustrated by the inhabitants of Balmoral Square Mansions. These people had simply gone indoors, forced into hibernation through age and decrepitude. But the dinosaurs were still alive. They made the occasional foray outside into their own rarified world safe in the knowledge that they were mixing with their own kind. They were still to be found on every local committee influencing the lives of their more modern and enlightened neighbours who were simply too busy working and exhausted to attend meetings on rainy Monday nights.

Nigel was sitting in a large armchair knitting. As the needles clicked, he repeated 'Knit one, purl one'. "Apologies, officers. My little hobby. Coming to the end of a line. Will lose count if I stop – have to unravel and start all over again."

Gunn looked on in genuine admiration, while Strawberry tried to guess what the indistinguishable woollen garment was meant to be.

As if reading the detective's mind Nigel supplied the answer. "It's a cardigan for our association secretary, Dorothea Hislop. She already has one of mine. Almost worn it out and, as her birthday is imminent, I thought I would do another as a surprise. Problem is I'm a bit behind schedule." He put what appeared to be a finished sleeve down, placed his hands in his lap and waited expectantly.

Strawberry had enlisted Gunn for this visit because he needed someone who would sympathise with the pair. Like many enlightened straight men Strawberry supported gay rights, but felt slightly uncomfortable among homosexuals. Perhaps it was a deficiency on his part. But he was certain Gunn would be equally unaware. She was far too feminine – too much of a real woman to know anything about that. How, he asked himself, could anyone with such magnificent breasts have the first clue about gay people?

But she had what Strawberry described as the 'truth

pheromone'. He had watched the reaction of people to her. It was as though she emitted a chemical substance that transmitted itself to people making them trust her. Whether it was about the recovery of their stolen TV set, or revealing their deepest, darkest secrets, people felt secure in confiding in her.

In Nigel Smail's drawing room he felt the power of that same truth pheromone working its magic. "I'm sure Dorothea will love your gift, Mr Smail," she said. "Stripes for the arms, but what will it be for the body?"

"Definitely not stars, dear," Nigel laughed. "I'm thinking something imperial like a purple rib. At this he produced several balls of wool from a sewing basket on a small table beside his armchair.

Jeremy was flitting around the room with the duster cleaning a series of photographic prints on the walls. Strawberry found the action distracting.

"Would you be kind enough to have a seat too, Mr Sheldrake? You also might be able to help us with our inquiries concerning the death of Arabella Pettygrew. The smallest detail could be helpful – no matter how irrelevant you might consider it."

Nigel pursed his small mouth as if in deep concentration. "Well, like everyone else in the street, Inspector, Jeremy and I have given the tragedy a lot of thought. We were speaking about it only the other night in bed."

Gunn gave her saddest puppy-dog look.

Encouraged, Nigel continued. "Well, it could be something or nothing, but are you aware that Arabella has a brother?"

Strawberry unearthed his notebook from his man bag.

"His name is Freddie Pettygrew. He lives in a place called Boca Raton. It's in Florida. Very chi-chi. Anyway, he comes over every summer to see Arabella without fail. Of course I'm not casting aspersions, Inspector. You understand I wouldn't dream of doing any such thing."

Nigel looked for reassurance at Gunn, who nodded understandingly. "He may have been already. I have no idea. As far as I know, he is Arabella's only relative and…" – here Nigel's mouth formed a small o – "…could stand to inherit her apartment – plus other property I believe she has, sorry, had somewhere in the city."

Strawberry's pen remained poised. "That's interesting, Mr Smail. Did Ms Pettygrew ever confide her brother's address to you?"

Nigel looked shocked. "You misunderstand, Inspector. I can't remember ever speaking to the deceased. She was a very private person and naturally, I would never intrude where I wasn't wanted. No, this is rumour I heard on the jungle drums, as it were."

Strawberry smiled. "Of course, sir, the famous Garden Association."

Nigel Smail inclined his head as a potentate would when acknowledging an inferior being.

"Anything else occur to you, sir, or to you, Mr Sheldrake?"

Jeremy shook his head. "Only what Nige's already told you, Mr Strawberry. The oldster didn't appear to socialise with anyone."

Strawberry closed his notebook. He was still feeling

slightly out of sorts following his panic at Gayfield Square. "Mind if I use your toilet, Mr Smail?"

Nigel waved in Jeremy's direction. "Show the detective to the cloakroom, will you, dear?"

Somewhat reluctantly, Jeremy trudged across the drawing room into the hall and wordlessly indicated a door with his feather duster.

There was no need to check for toilet paper. Nigel's cloakroom toilet possessed reams of it – finest luxury brand. Plus fresh heated towels. A soothing cinnamon scent hung in the air. Gays certainly knew about home comforts, he thought.

Turning to flush he stared into the face of Hamish Agincourt. The great walrus moustache was unmistakable. Though hanging in a miniature picture frame above the WC, it looked like an exact replica of the large oil painting in Marjorie Agincourt's apartment.

"I see you knew the late Hamish Agincourt," said Strawberry on his return to the drawing room.

Nigel smiled nostalgically. "Ah, Hammy. He was a first-class horticulturalist, you know. Learned a lot about plants during his military sojourns – particularly in Malaya. Had more time to devote to it after his illness."

Strawberry nodded. "During my interview with Mrs Agincourt she said he had been badly wounded in the course of his duties."

"Dear Madge," Nigel smiled indulgently. "Such a worrywart. No, I was referring to beriberi. He contracted a severe dose of beriberi, Strawberry. Knocked him sideways. Was never the same again, poor chap, but it proved a boon for us."

Strawberry looked politely at Smail. "In what way?"

"During his convalescence he became quite the expert in tropical plants and when he came back to Edinburgh he was invaluable to our little Garden Association. Leading light, Strawberry. Even introduced some of the more exotic varieties – though they couldn't cope with our dreadful climate. Poor Hammy – taken away from us far too soon." Nigel produced a silk handkerchief and dabbed his eyes.

"Thank you, both," said Strawberry, rising. "If either of you thinks of anything else, please don't hesitate to get in touch."

As Gunn followed suit, Strawberry caught Smail having a sneaky peak at his colleague's assets from behind his handkerchief. Did Nigel swing both ways? As Marjorie Agincourt might have put it – was he 'bipolar'?

MIAMI Airport. A collision of tribes. A hen party Florida style: a gaggle of young Southern Belles – luxuriant blonde tresses topped by Stetsons, swirls of backless, searing white taffeta to the ankles.

A posse of middle-aged businessmen hollering and hooting after three too many at the champagne bar. Jackets slung over shoulders in the subtropical heat, spreading sweat rings staining shirt armpits, bellies so big they couldn't see their tooled alligator cowboy boots.

A line of convicts shuffling in chains Indian-file through the main concourse – their outriders two US marshals toting pump-action shotguns.

This was the reason Freddie Pettygrew loved airports. What was the Shakespeare quote? *All the world's a stage. And all the men and women merely players.* Half a millennium too early perhaps, but he was sure the Bard would have appreciated airports too. The carousel of humanity constantly moving and ever-changing characters for Freddie's delectation as he sat wedged into the arse-tight bucket seats in departures taking in the show, his red rucksack by his side.

He believed in travelling light, especially where he was bound. A duty call. He wouldn't be staying long. No more than a couple of weeks. Just long enough to try and get a handle on Arabella's current madness – though he doubted that would be possible even with limitless time.

He also had his own life to lead. He had emigrated from Scotland to the US forty years ago in a bid to break free from the Calvinistic shackles of dour Edinburgh.

It had been a tough transition at first, taking any menial job that would pay the rent. Gradually he had picked up qualifications at night school and made his way from New York to a less hectic existence in Florida. It was there he had spent his professional career as a railway engineer.

The railway had made Florida. The sunshine state had been an uninhabitable malarial swamp until the turn of the twentieth century when a visionary named Henry Flagler tamed the Everglades and built his railroad. Everyone knew the story of the early settlers and their epic journey from the east coast across the hostile prairies to California. That was the stuff of Hollywood movie legend, but in Freddie's view Florida was an equally towering achievement in the development of the modern United States and a testament to the ingenuity and industry of the American spirit.

He and his partner, Jeanie C, had had their moments. But by and large they had been happy and lucky to live in Boca Raton – the place where Florida's railway revolution had started. Jeanie C had died suddenly eighteen months ago. Taken by a voracious cancer that had reduced her to five stones in as many weeks and in the end – despite the morphine – left her writhing in agony in a foetal ball. He had retired directly after the funeral and played a lot of golf in a bid to take his mind off Jeanie C's death and his loneliness. It hadn't worked.

The boarding call came over the tannoy. Freddie hitched his luggage on his shoulder and climbed aboard. He liked airports, but the same couldn't be said for flying. He could only afford economy which meant minimum legroom and the prospect of some snot-nosed kid kicking the back of his seat for eight solid hours. He got lucky; the kid didn't materialise. But this time the journey held an added element of anxiety. Thirty minutes into the flight he bought a whisky and took the letter from his pocket.

Writing was his sister's favourite – in fact only – mode of communication. She was too mean to use the telephone, especially at transatlantic rates. On the very few occasions some so-called emergency – usually involving the leaking roof – had prompted her to pick up the phone she made sure to reverse the charges. She had never owned a computer – far less a mobile phone. So e-mails and texting was an alien concept to her.

This latest epistle had arrived six weeks ago. That was the first hint of a problem. Arabella was a creature of habit. Her letters arrived every month as regularly as clockwork – meaning the next letter was two weeks overdue. He had tried phoning her and visualised the black Bakelite phone on the scarred hall table ringing through the flat. There had been no answer and he had tried several times.

His imagination started to work overtime. What if she had fallen and couldn't summon help? She also shunned the neighbours. What if she had become ill and been taken to hospital – too ill perhaps to give him as next of kin? Those fears had spurred him to book a flight a week earlier than his normal annual visit.

He opened the expensive notepaper, her only

concession to luxury, and reread the letter. The first clear sign that something had gone very wrong with his already crazy spinster sister was her handwriting. Elegant script was a source of lifelong pride to her. She had won prizes at school for her calligraphy, but the writing he looked at now was scratchy and disjointed, meandering without art or form across the page.

Perhaps more worrying was the fact that the content was rambling and at times completely incoherent. She referred to threats without any indication of what those threats might be, or their source. She addressed the plight of the illiterate, the incarcerated, the homeless. It seemed a garbled sermon addressing the miseries of the world – a subject Arabella had successfully managed to ignore for the past sixty-nine years until now. What had changed? Had she found religion? Was that the catalyst for this Damascene conversion from self-absorbed hermit to five-star Good Samaritan? Freddie didn't have a clue, but he knew he would have to try and find out – not least for the fact that he had invested a lot of time and energy in crazy Arabella and expected his reward perhaps sooner rather than later now.

August was Freddie's favourite time in Edinburgh. Festival time. The city came alive with street performers. Clubs and pubs stayed open into the small hours. The population doubled to a million for the month when tourists from all over the world invaded the city and the locals, either escaped on holiday letting out their homes for astronomical sums, or battened down the hatches and gurned about the overcrowding.

Freddie wasn't a great arts man, but once he had

sorted his sister out he meant to find the time to do a few golf rounds on the coastal links at the village of Gullane, or was it Gillane now? The locals had fulminated over the correct spelling, but more importantly pronunciation, of the name for years. Recently he had seen something on the internet claiming that a notable local golf club's members were so exercised by the issue they had enlisted the expert opinion of a professor in social history. After stating the pros and cons for each camp in forensic historical detail, the eminent academic had finally noted that the majority of the village's residents favoured the 'u' sound. Sky television commentators covering the Scottish Open held on the links course had also opted for Gullane. Freddie harboured the vain hope that the pretentious Gillane snobs had finally been put in their box as such affectation had been one of the reasons for his departure to the New World so many years before.

He disembarked into a cool early morning and a fine drizzle. He had been checking Edinburgh temperatures on his phone over the past few weeks and it had been full of record-breaking temperatures. Back to normal now, he thought. Not a patch on the amazing climate he had left.

Clearing customs, he rejected a taxi for the tram. Unlike most of the resident population, he liked the tram. He found its pace – you could probably throw your hat harder – relaxing. And he needed to be relaxed right now.

Getting off at the Haymarket stop, Freddie circumnavigated the ubiquitous roadworks and headed along the grand Victorian square to his sister's apartment.

During the short walk the rain increased in intensity

and by the time he arrived at the stair his trousers were sodden beneath his waterproof jacket.

As usual the main front door had not been closed properly, so grinning wickedly at the flap she would be in at his unannounced arrival, he ignored the entry phone and started climbing the steps. On route he had to squeeze past a buggy and an infant's bicycle on the second landing. New neighbours.

Arabella would no doubt be overjoyed at the prospect of screaming kids. He bet that topic would come high on her list of complaints. By the time he reached the top landing he was looking at his feet and breathing hard, so it took him a moment to take in the scene. Yellow and black tape cordoned off the entire landing and a notice on Arabella's front door warned potential intruders: CRIME SCENE. DO NOT CROSS.

Freddie had no memory of coming back down the stair. He was in a state of such shock that he didn't even notice the police car sliding into the kerb. One of the officers got out and walked up the steps to where Freddie was standing in a daze. The policeman spoke quietly though no one was around on the street.

"Sir, are you Mr Frederick Pettygrew?"

Freddie took so long to register the question that the policeman had to repeat it. "Freddie, yes. My sister. There are crime scene tapes across her door."

The policeman steered Freddie by the arm to the car. "It's best we explain at the station, sir."

The journey to Gayfield Square took longer than usual because of Edinburgh's seemingly permanent roadworks, and the influx of tourists oblivious to the traffic and crossing the roads like lemmings without any thought to personal safety.

During the drive Freddie tried several times to ask about Arabella, but each time the officer in the passenger seat simply smiled, declaring, "We'll soon be there."

Strawberry and Gunn were seated and waiting when Freddie was ushered into the interview room.

Strawberry had already prepped Gunn to take the lead. She was solicitous, but at the same time understood that bad news could not be sugar-coated. It had to be communicated in simple, straightforward language that could not be misinterpreted.

"Please sit down, Mr Pettygrew. I'm afraid I have some very distressing news."

Freddie was staring at Gunn as though he already knew what she was going to say but was willing a different outcome. After his attempted questions in the patrol car, now that the moment of revelation had come, he remained silent.

"Your sister, Miss Arabella Pettygrew, is dead. She fell from the roof of her apartment building last week. I am very sorry to have to give you such terrible news."

Even though his sister had often been an irritating incumbrance she was still flesh and blood. The colour drained from Freddie's face. He at last found a word. "How?"

It was Strawberry who replied. "We are examining a number of possibilities, Mr Pettygrew. It could be that your sister had a tragic accident…"

"She was on the roof doing her DIY stint, right?"

Although Freddie had been stateside most of his adult

life, Strawberry detected the underlying Scottish burr. "She was obsessed with that roof. I don't know how many times I warned her."

Freddie caught the assessing look Strawberry gave him. "You don't think it was an accident, do you?"

"At this stage we can't say. But the neighbours all say she was fit and sure-footed up there."

"So what are you saying – that she jumped! Never. Arabella might have been crazy and no doubt lonely, but she would never have committed suicide. Not in her DNA, Officer."

Strawberry paused. "We are tending more towards foul play."

"Murder! She was a nutbag with no friends, but equally no enemies. What could the motive possibly be?"

Freddie looked at both officers in turn. Their expressions were carefully neutral.

"Mr Pettygrew, my understanding is that as the only relative you would stand to gain a substantial inheritance following the death of your sister."

The colour was back in Freddie's face and rising alarmingly. "What is this? I only discover my sister's dead an hour ago and you try to hang a murder charge on me. I need a lawyer." Freddie was out of the chair, fists clenching. *If the table wasn't between us he would have a pop at me*, reckoned Strawberry.

"Please, Mr Pettygrew, we are trying to establish the circumstances of your sister's death," said Gunn, spreading her hands in a placatory gesture. "We're not accusing anyone right now. We need your help as one of the few people who really knew Arabella."

Freddie reluctantly sat down, but anger remained in his voice. He pointed accusingly at Strawberry. "I'm assuming you've seen my sister's place. It's a dump. Collapsing. Not even a shower. I had to go out to the public baths every day and that's been going on for years. It would cost me a fortune even to make it barely habitable. Some piece of real estate to kill for, Officer."

"What about her other property in Leith?"

Freddie gave Strawberry a sour look. "You have been busy. Pity you didn't devote more of your energies to letting me know my sister was dead. For your information I haven't seen the Leith flat for years. It's probably in the same state as the one she lived in."

"All right, but even untouched those assets could fetch you a million plus in a heated housing market like Edinburgh."

Freddie shook his head. "Oh yeah and you forgot Noodles." Strawberry looked askance. "Her freaking cat! Anyway, I only landed this morning. I wasn't even in the damned country when she died."

"We have established that, Mr Pettygrew, but just to play devil's advocate for a moment: you could have had her killed."

In spite of the situation Freddie laughed – though it was heavy with irony. "A hit man. A contract killer. You sound like a fictional detective in a second-rate TV crime drama."

"**WELL,** that went well." Strawberry was sitting in the police canteen with Gunn, going over the interview with Freddie.

"An unlikely candidate and the hit-man theory is a stretch, I will admit," said Strawberry. "But stranger things have happened. Remember the ice-cream wars? The Glasgow Gnoccis brought a hit man over from their home town in Sicily."

Gunn gave a blank look. "Okay, maybe before your time," said Strawberry, who for the first time wondered how old Gunn actually was. "Anyway, right now he's the only person with a motive. We'll put a tail on him and see what happens."

THE killer bought a poke of chips. Sometimes he opted for a tub of ice cream. It was all the same really. Either one was an irresistible lure to his victims. There were regular stories in the newspapers of ice-cream cones or chips being snatched from the hands of unsuspecting people by the predators swooping from the skies in their brazen attacks.

He hated them. They were no more than flying vermin. Fucking seagulls. They nested on tenement roofs all over the city – shitting on cars, shitting on people – and there wasn't a thing any member of the public could do about it. Tamper with any of their precious nests and you were in a world of trouble with the animal rights people.

He had seen a vain attempt to combat the birds when someone had put up a dummy seagull on a wire fluttering above a roof. That deterrent had survived a week until the seagulls had gotten wise to the fact that the newcomer was a dummy and presented no threat. They pecked and dive-bombed it to shreds.

How seagulls could be regarded as a protected species and safeguarded under law was a mystery to him. It was just another example of senseless wishy-washy liberal shit ruling the roost yet again.

Well, the council might be happy to allow these filthy brutes free reign to pillage bins and litter the streets of his beautiful city with rotting food and shitty nappies. But he was not.

Seagull Slayer – for that was his self-styled title, after all a superhero needed a touch of alliteration in the name – considered it his duty, no, much more than that – a solemn crusade – to clean up the city streets and return Edinburgh to its rightful place as the Athens of the North.

His most challenging decision had been the choice of balaclava. The Urban Classic Zipped Visor looked good and was one of the less expensive ones on the Amazon website. Then there was the Thermal Fleece Hood Police Swat style. Sexeee! He giggled at the name as he enlarged the image on his computer. The Trixes Skull Balaclava was a real temptation with its white skeletal mouth. A great statement – but sadly unsuitable for someone who needed to go about his business under the radar, or at least not under the eye of CCTV cameras. So it came down to a decision between the Mil-Tec Tactical model, featuring army camouflage, and the plain black Military Style Balaclava. He decided to go low-key and went for the plain black.

The headgear was currently in the boot of the car along with the weapon. He knew all the best locations to find them. The Grassmarket was teeming with the bastards simply because there were so many bins overflowing with the flotsam and jetsam of modern-day life on the hoof.

But it was also dangerous, especially at this time of year with the festival in full swing and people on the streets until all hours.

The West End was similarly productive as the bastards made their nests on the roofs of the flats and enjoyed dive-bombing the numerous bins that the council couldn't be bothered emptying. But the district posed the same kind of threat with an increasing number of houses being let out as Airbnbs and potential witnesses out and about until late.

Tonight he had opted for a series of grimy back streets well away from the festival epicentre – off Regent Road and overlooking Arthur's Seat.

He had reccied the area in daylight and was satisfied that there were enough escape routes in the event of discovery – even if it meant ditching the stolen car and legging it through Holyrood Park.

Now, under cover of darkness, he parked up under a bridge and took the balaclava and the cue bag from the boot. To the casual onlooker he would simply be some sad bloke on his way to play pool. Nor would the lateness of the hour arouse any suspicion. Many pool clubs were open all night to cater for insomniacs, night-shift workers, boozers, and plain pool nuts.

He placed the bag of chips on the pavement under a street light and close to four big bins. Then he retreated back under the bridge and into the shadows. He donned the balaclava, removed the air rifle from the cue bag and waited. So far he had bagged a dozen of the dirty buggers and his fame was spreading.

Over breakfast he had read a brief story in the *Hoots Mon* about his exploits, only it had slagged him off for being a 'perverted and cruel animal killer'. Later in the toilet, he used the page to wipe his arse.

He didn't have long to wait. A dirty great ugly bugger landed on the pavement and started waddling towards the prize. Cocky bugger, he thought, as he checked the area for people. Deserted. He raised the rifle and sighted on the target. The phut of the pellet missed the seagull and pinged off a rubbish bin. Shit. The bird took immediate flight, but only for a few yards landing clumsily on top of one of the bins. Remarkably the council had recently emptied them, so there were no tempting titbits available. It hopped down again, its webbed feet skittering in a noise that made his skin crawl over the bin's metal top and moved slowly towards the chips.

Greed, thought Seagull Slayer, greed was always going to be the undoing of these loathsome scavengers. He placed the thin stock of the rifle under his chin and tight against his neck. Steady the hands. Calm the breathing. Concentrate. Slowly squeeze the trigger. Bingo! This time the pellet found its mark hitting the seagull in the arse. The bird squawked, meandered drunkenly and tried to take off. Instead it belly-flopped and lay flapping its wings uselessly. Its beak snapped open and shut in a series of spastic clicks. It sounded prehistoric to Seagull Slayer – reminiscent of a muted version of the noise the Velociraptors made in the film *Jurassic Park*.

As he walked up to it, the seagull turned its head and one yellow feral eye appeared to glare straight at him. "Giving me the evils, you fucker." He raised his Doc Martens boot and brought it down on the creature's head. "Something else for your mates to eat." His laughter echoed through the dark tunnel as he sauntered to the car.

STRAWBERRY was on a rare night off with Fiona. He couldn't really afford the time what with the Arabella Pettygrew investigation, Operation Treetops, and now the seagull serial killer case adding to his already considerable workload.

Bert Rothesay wanted results and his patience was running out. Strawberry knew the signs.

The superintendent hadn't said anything for several days now. When the boss went quiet that was when you went to ground and held onto your hat. Rothesay was like a smouldering volcano slowly building up to an eruption and when he blew Strawberry would be directly in line of the fallout.

"Richard! Calling all interplanetary craft. Are you with us?" Strawberry suddenly realised that Fiona was speaking and he was ignoring her.

"Jeez, sorry, Fiona, you're right, I was on another planet."

"Well, pull your socks up, buddy – you're on planet McLuckie now."

They were walking down Lothian Road passing the historic graveyard bordering Princes Street. This was Fiona's last evening before she jetted off to Hong Kong for the international curling competition and here he was thinking about dead seagulls! *Get a grip, man!*

Silently he banned all thoughts of work for the evening and determined to give his girlfriend his full attention. Exhausted by his case-load, he felt he had been neglecting her lately and that would never do.

He had made a secret visit to a well-known jeweller in George Street and bought a very expensive ring. He planned to propose when she returned from Hong Kong.

"Back in the room," he joked as they passed a legless beggar holding out a cap containing a few coins. He scrambled for change knowing how sentimental Fiona got about the homeless. Nothing but a fiver. Keep smiling. He placed the note in the man's hat and sidelong saw the look of appreciation in her eyes. Worth every penny. "Come on, let's catch a drink before the show."

"I don't think we've got time, Richard."

"A quick one at your favourite place – in anticipation of your curling victory." The West End bar was a favourite watering hole for Edinburgh's young professional class, but the tourists had substantially increased custom.

They managed to squeeze into a booth in the corner, hip to hip. He could feel the heat of her body through her dress – a strapless red number.

He had a pint and she had a cocktail called A Scottish Mule whose ingredients included something called Copper Dog, strawberry liqueur, lime juice and ginger beer. They hurried from the bar holding hands as they weaved at a jog through the crowds to Rose Street and the venue.

A soporific heat enveloped them as they descended to the basement where the play was being staged. The place was packed, principally with older Scots, and they made it just as the performance was beginning.

The tragi-comic tale followed the efforts of a middle-aged female Elvis impersonator living with her mother in Aberdeen to make the big time – a world championship Elvis impersonator competition in Las Vegas. Dressed in Elvis's trademark star-spangled white costume, her Doric rendition of 'Are You Lonesome *The Nicht*' brought the house down.

Fiona was still laughing as they made their way up the stairs from the sauna-like atmosphere into the cooler evening air. They went to another pub in Rose Street thronged with American and Chinese tourists toting expensive cameras and selfie-sticks. Strawberry could barely hide the smirk as he watched a young woman sitting on her own photographing her plate of food. Where would this personalised idolisation end, he wondered? Would the self-obsessed millennials ultimately be snapping their ablutions on a smartphone to share with their friends? Look, mine's bigger than yours.

Thankfully Fiona was oblivious to his bias. She took a very different view being fully integrated into the 'me' generation. He had never discussed the issue with her, intuitively realising that she would think him an old fogey for his antiquated views.

Luck was with them and they found another seat at a table at the rear of the bar.

A couple were sitting over from them. The man, a large overweight individual in his early thirties, was perched on a stool and every time he leaned forward for his drink his jeans rode down and his bum-crack showed. It was particularly hairy. Fiona thought it hilarious, while Strawberry found the sight vaguely nauseating.

He had intended to subtly sound Fiona out on her personal plans for the future. But reckoned this was not the setting for a serious or romantic tête-à-tête. He decided to stay on safe ground.

"Excited about the tournament?"

"That would be an understatement," she said, almost bouncing on her seat at the prospect. "This could be my breakthrough, Richard. If I put in a good performance I can become a regular team member and, who knows, from there the Commies and Olympics."

Fiona looked radiant at the prospect. He could visualise an image of her, standing on a podium in a distant land, a gold medal round her neck, a tear glistening in her eye as 'Flower of Scotland', or the national anthem played.

"Aggh!" Fiona's triumphant reverie was shattered by an unexpected soaking. Bum Crack Boy had been returning with drinks from the bar when he stumbled and poured half his pint down her red dress.

Her dismay quickly turned to anger. "What do you think you are doing, you clumsy oaf?"

The man was clearly drunk and completely unrepentant "…Sa mistake. Keep your heid on, dear," he slurred in a Polish accent. Suddenly he was compounding the accident by dabbing at Fiona's dress with a none too clean napkin.

As he touched her leg, Fiona leapt up knocking into the man and that's when the remainder of his pint caught her full on the chest. She abruptly sat down again too shocked by the second dooking to make a sound.

For a second Strawberry stood riveted in place in stunned horror. The evening had suddenly taken a dramatic turn for the worse. Despite the fact that it had been an accident, the man had been rude and he knew he would have to say something robust. Fiona would expect a strong reaction, but at the same time he was a police officer and caution would have to be employed.

He moved towards the swaying drunk and held him by the sleeve. "You've soaked my girlfriend's best dress. She's due a proper apology, mate, not you coming out with smart remarks."

The Pole smacked Strawberry's hand away. "…Sa mistake, I say. Fuck off, mister, you and your beech."

Suddenly the Pole's companion was at his side launching an attack in broad Scots. "It wasnie deliberate, big man. Why don't you an' the wife fuck off? This isnae the pub for the likes o' fancy dans like you oniwie."

Fiona was on her feet again, dripping wet with a small puddle of lager pooling at her feet, but she had regained the power of speech and was incandescent. "Arrest the bastard, Richard. These people are foreigners. They have invaded Leith. A night in the cells will teach him a lesson."

Strawberry was aghast. His girlfriend had suffered severe provocation. That was patently true. But she had now revealed his professional identity and that made the situation ten times more difficult as any off-duty serving officer could testify.

"Ye hear that, Marek. He's a pig. You've spilt your drink over the wifey of a pig an' now he's gonna arrest ye. Wooooo." The woman, as drunk as her partner, feigned terror at the prospect.

"All right, that's enough, both of you," said Strawberry. "Any more of it and I will have you arrested."

Pub conversation had frozen as the customers were glued to the exchange. Strawberry looked over at the barman in a silent appeal. A skeletal youth with greasy hair in a ponytail, he was drying glasses and didn't seem to have any inclination to get involved.

"Listen, mate, I don't know whether you're a copper or not, but those folk are regulars here every Saturday – and I've never seen you or your wife before. My advice. You best leave."

"I'm NOT his wife," Fiona screeched as Strawberry guided the bedraggled figure of his girlfriend from the pub.

Fiona was ominously quiet on the walk to the taxi rank. Strawberry inwardly cursed the appalling turn of events. The evening had started so well and now it was in ruins and she was flying to Hong Kong tomorrow. But he couldn't think of anything to say to patch things up between them. She had expected him either to beat up the Polish drunk, or arrest him. Neither action could have been contemplated by a detective in his position, but he could never really explain that to her. She would never understand. As far as she was concerned, her protector, her gallant knight, had let her down – a lapse a woman like Fiona might never forgive.

"Hiya. *Big Issue*, please!" Fuck, another foreigner! Strawberry recognised the woman. She was dressed from head to foot in some black Middle Eastern garb and always occupied the same pitch on a corner of Princes Street. He waved her away with the moral blackmail of her forgiveness – "God bless you" – ringing in his ears.

He wondered miserably what she was doing trying to sell the paper at this time of night. Equally, he had noticed a foreign family, including some young children, bedded down for the night in the doorway of the House of Fraser. Lately he had been aware of a definite increase in the numbers of homeless people dossing down on Edinburgh's streets. What was happening to the city? But, more selfishly, what was happening to him?

They got back to the flat at midnight. Strawberry went to the bathroom.

By the time he had brushed his teeth she was in bed in her tartan winceyette pyjamas – a clear signal of her displeasure as she normally slept gloriously au natural. Her back was to him either asleep, or more likely feigning it: literally the cold shoulder.

He slipped in between the sheets careful not to invade her space and spent a largely sleepless night, finally nodding off an hour before the alarm jangled him awake at 4 a.m. He found the other side of the bed empty and blearily scrambled into his clothes. He caught her as she was about to leave.

"I'll give you a lift out, Fiona."

"I've already ordered a taxi. It will be here any moment." Her voice was muted, but he could still detect the hurt and recrimination from the night before.

He went out and paid the taxi off. Then helped Fiona, who was at least silently compliant, with her luggage into his own car. It was an ageing Ford and seldom used due to Strawberry's newly found passion for cycling. So he quietly thanked God when the engine fired first pop.

The twenty-minute journey was passed without a word being exchanged and Strawberry knew better than to push conversation. He could only hope that she would review the evening and come to recognise the difficulty of his situation during the forthcoming flight. After all, it would be long enough.

At the airport, polite but distant, she insisted on him letting her out at the drop-off point. He knew that in this mood there could be no debate with her. Any such course of action would merely escalate into a replay of the night before. Nor would there be the remotest prospect of mouth-to-mouth resuscitation. Instead he received a fleeting peck on the cheek and with a sad "Take care of yourself" she was gone.

Unshaven and unwashed, he arrived at the station in a state of extreme weariness – both physical and mental. He couldn't face the grubby nature of the men's showers. On the last occasion he had ventured near one after a sweaty cycle ride, he had changed his mind after seeing the amount of hair on the filthy mat. He was beginning to believe that the cleaners had abdicated all responsibility for the male changing rooms. He made a tired mental note to ask Gunn if the same was true of the female facilities.

HE got the phone call around mid-morning. It was like having a hangover and suddenly being smacked on the back of the head with a heavy blunt instrument.

"Raspberry, is that you?" Strawberry's heart sank. He would have recognised that voice anywhere – even without the attendant insult.

"Mrs Agincourt. How can I help you?"

"It's the other way round, Raspberry. Builders!"

Marjorie exclaimed the word as one might say 'Eureka!'.

Strawberry finally had to fill the intervening silence. "Builders, Mrs Agincourt?"

"Yes, yes. Polish builders. They worked for months in the apartment below Arabella renovating it for the new owners – Ross and Blunt."

"Ross and Blunt?"

"Are you going to repeat everything I say like some parrot, you stupid policeman? It's one of those modern relationships. Unmarried." Coming from Mrs Agincourt's mouth it sounded like a dirty word. "Ross is the man, Blunt is the woman. They have two very small, very noisy infants. Anyway, that's not the point, Raspberry. You have thrown me off track. The point is that they hired Polish builders to do work to the flat before they moved in. It took months. I'm sure they slept overnight in the flat on a number of occasions. Singing and laughing until all hours. The noise was terrible."

"I'm assuming you are talking about the workmen, Mrs Agincourt?"

"Naturally, man. Never mind your name, I have no idea how they ever allowed anyone as slow as you to become a policeman."

Ignoring the barbs, Strawberry pressed her to continue.

"Of course I tried to complain. I mean surely builders should not be staying overnight in the apartment they are working in. But every time I tried to catch either of them, Ross, or the woman, they managed to make some excuse and shut the door before I could have my say."

Strawberry found himself sympathising with the couple already. "My phone call is to alert you to the fact that the builders were there in the building all the time. I started thinking that perhaps Arabella had said something to upset one of them. Perhaps they learned she lived alone and decided to return and rob her after they had finished renovating the Ross and Blunt apartment. I have no idea, but the thought gave me the shivers. It could have been me they decided to bump off – after all, I have many more valuables than Arabella ever had in her shabby little flat."

Strawberry promised to look into it.

THERE was a solitary bunch of flowers for Arabella Pettygrew's funeral service. They sat on top of her plain wooden coffin looking weary as though they had been purchased at a motorway service station.

Strawberry and Gunn were in attendance along with young Angus Robertson whom Strawberry had assigned to tail Freddie Pettygrew. They were all in plain clothes and trying to make themselves inconspicuous at the back of the chapel. That plan was proving difficult, however, as there were so few mourners.

Freddie was seated on a pew at the front wearing what looked like a hired suit. When he rose for the minister, Strawberry saw he was wearing trainers. He clearly hadn't been financially able, or simply unwilling to invest in more appropriate footwear. Marjorie Agincourt had put in an appearance too. No show without punch, mused Strawberry. Her entrance was heralded by the tapping of the silver-handled walking stick as – dressed in the same oriental garb, pink turban included, that the detective had encountered on their first meeting – she doddered down the aisle.

Strawberry wondered if she ever changed, or washed for that matter. The idea of old women and smelly knickers entered his head. He looked guiltily at Gunn worried that his face had perhaps betrayed his thoughts. But she was looking around the chapel at the woebegone straggle of Balmoral Square Mansions residents who were present. There was the 'Lieutenant', Jock Witherspoon, looking a bit like an extra in *Dad's Army* wearing his uniform. Nigel Smail and Jeremy Sheldrake (thankfully not holding hands), the Tweedies, Peter and Marcy, and the Cruduckers, Fanny and Emile – though she was already showing signs of narcolepsy, drooping dangerously in her pew.

The minister's booming voice jerked her upright. It had a similar effect on the others comprising the motley congregation. He was a small, portly man with apple-red cheeks, but the power of his tonsils belied his diminutive appearance. The sound was deep, like the boom of a cannon.

"We are here today to celebrate the life of a friend and neighbour taken from us prematurely and in tragic circumstances."

The thunderous rumble of his Mons Meg delivery bounced off the walls of the small chapel. "Arabella Pettygrew was a very private person, an individual who was at peace in her own company and never happier than when she was walking in the hills and mountains of her native Scotland, snapping images of our breathtaking landscape with her simple Box Brownie camera."

Strawberry tried to shut down. He was still recovering from the upsetting nature of his parting with Fiona. She had been in Hong Kong for four days now and he hadn't received so much as a text from her. So he felt he could do without bland eulogies, but the foghorn nature of the sermon made it impossible. If he ever removed the collar, this guy could get a job as MC for a world heavyweight-boxing contest – 'Ready to ruuuuuumble'.

He noticed that Gunn was actually making notes. She had very neat handwriting and small, rather delicate hands. She had applied nail varnish for the occasion.

"And now Arabella's brother, Frederick, would like to share a few anecdotes about his sister with…" The minister's peroration was interrupted by a loud bang as the chapel door swung open on its hinges.

Dishevelled was a completely inadequate adjective to describe the four figures who stumbled into the chapel. One was clearly a woman with a narrow face and a furrowed brow. Two of the men had stubble heads while the third favoured a *Catweazle*-style. They wore a jumble-sale mixture of greatcoats, Parkas, camouflage jackets and oversize jumpers. Their footwear was equally eclectic featuring Doc Martens, trainers and gumboots while the woman wore a pair of Uggs splitting apart at the seams. Their grimy features made it difficult to determine age – and the unwashed stench deterred close inspection.

"This is a funeral service. Respect is due!" The minister's voice boomed from the pulpit at the intruders who stopped dead in their tracks bumping into one another like an unruly batch of skittles. In any other context, the scene would have been amusing, but after their initial surprise at the mighty voice of the small clergymen, one of the stubble heads took a step forward.

"We mean no disrespect. We are here to pay our respects to the miss. My name's Gav. This here's Laundry." He pointed at the *Catweazle* lookalike. "Then we got Glum Sue. Last but never least is Four-Fingers Bob." He pointed to the smallest of the men wearing a greatcoat two sizes too big. "We are homeless. The miss is…" – recognising his error he paused to correct the tense – "…was, she was like a saint to us. She helped us and we are here to remember her and pay tribute."

Like a magician, Gav produced a much better bouquet of flowers from inside his Parka, and head down, moved uncertainly forward and placed the flowers on top of the coffin. Then maintaining the same supplicant posture, he retreated to join the group.

During the interlude the onlookers had been stunned into silence. But now the chapel was abuzz with speculation and whispered questions as Arabella Pettygrew's neighbours tried to fathom how on earth the late hermit in their midst could have any connection with homeless vagabonds.

Predictably it was Marjorie Agincourt who led the prosecution. Leaning heavily on her silver-handled walking stick, she pointed a shaking liver-spotted hand at the group. Her voice – though lacking the baritone gravitas of the minister – accentuated the righteous indignation of Balmoral Square Mansions' crème de la crème.

"I don't know what you people are up to. This must be some kind of trick in order to obtain money – and at a funeral service of all places! But it won't work. In common with her neighbours, Arabella was a person of status. She might have been peculiar and solitary, but she had rank in Edinburgh society. A social standing that would preclude her from any association with people like you." Clearly spent from the effort of her tirade, Marjorie slumped down on the bench and looked around expectantly for support.

Peter Tweedie cleared his throat as though ready to launch his own brand of superiority. A rapid dig from Marcy quelled that urge. "We should not jump to conclusions," she said. "I doubt these people came all this way out here to solicit money. The idea is preposterous – particularly as they could do much better begging in the city centre."

'The Lieutenant' was standing ramrod straight with the glint of combat in his eyes. "I was almost in their position." He nodded at the men. "After the war a lot of men found it hard to go back to civilian life. If it hadn't been for my late wife – God bless her, she saved me from the drink – I might have found myself out on the street."

"Enough!" The minister's stentorian voice echoed off the rafters high above the chapel. "This is no place for an inquisition. This is a funeral service. These people have conducted themselves with dignity. That is all I would ask of anyone on such an occasion. None of us should rush to judgement. There but for the grace of God." He looked straight at Marjorie Agincourt. "Now the service will continue in the solemnity deserving of the deceased."

"Abide With Me" played as the coffin slipped through the curtains and into the fires beyond. In a moment of idle speculation, Strawberry wondered if the music was there to deliberately mask the whoosh of the fiery conflagration. After all, anyone opting for cremation would ultimately go the same way. He saw no reason why the living should be assailed with the Dolby surround experience of an inferno.

Strawberry and Gunn left the chapel and climbed into a fleet car used by the police for such discreet occasions. He saw Freddie's designated tail, Angus Robertson, pretending nonchalance as he smoked a cigarette under a tree. "He'll never emulate his old man," said Strawberry with a cruel hint of satisfaction.

"What do you mean, sir?" asked Gunn. She was in the passenger seat close enough for her perfume to be a pleasant distraction after the morbid proceedings of the funeral service.

"His father was Urquhart Robertson. He made chief constable – a bit before your time, I would imagine."

"And yours, sir, I would imagine." She smiled – and, despite his rank, Strawberry found himself smiling back.

Strawberry watched as the grey Stalag that was Edinburgh crematorium receded in the car's rear-view mirror: its sombre aspect emphasising the fact that every client entering its walls would never come out.

On the tree-lined avenue he caught a glimpse of Freddie Pettygrew in earnest conversation with the homeless people. He resolved to find out more about their connection to the dead woman.

ON a state of high alert, the patrol had passed through the poppy fields and now the swamp-land ended in a narrow lane.

It was a critical point for the Paras. The path allowed only single-file progress. High hedgerows flanked either side: on the one hand affording the soldiers much needed cover; on the other giving the Taliban an ideal opportunity for an ambush – either from the roofs of the guddle of ramshackle two-storey farm houses 500 metres away, or at the end of the natural 'tunnel'.

Lieutenant Four-Fingers Bob was in the lead. As the only officer present it was his decision. Stick or twist. Continue, or wait for air cover. Bob was not above taking advice from a more experienced non-com. He raised his arm and the patrol halted.

He signalled to the sergeant, who came forward in a crouching run. "What do you reckon, Andy?"

"Don't like it one bit, sir."

"Recommendation?"

"Hunker down here. Wait for air support."

"Agreed. Thank you, Sergeant. Rustle them up."

The sergeant crouch-ran back to the tail of the line and conveyed the command to the radio operator. Under sixty seconds later he was back reporting the negative news.

"Apaches are tied up giving cover in a major firefight 200 miles north. No gunship available for at least an hour."

Bob cursed his luck. They couldn't stay in such an exposed position for an hour. The decision had been made for him. Twist.

The line was 300 metres down the path when the machine-gun fire raked the ground beneath their feet and the rocket-propelled grenades exploded above their heads.

"The roofs," shouted the sergeant. The words were his last as a grenade exploded at his feet instantly vaporising what had been a man into a mist of blood and tissue.

A second machine gun opened up at the far end of the path. Ten Paras went down straight away. As the patrol scrabbled for what meagre cover they could find, Bob knew his men were facing a massacre. Up ahead, a Para was screaming, while the other casualties remained ominously silent. There was a lull in the deadly fusillade. The Taliban were on the move again. Experts at guerrilla warfare, Bob feared the enemy were deploying a pincer movement and closing in for the final kill.

Bob would replay the next few minutes later in his head and marvel at both the luck and lunatic bravery of the soldier who rushed past him.

Gav, one of the youngest in the company, was sprinting full out towards the enemy. The firing started again and he stopped, falling to one knee to return fire. Then he was off again and among the dead and injured Paras, seeking cover among comrades who were beyond help.

The screams of the injured Para continued. He recognised the runner and cried in agony. "Gav, I've lost my leg."

"No, it's over there, mate," Gav replied in the black humour of the Paras, pointing to the man's severed limb lying in the dust ten feet away. Gav hoisted the man on his back and stumbled back towards his besieged comrades.

The clatter of the Apache gunship arriving overhead drew a ragged cheer from the soldiers.

The Taliban were not around to hear it. Alerted by a walkie-talkie system of lookouts in villages miles behind, they had vanished like ghosts into the swamp-lands and poppy fields ready to fight the British Army another day.

The soldier Gav risked his life for died from his injuries in the helicopter five minutes later.

A year later back in civvy street, Gav threw the medal he received for his bravery that day into the Thames.

Back in civilian life Gav and Four-Fingers Bob became friends bound together by their shared history and their inability to recover from the horrors of Afghanistan.

It was an extraordinary friendship given the background of the two men: their paths to that hopeless and unwinnable conflict could hardly have been more contrasting.

Gav was born in Stirling's Raploch – one of a family of six children growing up on the poorest housing estate in Scotland. His father was an alcoholic who resorted to violence when drunk. The boy would hide under the bed with his fingers in his ears when the rows downstairs started between his parents. There were times when he would go without food for two or three days until his father won a game of cards at the pub. Then the family would dine on fish and chips. Gav escaped home at sixteen to join the army, but first he gave his father a hiding for knocking his mother about.

Four tours of Northern Ireland and Afghanistan followed with Gav proving himself an able soldier, rising to the rank of corporal following the ill-fated action in Helmand Province, which cemented the friendship of the two men.

Four-Fingers Bob earned his nickname – not through battlefield injury (though that would undoubtedly have been more glamorous) – but via a genetic abnormality. He was born without thumbs.

Fortunately for Bob, his parents were rich. His father was chief executive of a multinational company in the tobacco trade.

So Bob underwent an operation to substitute a healthy finger for each missing thumb. The procedure transformed his life and Bob made full use of his newfound dexterity launching into the daredevil sports of stock-car racing, skydiving and rock-climbing.

Never an academic and seeking new physical challenges, Bob left the comfort of his pampered existence in the Home Counties and joined officer training at the age of eighteen. Though the procedure to replace his thumbs was noted, he passed the medical with ease and joined the Parachute Regiment. He expected the jokes and the sniggering behind his back. It had been an accepted feature of his life for so long that he knew exactly what to do about it.

There is a brutal tradition in the Parachute Regiment called milling. Milling is a crude form of boxing lasting one minute. Ducking or dodging the blows is barred and, if you are knocked down, you have to keep getting up until the time has expired.

Bob engineered a bout with the man he knew to be his main detractor and beat the living daylights out of him.

When he resigned his commission after Helmand, Bob's pugilistic skills held him in good stead. At first he tried to adjust to civilian life by accepting a job as an account manager in his father's company.

He lasted a week. The job was a disaster on two counts. Bob was a useless salesman and he simply didn't believe in the product he was attempting to sell. He had smoked one cigarette in his life. That was at school and he was violently sick following the experience. He was also far too keen on physical fitness to succumb to something that hard scientific evidence linked to deadly diseases like heart failure and cancer.

Using his army experience, he managed to get a job as a security guard on the door of a luxury jeweller in London. He was a small, slightly built man and the addition of a smart suit rendered a non-threatening impression.

The thief should have looked at the small man's shoes. The shoes were the giveaway. They were polished to a shine you could see your face in. Army trained spit and polish.

The thief chose a quiet Monday afternoon near to closing time. Like most jewellers, customers had to ring an external bell, a staff member checked them over, and only after they had passed inspection was the door unlocked to allow entry.

The man aroused no suspicion – though he was casually dressed in jeans and a Polo jacket, he looked respectable enough. Once inside he browsed the locked display cabinets containing the most expensive watch brands. He showed no sign of nervousness as he admired the collections. Just another punter window-shopping for something he probably couldn't afford.

In one fluent motion the man reached inside his jacket and, producing a small hammer, smashed the Rolex and Omega display cases. He shovelled the contents into a cloth bag that had suddenly appeared in his other hand and ran straight at the door.

The staff had turned at the sound of shattering glass, but they were too stunned to move. One of the girls had her hands at her face staring in disbelief as the thief sprinted passed her. Further down the shop the manager came out of his trance and scrambled for the alarm behind his desk.

The thief was yelling and brandishing the wicked-looking ball-pein hammer as he charged towards the exit.

Bob was still standing at the door, his smart suit and earpiece intact. He ignored the staff who had emerged from their initial shock and were now shouting and running around like headless chickens. His entire focus was on the thief who was much bigger and broader than him.

As the man loomed nearer, Bob moved to block the door, simultaneously shifting his body weight so that – boxer style – he was balanced on the balls of his feet.

The thief let out a roar and swung the hammer down directly at Bob's head. Only Bob wasn't there any more. He jinked aside at the last second and as the man overbalanced with the uncontrolled fury of the downward swing, punched him in the kidneys. The roar converted to a scream as the robber dropped the hammer and collapsed like a sack of potatoes to the floor.

If the incident had ended at that point, everything would have been fine. As the court would hear later, the thief was struggling to breathe and was clearly completely incapacitated and no longer a threat or capable of escape.

But something had also happened to Bob. For an instant his eyes glazed and he was no longer in the jewellers shop. He was back in the dust and blood and chaos of a deadly trap. Men were screaming in agony all around him: their limbs dismembered, their guts hanging out.

In this dissociative state he didn't recognise the man on the ground as a common thief any more, but an enemy. Someone who must be eliminated.

He brought one perfectly polished shoe down on the thief's face in a brutal stamping motion. The man's nose exploded, the blood spiralling high in a slow-motion loop and landing on Bob's shiny shoes.

The staff grabbed him just in time before the thief suffered irreversible harm. The same could not be said of Bob.

The jewellery store had a high-profile reputation with a long list of very wealthy clients, which made it extremely sensitive to adverse publicity. The press had a field day with the story and the trial attracted a lot of publicity on a quiet news day. But rather than the thief, the more liberal elements of the press crucified Bob accusing him of barbaric and excessive zeal in carrying out a vicious attack on the defenceless robber.

Bob could have saved himself by revealing he was a Para veteran suffering from post-traumatic stress. His parents begged him to do so. He did none of those things, partly through loyalty to his former comrades and the regiment, but also because of his embarrassment and shame at suffering from a mental illness.

In the end the bad publicity forced the store to fire him, not that they were too concerned about the decision. After all, there were plenty of army veterans queuing up for such employment.

Bob – though desperately needing psychiatric help – was too proud to seek it. Too ashamed to accept the support of his parents, he went down a different path to homelessness and drug addiction.

He had been sleeping rough under a set of railway arches in London for several months when he bumped into Gav at a soup kitchen.

It was a bleak rain-sodden night. A few fires were flickering near the makeshift canvas shelters in a vain attempt to give some warmth to the rough sleepers under the arches. Spiralling downwards in serious physical and mental decline, Bob had to call upon all his remaining willpower to drag himself out of the stinking duvet and join the weary queue for food. A few more minutes and they would have missed each other. Gav had just received his helping at the head of the line and was making his way back when he spotted the skeletal figure.

He needed a double-take before he recognised his old platoon leader. "Lieutenant Bob, it's Gav!" he cried, attempting to clutch Bob's hand. Bob jerked backwards, alarm mingling with suspicion in his startled reaction. "It's Gav, sir – 2 Para Helmand. Remember?"

Gradually the light of recognition dawned in Bob's eyes. "Gav? Medal Gav?" he said in a faltering voice far from the resolute tone Gav remembered from Afghanistan.

"Yes, sir." Gav had been on the streets long enough to know the signs. What he saw here was a fellow Para in danger of going under. The *esprit de corps* unique to the regiment kicked in: once a Para always a Para. In that moment he resolved to do everything in his power to help his comrade.

That chance encounter and Gav's selfless decision probably saved both their lives – though the following months were hard.

Bob had experimented with drugs in a desperate bid to banish the psychological demons that beset him in the aftermath of Afghanistan. Unfortunately, the experiment turned into the craving for a constant fix and Gav, who had somehow remained clean despite all the odds, was determined to save Bob from his worst excesses.

He succeeded in part: managing to coax Bob to an outreach centre and a course of methadone in order to wean him off heroin. There were lapses, but gradually some of Bob's old character began to emerge. He started to eat more regularly, put on weight, and they both found sanctuary in a homeless shelter – albeit temporary – in Brixton.

The letter from one of Gav's five siblings, an older sister called Morag, changed everything. A nurse, she had finally managed to track Gav down through the social work department.

Even then the letter was a month old by the time he read it. "It's my mum, she's dying from cancer," he explained to Bob. "I've got to get back home and pretty quick by the sound of it. Why don't you come too?"

Bob said nothing. But the following night at King's Cross they jumped the barrier together and boarded the overnight train for Scotland.

It was a long night. They dodged the ticket inspector

by hiding for long periods in the toilets. On the last leg of the journey they abandoned caution and slept on the floor of a carriage. The guard undoubtedly saw them, but seeing their dishevelled appearance judged discretion to be the better part of valour and headed in the other direction.

They arrived at Stirling Station just after dawn on the kind of dreich morning Scotland specialises in, managed to scrimp together enough change for a cup of tea at a greasy spoon, and then humped their careworn kit the three miles to Gav's childhood home.

"Yomping again, thought we'd had enough of that crap," joked Gav as they trudged through the deserted Stirling streets to the housing estate.

"We never yomped anywhere in Afghanistan, Gav. You're thinking of the Falklands, mate. Thank God, we were too young for the Falklands."

"Right now I feel ancient enough to have been there," Gav laughed.

Reaching Gav's street, Bob could only think of one non-swear word to describe the place – grey. The two-storey council houses were grey. The abandoned settees and stained mattresses in the overgrown front 'gardens' were grey. Even the ubiquitous dog shit deposited by the roaming packs of feral dogs was so old it had turned grey.

During the past months he had witnessed at first hand the rancid underbelly of London in his descent. But somehow he had naively clung to the notion that the houses normal people lived in were largely clean and habitable places of basic comfort. He now realised this impression had been coloured by his privileged upbringing in the leafy avenues of Surrey.

Entering Gav's stair through the broken paint-stripped door, Bob was assailed by the malodorous stench of urine. A jumble of what looked like prams from the 1950s lay in the corner of the stairwell, while the area under the stair was crammed with black bin bags, which emitted the putrified stench of nappies and rotten food.

Gav was in the process of knocking on the door on the second landing when it opened. The woman was in a sky-blue Terry Towel dressing gown with tea stains down the front. Her face was stained with tears. Her reddened eyes indicated she had been up all night. She gave a long, shuddering sigh when she saw Gav, placing her head on his chest when they embraced. "Too late, Gav, I'm sorry. Mum passed away an hour ago."

"Give me a minute, Bob," said Gav as he walked down the lobby holding his sister. Bob sat on the stair staring at nothing as he heard the chorus of lament inside the flat.

Gav emerged thirty minutes later and picked up his kit. "I only came back to see my mum – and it turns out I was even too late for that. There's nothing but bad memories for me here, mate. How about we try our luck in the capital?" Bob nodded and an hour later they were hitching a lift to Edinburgh.

COMMANDO never knew his parents. He was born with learning difficulties and his drug-addicted mother was judged unfit to look after him. With no sign of a father around, the baby was initially adopted, but as his problems became more apparent his foster parents gave him up and he was abandoned to an orphanage.

Of course, Commando was not his real name. He earned it due to his predilection for wearing camouflage clothing. Leaving the orphanage at sixteen, he was supposed to attend an FE college to learn a trade. But he couldn't get enthusiastic about bricklaying, so he stopped attending the classes.

He became a regular sight in Edinburgh. Clad from head to foot in combat gear, he was always running somewhere, or in reality nowhere: jumping on and off buses – literally in his own world playing a permanent game of soldiers.

This make-believe world would have been fine for Commando, but for one important consideration. He had been eligible for a weekly payment from the government as an incentive for learning a trade. But when he stopped attending the college, the allowance was withdrawn, meaning he now had no money. This fact made him vulnerable.

Joining other poor souls dotted around the main streets of the city, he started begging for money to buy food. That made him a target for the unscrupulous criminals who preyed on the destitute.

Commando was just the kind of individual the two men were looking for. He was sitting on the pavement in his usual pitch on Lothian Road with a dirty blanket over his knees and an upended Glengarry cap at his side when the men sidled over.

The taller one with lank black greasy hair put a fiver in the cap. It was easily the biggest single donation Commando had been given in several weeks. After an average day, the cap normally contained coppers with a few fifty pence pieces and the odd pound coin glittering among the dross.

"Hey, thanks, mister," chirped Commando. "That'll get me a bridie at Greggs."

"You'll get more than a bridie with that, my man," said the tall man's mate. "I see you're an army man, neighbour. Respect for army." The man placed his hand over his heart.

Commando hesitated. The men didn't come from around here. They sounded strange. Foreign. Even so, he didn't like telling lies to anyone. So he went for what he reckoned was a compromise. "Well, I like the army, mister. Always have, since I was small."

"Of course, right," said the smaller man. "Me and my friend think army men deserve the best – much better than freezing your arse off on a pavement in Olden Reekie begging for a few pennies."

"Yeah, so how would you like to earn really money, Soldier?" said the tall man.

Commando looked confused. "Like what?"

"Like £10 a day mate," said the tall man.

Commando looked at what was in his hat – take away the fiver and he was lucky if he had a couple of quid in coins and that was after six hours.

"That would be good, mister."

"Good," said the tall man. "I thought you thought that would be good. So here's the deal, Soldier. We would need you to go on a special mission for us. It would be a secret mission just like in the army."

"Secret," repeated Commando as if the word conveyed all kinds of magical possibilities.

"Yeah, so secret that you couldn't tell anyone about it," added the smaller man.

"Aye, hush-hush," added the taller man.

Commando gave a slow nod. "Like when I jump on and off the buses. Nobody knows where I'm going and I don't tell no one either."

"Exactly," said the smaller man looking in bemusement at the taller man.

"Okay, so let's see you in this doorway."

The two men led Commando into the doorway of a closed gift shop. The smaller one kept lookout.

"I bet you got a big pocket in these combat trousers," said the tall man.

Commando beamed and lifted his camouflage jacket to display a large pocket at the front of his army fatigues.

"Everything okay out there?" asked the tall man. The lookout nodded.

The tall man produced a brown envelope no bigger than a video cassette. "Now here's what we want you to do…"

Later, the men discussed their latest recruit over a beer in a seedy pub at the bottom of Leith Walk. "The man is stupid," said the smaller man.

"Yes, he is, but he thinks he's on a secret mission. Anyway, tonight was a dry run. Sugar was the only thing in the envelope. We will try that a few nights and if there's no hitch, we'll hook him up to the real thing."

STRAWBERRY and Gunn were sitting side by side on a settee in one of the most opulent apartments he had seen in Edinburgh. They were in a drawing room double the size of Marjorie Agincourt's containing brand-new furnishings from high-end stores superior even to John Lewis.

The only impediment that would have prevented a double-page spread in *Ideal Homes* was the battlefield of toys spread across the floor including a trike and a wigwam in the large bay window. A small blonde girl emerged from it screaming like a banshee as she charged across the acreage of parquet floor. "Gwennie, please quieten down, poppet. Mummy has to hear what the police are saying."

There was a distinct absence of Balmoral Square Mansions' affectation to Agnes Blunt's accent, which made a welcome change. But she seemed to be putting on an act – employing her best Sunday voice.

It was a bit rough at the edges and her use of the word 'poppet' sounded artificial and out of place to Strawberry's ear. He placed the accent as working-class Edinburgh – Leith, Wester Hailes, or somewhere in the Lothians – Prestonpans perhaps, or Dalkeith.

He wondered whether she had moved up the social and financial ladder by partnering the businessman Jim Ross.

The background noise abated marginally as Gwennie leapt on the trike and did several circuits of the room at breakneck speed. Agnes Blunt smiled indulgently at her child before turning her attention to the officers.

"She's very intelligent for her age – makes her a bit hyperactive. We've got her down for the nursery section of St Hilda's, but intake is two months away, I'm afraid."

The woman gave a tired sigh. Gunn smiled sympathetically. "Must be tough, Mrs Blunt. I understand you have another child."

"It's Miss," corrected Agnes Blunt. "I decided to keep my own name. Daniel is eighteen months. It's not tough, Officer. It's more like a privilege to look after such poppets."

She was a small, rake-thin woman in her early thirties with dark hair falling past her collar and an unremarkable though strikingly white face hidden behind large black-framed glasses.

Children had arrived relatively late and the challenge was clearly taking its toll, despite her protestations, reckoned Brenda Gunn.

But Miss Blunt was clearly a woman who had firm convictions – and not an inconsiderable amount of money. Or at least her partner, Jim Ross, was not short of a bob or two. The couple's financial status was evident from the amount of work they had done on the apartment.

She had taken great pride in showing the officers around – much to Strawberry's barely concealed irritation. The place had been entirely renovated including three marble-floored bathrooms and a stainless-steel kitchen whose worktops gleamed free of any smudge or fingerprint.

"How do you get it so clean?" Gunn marvelled.

"Vinegar. I polish the surfaces every day." Had Agnes owned a chest, she would have puffed it out.

Strawberry grinned inwardly at the sister act and congratulated himself on his colleague selection. Gunn was shaping up to be a very good pick.

At the end of the tour Strawberry finally managed to get the interview on track. "As you know we're here because of the unexplained death of your neighbour Arabella Pettygrew. She lived directly above you and we wondered if you could throw any light on her movements leading up to the tragedy."

"We moved in very recently, Detective Inspector, so we didn't really know the lady."

"But you have been here for six months," said Gunn. "Didn't she introduce herself to you or vice versa? You know, breaking the ice with the neighbours? That sort of thing."

Gwennie was back in the wigwam talking to what Gunn assumed were the little girl's dolls. Blunt appeared momentarily distracted by her daughter's imaginary conversation.

"You know, the neighbourly thing?" encouraged Gunn.

Blunt gradually came out of her reverie and addressed Gunn's question. "Of course we said hello on the stair in passing, but both my partner and I are very busy people. Jim's away a lot on business. And the lady was a very private person. She didn't appear to welcome contact. I don't really know how Jim or I can help your inquiry."

Strawberry intervened. "Another neighbour told us that your renovation work took several months. Is that correct, Miss Blunt?"

Blunt grimaced at the memory. "Oh yes. The place was very old-fashioned. The previous owner was old and had done very little to update it. We had to pull up the floorboards and put in proper insulation… central heating, a new boiler, showers, gas fires. She sat in here in the winter with only a four-bar electric heater." Blunt shook her head in wonder.

"The neighbour claimed that the workers you hired were Polish and at times they slept in the empty apartment overnight. Is that true?"

The brow behind the large glasses wrinkled. "I don't think that's true, Detective, but I wouldn't really know. Jim took care of business with the workers and I had my hands full with the children."

"So you don't really know whether the workers slept here or not?"

A look of alarm appeared behind the glasses.

"That would be against the law, wouldn't it? Neither Jim nor I would do anything to break the law. We are law-abiding citizens, Inspector."

"I wouldn't concern yourself about that, Miss Blunt," said Strawberry. "We're not investigating some council rule here. This is an investigation into a suspicious death. Can we conclude that you are unsure about the workers' sleeping habits?"

Blunt nodded reluctantly.

"I am asking these questions because someone else has claimed that the workers made a lot of noise through the night. It was also claimed that they might have intimidated Miss Pettygrew, or worse."

Agnes Blunt was nonplussed. "If that's true, Inspector,

it's terrible. Poor woman and all alone too. If Jim or I had known we would certainly have called the police."

As Strawberry and Gunn left the building, a small, portly man with a Friar Tuck hairstyle was emerging from a Mercedes 4x4. He climbed the steps and went into the stair.

"Pound to a penny that's her partner," said Strawberry.

"Well, if it is, she definitely married… sorry, partnered him for his money," said Gunn.

BLESSINGS McKenzie had closeted herself in a cupboard at the top of a worn set of stairs in the west wing of the cathedral.

It was fifteen minutes past the witching hour of midnight and all she had heard in the last four hours was the wind – balmy for a change in Edinburgh – blowing through the vaulted upper reaches of the church.

She had come for the vigil provisioned with a supply of chocolate digestive biscuits and a Thermos flask full of tea. There was enough room in the cupboard for a collapsible chair and the naked bulb in the ceiling offered her enough light to read by.

First though, she had checked by switching the light on, closing the door and standing outside on the steps. Not a glimmer escaped from beneath the door. Her hiding place secure, her thoughts turned to the mystery of the silent bell ringers.

One of the strapping young men had left the room in the bell tower at 9 p.m. There had been a brief conversation that she couldn't hear – apart from the farewell goodnight. But she had heard the door being locked, presumably from the inside, on his departure and then his footsteps as he passed her cupboard.

She had sat immobile in her folding chair, clutching

her packet of biscuits to her chest, barely daring to breathe until the last of his footsteps died and the main door clanged shut.

That left two of them. But what were they doing at such an hour and why was the bishop still in his study? None of it made sense, but she knew it was imperative to find out.

Ruminating on the mystery, she unscrewed the Thermos and poured a cup. It reminded her of camping on the banks of Loch Ness on a Girl Guide trip when she first arrived in Scotland.

Besides the torture of midges, her most vivid memory was of tea; the smell, the taste. Tea always tasted infinitely better when drunk in the open air.

The idleness of her confinement triggered another entirely different and darker memory. She had been hiding then, too, as a child in Africa. She had run away from the orphanage and sought refuge in a tree. But her bravery had deserted her. When she heard the search party coming and the nuns' voices calling her name, she had panicked and tried to climb higher. Her footing had found a treacherous branch, dry and weakened by age. It had broken under her weight and she had fallen to the sun-baked ground breaking a leg and shattering her collarbone.

The pain had been excruciating. All these years later, she remembered it still. But even more painful was her memory of the nuns: severe in their censure of her efforts to escape.

Recovering in what passed for the infirmary – a bare room with a creaking overhead fan – she had drifted in and out of consciousness dreaming of her sister, longing for the comfort of her embrace. But her sister had never come.

Later, the nuns told her – with malice in their voices – that her much more beautiful and intelligent sister had been adopted by a rich and powerful family. That she had forgotten Blessings in her new and privileged life and she would never see her again.

Blessings had mourned the loss for a long time, but gradually when nothing more was heard, she felt her sister had indeed abandoned her and love turned to hatred for the betrayal.

The sound of footsteps on the stairs shook her from her dismal reverie.

Up or down? She strained to detect which direction they were coming from. But of one thing she was certain – they were drawing closer. She closed her eyes and counted silently to ten in a bid to control the rising anxiety.

Now she could hear, not only the plodding, but the laboured breathing accompanying the heavy footfall.

It suddenly stopped outside the cupboard and in her panic Blessings dropped the Thermos, which struck the stone floor with a crack that sounded like a pistol shot in the confined space.

The door was opened and there stood an equally startled Holy Smokes.

SEAGULL Slayer was tired of small news stories squeezed away, where the corrections or apologies went, at the bottom of page six. Like any superhero he deserved front-page headlines splashing his exploits in black ten-point bold.

Sitting at his computer eating cold baked beans from the tin in the squalid one-bedroom flat he called home, he had racked his brains for a solution.

He needed a big statement, something the authorities couldn't ignore. Something that would have the *Furst Meanister* raging in the Scottish Parliament. Something so outrageous it would be like what? Like setting wee Jimmie Krankie's knickers on fire as she chuntered on at the despatch box. He giggled at the image – and the germ of a plan began to form.

He was in another stolen car as nondescript as the last one and it was night again.

This time though he was much more nervous than on the previous occasion when he had shot the seagull in the arse and stamped its brains out. His hands were sweating as he gripped the wheel and he contemplated the next fifteen minutes.

As usual, he had carefully reconnoitred the target in daylight managing to gain access via an unlocked door in an overgrown area full of weeds at the back.

It had been the riskiest thing he had ever done, but he had worn a hard hat and a yellow bib – and had a meaningless printout in the pocket of his overalls claiming he was a gas company employee. Anyone with the most rudimentary knowledge would have immediately recognised the document as a forgery. But no one did. He was neither challenged coming in through the jungle at the rear of the building, nor in the building itself.

But now was the moment of truth. He got out of the car and took his equipment from the boot. On this occasion there was no cue bag, but a bolt-cutter and a much smaller package that easily fitted into an inside pocket of his anorak. He almost forgot the long-handled torch and quietly cursed his lack of concentration. The torch on a smartphone wouldn't be clever this time and should he have to escape in a hurry the last thing he wanted to do was leave such a clearly identifiable calling card behind.

Inside the building the ground-floor level was pitch-black necessitating the use of the torch. Its narrow beam picked out what had been an ornately tiled floor, now covered in dust and animal droppings.

The bannister on the stairs was still intact, but also covered in a fine filament of dust testifying to the fact that the building had been abandoned for some time without the presence of a security guard. Seagull Slayer had taken the precaution of wearing surgical-style gloves as fingerprints would have shown up clearly on the wooden bannister.

Walking along the landing of the second floor he let out an involuntary shriek and dropped the bolt cutter as his face was suddenly caressed in the darkness. His hands shot up in panicked defence and came away with a skein of cobwebs.

On the third floor the stygian gloom was relieved by a faint glimmer of light and he heard the skitter of their feet on the roof.

His torch sought out the ladder and he climbed up to the skylight.

Now came the hardest part. The part where one slip and he could fall from the ladder and badly injure himself or worse. He shuddered at the possibility of lying helpless with a broken back waiting to die in this place. But his hatred was greater than his fear.

Placing the torch in a pocket, he leaned his bodyweight tight against the ladder and slowly raised the bolt-cutters above his head. He had already located the padlock in the torch beam and now he worked from memory and the glimmer of light from above.

The blades missed the chain on his first try and he almost lost his balance. Breathless and sweating hard, he steadied himself against the ladder and shakily raised the cutter again. This time the blades found the chain. He opened the jaws and, summoning all his strength, clamped the blades down. Metal bit into metal – and stuck there. He swore, unclenched the blades and pushed down until his hands shook with the exertion. He had to carry out the same exhausting manoeuvre three more times before the chain finally gave way and the padlock fell past him to the landing below.

It took several moments to halt the shake in his shoulders and regain the strength in his hands. Finally, he pushed the skylight upwards and thrust his way onto the roof.

He put on the balaclava and substituted the bolt-cutters for the torch. He swept the beam in an arc around the roof until he located them.

There was the scrabbling sound of some movement among the adults, but nothing chaotic. That would happen soon. He giggled at the thought.

He removed the small package from his pocket and shone the light on the acetylene burner. As he moved quietly towards his targets, finger on the trigger, his only regret was that flame-throwers were not yet available online.

The fire brigade got the call around 3 a.m. and three engines were despatched in as many minutes. By the time they arrived a substantial section of the roof of the abandoned Victorian library was ablaze, but the chief officer reckoned they would be able to contain the fire and save the building if they acted quickly.

The extendable ladders were deployed and the fire fighters went up unhesitatingly. They had already been briefed that the building was presumed empty, so their job would be relatively straightforward. In the unlikely event of a vagrant inhabiting the building, the chief officer had already employed a loud hailer warning anyone inside to come out immediately.

So the firemen didn't expect any casualties as they climbed towards the conflagration. Instead, they were assailed by an unholy shrieking and then dive-bombed by a series of adult seagulls.

Fortunately, none of the firemen fell and their

helmets, gloves and breathing apparatus saved them from being bitten or scratched as the birds' ferocious attacks intensified.

Suddenly they were aware of the stench of burning flesh and the first of the chicks, ablaze and spinning like Catherine wheels, began to rain down from the infernos that had been their nests.

BERT Rothesay had a copy of the *Hoots Mon* on his desk when Strawberry entered his office. He said nothing, merely flipped the newspaper around so Strawberry could see the front page.

The photographer had been brilliant, if indeed that was the appropriate word, in capturing the atrocity. The colour picture showed a fireman on a ladder with the roof of the Victorian building at the upper edge for context.

But the appalling focal point was at the centre of the image – a drizzle of incinerated chicks in a death spiral plummeting past the fireman's helmet – and carefully circled by the graphic artist just to make sure the reader literally got the picture. The headline drove home the message *Seagull Killer Firebombs Baby Chicks* with the accompanying strap line *Animal atrocity ignites Sturgeon's fury*.

The silence expanded. Strawberry knew the game. Like many in senior management Rothesay used the silent treatment as a method of bullying a subordinate, knowing that finally the individual would break and gabble a confession.

But he was too tired to gabble. His gabbling days were over. Additionally, unlike most of the population, he didn't collapse in paroxysms of grief at the sight of a few cremated chicks.

"I'll get a senior officer to follow it up as a matter of urgency, sir," was all he said.

Rothesay shook his ponderous head seemingly in sorrow rather than anger. "This isnae a joke about KFC, and I'm no Colonel Sanders. This is real life, or at least real politics and it's not only the chicks that are getting roasted. I'm getting it from all quarters, Strawberry – from the council and the animal rights groups to the *Furst Meanister*. Right now she owns the pulpit of public opinion. She's like a latter-day John Knox. Holier than thou. Righteous in her right-on indignation. So these bloody seagulls are the number one priority if we want to keep our jobs, laddie. More important than Operation Treetops, or any number of pensioners taking a heid dive off a roof. That's the truth of it, so this madman has to be caught. If you think you have the man for the job, fair enough. You are in charge, but remember exactly that – you are in charge and if your senior officer fails then it is your head that will roll. Now get out and get to work."

Needing to calm down after his own roasting at the hands of Bert Rothesay, Strawberry decided to cycle to Balmoral Square Mansions. He found Dougie Nichols still on surveillance duty, but in what appeared to be a state of torpor.

He shook his head dismally when Strawberry asked for a progress report. "Quite frankly I'm beginning to wonder if we've got the right street, far less the right address. I've seen more action in a funeral parlour."

"Okay, we've still got to the end of the week," said Strawberry, "so the team will have to stick it out. But you've earned a get-out-of-jail card, Dougie."

Nichols tried to disguise his suspicion as he studied his rival's face. "The boss is getting all kinds of flak over the seagull killer case, so I'm putting you on it as a matter of urgency. Take anyone you want, but just find the bastard and shoot him if you have to!"

The first thing Nichols did when he got back to Gayfield Square was check the duty roster. His finger traced down the list of names until it alighted on PC Derek Murch: the officer who had been so exercised by the seagulls. He had probably been joking when he requested permission to shoot them, but then again there was the possibility that he had carried out the threat. Anyway, as Nichols had no other leads, it was a place to start.

It was impossible to know exactly when the seagull killings had begun, so he confined himself to two dates: the newspaper report of the seagull stamping, and the torching of the nests.

Murch had suffered from sunstroke on the afternoon before the first atrocity, so, after yawning in technicolour down a toilet bowl most of the day, it seemed very unlikely to Nichols that Murch would have been out that night shooting seagulls in the arse. But he had been off duty on the day of the arson attack.

IT was raining for the first time in three weeks when Dougie Nichols got in the unmarked police car. A sudden intense summer shower of big, splattering drops that necessitated the use of the wipers at full speed.

As Nichols watched several months of dead bugs gradually disappear from the windscreen he pondered his approach to the delicate situation of investigating a fellow police officer.

Murch had gone on duty at 2 p.m. with the surveillance team. It was now 3.15 p.m., which meant he was away from his flat and Nichols knew he lived alone. His one-bedroom flat was on the south side of Edinburgh in a side street off Morningside Road.

Nichols drove past the tenement and parked fifty yards further on. He strolled back to the main door of the apartment building and found it unsecured – hardly uncommon for communal stairs in the city. There was no sound, or sign of anyone being at home in the flats. Most people would still be at work and any mothers would be on the afternoon school pick-up run.

He went up the stairs to Murch's flat on the second floor. He looked through the letter box and saw a slew of envelopes on the floor. He lifted the doormat, but found no key under it.

He was pushing the mat back in place with his foot when the front door of the flat opposite opened. The old woman had a full head of snow-white hair, but her eyes conveyed a bright sparrow-like alertness.

"Derek's a policeman," she said. "Out all different times of the night and day. He left two hours ago. Is it urgent? Can I give him a message?"

She was assessing Nichols as though he was a burglar. In a way, thought Nichols, he was; a colleague engaged in a clandestine operation against a fellow officer aimed at seizing any incriminating evidence he might discover. "No message, thanks. I'm a friend. Just passing by and I thought I would call in on the off chance."

"You could have saved your legs. The bells at the bottom work, you know."

Nichols nodded. This old dear was as sharp as a tack. Even if she had known how to use one, she had no need of a smartphone camera. He knew without question that if she was asked to supply an identikit picture of the suspicious man who had called on her neighbour, she would have him down to a tee. More importantly, Murch would be informed by her of the mysterious visitor the minute she heard his footsteps on the stair.

Cursing his stupidity he got back in the car and headed to the place he should have gone first.

The shower had abated to a drizzle by the time he reached the Blackfords and parked at the tennis and bowling club. He looked down the hill at the allotments. They were deserted. He knew that one of them belonged to Murch, but which one of the fifty-odd plots might it be?

He walked along the wire perimeter, wracking his

brains for a clue, and vowing that this time he wouldn't be caught out by a nosey neighbour. He recalled that Murch had once come into the station with a basket of tomatoes he shared out, urging his colleagues to taste the difference between supermarket-bought and allotment-grown. Nichols, who liked tomatoes, remembered trying one and commenting on how sweet it was. Tomatoes could never survive in Scotland's godawful climate. So that meant Murch grew them under greenhouse conditions.

Nichols walked onto the path beside Blackford Hill. The scree of loose stones scrunched under the leather soles of his shoes as he patrolled the allotment perimeter looking for a greenhouse.

He spotted four. One of them was devoted to what looked like peas and a second appeared to specialise in onions. The third and fourth greenhouses featured tomatoes, but one was a relatively well-built affair, while the other was a shambolic lean-to.

Nichols opted for the shambolic, but what clinched it for him was the saltire hanging limply on a pole above the plot. Murch was nothing if not a patriot. Nichols slowly did a 360-degree turn. It was still drizzling and he could see no one, either on the hill above, or in any of the allotments.

Climbing the wire fence, his leather shoes slipped a couple of times and he tore a jacket pocket as he struggled for purchase, but then he was on top and dropping down on the other side.

He almost turned an ankle on the heap of tins he landed on. They had been hidden in the undergrowth near a clump of wild raspberries. "Bloody litter lout," Nichols muttered, picking up one of the tins. It was dented in several places, but the marks were small and looked very specific. A remote memory stirred, but refused to announce itself. Nichols dumped the tin among the rest.

The shed door was on a latch and unlocked. Inside, there was a row of narrow wooden shelves sprinkled with earth and a clutter of plastic garden pots of various sizes alongside a rusting trowel, a hoe and a pitchfork with a bent tine. A bundle of newspapers shared a table in the corner with an array of dead spiders, a jar of instant coffee and an electric kettle that had seen better days. Under the table were three sets of long drawers. Nichols found the air rifle in the second.

THE piercing clamour of emergency service sirens disturbed the slumbering residents of Balmoral Square Mansions.

Unfortunately, a good proportion of them were already awake even at such an ungodly hour: such is the curse of advancing years where the tendency is to waken ridiculously early, despite the fact there is nothing to get up for and precious little prospect of doing anything vaguely productive in the tediously long day ahead.

Thus Marjorie Agincourt witnessed the entire pre-dawn drama as the convoy of blue flashing lights – a police car, an ambulance and a second following police car – sped down the deserted street ending in a perfectly orchestrated halt outside the cathedral.

Laden with the paraphernalia of medical aid, the two-man ambulance crew moved briskly into the building, while several policemen stood sentry outside.

Marjorie picked up Hamish's field glasses and focused on the front of the church, which was intermittently bathed in the strobe lighting of the emergency vehicles. She didn't have long to wait.

Minutes later a stretcher emerged. They were moving quickly and Marjorie's vision through the lenses swam as she attempted to steady her rheumatic hands to catch up with the movement. She managed to zero in for a second before the stretcher disappeared into the back of the ambulance – and gasped.

She only got a glimpse of an arm protruding from the blanket. But she would have recognised the material and the ring on the finger anywhere. It was a white cassock and the ring, with its single sapphire signifying the wearer was wed to the church, could only belong to one man. It was the bishop!

The paramedics went into the church again and seconds later emerged with a second stretcher.

Though still in shock, Marjorie was determined this time and held the binoculars steady. In the intermittent light of the strobe she glimpsed a face on the stretcher that was vaguely familiar. Marjorie could not be certain but it appeared to be a coloured woman. What was her name again? Precious? Princess? Those African names were so absurd and they all sounded the same. The ambulance and police cars performed a precise U-turn and sped back down the street.

They were halfway along Murrayfield when Marjorie remembered. It was Blessings. Blessings Mckenzie – the church provost.

THE Garden Association had called an emergency meeting. It was the Tweedies' turn to host so there was fresh ground coffee on offer in small pearl-white china cups alongside a range of superior biscuits from Jenners.

Peter and Marcy had recently returned from a brief holiday in Barbados to top up their year-round tans. They were both dressed in white chinos and linen shirts. Marcy – wearing gold at her throat and wrist – was handing out the coffee, while Peter was attending to the seating arrangements.

As befitting their positions, Nigel Smail and Dorothea Hislop were already ensconced at the front of the drawing room, while the other residents drifted to their designated places.

The problem was that the various sofas and armchairs were so comfortable they invited a somnolence not to be found at, for instance, Emile and Fanny Cruducker's home. In fact Fanny was already barely conscious and the meeting had yet to begin.

As the use of a gavel was out of the question on the surface of such an expensive table, Nigel confined himself to raising his voice.

Apologising for the sudden and unscheduled nature of the meeting, he explained that it had been called as a matter of urgency due to the continuing presence of the amateur gardeners.

"We are all now extremely concerned that the council seems to be ignoring our request," huffed Nigel. "There is no sign of the original gardeners returning. Meantime, the amateurs are still *in situ*, lopping off branches and beheading bushes with impunity.

"Well, enough, I say. I know the council leader personally having carried out various legal assignments with him during my professional life. So with the support of the members, I propose meeting with him early next week in order to settle this unfortunate state of affairs."

The members – fewer than normal because of the last-minute nature of the meeting and singularly lacking the presence of Marjorie Agincourt – grunted their assent.

Nigel bobbed his head in a parody of obsequious gratitude.

"There is only one other item on the agenda." Nigel grimaced. "Strictly speaking the subject doesn't fall within this association's remit, but as no other local residents' group exists to tackle the issue…"

"For God's sake, spit it out, man!" cried 'The Lieutenant' Jock Witherspoon. "We all know it's dog shit!"

"Thank you, Mr Witherspoon. Personally I would have put it more delicately," said Nigel. "But it is the issue of dog excrement. Dorothea has raised the matter because of an unfortunate incident she witnessed the other evening when an owner allowed her animal to void its bowels and then simply left the mess." Nigel gave Dorothea a pleading look. "Since it's your motion, Dorothea, would you like to expand on the problem?"

Dorothea was happy to. Even though the subject of dog fouling was less than pleasant, at least it would, however temporarily, take her mind off the real reason for her anxiety.

The warning had come three nights ago and she had heard nothing since. She had no way of contacting the anonymous party. That wasn't how the arrangement worked. But the situation was now becoming critical.

She had received an avalanche of texts and increasingly desperate phone messages from customers demanding to know when normal service would be resumed. She didn't know how long they could hang on – or how much longer she could. The house was clearly 'unsafe' but when would it be safe to return without the all-clear?

She willed herself back to the present and offered an apologetic smile to her audience. "As Nigel says, if we the Garden Association don't take on this challenge, no one else will. The problem of dog fouling in Balmoral Square Mansions and the surrounding streets in the West End has become acute. We can't have our beautiful streets besmirched in such a disgusting way. I speak as a responsible dog owner. So I would suggest that we set up some kind of monitoring arrangement – strictly lawful of course – to try and get the thoughtless owners to clear up after their animals."

'The Lieutenant' raised his hand. "A patrol is what we need. I'll volunteer to arrange a rota of residents equipped with baggies in case the culprits make the excuse of not having any. If they refuse then we name and shame the buggers. Names posted on the lamp posts."

Dorothea could not recall hearing such a round of applause at any previous association meeting. Forcing themselves out of the luxurious seating, the members waved their invitations.

"About time," cried Jeremy Sheldrake.

"Take back the streets from the dirty louts," shouted a ruddy-faced Peter Tweedie. "Make them clean again," chirped a reinvigorated Fanny Cruducker.

Perhaps this show of solidarity was at a small local level on a relatively insignificant subject, but Nigel was reminded of the scenes in the House of Commons when MPs waved their order papers following a nationally important vote. He suddenly felt an uncharacteristic warmth towards his neighbours. Long live democracy, he thought. Long live Balmoral Square Mansions!

On the way back to her flat and the evening walk with her dogs, Dorothea returned to her dilemma.

There was an additional and even more immediate problem with the house. It was in the basement. That would have to be resolved very soon. If the problem got out of the basement and made a commotion – worse still, if the problem escaped from the house – that would spell disaster.

So Dorothea knew, if radio silence continued, she would be forced to use her initiative – probably within the next twenty-four hours.

THE Seagull Slayer had read the *Hoots Mon*'s front-page story with a mixture of satisfaction and frustration.

He was pleased that at last his actions merited the sort of exposure his exploits justly deserved. But at the same time he was increasingly incensed at the uncomprehending hostility shown towards his heroic stand.

Did the public really think he was a heartless monster for combatting a menace that threatened to turn the historic streets of a world-famous tourist destination into one big, festering rubbish tip? From what he heard in walking around Edinburgh the reverse was true. The ordinary citizenry considered seagulls to be verminous scavengers harbouring heaven knows what kind of filthy human health hazards.

No, the people were overwhelmingly on his side. As usual it was the press, the media, the namby-pamby animal rights groups and the liberal establishment who castigated his actions. And no one was more vocal in that castigation than the *Furst Meanister*. If only he could use a flame-thrower on that wee Jimmie Krankie! Never mind your Scottish Independence, Nicola. That really would make global headlines.

Yet he was already planning the next grand statement in his campaign and it made frying baby chicks look like, well, chicken feed.

The battery had a series of wires sticking out of the top. It was lying on the desk next to his computer. He had carefully followed the instructions on the specialist website. They even had a video taking you step by step through the assembly procedure. It would be easy to rig – and then – party time!

HE was standing at the foot of the Royal Mile on yet another sunny day beside an ice-cream kiosk. He had bought a cone as a prop in a bid to look casual and allay any suspicion that he might be loitering with intent.

Almost immediately, he discovered it didn't work. If only he smoked. A cigarette was an ideal prop that never melted, he thought, as he licked feverishly around the cone's perimeter. It was hopeless. The ice cream was running down his bare arm. His hands were sticky now.

He searched for a bin. Of course there was no bin. There would be no bins within a half- mile radius of the building. Bombs could be concealed in bins. He couldn't throw the cone on the ground. That would attract attention. Worse, a seagull might be attracted to the abandoned food. He didn't think he would be able to handle a situation like that without losing it.

A tourist coach was pulling into the nearby car park in Holyrood. It disgorged a horde of Japanese tourists who invaded the area surrounding him as they chattered excitedly while machine-gunning the parliament with their expensive cameras.

Ah, the Scottish Parliament – there was a tale of bureaucratic bungling by the authorities verging on criminal malfeasance. Designed by some highfalutin

Spanish architect and delivered three years late at a cost of more than forty times the original budget.

The fancy-dans called it postmodern, whatever that meant, and reckoned it was a 'sympathetic' fit with the dramatic backdrop of Arthur's Seat and the hills of Holyrood Park.

As he watched the police guard on the entrance, Seagull Slayer wondered whether Prince Charles – royal champion of architecture for the common man – had it on his list of ugly carbuncles. From Seagull's point of view the building's exterior looked like a heap of balsa wood thrown together by a toddler.

The TV images he had seen of the debating chamber were equally dire. The MSPs sat at small individual wooden desks like primary-school children. They behaved in much the same way.

Dumping his half-eaten ice cream in a passing Japanese tourist's open tote bag, he moved from his position at the ice-cream kiosk across the street, past the pond towards the armed police at the entrance.

Even though he carried nothing upon his person to suggest homicide, he knew he was taking a chance.

But he wanted to see and hear the woman live, in the flesh, as it were. He knew he might be out of luck purely from the fact that he was attempting to get a ticket on the day. Demand might exceed supply. But disclosing identity by pre-ordering online would have been far too dangerous. Taking a chance on availability was the only way.

His luck was in. Tickets were available. Then, masking his impatience by reading a pamphlet of Disneyesque simplicity outlining the devolution story, he joined the queue to go through the airport-style security.

It appeared to be exclusively foreign with the Japanese contingent being joined by Americans, Germans and Scandinavians. He strained, but failed to hear a Scottish accent.

Perhaps the native population were so disillusioned by politics they had opted out. Was this eye-wateringly expensive carbuncle simply window dressing for an international audience: inhabited by windbags and self-serving carpetbaggers presiding over a democratic chimera?

Nearing the front of the line he could feel his pulse beginning to race. A German woman was being told off by a security guard for not paying attention. The man was large and fleshy with a beard you could have hidden animals in.

Seagull Slayer concentrated on beards, anything to take his mind off the next few seconds. Beards, not stubble or a neatly trimmed full set, but shaggy, long, wildly extravagant face hair like the American band ZZ Top favoured, were all the rage in Scotland. Maybe it was the fact that the men were all ginger, or behemoths attempting to deflect attention from their obesity that was fuelling the craze.

"Next!" It was his turn. The big, bearded fat guy was calling him through. Standing at the entry to the metal detector he could feel the sweat glands in his armpits and groin working overtime. Not the face, he prayed. "Come on, pal. We've not got all day."

He moved through the gate and the alarm went off.

Christ, could it detect panic? Another guard approached him with a body scanner. "The watch, bud." Seagull looked down at his wrist. The fucking watch. Trying to keep his hands from shaking he removed the watch, placed it in a tray, and came back through the gate. This time he was waved straight through unhindered.

Sitting in the public gallery he had a perfect view of proceedings. The MSPs were already in place, many of them fidgeting as they strove to fit their considerable arses into the school seats. Then the main players entered.

First, the presiding officer, the Scottish Parliament's answer to the Speaker in the House of Commons. Then the party leaders and, finally, there she was: Nicola, Queen of Scots.

From his vantage point in the gallery he estimated she was only about 100 feet away. If only he had a gun. The opposition had raised a question about the testing of five-year-olds in primary school. Snappy as a cornered badger, Nicola was on her feet barely pausing for breath as she crashed through her practised responses.

There followed a lightning quick follow-up of her government's so-called achievements; free university education, free baby boxes for all new mothers, free sanitary products for all college students – the freebies just kept on coming.

Like many others, Seagull wondered where the money was going to come from to pay for this jumble sale of second-rate populist ideas since the economy was tanking.

He switched the sound off concentrating instead on his target. At five-foot-four she was an inch shorter than Angela Merkel and two inches shorter than Theresa May.

The runt of the female leadership litter. But she looked slightly chunky like a hedgehog, or maybe it was the hairdo that summoned the simile. And if the prickliness of her character was anything to go by she would put up a fight. Seagull considered these things as he slipped out of the chamber and headed back up the Royal Mile.

COMMANDO was on the buses again, or more specifically, one particular bus.

His new friends and benefactors – the two dark-haired men who had made him such a wonderful offer of £10 a day for his services – did not mind how many buses he jumped on in the course of his adventures. They only had one stipulation. That at four thirty each afternoon, he caught the no. 3 bus in Princes Street going to *A-Patch* territory. The scheduled time for the journey was fifty minutes which – even accounting for excessive traffic jams or roadworks – allowed more than enough time for him to get to the address by 6 pm.

The taller of the two men met him behind the bandstand in Princes Street Gardens at 4 p.m. on the first day of his secret mission.

Commando didn't read people well. That had been a large part of his problems in the orphanage and later in college and then in the rough and tumble of life on the streets. But he sensed a change in his new friend. He wasn't so friendly as on their first encounter. There was no attempt at humour and he seemed – and Commando was personally acquainted with this sensation – nervous.

"You know what you have to do." It wasn't so much a

question as a command from the tall man. Commando nodded, bewildered at this change of personality.

"No my friend. Toy dogs in cars nod. Tell me what you have to do." Commando recited his instructions including the name of the high-rise Saltire Court and the flat number 703.

It was the tall man's turn to nod. Commando decided it might be imprudent to mention toy dogs in cars.

"Okay, Soldier, now I am going to show you a photo of the person you will give the envelope to." He produced a small passport-size colour photograph.

Commando knew the kind: you got them in curtained booths in supermarkets or train stations. He smiled to himself at a memory long ago on a rare trip from the orphanage when everyone got their picture taken at a kiosk in a bus station. He had kept getting the stool height wrong, or moving at the precise second he had to stay still. None of his five photos was any good: two featured him headless, two got the blurred side of his face in a panicked grin, and one simply showed the background as he had bent down to pick up his change as the light flashed.

"Come on, man, pay attention," ordered the tall man misunderstanding the reason for Commando's smile. He jabbed a nicotine-stained finger at the photo.

Commando saw the image of a small dark-haired woman staring unsmilingly into the camera. Her cheeks were sunken as though malnourished and the only colour in the photograph was the bright green supermarket uniform she was wearing.

"Now this is very important. You only give the envelope to this woman – no one else. If anyone other than her opens the door ask specifically for Glum Sue. Have you got that?"

"That's a funny name," said Commando, staring at the face in the snapshot.

"Yeah, well, she's got bad teeth, doesn't smile a lot. Anyway, her name's got nothing to do with your mission. Just concentrate on what you have to do – and bring her photo back to me. We don't want it falling into enemy hands."

The tall man thrust the envelope hard into Commando's midriff, winding him. "Okay, hide that in your army drawers. Remember, this is a very important mission, Soldier. Fuck this up and there will be no more tenners. Plus, you could get into a lot of trouble. Now catch that bus pronto."

Commando was still recovering on the bus from what had effectively been a punch in the guts, so he never noticed the tall man's smaller accomplice board a couple of stops later. It would have been difficult to tell anyway as the man had a baseball cap pulled over his eyes and was dressed completely differently from the first meeting.

Following instructions, Commando got off at the appointed stop and walked through a dilapidated shopping centre – most of the businesses were boarded up and scarred with graffiti – to a rear entrance. Then he turned and walked past a playing field – deserted apart from a burnt-out car minus the tyres and a couple of women pushing prams around the perimeter of a football pitch – towards the high-rise.

Saltire Court rose for ten storeys – literally a monumental folly to the architecture of the 1970s – and a scabrous impediment to the Pentland Hills fanned out in a glorious panorama behind. Washing lines, disused furniture, an abandoned TV set – even a car engine littered the balconies as Commando gazed up at the tower block.

Once upon a time there had been functioning lifts, but they had ceased operating long ago. Commando didn't really mind. He ran everywhere anyway and jogging up the seven floors helped ease his aching stomach.

There was no bell or nameplate on 703. Somebody had used a sharp instrument to carve the number into the wood of the door.

Commando knocked on the door, tentatively at first, then – when there was no response – louder, shaking the flimsy structure.

"Right. Hold your horses!" yelled a female voice. The sunken creature from the photograph opened the door three inches on a chain and stared suspiciously at Commando. "Where's the fire, chum?" she demanded.

"No fire, Miss Glum Sue," Commando said.

The woman looked more closely at Commando and her sallow demeanour broke into a smile. Commando tried not to shudder. He had never seen such a set of tombstones in his life. The teeth that were not missing or broken were a mud-brown colour. Glum Sue switched off the Halloween grin. "I take it you're the new recruit. Got something for me, sonny?"

Commando fumbled under his camouflage jacket for the envelope secreted in his combat trousers.

"No on the landing, you balloon." Glum Sue gripped his arm with surprising strength and hauled him into the flat. She led him down a bare lobby with green institutionalised walls and into what he could only guess was the living room.

There was not one item of furniture that was not broken. A large table – where clearly all the meals were taken and rarely cleared away – was balanced with a bundle of newspapers under a leg. Two beige stained settees squatted on the floor at precariously canted angles having lost a set of castors each.

A man with a blanket over his head was asleep on one of the settees, while two pit bulls lay on the floorboards at his feet. As Commando entered the room the dogs skittered across the wooden boards towards him. "Sit down. They'll no' hurt you. Joshua, McGregor: behave now," commanded Glum Sue.

Commando perched on the settee opposite the sleeping man, while the dogs sauntered over. One of them nudged his head into Commando's balls. He could feel them shrink as the dog continued its inspection.

"Joshua! Off, you dirty bastard!" Glum Sue hauled the animal away by his studded collar and kicked him in the arse as he reluctantly retreated to his previous position. After a brief sniff at Commando, McGregor lost interest and joined the other dog.

"Davie, we've got company. Waken up, you lazy bastard."

The sleeping man moaned and reluctantly removed the blanket. Despite his scruffiness and the sores at his mouth and nose, he had blond hair and regular features, which looked as though he might be handsome under the ingrained dirt.

"Say hello to the new delivery man, Davie," said Glum Sue.

Davie grunted, but rose to a sitting position and appeared to take a new interest in the information.

"All right, let's have the package, mister."

Commando retrieved the envelope and Glum Sue snatched it, running into the pantry-sized kitchen. She opened the envelope with her back to Commando so he could not see its contents. But he saw her dab her finger into it. She turned and gave Commando her tombstone smile. "That's fine, wee man. Now you better be off and catch your bus. Remember, straight home now."

The flat door crashed behind him, but as he moved along the landing to the stairs he clearly heard the woman's instructions. "Davie, get Laundry on the mobie. We cannie be late, or else."

Commando had to sprint for the bus. Mission accomplished he thought as he sat on the top deck staring at the stark grandeur of Salisbury Crags: its cliffs burnished gold in the sunset.

He fished in his pocket for the photograph of Glum Sue. The tall, dark man had been insistent on getting the snap back. That was the last detail for the night.

Commando had been too preoccupied to see the small man in the baseball cap. He had watched from the shadows of the tower block as Commando boarded the number 3. He hit the speed dial on his smartphone to relay the news.

THE emergency phone on Superintendent Bert Rothesay's desk rang. It was the chief constable's direct line.

In the five seconds it took for Rothesay to pick up, a variety of dreaded possibilities sent the neurons ricocheting around his brain like a pinball machine. A terrorist attack on the tourist hordes at Edinburgh Castle? A plane crash killing hundreds at the airport? A multiple car pile-up on the new Forth Road Bridge? He was wrong on every count. But it was still a disaster beyond imagining.

The voice on the other end was so tense it took Rothesay a moment to recognise it indeed belonged to the chief constable. When he did, what his boss said was so incredible it was hard to believe.

"Rothesay, put Sky on, they're running it live."

Hearing the strained urgency in the command, the superintendent needed no second bidding. He put the TV on and the live news images flickered across the screen.

They were jumpy and taken at distance. Aerial shots from a helicopter, thought Rothesay, and a second later the camera confirmed the fact by showing a rooftop.

There were three figures on it. One was a man who appeared to be holding another man. He was waving what looked like a gun, but the camera shots were at a distance so it was hard to tell. The images were blurred and jumped back and forth like a home-made movie. The camera then panned shakily to a third figure even further away. It was a brief glimpse not helped by the vertiginous jerking motions of the camera. It was the figure of a woman sitting on a chair in the background. Somehow she looked eerily familiar. The news caption running under the pictures removed any doubt. It was the First Minister!

Rothesay suddenly felt very sick. He was dully aware that the chief constable was speaking rapidly and utter concentration was required.

"You know what to do. Code Red. Armed response team – and get a negotiator."

The line went dead. Rothesay stared at the receiver for a full minute as if it might suddenly come alive, rise from its cradle and beat his brains out. He almost wished it would.

He slapped himself hard in the face and made the Code Red call. But what about the fucking negotiator? There was no professional negotiator within the ranks of Police Scotland: the budget cuts had seen to that. *Come on, man, think fast.*

An idea was swimming around at the edge of his consciousness but refusing to surface. He forced himself to calm down. What personnel were at his disposal? What cases were running? Who could he call upon immediately? Strawberry's team. That constable the man was always going on about. A good listener. A sympathetic ear. She would have to do. He picked up the phone again.

THE Seagull Slayer had graduated to a proper gun and a proper gun meant proper violence.

He had arrived at the target just after dawn parking on the other side of the square. Judging from the avalanche of newspaper reports, the building was not currently habitable. Vital structural repairs costing taxpayers a million pounds were urgently required, so everyone had moved out. And the workmen had moved in. But they wouldn't turn up until at least seven thirty going on eight. That only left one – maybe two at most – security guards. He had more than enough time to make the morning newsreels.

He got out of his third stolen car, put on the yellow bib, hung the lanyard around his neck (he had improved the forgery by encasing it in plastic for this special occasion), and hard hat in one hand, he clutched her arm with the other and walked towards the most famous political address in Scotland.

An old man answered the door. Seagull Slayer had donned the balaclava and she was standing out of the old man's eyeline to the side of the door with a blanket over her head. No need, he reasoned, for immediate mayhem.

"Morning, mate. One of your neighbours phoned about a smell of gas. Thought we should give it priority." Seagull laughed – as if to convey that a call about such an eminent address could be regarded as anything other than priority.

The old man was more diligent than Seagull expected. "I'm the porter here. Responsible for the building's security. Let me see your ID, please."

While the porter was fishing for his reading glasses, Seagull produced the gun from inside his helmet and prodded the man in the chest.

"Okay, Dad. Me and this lady here" – at that Seagull grabbed her arm and brought her into view flicking the blanket away like a conjurer – "are going for a promenade on the roof. You are coming with us. Just do as you're told and no one will get hurt. First off, we'll need a chair for the lady."

In a state of shock, the porter stumbled ahead up the stairs.

The interior was covered in dust-sheets and scaffolding, but the Georgian splendour of the building peeped through on the sections that had already been renovated.

Getting her onto the roof was no easy task what with having to encourage the porter as well by prodding him from time to time in the back with the gun barrel.

But they made it and Seagull Slayer celebrated by shooting a couple of seagulls as they walked inquisitively towards the intruders. One fell where it stood with its head missing. The other spiralled from the roof to splatter on the steps of the building. Seagull Slayer whooped. "That will make a great photo for the first editions. What do you think, Nicola?"

Seagull Slayer giggled. "Cat got your tongue, *Furst Meanister*? She's not saying much, is she, Mr Porter Man?" The porter, who was shaking with fright with his hands in the air, said nothing either.

THE stately elegance of Charlotte Square had been transformed into a scene from a New York crime drama by the time Strawberry and Gunn arrived.

"Every patrol car in Edinburgh must be here," said Gunn as a fleet of police cars, blue lights flashing, cordoned off Bute House. They outnumbered the outside-broadcast television vans, but only just. The vans with their distinctive antenna and gaudy logos had been corralled fifty yards away outside the National Records building.

The newsprint foot soldiers had fared marginally better sneaking over the garden railings to within twenty yards of the building, but a phalanx of police officers, arms interlocked, were ready to repel anyone threatening to breach the tapes.

As they climbed from their car, Strawberry raised his eyes to the surrounding rooftops. "Every police marksman in Scotland too by the looks of things." Gunn followed his gaze and saw the distinctive black baseball caps of the armed response unit dotted around on vantage points high above the eighteenth-century garden square.

Strawberry nudged Gunn as he spotted the small, burly figure of the chief constable walking towards them with Bert Rothesay in close attendance. Rothesay was carrying a loud hailer.

Strawberry looked directly into her eyes. "This is dangerous, Gunn. It's a job for a trained negotiator. You don't have to do this."

Gunn looked directly back at him. "I don't think I've ever done my impersonation of Gloria Swanson in *Sunset Boulevard* for you." She fluttered her eyelashes, adopted a coquettish pose, and went American. "All right, Mr DeMille, I'm ready for my close-up."

Strawberry and Gunn were standing in the middle of the square. The other police officers had withdrawn to their patrol cars – although the marksmen were still in position.

The chief constable and Bert Rothesay were in the gardens in a discreet corner in constant radio contact with the leader of the armed response unit and Strawberry and Gunn, who both wore earpieces – and bulletproof body armour.

Left to the dramatic stage, Gunn was given the green light to begin. The echo of the electronic loud hailer sounded unnaturally loud in her ears as she addressed the seagull killer.

"No one needs to get hurt here today. Tell us what we can do for you, but please release the First Minister and the porter. They are both innocent. Neither of them has done you any harm."

For a long moment Gunn believed there would be no response. But then the seagull killer moved towards the edge of the roof with the porter in front of him. He had his arm around the man's neck and the gun at his head.

"Innocent, you say. No harm, you say." The seagull killer's voice, dripping with sarcasm, carried clearly across the square.

The TV and radio mikes would have no difficulty picking up the message and relaying it live to the waiting world. The idea of such a platform – the oxygen of publicity for a madman – made Strawberry sweat under his Kevlar vest.

"She…" – he waved the gun generally in the direction of

the figure sitting in the chair behind him – "…she is the one responsible for the rules. She gives the orders and everybody jumps. She…" – his voice was rising to an alarming pitch – "…likes fucking seagulls. The vermin that carry diseases. The scavengers that are turning this beautiful city into one big rubbish dump with filth scattered all over our historic streets. She's protecting these disgusting creatures, so she is not innocent and she is causing us great harm. That's why I am here today. To make a statement."

Gunn felt her hand tightening around the loud hailer. This was going wrong. She had to somehow lower the temperature, calm the man down before things got out of control. She decided to change tack. Try to take the spotlight off the First Minister.

"Please release the porter. His name is James Ballantyne. He is seventy-eight years old and a grandfather. He has nothing to do with your quarrel."

The seagull killer suddenly stepped away from the porter and there seemed to be an audible sigh of relief from the watchers in the square. "Well done," Strawberry whispered in Gunn's ear. The words had barely escaped his lips when the madman ran towards the First Minister. A flame suddenly erupted from his hand.

Everything happened so quickly that Strawberry could only comprehend what he witnessed later. Fire suddenly engulfed the figure, an inferno which consumed her at lightning speed before she fell soundlessly from view on to the flat roof.

Then Strawberry heard something he had never heard before and doubted he would ever hear again. It was a collective gasp and it came from the ranks of the assembled press. The hard-boiled camera crews, the urbane news anchors, the harried scribblers, the outrageous paparazzi: these flint-hearted peddlers of a thousand stories of death and destruction – normally Teflon-coated in their hard-nosed indifference to pain and suffering – for a second forgot their *raison d'être* – the story. As the First Minister was engulfed in flames, becoming a live funeral pyre before their eyes, the Fourth Estate lost all semblance of professionalism. Like everyone else hypnotised by the horror they suddenly became human in their anguish.

"Shoot the bastard!" The media were jolted from their paralysis by the chief constable's outraged command from a distance of thirty yards. Their microphones picked up the ordered death sentence as clearly as they had the madman's message.

Within twenty-four hours it would go viral on YouTube and every other major video-sharing website. The chief constable would resign a day after that.

Three marksmen had been designated to take the shot should it come to that. In the pre-ordained briefing they were simply codenamed Hit 1, Hit 2 and Hit 3. The choice of shooter was to be determined by the position of the target on the roof in relation to the marksmen at the precise second of the command. Seagull Slayer was nearest the cross-hairs of Hit 2 when the order came. The officer fired without hesitation and the bullet travelling at 2,500 feet per second – more than twice the speed of sound – hit the target in .5 of a second.

A crimson starburst bloomed on the chest of Seagull Slayer. The gun fell from his nerveless fingers and he plummeted from the roof to land on the steps of Bute House beside the mangled corpse of the seagull.

IT was a recurring dream. Nicola was Catherine the Great, Empress of Russia and she was in her boudoir. But someone else was in the room too – and they were imprisoned in an iron cage.

The only thing that ever changed in the dream was the occupant of the cage. Sometimes it was Ruth Davidson. Sometimes it was Patrick Harvie. More frequently in recent dreams it had been Alex Salmond. But on this occasion it was her second in command, John Swinney. He had clearly displeased her in some way.

As with all dreams the details were sketchy at best, but she found herself moving towards the cage to do some terrible damage to the inmate when she woke up in a thrash of bedclothes.

Christ, the dream had been so vivid! Nicola lay quietly for a moment trying to compose her thoughts: attempting to rationalise the dream's meaning.

It was true that in the few flights of fancy she allowed herself, the First Minister considered she had a lot in common with Catherine the Great. For a start they were both physically small women. They both completely dominated their respective courts – despite the fact that they were separated historically by 250 years. And they were both utterly ruthless.

Catherine had indeed imprisoned her hairdresser in a cage in her room for three years fearing that he might betray the fact that she wore a wig. She also murdered her husband to take the throne and Nicola was seriously considering hanging her long-time mentor Alex Salmond out to dry.

The answer as to why it had been Swinney's turn for the cage was more explicable. She had argued late into the previous evening with him debating the reasons for the parlous state of the nation's health service and the fiasco of Scotland's education system – a disaster that was Swinney's personal remit – before being ferried in her personal limousine to her new temporary quarters in the New Town. She had to take a large whisky to calm herself down – and that had been her undoing.

Leaning over to the alarm she had failed to set she suffered the second shock of the morning. It read 10 a.m. when her normal rising time was 6 a.m.! Why had her new PA not made contact? Nicola vowed there would be hell to pay for this. Heads would roll starting with the useless girl Kezia!

She attempted to move and groaned. Her head was bumping from the unaccustomed alcohol and she was temporarily disoriented by her surroundings. It took a few seconds to remember that she had been forced to decamp a few weeks earlier to an apartment in the New Town because of the emergency repairs currently ongoing at her official residence.

Pursing her small mouth in a moue of annoyance at the continuing inconvenience, she made a concerted effort, threw off the covers and, ignoring the hangover, walked purposefully to the en suite bathroom.

Nicola walked purposefully everywhere. Television pictures did not exist showing the First Minister walking in any fashion other than purposefully. It was in her DNA: a signature image of her intent and resolve. On occasion she might add a plastic A4-size folder (never moleskin or leather; she was, after all, a woman of the people) at the hip of her perfectly tailored two-piece business suits. But the stride never changed.

A sudden crash as the bedroom door imploded interrupted her toilet.

Nicola emerged from the en suite to see a posse of armed police officers with a battering ram in the room. Immediately behind them stood her PA Kezia, but only for a moment. On seeing the First Minister, she promptly fainted.

Nicola took more than a little satisfaction in dousing Kezia's face with a glass of water. The woman spluttered and came round. Then looked at her boss as if she was seeing a ghost. Then hugged her in a fierce embrace.

"You're here! Everyone thought you were dead. Thank God, First Minister. I thought you were gone. You are on the roof. Live pictures on every channel – even the Catalonian one you had installed. Burnt to a crisp."

The First Minister's eyes held a puritanical glint. "Kezia, have you taken something? You know my views on drink and drugs. I can't have a sozzled PA. Remember, you're still on your probationary period."

"No, no, First Minister. Let me turn on the TV." Pushing the police officers aside, Kezia darted across the bedroom, almost tripping over the bed in her haste to get to the set.

She hopped from foot to foot as she waited for the picture. The Sky report was no longer live, but they were streaming repeat images on a continuous loop from the roof of Bute House.

For the first time in her life, the First Minister gawped. The TV pictures showed someone that looked the spitting image of herself being incinerated by a lunatic with a blowtorch. A lesser person would have collapsed. Instead, Nicola emitted one carefully chosen expletive – "Shite". You could take the girl out of Ayrshire…

STRAWBERRY and Gunn were sitting across from Superintendent Bert Rothesay in his office. All three looked exhausted from the drama of the morning.

In violation of Gayfield Square's no smoking rule, Rothesay had a pipe in his mouth – though it was clearly unlit.

A bit like a baby's dummy tit, thought Gunn – a comforting prop to stop the possibility of spontaneous screaming. After a while he removed the pipe and placed it carefully on the desk. It was a slow, measured action aimed at counteracting the internal riot he was presently experiencing.

He cleared his throat. "I got you both in because I feel it's only right that you should be the first to know what happened this morning before the shit hits the fan." He paused again, stealing a forlorn glance at the pipe. "But first I want to commend you both for the courage you showed, especially you, Gunn. The man had a gun and neither of you hesitated to put yourself in extreme danger to resolve the situation."

Seeing her blush, Rothesay went quickly on. "It was a dummy, a mannequin. The figure on the roof. He torched an effigy of the First Minister. She was sitting in a chair. Her legs were covered with a blanket. At that kind of distance she looked like the real thing. Her arm even moved. The crazy bastard had rigged a battery in her back."

The superintendent looked as though he might actually cry. "We received a report early in the morning of a break-in at a woman's clothes shop called…" Rothesay had to look at his notes. "Tattie Scones."

Strawberry looked uncomprehendingly at Rothesay. "Sturgeon's clothes designer," volunteered Gunn. "It's a wee boutique shop at the Links. I pass it every day on the bus coming into work."

Rothesay nodded. "The seagull killer put the front window in and took the dummy. It was an exact life-size replica of the First Minister. A Madame Tussaud's lookalike in every detail. Apparently the First Minister goes there for all her outfits. Great publicity for the frock-maker I suppose, so she had the dummy made."

"And, unable to kidnap the real thing, the seagull killer stole the dummy for his 'statement,'" said Strawberry.

"Exactly, but at the time our call handler simply thought it was some kind of student prank and put it at the bottom of our priorities," said Rothesay. "A perfectly reasonable conclusion, but it's being seen as a major fuck-up by Police Scotland – and we've already made a few of these recently."

"So where was the real First Minister, sir?" asked Gunn.

"At her new digs safely tucked up in bed. Apparently she had a couple of nips last night and slept in. Her new PA failed to contact her." Rothesay shook his head in exasperation. "I suppose when everything kicked off she was taken in like the rest of us."

"Anything suggesting a motive, sir?" asked Strawberry.

"They found a letter on him," said Rothesay. "It was a long, rambling affair, hand-written and at times indecipherable. Essentially though it claimed that his young child had had an eye poked out by an adult seagull in a frenzied attack after she found a baby seagull on the ground. Apparently it had fallen from its nest."

Rothesay spread his arms in resignation.

"Of course, the worst thing about this entire fuck-up is the needless waste of a life."

Strawberry's brow furrowed. "Well, there might have been extenuating circumstances, sir, but the man was mad. It would only have been a matter of time until he actually did kill someone."

"I wasn't referring to the seagull killer," said Rothesay. "The porter died from a massive heart attack an hour ago."

DOUGIE Nichols was reading the *Hoots Mon*. The latest edition was hot off the press in more than one sense of that cliché. *Deadly Hoax – police hoodwinked in Sturgeon rooftop drama* – screamed the headline.

"Well, at least the real thing wasnae cremated," Nichols muttered as he read the report in the Gayfield Square canteen.

A loyal supporter of the SNP and its present leader, Nichols was relieved at the outcome. He was also pleased for a personal reason. His girlfriend, Brenda Gunn, had received heroic treatment from all the papers, especially the tabloids.

Walking through the train station on his way to work earlier in the morning he had stopped at a newsstand and shuffled though the papers. Every one had a photo of Brenda on the front page standing in Charlotte Square, loud hailer at her lips, attempting to talk the seagull killer down from the roof.

The reports were united in their praise of her courage. *Brave Brenda*, *Gunn is the Real McCoy*, *Our Glorious Girl in Blue* were only a few of the phrases employed. An editorial comment in one national Scottish newspaper was even calling for her to be awarded the George Medal for her bravery.

Nichols had left the station with an extra spring in his

step. The only irritating thing about the whole episode was that Strawberry had also been in the photographs standing by her side.

Later at his desk, he cut Strawberry out of the front-page image in the *Hoots Mon* and put the clipping in his drawer. He hadn't been able to speak to Brenda yet to offer his own congratulations as she was currently doing the rounds of the TV stations. He vowed he would try to catch her later on the sofa with Holly and Phil in ITV's *This Morning* programme. He only prayed that Strawberry wouldn't be there too.

Right now though, it was back to the serious business of police work and an interview with PC Derek Murch. The good news as far as Nichols was concerned was that Murch had not turned out to be the seagull killer.

When a member of the armed response unit removed the killer's balaclava on the steps of Bute House the face of an as yet unidentified John Doe stared sightlessly back. However, Murch would still have to be interviewed under caution for possession of an air rifle. Nichols had already established from records that the officer did not have a licence for the air gun and that was an offence.

Nichols felt the tension the minute he entered the room. Murch was alone. The PC had not felt the need for a federation rep and Nichols was grateful for that as he wanted to keep the whole affair unofficial. But Murch looked distinctly uneasy as he rose quickly and stood to attention. Nichols signalled for the man to sit down.

"I expect you know what this is about, Murch."

"No, sir, not exactly. I know that you were out at my flat a couple of days ago."

"Ah yes, your alarm system."

"Sir?"

"Your neighbour, Murch. I can't imagine anything escaping the eagle-eyed attention of that lady."

Murch nodded bleakly. "She certainly does keep the stair in order. If you forget your turn for washing the landing there's a note posted through the letter box the same afternoon, night duty or not. And any noise after 10 p.m. is a complete no-no."

Before he got full chapter and verse on communal tenement life, Nichols thought it best to move directly to the crux of the matter. "After my visit to your flat I went round to your allotment, Murch." The PC appeared nonplussed. "I did that because I harboured suspicions that you might conceivably be the person responsible for the seagull shootings."

Murch gave an embarrassed laugh. "Sir, what I said in the garden was a joke. I was tired of being shat upon by these bloody things every day."

"Yes, I see that now, Murch. But I found an air rifle in your shed and I had you firmly in the frame for the shootings right up until the real culprit was shot dead yesterday on the steps of the First Minister's official residence. But I must still ask you – given that you do not have a certificate for an air rifle, and that is an offence, Murch – why do you own one?"

Murch flushed and studied his hands. Then he crossed his arms in a defensive posture. "I'd prefer not to say, sir. It's a private matter. I'm not doing anything wrong."

"You are if you don't possess a licence for the air gun – and I already checked, Murch. Look, if there's a rational reason for you having the thing, which isn't harming anyone, I can overlook the licence issue, Murch. But you must tell me."

"The only thing I've ever wanted is to be a member of the armed response unit." Murch appeared stricken by the admission as if he had confessed to some terrible deviance. He went on. "It's a personal thing. I didn't want anyone to know. I applied a while ago, but my shooting wasn't nearly good enough. So I got the air rifle in order to practise privately – away from the guys at the station. You know what it can be like."

Nichols knew all right. Then he started putting the picture together. He thought back to his visit to the allotment and the dented cans and it all made sense. "So you were doing target practice on the allotment trying to improve your accuracy by shooting tin cans?"

Later, at his desk again, Nichols reflected on the interview with Murch. Judging from the tin cans the bugger couldn't hit a dead dog if he was holding it by the tail. He was also completely temperamentally unsuited to the duties of a police marksman where life or death decisions were taken in a split second. Armed response unit? Nichols shuddered at the thought. He wouldn't let Murch loose with a pop-gun in a chicken coup. It was back to Balmoral Square Mansions and the surveillance team for him – and for me, he thought, just as soon as he had a quick look at Brenda on the *This Morning* sofa.

THE incident happened on the third drop. Commando had got off the No. 3 at the same stop and followed the same route through the shopping mall and past the field. He was in sight of the high-rise when they ambushed him.

Half a dozen kids on choppers: no older than twelve and not much taller than their bikes. They emerged from an alley under the tower block in drill formation and then fanned out and came sprinting at him from all sides.

The speed of the attack and its fierce intensity took Commando by surprise. As he dodged the bike heading straight at him, he was smacked in the back by a second chopper. The impact buckled his legs and he fell forward smacking his head on the pavement.

Then they were on him like a pack of feral animals pummelling him with their small fists and tearing at his clothes. Dazed from the blow to his head, Commando could do nothing to stop the onslaught as they ripped off his combat jacket. "It's here," he heard one small voice pipe up. A frenzied scrabble of fingers ensued as the pocket in his combat trousers was rent asunder and the envelope was removed. Then, with a fleeting kick that fortunately missed his balls, the gang were on their bikes again and flying back through the alley to the warren of flats that lay beyond.

Why he forced his bruised and battered body to climb the seven floors to Glum Sue's flat when there was no longer any delivery to make was a mystery. Perhaps in his mind a soldier had to complete his mission – even if it was a failure.

If Commando expected tea and sympathy he was in for a disappointment. There was a full welcoming committee on the landing waiting for him as he dragged himself up the last few steps.

The pit bulls Joshua and McGregor were tethered with fraying ropes to the railings: a confinement they did not care for as they strained wildly at the end of the leads employing their heads as battering rams upon the neighbours' doors. Glum Sue and Davie looked as if they had been doing strenuous exercise too. They were both sweating profusely and Glum Sue's eyes held an unnatural, disconcerting shine. "Where the fuck have you been?" she demanded, seemingly oblivious to his injuries. "You're fifteen fucking minutes late."

"I got attacked. Kids on bikes. They stole my jacket."

"What about the envelope?" Glum Sue was like a kettle coming to the boil and her eyes looked as though they were in danger of popping out of her head.

"That too," admitted Commando. "Look, they tore my combat trousers."

Davie, who appeared to be having difficulty following the conversation, unzipped his flies and pissed against the landing wall. Glum Sue's face was now a deep crimson. "They tore your combat trousers! I'll tear you a new scrotum, you fucking cocksucker! Better still, I'll get Joshua and McGregor to do it for me."

As Glum Sue crossed the landing to the tethered dogs, Commando knew it was time to go. "I'm sorry about the envelope," he shouted, retreating down the stairs appreciably faster than he had climbed them.

HOSPITALS engendered similar emotions in Marjorie Agincourt as police stations. They were the kind of places – albeit depending on the day or time – where one would find the dregs of society.

For instance she knew, from reports on Radio 4's *Today* programme, that hospitals were the haunt of drug addicts and violent hooligans at weekends. Late on Friday and Saturday nights – after the pubs and clubs had disgorged their rowdy clientele onto the streets – A & E departments often became battlegrounds for the drunk and disorderly with hard-pressed medical staff fighting rearguard actions in order to maintain any semblance of care or order.

Therefore she had chosen to visit the bishop in broad daylight during the week. Alighting from the taxi, however, she remained tentative as she entered the vast building on the outskirts of Edinburgh.

An advance phone call had established very little information as she could not claim to be a relative. But when Marjorie finally managed to get through to the ward, the nurse's use of the word 'critical' about the bishop's condition made up her mind.

Despite her fears, she was determined to be at his bedside. Her resolution had nothing to do with religion, as Marjorie Agincourt could never have been described as religious. Agnostic might have been a more accurate term, though she was ignorant of the word's meaning, but Marjorie undoubtedly hoped that her precious Hamish was in the care of some higher celestial being.

Her concern for the bishop was solely based on a long-term friendship. Each had arrived in the precinct of Balmoral Square Mansions at the same time and had met quite by accident at a floral event hosted by the church. A purely secular friendship had bloomed and grown with the passing years and Marjorie had become even more reliant on the bishop as a trusted confidant after Hamish's passing.

Employing the confident arrogance of her colonial past, Marjorie collared a porter to secure a wheelchair and progressed along the seemingly endless corridors to the ward.

However, even Marjorie's unflinching self-belief could not get her beyond the double doors of the Intensive Care Unit. Inside, the small corridor was bathed in a calming green glow reminiscent of the illumination on the dashboard of a motorcar, or the instrument panel of an aeroplane. The same muted lighting enveloped the half dozen patients who lay motionless in beds behind the long glass windows.

A nurse emerged from the unit and in the soft, but implacable tones of a gatekeeper for those hovering between life and death, informed Marjorie that there was no prospect of visiting the bishop.

She relented slightly at seeing the old woman's anguish and confided that the bishop remained 'unconscious' and the next twenty-four hours would be 'vital' in the outcome.

"He suffered a very heavy fall, so as yet the doctors have no way of knowing the possible damage caused."

With that, she disappeared back inside the unit. Marjorie was wheeled back along the endless corridors. She had failed in her effort to see her friend and the weight of that failure lay heavy with her. This could well be the last opportunity she would have to see the bishop to say goodbye.

Back at reception a sudden thought struck her as the porter helped her out of the wheelchair.

She weighed up the nurse: a young woman barely out of college, or university – wherever it was nurses went to be trained these days. That meant one of two things: she could either be uncertain, malleable and eager to please, or a politically correct stickler for the rules as so many young people – what was the word for them? Menials? Milooniels? – were nowadays.

"Just a minute, Porter, I want to speak to the nurse." If there was a flicker of impatience for this cantankerous old woman who had ambushed him – and was now detaining him beyond the end of his shift – the porter did not show it. He kept hold of her walking stick and pushed her over to the desk.

"Young lady, I wonder if you can help me. I've already been disappointed once tonight in my efforts to see a dear friend. I didn't realise he was quite so ill and couldn't receive visitors." Marjorie attempted a sob, though age had dried up her tear ducts. Anyway, weeping was not her forte, never had been. The sob emerged half formed like an embarrassed cough, but the young nurse bought it: eager to please.

Marjorie went on: "I rarely manage to leave my

apartment. So as not to make my journey entirely wasted, I have another friend who is a patient here. Her name is (and here Marjorie managed to remember very well) Blessings McKenzie." She also managed to avoid any reference to Blessings colour – an observation she knew went down very badly with today's liberal youth.

The young woman gave Marjorie an endearing smile. What a wonderful old lady. Good Samaritans were in short supply in twenty-first-century Britain where a pitiless right-wing government was cracking down on the weakest: the poor, the disabled and the homeless.

Her finger ran down the ward lists stopping halfway down the third page. "Your friend's in orthopaedic – a broken leg, hopefully not too bad, dear. Visiting hour still has fifteen minutes to run. Ron, could you take this lady along to Ward 20."

Ron, the porter, gave Marjorie back her walking stick, which she waved regally at the young nurse, and they set sail once more down another long corridor.

This time access was straightforward. A few visitors were still dotted around the ward, either sitting in conversation, or about to take their leave. None of the patients looked particularly ill, thought Marjorie, as she scanned the beds for a black face.

Identification was simple. Blessings McKenzie was the only patient of colour in the ward – though there were a number of black nurses. She was in the fourth of six beds on the left-hand side of the ward. Her entire leg – encased in plaster from the foot upwards – was hanging in mid-air in a sling. She looked very uncomfortable and not a little grumpy.

Adopting her Sunday smile, Marjorie had Ron carry out the docking manoeuvre to park the wheelchair at the side of Blessings' bed.

"Can I have five minutes to talk to this lady alone, please?" It wasn't so much a question as a dismissal and Ron retreated in the knowledge that he would now certainly miss his bus to Penicuik and have to wait an hour for the next.

With the aid of a pulley, Blessings McKenzie hauled herself into a sitting position grimacing at the pain as she stared at the old woman who was beaming at her. Her face was vaguely familiar, but Blessings couldn't place where she had seen her.

Marjorie answered the question for her. "I know we don't know each other. You must be wondering why I am here?"

Blessings remained in listening mode: her features carefully neutral.

"My name is Marjorie Agincourt. I live in Balmoral Square Mansions and I am a friend of the bishop."

Her broken leg was causing Blessings too much pain to show relief, but she was mentally relieved at the information. "I think I remember seeing you around the square," she said. "But never in the church."

Marjorie didn't know whether this last comment was a rebuke or not. She didn't much care. She had the hide of a rhino.

"Anyway, what can I do for you, Mrs Agincourt?"

"I tried to see the bishop tonight, but he was too ill for visitors. I wondered whether you could put my mind at rest and tell me what happened?"

"I don't understand," said Blessings.

"I heard the sirens that night. I was at my window when the ambulance arrived and I saw the bishop being taken out of the cathedral on a stretcher. It was a dreadful shock for me. As I said, we have been friends for years.

"Then a few minutes later I saw you going into the ambulance on another stretcher. According to the nurse I spoke to in the Intensive Care Unit tonight, the bishop is in a critical condition. This was possibly my last chance to say goodbye…" For once in her life Marjorie trailed off leaving Blessings to fill in the silence.

"I'm sorry to hear the bishop is so poorly. They didn't tell me. I've been in great pain with this leg. I'm tired now so you should go."

"But what happened?" Marjorie's voice had risen to a pitch transgressing the calm of visiting hour. A nurse turned to look reproachfully at the source of the noise.

"An accident happened. We fell. That's all."

Blessings McKenzie eased herself back down into the pillows and closed her eyes. The audience was over. Marjorie Agincourt had been rejected twice in the same evening. She couldn't recall any such thing ever happening to her before.

As Ron wheeled his indignant passenger back along the corridor to the exit, Blessings McKenzie lay deep in thought. She knew one thing for certain. If she didn't get out of here very soon everything she had worked for would be gone. Disaster threatened to overwhelm her.

COMMANDO might have been slow in the way society judges people who think differently from the norm, but he was street smart.

Smart enough to know that his missions on the No. 3 bus had come to an abrupt end and therefore his daily £10 was also forfeit. Smart enough to intuitively understand that the two dark-haired men now posed a very real threat, so he thought he might take a holiday from his usual pitch on Lothian Road.

He migrated the two miles to Morningside and a pitch outside Waitrose where the pickings were about the same. There was a pretty solid principle all rough sleepers and homeless people quickly became acquainted with: the wealthier the area, the poorer the return in the begging bowl. At least, though, he was safe.

That was his reasoning until 1 a.m. the following night when the dark-haired men caught up with him.

They didn't hurt him straight away. That would have defeated the most important purpose of their nocturnal visit. First, they had to find out what had happened to their consignment and those responsible for stealing it.

So the steel toecap of the tall man's boot did no more than tickle Commando's nose. He woke immediately and stared up at the men, subconsciously wrapping himself tighter in the filthy blanket.

"We've been looking all over for you, Soldier. I think you owe us an explanation." The tall man's voice was soft, almost kindly.

But Commando knew better. He looked around. Morningside Road was dark and deserted. Only the traffic lights showed movement and that dreadfully slow. Commando wondered idly if they changed at a different rate at night. Anything that could take his mind off this encounter would be good, he thought.

"You do have a problem with concentration," said the tall man. "I noticed that the first time we met." He grabbed Commando by the front of his T-shirt and hauled him into a sitting position.

The smaller man spoke. "We need to know who took the envelope. We need to find them and get our goods back."

"Yes," said the tall man. "We also need to teach them a lesson. The same lesson we had to give Glum Sue."

"They were young kids on bikes," said Commando. "They came from somewhere behind the tower block. Knocked me down. Stole my combat jacket. I'm cold without my combat jacket."

The tall man looked at his smaller colleague with regret. "It's always the same. Why does everything have to end like this? Can you tell me that?" In the same instant he drew back his fist and smashed it into Commando's stomach. Commando's body went into spasm and he vomited on the tall man's boot. He wiped it off on Commando's blanket.

"Stand him up," ordered the tall man. "I need to see where I'm hitting him."

The smaller man pinioned Commando's arms behind his back and dragged him to his feet. He produced a cosh from his coat pocket. He yanked Commando's hair forcing his head up.

"You need to look at me, Soldier. This is an important lesson. When people let my colleague and me down there has to be consequences – otherwise we would go out of business. You understand?" He gave Commando's hair a final tug. "I'll need to be careful here. Try to avoid the kidneys. That could be fatal."

The first blow landed just above the right knee and Commando screamed. The noise echoed down the street. "Gag him," ordered the tall man. The smaller man stuffed a dirty handkerchief into Commando's mouth. The second blow went to the solar plexus again: Commando's head dropped and his vision swam.

The tall man was lining up the area above the left knee when he shot forward. The force of the impact dislodged the cosh from his grasp and it clattered to the pavement several feet away. A large, heavy weight in his back drove him to the ground. The sudden pressure of an additional weight landing pinned him there. Gav's kitbag lay full-square on top of the man with Gav behind it bracing his knees into the pack.

After the initial shock of the attack the smaller man leapt for the cosh. But Four-Fingers got there first swiping the weapon upwards to connect with the man's nose. There was a crunch of bone and the man fell backwards clutching his face.

The tall man was thrashing and cursing on the ground in a vain bid to get up. "Whoever you are, you don't know what you're messing with, you fuckers. I'll have you both."

Gav mashed the tall man's face into the gravel of the road and pushed it from side to side until he could see blood.

"There's nothing you could do to us that hasn't been tried before, mate. All I see here is two thugs beating a homeless guy and that's cause enough for us to mess with you."

Gav gave the man's head a final shove into the dirt, then rose with his pack. "What say we get this man out of here, Bob?" Four-Fingers nodded and supporting Commando between them they walked down the road towards the dark silhouette of Blackford Hill.

THE offices of Grimwood and Doon, solicitors and notaries, lay off Constitution Street behind the old Corn Exchange.

The establishment had seen better times. In its heyday the firm had been at the centre of a thriving commercial port, acting as the legal lubricant for wealth-creating deals in the expanding grain and agriculture markets of the Americas.

Today there remained little sign of that lucrative past.

As Freddie Pettygrew sat in a rickety chair he surveyed the room. The high ceiling with its ornate egg and dart coving looked as though it had not seen a lick of paint for half a century. The once grand space was now no more than a storeroom stacked with boxes and filing cabinets.

An antique desk lay between himself and James Burnett Grimwood. As the other name on the weathered brass shingle – Doon – had passed away at the dawn of the new millennium, J. B. Grimwood was the sole surviving partner. He looked as old as the desk.

Mr Grimwood paused and cleared his throat. The procedure took a long time and when he finally spoke, it was with a voice that sounded as if it needed oiling. "I knew your father, of course. He liked the outdoors – mountains and such – could never quite understand that."

Mr Grimwood seemed to go away, lost in a private

reverie, either about Freddie's father, the alien nature of the countryside – or something entirely irrelevant to this morning's proceedings.

Freddie checked his watch. Time might stand still in the antediluvian world of Grimwood and Doon, but he wanted out of here asap. He had important business to attend to. He decided to kick-start the conversation.

"The will, Mr Grimwood?"

"Ah yes. Yes. It was – I must say – a great surprise when your sister made an appointment. I hadn't seen or heard from Arabella for many years, normally dealt with her papa you see, so it took me by surprise."

Freddie tried to stay as still as possible on the rickety chair. "What exactly took you by surprise, Mr Grimwood?"

"The fact that she wanted to see me and your father…"

Freddie could not bear the agony of this circumlocution any longer. "So she came to visit you?"

"Oh no. My dear fellow. She died. Such a tragedy. How does one come to be on a roof at that stage of life?" Mr Grimwood was shaking his head at the incomprehensible nature of the idea.

Nearly there, thought Freddie. *Must remain patient.* "So she never made the appointment. Is that what you are saying, Mr Grimwood?"

The lawyer gave a rusty chuckle that threatened to break into a cough. "That would truly have been a miracle, Mr Pettygrew. No. No. Your sister's appointment with me was for the Wednesday, but she fell from the roof forty-eight hours earlier on the Monday."

Freddie chose his words carefully. "What was the agenda for that meeting, Mr Grimwood?"

The cocoon of bluff buffoonery suddenly evaporated. "I couldn't possibly divulge that information, Mr Pettygrew. What is said between a client and her lawyer is strictly confidential and remains so – even if the client is no longer extant. Now, to business."

Grimwood stared at the document in front of him. At least the question had got the old buffer on track, thought Freddie.

"Arabella Pettygrew's last will and testament is exclusively in your favour, Mr Pettygrew. Having no other living relative, she stipulated in this document that as her brother you should inherit her property in Balmoral Square Mansions and a second apartment located in Leith. Various sundries are also stated including a Box Brownie camera, a photograph album and a small selection of books. I believe those items are presently in the possession of the police, but they will be returned to you as soon as their inquiries are concluded. Oh yes – almost forgot."

The lawyer shoved a stack of dusty legal tomes aside to reveal a bronze bell showing the verdigris of neglect if not age. It rang clearly though, and a moment later an elderly woman entered the room with a cat on a lead.

"Cats are not very biddable, I'm afraid," said Grimwood.

"They're not known for it," agreed Freddie, looking at the creature with distaste.

"I think its name is Noodles," said Grimwood. "Anyway, it's an additional sundry."

Freddie did not see Angus Robertson sitting in the window of a café across the road. He was too busy corralling Noodles and checking which bus would take him to his newly acquired property.

A cat on a lead. Now there was a novelty, thought Robertson, although he had once seen a woman in the West End walking a cat as you might a dog – on a lead. Perhaps such behaviour was more commonplace in the USA. Americans always seemed to set the trend in wackiness. At any rate, this case was becoming increasingly bizarre.

As the bus approached the stop, Robertson sauntered across the road, getting on two passengers behind Freddie.

He was within a second of making a big mistake as he automatically reached for his identity card and the free transport its production entitled him to. Then had to suffer the grumblings of the driver as he searched his pockets for change.

Fortunately for him Freddie was too preoccupied trying to get the cat to sit still to notice him.

He was still festering over the mystery of his late sister's appointment with Grimwood. The old codger had protected his client's sacred confidentiality literally to the grave.

But Freddie had a good idea what the agenda of that proposed meeting would have been. His beloved sister had been on the brink of changing her will. Cutting him out in favour of the National Trust or some bloody cat charity. After all, she was as crazy as a bag of snakes. Her last letter to him proved it.

Well, providence, or some madman, had intervened to scupper her plan. He had the flats. He had a right to them. He had earned them after all these years of running back and forth playing nursemaid to an eccentric old spinster. It was time to celebrate – and perhaps play his own little trick on Arabella.

Freddie alighted halfway up Leith Walk and entered a stair on the main road.

Robertson went into a newsagent, bought a *Hoots Mon* and pretended to read it on the other side of the road. He waited five minutes then crossed. Remarkably the stair door was locked and Robertson had resigned himself to a prolonged period of observation, when he saw Freddie looking out of the window of the ground-floor flat.

Robertson moved as casually as possible behind the hedge bordering the flat's front garden. A couple of minutes later he walked past the hedge and the stair door pretending to look back for an oncoming bus. As he did so he glanced through the window of the flat. Freddie was no longer there, but Robertson saw enough to necessitate a call to Strawberry.

"Sir. Am I correct in saying that Freddie Pettygrew told you his sister's Leith property was a dump?"

"That's right, Robertson. He said it was in the same state of dereliction as her apartment in Balmoral Square Mansions." Strawberry tapped his fingers impatiently on his desk. "Come on, man, what is it?"

"I'm outside his newly inherited flat, sir. The front room looks as though it's been freshly decorated and there's every mod con including expensive-looking furniture and a dirty great TV on the wall."

An hour later Freddie left the flat carrying a large black bin bag. He flagged down a taxi which set off back down Leith Walk.

Robertson managed to whistle up another taxi with the driver doing a smart U-turn. He showed his ID card and the driver blanched. "Never mind that, I'm not on traffic duty yet," said Robertson, "though I might be if you lose that taxi."

Robertson guessed that Freddie was returning to his lawyer's office for some reason. He was wrong.

The taxi went straight down Leith Walk and onto Newhaven. Halfway along the quiet road past the harbour known as Starbank, the taxi stopped and Freddie climbed out.

"Keep driving," ordered Robertson and as his cab passed Freddie's parked taxi the policeman looked back in time to see Freddie throw the black bin bag over the sea wall. It was about twenty yards away and Robertson couldn't be certain, but he thought the bag twitched slightly.

Only Freddie knew that Noodles was in the bag along with a couple of large bricks from his newly acquired back garden.

GOOD as his word, 'The Lieutenant' Jock Witherspoon had taken charge of the dog-patrol rota.

The volunteers had been equipped with a liberal supply of doggie bags – financed from his army pension though he was sure the Garden Association would reimburse him. He had even had a batch of name-and-shame posters printed with the appropriate underlined blanks waiting to be filled in with the names and addresses of offenders.

Preparation was important in carrying out a successful mission. But command was essential – and he was the man to lead the mission and secure the goal of a dog-dirt-free Balmoral Square Mansions.

Who knew – the mission could be expanded to the entire West End. Ultimately, if the scheme went national, there might even be an MBE in it. If posties and lollipop ladies could make the Queen's honours list, a dog-dirt campaigner was surely in the same bailiwick.

Fired with the zeal of the righteous, he took the first night shift. He was on duty at 11 p.m. promptly as he knew this was the final dog-walking hour before bedtime for owners. Sure enough, it looked like Crufts on tour in Balmoral Square Mansions.

His first encounter was Dorothea Hislop with her Labradors, Ebony and Ivory.

"Acting as backup," 'The Lieutenant' joked as her charges sniffed his legs before searching out more interesting smells on lamp posts.

Dorothea smiled benignly. Witherspoon was a harmless old pongo, but he might be very useful to her in the near future. "I'm not sure these boys would be much good to you," she said, indicating her dogs. "But I'm on tomorrow night."

"Excellent. Meantime, all quiet on the western front."

"Carry on, 'Lieutenant'," she laughed.

He walked along the street towards the cathedral – though shrouded in darkness its towering presence dominated Balmoral Square Mansions and the surrounding West End streets. Then he cut along the footpath – made uneven by the unhindered growth of encroaching tree roots – by the side of the church.

This was a favourite spot for dog-walkers who often used the grass area within the church grounds for exercising their pets.

A small, attractive dark-haired woman with a Westie emerged from the grounds. He recognised her as a relatively new neighbour in the street though she seemed a private person. He had never seen her at the Garden Association meetings, or the annual garden event.

He nodded amiably and noticed the tied black baggy she was carrying. Job done, a responsible citizen, if only everyone could show the same kind of civic responsibility, he thought, as the woman deposited the baggie in a bin.

He turned at the end of the path, deciding this would be the boundary of his patrol, and retraced his steps back towards Balmoral Square Mansions.

Emile Cruducker, the small, bespectacled American, was walking a Chihuahua. The creature was a snappy little bugger no bigger than a hamburger. Neither use nor ornament in 'The Lieutenant's' view. He couldn't imagine it shitting anything. But he gave a congenial wave. "What's his name?"

"It's a female: Trinity," said Emile who peered suspiciously at Witherspoon as though he had no idea who the man was.

'The Lieutenant' felt obliged to enlighten him. "It's Jock Witherspoon: out on dog-dirt patrol?"

The fog lifted. "Of course. Yes. Dog patrol. Very good. Found anything?"

'The Lieutenant' shook his head before realising that Emile probably couldn't see that far. "Not yet, but the night's young."

Emile appeared confused. Perhaps being American, he hadn't heard that expression before.

"Anyway, goodnight," he said.

'The Lieutenant' continued on his round walking back along the street in the direction of Haymarket Station.

The night air held a century-old smell particular to Edinburgh: the tang of malted barley and hops coming from a nearby brewery. What he would do for a pint right now. In future he would bring a radio and listen to the news if it was going to be as uneventful as this.

A white dog the size of a small horse was coming towards him with a man attached. He recognised him as a Russian neighbour – a tenant who did something professorial at one of the universities and rented an apartment in the street.

The number of rentals was an increasing trend in Balmoral Square Mansions along with the citywide explosion of Airbnbs. Personally, Witherspoon had no problem with people renting as they often became energetic assets to the community, but Airbnb was something else entirely. There were already terrifying reports of visiting hen and stag groups having all-night 'raves' in Airbnbs in nearby streets.

He wasn't quite sure what a 'rave' was though the word sounded disruptive. It was only a matter of time before the problem arrived in Balmoral Square Mansions. Then the dog-dirt patrol might have to widen its remit to noise abatement issues.

"Good evening," said the Russian, doffing a tweed-patterned cap.

Witherspoon, who had encountered the Russian in passing before, observed the man's perfect manners and a clear willingness to fit in.

"Hello. He's massive," he said.

"Yes, he is the one taking me for a walk."

"What do you call him?"

"St Beaufort Le Grand. My wife is French Canadian," said the Russian by way of obscure explanation. "But I call him Bowf. It's shorter."

Both men laughed and Bowf pricked up his ears. With a touch of revulsion Witherspoon noticed that the inside of the dog's massive ears were pink.

Despite his best intentions he found himself speaking slightly louder and more slowly. "Maybe you have heard. We are starting dog patrols. Patrols to catch people who do not clear up their animal's mess."

"Ah yes. Dorothea – the owner of Ebony and Ivory – we meet all the time on our dog walks. She told me." The Russian nodded sombrely. "It's a good thing you do."

Witherspoon acknowledged the compliment with an accompanying nod.

"Of course, I need a bucket – for the shit," said the Russian, laughing uproariously.

Bowf's growl alerted the men and they turned to see a brown and white spotted dog streaking towards them. It skidded to a halt three feet away, appeared to change its mind about saying hello to Bowf as his hackles rose, then defecated on the pavement before rushing back the way it had come.

In the distance Witherspoon saw a blonde woman calling "Rommel" before she turned and sauntered off in the opposite direction.

"Madam, your dog. You must clean…" But the woman had disappeared into one of the apartment buildings leaving 'The Lieutenant's' plea hanging in the air.

Rommel was still on the street and Witherspoon gave chase. *If I get his name tag, I'll be able to collar her*, he reasoned as he ran towards the dog.

Rommel took off, darting around the corner. His breathing coming in ragged gasps, Witherspoon rounded the corner to see the dog waiting for him.

The minute he spotted the man he was off again. *The bloody thing thinks it's a game*, he thought, hands on knees fighting for air.

Rommel ran up an alleyway leaving his pursuer stumbling on behind. The alley led to a series of back gardens belonging to the properties on Balmoral Square

Mansions. He was in time to see the dog's tail disappear over a fence into the first garden.

The gate was an easier way through. It was unlocked and he puffed through gratefully latching it behind him in case Rommel planned a sudden U-turn in his game of chase.

Moving over a series of low walls separating perfectly manicured lawns, Witherspoon was acutely aware that he was trespassing. Thankfully the rear windows of the properties were in darkness.

Most of the elderly residents would be asleep and the majority were also Garden Association members who had voted in favour of the dog-dirt patrol. Even so, he was breaking the law. It would only take one recalcitrant neighbour to complain and his position and the future of the campaign would be in jeopardy.

Moving with greater stealth, he negotiated another low wall into a neglected garden overgrown with weeds.

He saw the dog. It was squatting in the middle of a yellow dead patch of grass busy doing its business again. He managed to collar the beast while it remained engaged.

"Christ!" He couldn't help the expletive: the stench of the creature's deposit was abominable.

The prolonged wail jerked him out of his olfactory discomfort. It was the sound of a human in extreme distress. It was coming from the rear of the property.

Still clutching the struggling Rommel, Witherspoon approached the sound wishing fervently that he had equipped himself with a torch as well as the doggie bags.

He crept down a series of dilapidated steps into a small courtyard of fractured concrete. Looking upwards he could see what appeared to be an old mattress stuffed into the space where a windowpane should have been.

Suddenly the anguished cry came again so close he jumped, releasing Rommel in his fright. He stared at a black face staring out at him through the bars of the basement window.

The girl – for that's what she appeared to him, though she might more accurately have been termed a young woman – was clearly distressed. He couldn't make out what she was saying: the language seemed so garbled he wondered whether she was actually speaking English. But he knew she was in trouble and he had to get help.

Hoping she would understand his signalled intention, he rushed back through the gardens noting idly that Rommel had vanished. That particular problem would have to wait for another day – though he now knew the beast's territory given the state of the bare patch in the weed-strewn garden.

Turning the corner into the alley he saw the gate was slightly ajar offering a view of the street beyond. He was sure he had shut it behind him.

The thump on the back of his head foreclosed further conjecture. Vision narrowing to a pinpoint like a closing camera shutter, he saw a glimmer of dogs under a flickering street lamp – wraith-like shadows fading – then blackness.

ANGUS Robertson had failed in his duty. He had lost Freddie Pettygrew. He was standing to attention before Strawberry in the borrowed office of Bert Rothesay. "You might have achieved distinction at Tulliallan, but this isn't college any more, Robertson. This is the real thing." Strawberry gave the young officer a baleful look. "You were given one simple task to perform and somehow you managed to screw it up."

Robertson said nothing. There was nothing to say. His last sighting of Pettygrew had been at the harbour wall throwing a black bin bag into the sea. After that he had lost contact with Pettygrew's taxi and – although he had returned to Freddie's newly acquired property in Leith and watched it for several hours – the man had not turned up. Now no one knew the whereabouts of one of the prime suspects in Arabella Pettygrew's death.

Robertson couldn't find his arse with both hands, concluded Strawberry. The only consolation in this sorry state of affairs was the roasting young Angus would receive from his father, Urquhart – the former chief constable. Strawberry would have paid good cash money to be a fly on the wall in that household when the old man found out.

"You have some atoning to do, Robertson," said

Strawberry, "and I think I have just the job for you to begin that process."

Strawberry had Robertson in tow and they were back at Arabella Pettygrew's flat. The detective still could not be certain that the woman had not tripped, or taken her own life. He had returned to the scene to carry out an experiment and young Robertson was going to be the guinea pig.

They were both standing on the landing at the bottom of the ladder leading to the roof. "Okay, Robertson. Here's my problem. I'm trying to work out how the deceased came to have those marks on her legs. Any ideas?"

"It's possible she might have preferred to climb the ladder backwards, sir, and she could have struck the back of her legs on the rungs."

"A reasonable theory, Robertson. Let me see you try it."

Robertson began to climb the ladder backwards. The strain on his arms became so great that he gave up after the first six rungs.

"You struggled and I'm giving you the benefit of the doubt by saying that you're a fit young man," said Strawberry. "Additionally, you're a third of Pettygrew's age. So, fit as she undoubtedly was, she didn't climb the ladder in the manner you suggest. Though she might have exited the trapdoor backwards. All right, monkey up the pole again. Let's see you execute that movement."

Robertson went up the ladder once more. Turning round at the top, a feat of gymnastics in itself, he hoisted himself through backwards with his arms. Once more it was a strenuous procedure far beyond the capabilities of a sixty-nine-year-old woman no matter how fit she might have been. But Robertson cursed as he caught the back of his hamstrings on the edge going over.

"All right, drop your drawers, man," Strawberry said as Robertson returned to the landing.

"Sir?"

"It's not a penance for losing your man, Robertson. I just have to check something."

Robertson reluctantly lowered his trousers.

"All right, turn round, man," Strawberry commanded. Robertson now looked distinctly uncomfortable as he slowly turned round.

"It's all right, you're not my type," said Strawberry as he bent down to study the back of the young officer's legs. "No marks, Robertson. I think she was hit with something. I think she was murdered by a person or persons unknown."

PARKLAND as night falls. Silhouettes meandering uncertainly through the trees to a series of benches behind the swings.

The Polish workmen on a rare night off and celebrating their leisure in time-honoured fashion in a park near Leith drinking and singing. They had been on the same benches for several hours and as the beer continued to flow they became increasingly loud. The singing was their happy drunk stage and the precursor to the argumentative drunk stage, closely followed by the fighting drunk stage.

It was their traditional idea of a good night out and the foreman Marek was leading the carousing. While drinking outside on a warm summer night was perfectly acceptable in their homeland, the hard-working, hard-playing incomers had not seemed to grasp the fact that it was against the law in Scotland – or they simply didn't care.

Either way, inebriated Polish men with a penchant for public disturbance had been a problem for the police ever since the arrival of the first EU migrants. Most of the time they simply fought each other and the native inhabitants were safe from assault, if sleepless from the boisterous shenanigans.

Marek had broken off leading the chorus of a

particularly loud song to regale his comrades with the story of his encounter with a polis and his girlfriend. "Sa was in a pub in Rose Street. I was hosting Sandra. You know Sandra, the one with the *duzi piersi*."

The men roared lustily. "You must learn to say it in English, Marek," said Aleksander. "If you mean big tits, say big tits."

"OK. Sa, I was hosting Sandra with the big tits and I was getting a drink at the bar. Getting back I spilled my beer on this girl – another one with *duzi piersi*." More loud appreciation.

"Oniwie, she didn't like it. I tried to – how would you say – damp her down. She doesn't like that either. She stands quick and the rest of my beer spills on her dress. Then her boyfriend – he's in my face space. Then Sandra gets angry. Then I find this man is polis. His woman says him to arrest me like I'm Polski and always causing trouble. It's hot now. Sandra going crazy. Her *duzi piersi* shaking with the anger."

His audience howled their appreciation.

"Oniwie, I'm thinking this polis gonna put me in the jile. Then they see my record. Send me back home. Sa very bad. I expect worst.

"Then the barman says to them to get out. That Sandra and me are regulars. Other two must go. And they do. Sa I beat the polis. That night Sandra and me get very drunk and dance the polka."

The raucous cheers of the men were greeted by a series of lights going on in the tenement windows above the park, a disembodied male voice somewhere above yelling "Stop the fucking noise, people are trying to sleep here."

The men were too drunk to care and the decibel count continued for another twenty minutes until two police cars turned up.

A few of the men managed to stagger away in the darkness, slinking behind the public toilets before jogging haphazardly – stopping only to vomit en route – towards their rented flats in Constitution Street.

Marek and Aleksander were not so lucky and thirty minutes later found themselves in the police station. As the pair were being processed through the system Strawberry emerged from his office. He recognised the big Pole with the hairy arse-crack immediately – though Marek was too far gone to recognise him.

Later, as they were taken to the cells to sleep it off, Strawberry spoke to the desk sergeant. "Drunk and disorderly?"

The sergeant nodded.

"I've come into contact with him before – socially, as you might say," said Strawberry. "Find out about the big one. Let me know what you can get on him before we have to let them go."

When Strawberry checked in the following morning the men had already been released and a new intake was being dealt with.

The harassed desk sergeant looked as close to apologetic as he was going to get during the city's busiest month when thieving reached record-breaking levels thanks to the easy targets provided by mass tourism.

"Had to let them go, Strawberry. You know how it is. This place is a revolving door in August. Ten in, ten out. We just don't have the cell space to hold the bastards."

"Budget cuts. Tell me about it. It's the same for the toilets."

The sergeant gave Strawberry a strange look. Plain clothes were on a different planet. That had been the case as long as he had been a copper, coming up thirty years now. He ignored the remark and got down to business. "That information you wanted. He goes by the name of Marek Wójcik. Foreman of a gang of Polish builders. He's a bruiser. Been on charges for assault and battery. But almost exclusively beating up other Polish guys. The charges are always dropped once the victim sobers up."

"You said 'almost exclusively'," said Strawberry.

"That was another one that was dropped last minute," said the sergeant. "Involved a woman he was seeing. She had a black eye and a bent nose. Apparently we tried to get her to press charges, but she changed her story with the classic 'I fell down the stairs' line."

Strawberry nodded. He had heard the scenario so many times: cold reason being overwhelmed by blind emotion. Endlessly hopeful and forgiving women going back for more, until it was too late and the perp went too far.

As Strawberry headed for the door a thought occurred.

"You said he was a building foreman. Any ideas where they did recent jobs?"

The sergeant checked his information. "According to this, mainly around the New Town and Stockbridge."

"Specific streets?" asked Strawberry.

Balmoral Square Mansions came up third on the list.

HE wasn't looking forward to reacquainting himself with the woman. Strawberry didn't like women with dirty mouths. They were invariably more difficult to control than men. More unpredictable. And Marek's amour was undoubtedly in that category.

Sandra McGinty lived in a small, weary flat in Constitution Street. Her surroundings suited her character: grungy with a hint of Beelzebub featuring black curtains and, from what he could see through the open bedroom door, a variety of crucifixes and black satin sheets. Very sixties, kinda Charles Manson.

Of her boyfriend, Marek, there was no sign, but Sandra was putting a brave, if belligerent, face on it. "I haven't seen the bastard since he did this," she said, pulling up her long-sleeved T-shirt to show a series of angry-looking sores.

"How did he do it?" asked Brenda Gunn, looking carefully at the wounds.

"Cigarettes. When the bastard got drunk or angry he took it out on me. Used me like a fucking ashtray. Stubbed his fags out all over my body – even on my arse." She was about to drop her tracksuit bottoms when Strawberry intervened quickly.

"Okay, Sandra. If you want to bring charges of assault we can have you properly examined by a doctor.

Meantime, we need to know where Marek is; it's of the utmost importance."

"Why is that?" she said, jutting her chin out and staring at Strawberry with the same defiance she had shown on their first encounter. Drunk or sober, she was a wild one.

"He's a prime suspect in a murder inquiry. He was the gaffer of a Polish team of builders when they were renovating a flat in Balmoral Square Mansions. An elderly woman fell from the roof of that building in suspicious circumstances, so we need to trace your boyfriend."

Sandra sneered. "Well, good luck with that, copper. The bastard came in and took his things last night. Left without a word."

"Any ideas where he went?" asked Gunn.

Sandra gave a sullen shake of her head. "Don't know. Don't care. He's always been a funny bugger ever since I've known him. One minute sunshine, the next shite. And very superstitious. I think it was his religion. He was a Pape."

"How long did you know him?" asked Gunn.

"A couple of years. It was off and on. I'm really no' bothered. Are you his new squeeze?" Sandra pointed at Strawberry. "Last time I saw him he was wi' this blonde piece. Punching way above his weight."

"We're asking the questions here," said Gunn, noting Strawberry's discomfort. "How did you meet Marek?"

"Fush," said Sandra.

"Fush?" echoed Gunn.

"The fishing industry," Strawberry clarified.

"That's whit I said, copper. I wiz working in a fush factory at the time and he was on the trawlers. A met him at the harbour. Said he came over for a better life – tae make mair money. He went intae the building trade cos it paid better. But he missed the sea. He would come over aw maudlin in his drink and talk aboot the comradeship o' his mates on the boats. Telt me he'd go back there one day."

"Do you remember the boat he worked on?" asked Strawberry.

Sandra scratched her head. Her hair looked lank and greasy. Strawberry thought he saw something move in it. His stomach did a slow flip. He wondered when she had last had a good wash. "It was something like happy, or glad. Wait a minute. Merry! That was it, the Merry something or other."

THE *Merry Guddler* was drifting late at night in the middle of the North Sea by the time the patrol vessel caught up. The weary lookout got the fright of his life when the searchlight beam illuminated the trawler and a megaphone announced they were about to be boarded.

The sea had been relatively calm, but Strawberry was still feeling the bilious effects of the constant rolling motion as he clambered aboard the fishing boat. Apart from the startled lookout, the rest of the crew were below decks dead to the world and their first indication of a police presence was a series of torch beams trained on their faces. Despite a comprehensive search of the vessel, Marek was nowhere to be found.

Unable to get a signal from his mobile, Strawberry employed the patrol-boat radio to transmit the news to shore.

"I reckon we took the bait hook, line and sinker, Gunn," he reported as the boat gave another gentle roll and his stomach went with it. "Sandra deliberately planted the seed that led us in the wrong direction. God knows where her boyfriend is now."

"That figures, Strawberry," she said. "Sandra suddenly became very coy and refused to press charges when we got her to the station. But the police doctor was on hand.

He talked to her and managed to get a look at the burns on her arms. They were caused by a cigarette all right. But they were old and he believes they were self-inflicted."

EDINBURGH'S Mediterranean summer was finally faltering. Raindrops the size of florins spattered the cobblestones as Strawberry and Gunn drove down East Market Street past the taxi rank at the rear entrance to Waverley Station. Bracing themselves for the cab run, a straggle of desultory travellers, newly disembarked from a King's Cross train, emerged at the top of the steps to the echoing soundtrack of a tannoy announcement.

The police headlights picked up the figures a hundred yards ahead sheltering under one of a series of stone arches. "Three of them," said Gunn.

Strawberry squinted through the windscreen. "They've picked up a mate. Probably army too. Let's go in with respect. It's the least men like this deserve."

Gunn appraised Strawberry. His voice held no trace of sarcasm. Had he been in the army himself, or was there army in his family? He was known at Gayfield as a politically correct pain in the arse, but perhaps there was more to him: hidden layers she had not expected.

They parked across the street from the men and Strawberry and Gunn ran through the downpour to the embrasure. Gav was roasting sausages over an old iron brazier, while Four-Fingers and Commando were hugging tin mugs of tea, sitting as close to the fire as possible without becoming burnt offerings themselves.

"Good evening, gentlemen," said Strawberry. "Apologies for interrupting your supper, but we're police officers investigating a potentially serious crime."

"Detectives Strawberry and Gunn," acknowledged Gav. "We saw you at the funeral. Freddie Pettygrew told us who you were. This is Commando. Like us, fallen on hard times."

"Paras too?" asked Gunn.

"No," said Four-Fingers. "Just a buddy needing a hand."

Introductions made, Strawberry cut to the chase. "At Arabella Pettygrew's funeral you (he indicated Gav) made an emotional speech about her. You clearly held her in high regard."

"We both did," interrupted Four-Fingers. "More than us – a lot of homeless people owed her a debt of gratitude."

"Why was that?" asked Gunn.

"She was good to us," said Gav.

"In what way? You need to be more specific," said Strawberry.

"That's not going to be possible, Officer," said Four-Fingers. "She was a Good Samaritan – that's all you need to know."

Their intransigence was understandable, their loyalty admirable, but Strawberry could feel his irritation building.

"Not happening, men. This is a police investigation into a possible murder. Let me spell it out for you. Both Gav and you admitted knowing Arabella Pettygrew. Coming into contact with her for some reason you seem reluctant to specify. You must tell us that reason because right now I have both of you down as suspects in her murder."

Gav placed the fork in the fire staring into the flames as the skewered sausage was incinerated. "How do you make that out, Detective?"

"Your army records are highly commendable. You were awarded a medal for your actions in Afghanistan, Gav. And you, Four-Fingers, led the patrol selflessly in that encounter. But you both have a history of violence. Admittedly, you in defence of your comrades, Gav, but, Four-Fingers, you have a record of excessive overreaction while in the employ of a jeweller. From the reports we have read you seriously injured the burglar in the course of detaining him. That makes both of you persons of interest in our inquiry."

"Why can't you tell us?" asked Gunn.

"Everyone knows that Miss Pettygrew was a very private person," said Four-Fingers. "She did not want what she did broadcast to the world. She made us promise. We gave her our word that we would never go against her wishes. In honour of her memory we cannot break that promise."

Gunn looked at Commando. "What about you? Did you know Arabella, Commando?"

Commando glanced sidelong at his friends, who stared steadfastly into the embers of their guttering barbecue.

"No, miss. Not that lady. I'm on the buses a lot going places. Don't know people. Glum Sue and Davie (he hesitated), the two dark-haired men and my friends here. That's all, miss."

"**WHAT** do you think, Gunn?" The detectives were in the car again driving to *A-Patch* territory to make a surprise call on Glum Sue and any other bodies they might find in the squat she called home.

"I can't see either of them murdering an old woman. Okay, they were both trained to kill in the army, but Gav was decorated for an action aimed at saving a comrade. Four-Fingers might have lost it with the thief, but he was probably suffering from post-traumatic stress and the situation he found himself in in the jewellery shop triggered his violent reaction."

Strawberry pondered her response. "I agree about Gav, but isn't there a question mark about Four-Fingers? I read the court report and saw the photographs. He made a mess of that guy's face – and if the other staff members hadn't hauled him off, he might have killed him."

"Yes, but he was in a conflict situation there. Arabella Pettygrew was no threat to anyone. If she was murdered it was in cold blood. Given Four-Fingers' background, his fight to overcome his disability, I just don't see it. Then there's this whole Para honour thing: promising Arabella they would maintain her privacy. It might not suit us, sir, but I don't think it puts either of them in the frame."

"What about Commando?" Strawberry asked. "He

looked very shifty about the question. He was certainly lying. He definitely knew her, but he took the line of his army buddies."

They stopped at a light on Colinton Road. Strawberry stared into the gathering gloom. Under the harsh sodium glare he looked drawn from the strain of the workload. But there was also a haunting sadness in his eyes.

Gunn took a chance. "The *STV* news had a bit on the Hong Kong curling championships the other night. It was only a snippet, but Fiona was on. It looks like Scotland are doing well – into the quarter finals."

Strawberry sniffed. "I wouldn't know. I've been too busy to watch much TV lately. Anyway, I'm glad they're doing well."

Conversation closed. Congratulations, Brenda: next time try engaging your brain before you put both feet in it.

In fact Strawberry had heard nothing from Fiona since she had arrived in Hong Kong four days ago. He could understand her commitment to the competition and the hurt she felt over their last evening together. But surely that anger had worn off? The lack of a phone call – even a brief text – was upsetting.

DARKNESS had fallen by the time they arrived at Saltire Court. "Count the wheels," said Strawberry. "We might have to catch the bus back."

The door of 703 was wide open: more accurately it was hanging off its hinges and the handle was lying on the lobby floor. At times like this Strawberry wished he was armed.

Signalling Gunn to wait, he moved down the hall disappearing into the lounge. Seconds later he reappeared waving urgently.

The first thing Gunn saw was the figure of a small, skeletally thin woman – eyes shut, mouth wide open – lying prone on a broken settee. The second was the bodies of two dogs splayed in a corner. The floor surrounding them was slick with blood.

"They're dead," said Strawberry. "Throats cut. The woman's got a pulse. Phone for an ambulance."

While Gunn was on her mobile, there was an explosion of breath and the woman suddenly sat upright. She looked around her and then attempted to get up. Strawberry took her arm in a bid to help, but she shrugged it off in alarm.

"Who the fuck are you?"

"Police officers," said Strawberry producing his warrant card – though he knew, judging from the state she was in, that he might as well have shown her a supermarket loyalty card. As if to underline his suspicion, she began tottering, threatening to collapse.

Gunn stepped forward. "What did you take? We need to know now."

"Who the fuck are you? You police, too?"

Gunn nodded. "I'm getting an ambulance. But they need to know so they can help you."

"No ambulance. Don't need no help. Just a wee bit of spice in ma tea." Glum Sue suddenly emitted a high keening sound as she pointed at the dogs. "They're deed, are they? Joshua and McGregor. They came in with a knife. I thought they were going to kill me. The dugs tried to protect me. Poor wee bastards."

"Who came?" asked Strawberry.

"The two of them. Don't know their names. Never known that. Both dark-haired bastards. Ask me, they look like fucking Romanians."

"Why would they do this?" asked Gunn.

Between the anguished wail of her continuing lament Glum Sue outlined the story. "Punishment. That feil wee bastard Commando fell doon on the job. Got ambushed by a bunch of kids. They stole the package. The dark-haired men blamed us. Working for Holy Smokes, nae doubt."

"Who the hell is Holy Smokes?" asked Strawberry.

"It's a nickname for the bishop," said Gunn. "Dougie Nichols told me."

Strawberry paused. He was having difficulty taking in this new information. "You mean the bishop along at the cathedral in Balmoral Square Mansions?"

Gunn nodded. "He's unconscious in hospital.

Apparently he had an accident. He fell down the stairs in the church."

Strawberry looked at Glum Sue. "Let me get this right. You said a minute ago that the dark-haired men – 'the Romanian bastards' – worked for Holy Smokes, also known as the bishop. What exactly are you inferring?"

A wary look crept over Glum Sue's countenance. The drug was wearing off. These bastards were police. She had said too much.

Reading her thoughts, Strawberry intervened. "We're investigating a possible murder. We're not here to arrest you for drug possession – or even peddling drugs." That can happen when the Pettygrew case is wrapped up, Strawberry silently vowed.

"What murder? I know nothing aboot any murder."

"A pensioner named Arabella Pettygrew fell from a roof a couple of weeks ago. We have since spoken to a number of homeless people including Gav and Four-Fingers. I think you know them."

Glum Sue grudgingly acknowledged her acquaintance.

"They said that Miss Pettygrew had helped them and many other homeless people. Did she help you?"

"A was at her funeral," said Glum Sue, admitting her acquaintance with Arabella Pettygrew.

"Aye, she was a nice woman. She gave me food. Never money, mind. She knew I liked the wacky baccy too much. She would never have wanted me getting stoned on her money."

Two paramedics appeared in the doorway. Strawberry and Gunn made way for the ambulance men as they helped a reluctant Glum Sue to her feet.

The officers were on their way out when a thought occurred to Strawberry.

"Who else lives here?"

"Folk come and go," said Glum Sue, whose body language strenuously indicated she didn't want to go anywhere with the ambulance men.

"Okay, but anyone who's a bit more permanent?"

"Davie Affyer, I suppose. He often dosses doon on the settee efter a session."

"Where is he now?" asked Strawberry.

"Oot an' aboot somewhere," said Glum Sue vaguely. "He's always on the move. A right bampot. Too much jail. No' enough school. Cannie read nor write, poor bastard."

"That's an interesting name he's got. I've never heard that one before," said Gunn.

"Whit, Davie?" Glum Sue gave a sour laugh.

"No, Affyer."

Glum Sue gave Gunn a pitying look. "That's no' his real name. He goes by that cos he's always aff his heid on the drugs. Affyer. Geddit?"

Gunn gave a patient smile. "So what's his real name?"

"How would I know? Maist of us go by street names anyway. Do you really think ma first name's Glum?"

STRAWBERRY was in the communal gardens with Nichols reviewing Operation Treetops.

Though he was in overall charge of the surveillance and Nichols was answerable to him, he felt distinctly uncomfortable at these meetings: after all, they shared the same rank and had been diligent rivals since Tulliallan.

"We're at the end of our rope on this, Dougie," he said noting the hang-dog look of the troops. "The old man's getting too much flak from on high. There are people in this street who have the ear of the authorities. If we can't get a result within the next forty-eight hours he'll pull the plug. I don't need to spell out what that means for our record."

Nichols looked disconsolately through what was left of the trees at the target address. "Not a bloody thing has moved there since we started this operation, Dick. It's spookily quiet. Like someone put the word out on us and they've known all along."

Strawberry pondered the suggestion. "You mean somebody watching us? That's an interesting point."

Strawberry drew Nichols away from the team. "Look, this could be nothing, but I was interviewing this druggie yesterday about the Pettygrew investigation. She made some vague claim that Holy Smokes, sorry, the bishop along at the cathedral was the drugs kingpin behind the whole operation."

Strawberry expected Nichols to shrug and laugh off the idea. He did neither.

"I heard he was called Holy Smokes, too. One of the guys said he was known as that among the homeless community. He thought it was a joke on the bishop's position – you know, the American saying 'Heaven's above'. I reckoned it might have been a reference to him being like the Pope. Whenever they elect a new one, there's white smoke comes out of a chimney."

"Wrong outfit," said Strawberry. "The bishop's Episcopalian, not Catholic."

"Okay, Dick, I stand corrected." Nichols took a deep breath, clearly counting to ten on the smart-arse response.

"The point is," said Strawberry apparently oblivious to the hostility, "that the nickname might have more sinister connotations. Anyway, it's our last roll of the dice.

"There's only one problem. I checked with the hospital and so far he's failed to regain consciousness. Unless he wakes up, we're knackered."

IT was closing on midnight. Dreever was in the bell tower. The information about Holy Smokes had been passed on – as had the final deadline. Forty-eight hours to go until the plug was pulled.

The news engendered mixed emotions. On the one hand, he would be glad to get back to regular hours and bed at a civilised hour. On the other, his sense of professionalism balked at failure.

The surveillance was coming up for two weeks. All that time, patience and exhaustion for nothing. The thought was galling.

He knew an ex-SAS bloke who had been camouflaged as a bush for six weeks in Irish bandit country staking out an alleged IRA safe house during the Troubles. He couldn't imagine the sheer bloody-minded determination and stamina that must have taken. The result had been the same, a big fat zero.

Dreever consoled himself that the soldier must have felt even worse than he did. He felt himself nodding off and moved away from the observation turret to stretch.

Midway through the exercise he saw the woman with the two Labradors. She usually took them out at eleven. She was nearly an hour late. No difference, the territorial buggers would still shit in exactly the same place – near the railings beside the garden – and she would clear the mess up after them as she had done for the past two weeks he had been observing the ritual.

She dumped the two baggies in the large black bin as usual and then turned back the way she had come down the street. Then she stopped under a street lamp and looked up and down the street. The street was deserted. Corralling the dogs together with both leads in one hand, she took a last look in both directions before moving up the four steps to the target address.

Dreever picked up his binoculars and zoomed in on the figure. She produced a key and went inside. Dreever went for the two-way radio and uttered two words: "Happy trails."

DOROTHEA had run out of options. Jock Witherspoon – the interfering old *Dad's Army* bastard – had stumbled over the girl during his dog-dirt patrol. She had witnessed the encounter from the trees at the back of the garden jungle. When he rushed from the courtyard she knew he had to be stopped. He was breathing so heavily from his exertions he never heard a thing as she crept up behind him. The branch was heavy enough to lay him out on the first strike.

Then grabbing him under the oxters, she dragged him back into the jungle garden and laid him out face up in the old shed near the back wall.

She checked his pulse. Thready. She didn't like the sound. Murder was not part of the plan. But, if he didn't die, he had to be detained for a short period of time – long enough for her to do the deals and get out. Reluctantly, she cinched his hands behind his back with an old piece of rope, applied a loose gag using a relatively clean cloth and turned him onto his front again.

Hopefully the bugger wouldn't suffocate – and when she was clear she would make an anonymous call to the cops. She locked the shed door. The girl would have to be sorted out very soon, but not tonight. She hurried from the garden back to her flat. There was a lot to do.

She hadn't checked on Witherspoon for twenty-four

hours. *One thing at a time, Dorothea.* She didn't allow herself to think about it as she moved down the corridor to the basement stairs. Since his wife died, he lived alone. No alarm had been raised in the intervening hours since the ambush and his imprisonment in the shed. Maybe he would survive – and maybe her plan would succeed. Either way, she was on her own now.

There had been no contact from the controller, or 'robot man' as she called him, since the cryptic metallic-sounding message, 'Don't let the dogs out'.

That was seven days ago. She had no clue about what might have befallen him. But she had been forced into action and there was no going back.

She heard the girl as she unlocked the door. She was lying on the camp bed moaning. The reek of body fluids was overwhelming. Dorothea put a handkerchief to her mouth. There was vomit on the floor and the bed sheets.

She picked her way across the floor carefully. The place was a tip with empty pizza boxes, beer cans and unwashed clothes littering every surface. More importantly though, sometimes the girl used the bucket for her ablutions, sometimes she missed – and sometimes in her drugged stupor she forgot altogether and did it on the spot.

The room was a health hazard. The metallic voice's orders had been specific. Keep her imprisoned and addicted until otherwise instructed, but monitor her condition. She must not die.

Dorothea felt the girl's forehead. Damp, but not hot or fevered. She produced the syringe from a coat pocket and tested it: a small stream of translucent fluid rose in a lazy arc spotting the filthy bedcover in its descent.

She was no doctor. There was a risk, but it had to be done if the plan was to succeed. Dorothea raised the girl's arm, slapped it until the vein stood out, stuck in the needle and depressed the syringe. She released the girl's arm, which flopped onto the bed.

The girl's moaning ceased almost immediately and within a minute she was snoring softly. A mild sedative, no more than that. Dorothea fervently hoped it would buy enough time for the transactions to be completed.

Back at her flat she switched her mobile back on. It had been silent for seven days as she remained incommunicado. She opened it to messages. The inbox was full.

She stopped counting the unopened messages at two hundred. The first hundred. No more. Spread over a day that should work providing she gave precise instructions about pick-up times. She would also make it abundantly clear that anyone who ignored the instructions and turned up early in their desperation would go away empty-handed. Queues, or people loitering around outside, would signal disaster. The hundred selected, she deleted the rest and set about composing the replies for each recipient. The code for all-clear coming at the end: 'the dogs are out'.

STRAWBERRY had returned to Arabella Pettygrew's apartment. He had cycled from his flat in Woodburn Terrace. The ride was bracing.

The sun was setting as he crested Church Hill and freewheeled past the Links; the trees in full canopy, though the first hint of autumn bronzed the leaves.

He needed to clear his mind of the chaos of the past two weeks. To blow the mental cobwebs away and look again afresh at the potential crime scene: renew his search for vital clues that he had possibly missed in the surge of activity immediately following the death.

As he stood in the time capsule that was now the spinster's flat, he ran through the list of suspects once more.

Her brother, Freddie – an outside bet perhaps, but he had lied about the flat in Leith. According to Angus Robertson, it had been recently renovated. Judging from the state of this flat, he would have bet his pension that Arabella was not responsible for modernising her Leith property. It simply made no sense to live in a crumbling, barely habitable dwelling yet spend money doing up a place that you did not rent out or live in.

The logical conclusion was that Freddie was responsible for the upgrade. So the jury was out on Freddie Pettygrew.

Marek, the unruly Polish builder – and his workmates – were also in the frame. Strawberry had personal knowledge of Marek's temper. He had been surprised to discover that he was the same man who had insulted Fiona on their ill-fated night out during the festival. Strawberry had witnessed the fact that with a drink in him, Marek could go from 0-60 in a few seconds. Whether he possessed a short fuse sober was debatable as was his ability to murder a defenceless old woman. But his complete disregard for what he had done to Fiona and, more importantly, the alleged assault of a woman raised grave suspicions. Additionally, the big Pole was nowhere to be found.

Following the wild goose chase to the *Merry Guddler*, his building crew had been located working at a New Town address.

His mates had closed ranks declaring he was probably off on a bender and would turn up again soon because he needed the money.

Strawberry didn't believe a word of it. Like Freddie Pettygrew, Marek had now disappeared which made the whereabouts of two of the prime suspects in the case unknown.

Gav and Four-Fingers were also persons of interest who could not be ruled out. Professional soldiers, yes: the safety catch firmly secure on their actions in military service. But they were trained in violence: after the trauma of Afghanistan and its mental scars, had they lost their moral compass?

Then there was Glum Sue. She had been evasive about her relationship with the deceased. She was also a drug addict and drug addicts were notoriously unpredictable in their behaviour.

Perhaps Arabella Pettygrew had refused to bankroll her addiction once too often when Sue was in a desperate state craving an immediate fix. What might have happened then?

The incontrovertible truth was that the Polish builders had the opportunity for homicide because they had literally been on site. The information that their foreman, Marek Wöjcik, had a record of violence made him particularly interesting.

The homeless people also had the time and opportunity to commit the crime because of their admitted, but as yet unclear, association with Arabella Pettygrew.

Strawberry walked down the hall and into the small lounge. He gazed from the small balcony window across the communal garden and the historic city rooftops as the dying sun turned the sky orange in its final dazzling display of the evening.

Edinburgh was his city. His beat. His responsibility to enforce the law and protect its citizens. Failing that, it was his sworn duty to bring to justice those responsible for their heinous crimes. That was when the whispering started again. At first too low to register; a trembling susurration like the stirring of autumn leaves, yet gradually gaining the sound and semblance of a meaning he knew only too well: 'Where are you? I tried to wait. I'm still waiting. Please. Please find me. Have you given up?'

"Never," Strawberry said aloud, the vehemence of his promise echoing through the apartment. "I will find you no matter how long it takes."

Shaking his head in a bid to still the insistent voice, he retraced his steps down the hall. The light was fading fast and in the gloom he bumped into the scarred table. The book he had retrieved from the floor and placed there only two weeks previously, but which felt like an age ago, fell face up. Strawberry bent down to pick it up and saw the passage underlined in red felt pen.

THREE WEEKS EARLIER
Day 7

ARABELLA was walking in the hills with her father. Her hair was long and blonde and in curls and she was skipping. She was a child. It was mid-winter but she was wearing her green and white checked school summer dress with white crocheted socks to the knees.

The hills didn't look like the ones in Edinburgh she knew so well. They seemed alien and shrouded in mist.

The mist suddenly disappeared revealing impossibly high, jagged mountains. The snow was up to her knees and she ploughed through it in her bare feet.

The wreck of a plane appeared beneath the scree of a bleak hill. "Spitfire," announced her father in a voice full of wonder. "Teatime," he said.

She was in the flat eating scones at the family table with jam and cream on top. Then she was on the bleak hill again at the dinner table in the midst of the wreckage. "Take a picture, Arabella," said her late father.

She looked down and the Box Brownie was in her hands. There was a blinding flash. Then she woke up.

In reality, she had been in the hills many times with her father and they had found more than one crashed plane.

Several hundred were scattered all over the Highlands her father had told her.

There had been signs of disturbance at a number of these sites indicating that souvenir hunters had taken bits of the wreckage as mementos.

That was wrong, he said. The crash sites should not be disturbed. They should be treated as war graves with the same respect as that extended to the dead on sunken ships.

The dream was a bit of a curate's egg, her papa would have said. Strange in parts, but overall good: especially good in that it reunited Arabella, however fleetingly, with the memory of her father.

She missed him. Women who had never married, or experienced a stable, long-term partnership with a man, invariably missed their fathers. He had been the only man in her life who truly cared for her. After all the recent unpleasantness, the dream gave her hope that today would be a turning point for the better.

As she rose with renewed optimism she could have had no conception of how counterfeit that emotion would prove to be. Arabella Pettygrew had one week to live.

The intercom buzzer interrupted her nostalgia. Still in her dressing gown she had to go down the three flights to sign for the recorded delivery letter. That was the way of service these days. Postmen no longer climbed stairs, but dumped the mail in the communal stair entrance.

The changes amazed Arabella. She had been brought up in an age of duty and deference. A time when society had structure and everyone knew their place on that pyramid. Arabella and her family might not have been at the apex, but as residents of Balmoral Square Mansions they sat far higher on the continuum than tradesmen, shop workers, bank clerks, or postmen.

She squiggled her signature on the electronic hand-held device giving a bemused chortle at the perfunctory "Thanks, Mrs" from the postman.

Over the years transactions such as this had become increasingly extraordinary and foreign to her. Perhaps that was one reason she had turned inwards, increasingly avoiding human contact, becoming in reality a hermit.

Also, possibly because she had been single and reliant upon herself for so long, self-interest had become her watchword, the leitmotif that guided her existence.

Such a solitary condition – without the checks and constraints on inconsiderate behaviour provided by a partner – through time became an incubator for selfishness.

Back in her apartment she unearthed a letter-opener from the bric-a-brac in the hall desk and slit the envelope. It was a letter from her bank.

What she read was so distressing and incomprehensible that Arabella dressed immediately and called a taxi.

There was a long queue in the bank, which only increased her anxiety, and by the time a teller became available her agitation overwhelmed any attempt at good manners.

"I must see the manager immediately," she demanded.

"What's it about?" asked the young man whose accent clearly marked him as foreign – and disinterested at that. He was only half listening as he appraised an attractive young woman behind Arabella in the queue.

"It is about an error – a massive error on the part of the bank."

Totally unimpressed, the clerk continued his callow interrogation. "What error?"

"Look, I will not conduct a conversation in public." She waved at the lengthening line of people behind her. "I insist on speaking in private to someone in authority."

Bored rather than concerned, the young man signalled another older female employee over. "She wants to see the manager."

The older woman steered Arabella into a cubicle indicating a seat. "Now, madam, what seems to be the problem?" At last some service thought Arabella producing the letter.

The woman scanned the letter before returning it to Arabella. "What is your question, madam?"

Wasn't it obvious? Arabella blustered finding difficulty in getting the words out fast enough. "I want to know the meaning of this letter. The impertinence and falsehood contained in it. That is my question."

"Let me take a look at your account, madam," said the woman, her fingers clicking expertly across the keyboard of her computer.

Arabella's fingers drilled an unconscious counterpoint on the table as she awaited the woman's profuse apology.

Finishing her investigation the bank employee looked levelly at Arabella Pettygrew. What she saw was a flustered old woman from another age and class. Someone out of her depth in the modern world with its accelerating speed of change.

"I apologise if you think the letter is impertinent,

Miss Pettygrew, but there are no, as you put it, falsehoods contained in it. It is an entirely accurate representation of your financial situation. Your account is overdrawn by a thousand pounds and you have no overdraft facility with us."

"That's impossible. I have £50,000 deposited with this bank."

The clerk shook her head. "That was three years ago, Miss Pettygrew. Do you do online banking?" The bank employee might as well have been speaking Martian.

"Online? Computers? I don't have a computer."

The clerk nodded professionally. Her aquiline features held not one scintilla of sympathy.

"That is unfortunate because had you checked your account you would have seen that a direct debit has been in place for the last three years for the amount of £1,388.32."

This was all too confusing for Arabella. "A direct debit? What does that mean?"

"It means that £1,388.32 has been withdrawn from your account every month for three years – made payable to a Mr Frederick Pettygrew."

Day 6

SHE had spent a sleepless night listening to her apartment creak like an old galleon as her brain raced with the knowledge of her brother's betrayal.

How could he have done such a thing? More importantly, how had he accomplished the fraud?

Her memory, once a source of pride like her handwriting, had begun to fade in the past few years. Could it be that she had unwittingly signed something, or indeed agreed to something that she had since forgotten?

Finally, exhausted at wrestling with the conundrum, she fell into a troubled sleep. She was wakened by the weight of her cat lying on her feet for warmth.

Knowing there was no point in remaining in bed in her present state of mind, she got up and dressed. The apartment was too cold to linger in her nightclothes.

Having forgotten to buy milk amidst the drama of yesterday's events, she made do with black coffee. She had no desire for breakfast feeling nauseous from her brother's duplicity.

The old record player was on a dresser in her bedroom. She took the LP from its sleeve, wiped it on her cardigan and put it on the turntable. The mellifluous, soaring sound of Debussy's *Clair de Lune* flooded the room: its calming effect gradually taking hold.

She had to try and find out the reason behind her brother's actions. She couldn't face the prospect of phoning him. There was the strong probability that he would deny all knowledge. The conversation would quickly descend into a shouting match with him doing all the shouting. She knew his tactics of old.

Found out in a lie, he would react in classic bullying fashion turning defence into attack, escalating the argument into a tirade of personal abuse aimed at undermining her confidence and ultimately turning the tables, accusing her of being in the wrong and mismanaging her own finances. She would write instead, but meantime she would take positive action.

Picking up the black Bakelite receiver she dialled her lawyer. An interminable age seemed to pass before her call was answered. She had not visited the offices of J. B. Grimwood for many years, but she recognised the voice of his loyal retainer immediately.

Years went by, but time stood still at solicitors and notaries Grimwood and Doon – as did the staff. It was a world preserved in aspic. The woman had been with the firm while her father was alive and that was a good thirty years ago.

Arabella conjured a picture of her – small and stooped even then with a severe grey bun. In all probability she would look exactly the same.

After introducing herself as a long-time client, Arabella asked if she could speak to Mr Grimwood to be told he was otherwise engaged. "Can I ask the nature of your enquiry, madam?"

The subject was sensitive and Arabella was loath to discuss her business with Mr Grimwood's secretary. But she needed to see her lawyer quickly and baiting his mastiff might well extend her wait, if not scupper it altogether. She guessed that messages could well go missing, be forgotten, or simply not passed on in antiquated law firms like Grimwood and Doon.

"I need to change my will," said Arabella. "It's a matter of the greatest urgency."

"Mr Grimwood could be available next Wednesday morning at 10 a.m., madam. Would that suit?"

"Perfectly well," said Arabella hanging up. She sat down quickly. Her pulse had quickened at the idea of the extraordinary step she was about to take.

To cut her only surviving relative out of her estate was a momentous decision. She wondered what her papa would have said. The idea brought her close to tears. But Frederick had brought this upon himself through his chicanery. She was right and she resolved to go ahead.

Arabella let the soothing strains of *Clair de Lune* wash over her. She felt herself calming: Debussy's music was a balm to the soul.

As the piece reached its crescendo her bedroom floor began to vibrate to a frenzied thumping. The vituperative screams of a harridan followed. "Turn that fucking noise off. My children are trying to sleep."

Heavens, it was the new woman from downstairs. This was the second time she had complained about the music. The family had only been in the building for a few months and they were already proving extremely difficult neighbours. The banging and screaming continued until Arabella turned down the volume. It had already been low and it was 9 a.m. How long did young children sleep, she wondered – and wasn't she within her rights to play her music in her own apartment during the day?

It was no good. The mood was ruined. Arabella plucked at the stylus, but in her haste, the needle dragged across the vinyl scratching the record. "God, now look at what that woman's made me do!"

Arabella spent a fretful day walking – though pacing would have been a more accurate description – in the city's parks.

Hills were beyond her now. Perhaps not the relative gentleness of what she termed urban hills like the Blackfords or Corstorphine, but the Pentlands and the wilder climbs on the city outskirts – expansive and wide open to the elements – were too challenging.

Where once, she wouldn't have thought twice about scaling Arthur's Seat, she was now forced to listen to her body and the signals of mortality. Her limbs were seizing, her blood was thinning and she felt the cold more intensely.

Arabella had much to consider as she trod those familiar paths. Freddie's treachery was already a receding anxiety. She had made up her mind on a course of action and her mental fortitude was strong enough to relegate the problem until the meeting with her lawyer.

The neighbours were a different proposition. Marjorie Agincourt had been a source of annoyance for many years. The problem had escalated since the death of her husband. Before that Marjorie had been too wrapped up in her beloved Hamish to bother about the strange spinster upstairs. Arabella's mouth twisted in a cruel smile. If only she knew, the knowledge would devastate her.

But Arabella intended to harbour that secret as the ultimate nuclear option, though Marjorie's behaviour of late had made her finger itch on the metaphorical button.

With more time on her hands Marjorie had become intrusive and critical. If they met on the stair or outside the woman never missed an opportunity to offer some snide comment about the superiority of her apartment over Arabella's.

More infuriatingly, she always supplied the unsolicited answer.

"If the roof is leaking you must call upon professional tradespeople, Bella. After all, the roof is a communal responsibility. If you can't afford the bill perhaps you should sell that property of yours in Leith."

Lately the criticism had become more overt and threatening. The last time they had 'bumped into each other' (Arabella was certain Marjorie had been waiting behind her door to ambush her) Marjorie had said she was considering phoning the council to complain about the dangerous state of disrepair to the roof.

"If a slate, or part of the chimney fell on a passer-by fatally injuring them, it wouldn't just be you who would be held responsible, Bella. It would be all of us – criminally responsible."

So Arabella did her best to avoid Marjorie Agincourt, but she was now facing another problem.

Shona McPherson – a friend since Arabella had first moved into her apartment in Balmoral Square Mansions

– had sold her apartment downstairs moving to a smaller flat in Morningside.

Arabella had not seen her new neighbours for many months. But she had heard them, or rather the unholy racket their builders had made in renovating the property.

From eight in the morning until seven at night, weekends included, the Polish builders knocked down walls, ripped up floors, humped iron radiators up the stairs – and generally shredded the tranquillity of the apartment building with their electric drills and sledgehammers.

There were even times when they stayed overnight drinking and singing, sometimes involved in heated arguments, into the early hours. On these occasions, acutely aware of their roughness and proximity, Arabella remained in a state of wakeful distress.

Of course Marjorie Agincourt had taken immediate action and the late-night carousing had died away.

But when Agnes Blunt and Jim Ross finally moved in, there was no apology for the months of disruption. And now they had the cheek to complain about her music when their brats thundered around their apartment all day long!

Day 5

DEBUSSY would have to stay on hold until she resolved the problem. It pained Arabella to deny herself this daily panacea, but she would bring the issue of her difficult neighbours up with the lawyer and hope for a legal solution.

Meanwhile, between the thunder squalls of the brats downstairs, she was enjoying reading a novel she had discovered by chance while browsing the shelves of Morningside public library.

It was a psychological crime thriller by Ruth Rendell called *A Judgement In Stone*. The story had intrigued Arabella from the start when – flying in the face of universally received wisdom – the author revealed the murderer's name in the opening sentence of the first page. Chutzpah didn't come much bigger or bolder than that, she decided.

She could barely wait to get home with her find, especially as the library was so NOISY. When had libraries become alternative locations for nurseries and playgroups, she wondered?

The children's section at the rear of the building was full of infants and mothers. Good. Reading was to be actively encouraged in the younger generation. But the mothers were reading out loud to their children and at times they were even singing nursery rhymes. Bad.

Arabella had made the mistake of commenting on the noise to one of the librarians – a hippy type with a mournful face and long, dark, greasy hair.

"In my day libraries were places of quiet reflection and study," she said.

If anything, the hippy looked even sadder as he informed her that libraries had changed a bit since her day. They were now 'places of inclusion for all the community'.

Now in her apartment she raced through the novel and finished it as night began to fall. Many people would think it was a waste of a day, but finding such an engrossing read was a rare luxury for Arabella akin to gorging on a box of chocolates at one sitting.

She had been particularly struck by some thought-provoking lines at the beginning of the novel and went to the extent of underlining the words in red pen.

Normally she would never have done such a thing. She viewed books as precious (even if nowadays they could be purchased at knock-down prices in supermarkets) and their defacement – even folding a page corner – as sacrilege.

On this occasion though she made an exception because of the sheer philosophical power of the author's observation – and its relevance to the plight of a new friend. She determined to visit him and her other new friends the following evening.

Day 4

IT would perhaps be too simplistic, too much of a hackneyed cliché – and almost certainly not recognised by the woman herself – to describe Arabella Pettygrew's character transformation in the last few months of her life as a Damascene conversion. After all, at best she only possessed a rudimentary knowledge of the Bible.

True, at the behest of her father she had attended bible class every Sunday morning as a child. But a bullying incident involving a fat ginger-haired classmate called Kenneth and Arabella's nose on the wrong end of a fiercely wielded bible had put a premature halt to her religious studies.

Her blood-encrusted nostrils and beseeching sobs had finally swayed her father into relenting and cancelling Sunday school altogether.

Those many years later Arabella still recalled with a kind of fond affection the freckled fatso whose vicious action had saved her from those endless boring Sabbaths.

Additionally, she still retained many of the unsavoury traits that had marked her personality from the outset: an innate feeling of superiority, the inviolable rightness of her views on everything, an untrammelled rudeness to all and sundry.

However, notwithstanding those frailties, something did happen to blunt the sharp edges of her acerbic nature and reveal an unexpected humanity.

The event had occurred a month previously. It had been just before the hot spell. She had been on her way to catch a late evening train at Waverley Station to visit one of the very few old school friends she kept in contact with in York.

A heavy downpour had made the pavement slick and hazardous. In danger of missing her train she was trailing a piece of carry-on luggage with a dodgy wheel and trying to move quickly down the incline outside the station's main entrance.

With half an eye on the wonky case, she did not see the raised paving stone and tripped, falling face-first onto the kerb.

She regained consciousness to a terrible smell. As her faculties gradually returned she saw what seemed to be a canvas roof above her. It was difficult to be sure because only one eye was working, the other was swollen shut and when she raised a shaking hand to her head she touched what felt like an orange-sized lump.

"I'd be careful there, dear. You've taken a sore one. Best to lie still." A dirty hand emerged from the darkness and gently removed her hand from her head. His movement evoked the stench again and as the vision in her one good eye became accustomed to the gloom she identified three men beside her in a makeshift tarpaulin tent.

"What happened? Who are you? I feel so ill."

The filthy hand patted hers again. "You were in too much of a hurry, love. You went skiting your length on the pavement – smacked your heid and conked out."

She remembered now. The train. The visit to her friend. She groaned and made a feeble attempt to get up.

"It's all right, dear. Just lie still in case you've broken something. Four-Fingers has gone to get help."

The man gently raised her head bringing a bottle of water to her lips. Despite his smell, she drank gratefully looking beyond his shoulder at a younger man sitting in the corner nursing a beer can. The man followed her gaze.

"That's Davie. Oh – and I'm Gav." He sensed her revulsion at the smell. "Apologies, dear. We're sleeping rough tonight."

"Make that every night," laughed Davie.

Gav nodded. "It's a good spot. There's a public toilet across the street. One of the few left in Edinburgh. We climb the railings at night for a pee when it's closed. And we get the chance for a wash when it's open during the day."

The sound of the ambulance siren split the silence of the night awakening a debilitating headache. The pain precluded further conversation as Arabella was placed on a stretcher by the paramedics. She managed a final question. "Why did you look after me?"

"Only a few people around at this time of night, dear: most of them drunk," said Gav. "I suppose the ones that weren't were in too much of a hurry to stop. We had to get you off the pavement."

That's how Arabella had met her homeless friends. As it turned out – though she had badly bruised her face – her injuries were superficial and she was released from hospital within a few days.

But the young doctor tending her left her in no doubt of her lucky escape. "If these men had not got you out of the cold, things could have been much more serious," he said. "After the shock of a fall like that outside and late at night the body temperature, especially among the elderly, can plummet resulting in hypothermia." Seeing her alarm, he stopped and wished her a speedy recovery.

But she had received the message loud and clear. For whatever reason a fair number of upstanding citizens had chosen to walk by the old woman lying unconscious and bleeding on the pavement. Yet three homeless men – among the poorest and most shunned human beings in society – had taken her in. They had saved her life and she vowed to repay that debt.

She remembered the first taxi journey. The driver must have thought her mad. But he followed her instructions to drive around the city past the haunts of the homeless until she found them.

It had taken some time. There was no sign of their makeshift tent outside Waverley Station. The driver cruised down the Royal Mile and then doubled back along the Grassmarket without success – though Arabella witnessed many people sleeping in doorways on cardboard, or their obscure shapes hidden beneath mounds of filthy blankets in the cobbled closes and vennels of the old town.

Further along Princes Street in the shadow of the world-famous castle, an entire Eastern European family – parents and young children – huddled together in the doorway of the House of Fraser.

Under cover of darkness the Festival City of Edinburgh, historic mecca for wealthy tourists, became a city of the dispossessed. The brutal, fetid reality of what she was seeing perforated the bubble of her own privileged, smug world and she realised that Balmoral Square Mansions could be a million miles away as far as these people were concerned.

Finally, she found the men sheltering under the overhanging wall of a graveyard beside King's Stables Road. Their surprise was evident, but their spirit remained as generous as ever.

Since that night Arabella had taken many late taxi rides visiting the men regularly with gifts of food she had purchased en route from supermarkets.

They had introduced her to other homeless people including Glum Sue and Laundry. But Gav, Four-Fingers and Davie were her obvious favourites.

Finally, in a gesture that would have been undreamt of before her first dramatic encounter with the men, she invited them to sleep overnight at her apartment.

There was only one rule: no drugs or alcohol. She was a bit suspicious of the younger one, Davie, but they were all as good as their word.

Seventy-two hours before Arabella's death, all three of them could have been found sleeping on the glass floor of the back room.

Day 3

HOMELESS people in Balmoral Square Mansions! Inhabiting the same building: staying overnight in a spinster's apartment hatching heaven knows what kind of skulduggery!

Marjorie Agincourt was the kind of person who could find many things to become outraged about. But the idea of filthy, begging, thieving ragamuffins being under the same roof as her was beyond the pale.

Arabella Pettygrew had always been eccentric – a bit of a rum character – but this time she had clearly lost her mind. A single woman of a certain age allowing the homeless – and men at that – to, what was the expression, 'toss down', overnight in her home was madness beyond reason. Apart from the issue of her reputation, Arabella had put everyone else in the building at risk. They, she – Marjorie – could be robbed of her possessions, worse, murdered in her bed by these unscrupulous wasters who were now skulking two floors above.

Marjorie should have known. The signs of irrational behaviour on the part of her neighbour had been increasing over the past few months. Her visits to the roof, the wayward nature of that cat of hers out all hours and then returning with some foul 'gift' it often as not dropped on the stairs, the clandestine taxi trips late at night had become a regular occurrence.

Marjorie had been patient. She had witnessed the strange goings-on without comment.

But this morning she had smelled their stink on the stairs as they left. It was still there, quite literally a lingering bad smell. The entire stair would have to be fumigated. That would be Arabella's first job after she got a flea in her ear.

Marjorie struggled with a heavy dining room chair into the hall placing it near her front door. Then she brought her morning cup of Earl Grey tea and sat down to wait. An hour later, she heard the door at the top of the stairs open and close.

Her movements were arthritically slow. Arabella was almost out of the front door before Marjorie managed to open her own door. "Arabella, a word if you please."

Arabella knew that tone and the implication of Marjorie using her proper name. In Agincourt's book, this was a serious transgression of building rules. She also knew that Marjorie had been waiting – heaven knows how long – behind the door to ambush her. Given those perfectly logical deductions things did not augur well.

Arabella tried to smile. "How can I help you, Marjorie?"

"It's not about helping me, Arabella. It's about helping yourself."

Arabella gave Marjorie her best bemused look, but said nothing. Whatever was coming would come irrespective of any response she might make. She was certain the bloody woman had Tourette's and the older she got the ruder she became.

"A woman of your social standing can't be seen associating with toerags, far less allowing them under your roof. Think of your reputation, Arabella. Think of the reputation of the street. I've held my tongue for long enough. You must put a stop to this behaviour or else…"

Marjorie left the threat hanging. Arabella had experienced this ruse on a number of occasions over the years. She considered simply walking away. But she was tired. She didn't want the prospect of Marjorie waylaying her again when she returned – and she would. Marjorie Agincourt was like a dog with a bone. When she got an idea in her head she would not let it go.

"Or else what, Marjorie?"

"Or else I'll have to consult with the neighbours. These people are dangerous, Arabella. It's bad enough they're on our streets. We can't have them in Balmoral Square Mansions – and we certainly can't have them polluting the stair."

Perhaps it was because she was tired and drained from the events of the last few weeks that Arabella did something completely uncharacteristic with her formidable neighbour. She bit back.

"I can have whoever I like in my home and it is no one else's business, so I would thank you to keep out of my affairs." With that Arabella moved onto the street knowing that Marjorie would have the last word.

"I will be contacting the council to report the perilous condition of the roof, Arabella. That is everyone's business!"

Day 2

ARABELLA returned late that night to find a brusque note through her letter box from Marjorie Agincourt.

It required her to either clean the stair herself, or engage someone to do so *as soon as possible due to the unhygienic and polluting effects upon the common stair through its use by your unsavoury house guests.*

She threw the note in the bin and looked for the solace of Noodles. "Out on the tiles again, old boy," she cooed as the cat emerged from under her bed slinking round her legs. She saw an exiguous blood trace and a stray feather particle around his whiskers as she bent down to fill his saucer with milk. Red in tooth and claw.

She had long since lost her disgust for his habits. When you loved an animal you overlooked its base inclinations. It was after all the natural hunting instinct of a creature related to much bigger feline beasts of the wild.

But now she would have to search the flat for any more substantial traces of his present. She was midway through her inspection in the kitchen when the intercom rang.

She checked her watch. It was almost midnight; who could it possibly be at this hour? Even more disconcerting was the insistence of the person. It was almost as though they were leaning on the buzzer.

She picked up the receiver. The torrent of abuse began before she could say hello. "It's Jim Ross. My children are traumatised. Having nightmares because of your fucking cat."

Arabella stuttered. "Sorry, I don't understand."

Jim Ross steamed on, oblivious to her intervention. "Agnes and the children came back to find a disembowelled bird on our doormat. Its fucking head was missing."

He was screaming down the intercom. She imagined a sheen of spittle on the external microphone from his uncontrolled invective. "That was your fucking cat. So what are you going to do about it?"

"I – I am…" But Arabella's attempt at an apology went unheard.

She heard him slamming the main door and stomping back up the stairs. Heavens, what if he started banging on her door?

She had thought it best to allow a cooling-off period after the morning run-in with Marjorie, and had not invited her homeless friends back tonight. If he came up to her door, there would be no option, she would phone the police. Then she heard his door below crash shut and let out a shuddering sigh of relief.

The incident had shaken her badly and she paced the floor for the next thirty minutes, her nerves jangling with fright.

Then she heard the door below open and waited, hardly daring to breathe, for the sound of his footsteps. They retreated down the stair.

She went through to her lounge and peered out of the balcony window. She saw the bald, portly figure of Jim Ross getting into his expensive silver car. The lights came on, the powerful engine revved, and the car gunned down the street turning left at the end away from the city centre.

She went to bed cold and disheartened. The flat seemed colder and more lonely than ever tonight. The culprit crept onto the bed beside her mewing pathetically as if to apologise.

She was nodding off when the insidious sounds began. At first in her semi-conscious state Arabella found it difficult to discern what the noise was. It was like having a radio on too low, or more accurately trying to tune into a foreign station. It sounded like a murmured conversation.

Arabella raised her head from the pillow and concentrated on the sounds. It was the voice of the woman downstairs and she was talking to someone else. The voice was smaller. It was the voice of a child.

"It's all right, Gwennie," she heard. "Ssshh, Mummy's here, poppet. There's nothing to worry about. The old woman and her cat can't harm us. She's an evil witch. Witches are always ugly and old and they always have a black cat. But it's all right, Gwennie, Daddy will protect us from the witch. I know, let's sing a song to keep her awake."

Then the singing began, low at first, and gradually rising in volume as the child's enthusiasm for the game increased.

"...itsy bitsy spider
Climbed up the water spout.
Down came the rain

And washed the spider out.
Out came the sun
And dried up all the rain
And the itsy bitsy spider
Climbed up the spout again."

They giggled as the child insisted "Again, Mummy". They began the rhyme over again. The lullaby was designed to soothe and calm the nerves. But Arabella Pettygrew had never heard such a chilling version. It sent a shiver of apprehension down her spine.

Day 1

SHE spent a sleepless night trying to work out how she would tackle this new situation.

Yes, she could contact the authorities and make a complaint about harassment. But how seriously would that complaint be taken?

The new neighbours would also give their side of the story about the dead bird and the trauma it caused their children.

The most likely outcome would be a draw: where the authorities, judging the incident a minor issue, would take no further action. Such a result could – at the very least – lead to a cold war, or intensify their hostility towards her. The thought of Jim Ross screaming down the intercom brought her out in a cold sweat.

Another route would be to sue for peace: apologise for the upset caused with the promise there would be no repetition.

That would mean boarding up the cat flap and keeping Noodles permanently housebound, or getting rid of the best friend she had.

Then she thought about Agnes Blunt's incitement of her child: the callous manipulation of her own daughter to punish her. The sinister use of a lullaby made her blood run cold.

She had lived her entire life in this apartment. Why should she kowtow to their rules: become a prisoner in her own home because of the bullying edict of people who had hardly been in the building five minutes?

She also had new friends she could call upon *in extremis*. The homeless men Gav and Four-Fingers had been in the army. That much she knew through general conversation.

They had not expanded on their experiences. Arabella had seen the reluctance in their eyes and respected their silence. But every sense told her that, despite their circumstances, they were brave, honourable men.

In normal circumstances she would never willingly take advantage of their friendship. But if events did escalate and turn ugly, she knew they would come to her assistance.

The thought cheered her and Arabella rose early that morning tired, but resolute. She would not knuckle under to the awful new neighbours or Marjorie Agincourt.

She would inspect the roof – not because of Marjorie's thinly veiled threats – but because it was the right thing to do. She would then make her own decision as to whether to call in professionals – or not. If she did, it would not be cowboy operators like the Duncan brothers. Then she, Arabella Pettygrew, would be the one informing Marjorie Agincourt about her choice for the job – not the other way round.

She dressed and checked the weather. It was early but looked as though it would be another fine day.

She was about to go onto the landing for her expedition to the roof when she stopped. Photographic evidence would be necessary to show the others its present state. She scoffed at the thought of Jim Ross, far less Marjorie Agincourt, venturing up the ladder.

But where was her faithful Box Brownie camera? It had been a long time since she had used it. The memory of better times: sepia-toned images of a thousand Scottish hills and lochs lightened her step as she searched the jumble of her apartment.

She found it in what she quaintly termed the sun lounge at the back of the flat. She really should make the effort to do something with the room when the roof was repaired, she thought. It was potentially the best space in the house – though it was an unpainted shell at the moment, lacking any furniture.

She found the camera on the floor in a corner opposite the set of ladders. She remembered capturing a particularly vivid sunset with it through the glass cupola.

As she bent down to pick the camera up, Arabella found herself staring down through the glass floor at the landing below. The image she saw was so unexpected that she froze for a moment in surprise. Then for the first time in years her face broke into a genuine smile as she focused through the viewfinder and tripped the shutter.

DARKNESS was falling quickly as Strawberry picked up the book. He had to use the torch on his smartphone to read the lines that had been marked. *Literacy is one of the cornerstones of civilization,* he read. *To be illiterate is to be deformed. And the derision that was once directed at the physical freak may, perhaps more justly, descend upon the illiterate.*

What was so important about this paragraph that had made Arabella Pettygrew mark it? She did not seem the type of person who would vandalise a book.

Preoccupied by the puzzle, he only heard the movement behind him when it was too late. Half turning, he took the force of the blow on his forehead. He was unconscious before he hit the floor.

A cold draft brought him back to his senses. It was difficult to see where it was coming from as he was being dragged backwards across the floor.

It felt like night air intruding. Someone was behind him pulling him by the collar of the jacket. The pulling stopped abruptly and the back of his head smacked the floor.

The sensation of sickness and disorientation threatened to overwhelm him. Then he was being hoisted under the arms and he made out the source of the draft. It was a small French window, but it was too dark to see anything beyond. His vision was swimming and he remained groggy from the blow to his forehead. But memory returned.

He was in Arabella Pettygrew's apartment late at night. He had been reading a marked passage from a novel when he was attacked by an unknown assailant who was now attempting to do what?

As if to answer his unspoken question Strawberry felt the chill of the night air like a slap. His back was against something hard and cold. Stone. A narrow stone column. More than anything he wanted to vomit.

Suddenly he was being hauled upright and Strawberry saw his attacker for the first time. He looked and smelled vaguely familiar: a smaller, younger man with blond hair and the body odour of a yak. Recognition could come later, if there was a later. Right now Strawberry recognised only one imperative – survival.

The man took a pace back leaving Strawberry swaying drunkenly. A second later he was lunging forward with both arms fully extended. But the target – Strawberry's chest – was no longer there. The detective had slumped to a sitting position. Cursing, the man grabbed Strawberry again under the arms.

As he attempted to raise him, Strawberry wrapped his arms around the man's legs. The attempt was feeble and the man punched his arms away before punching Strawberry in the face.

This time the detective vomited. The violence of the action cleared his head and his brain clicked into gear. He was on the small balcony outside Arabella Pettygrew's living room. He had watched the orange sunset from the same place only a couple of hours ago – with one critical difference. He had been inside the room looking through the French window.

Now he was outside and the drop to the pavement below was long and unsurvivable. This bastard was trying to kill him.

The man came on again – the kick aimed at Strawberry's stomach – but connecting with his knee. Strawberry screamed and retched. He was in a foetal position lying on the narrow balcony ledge. The man struggled with the shape and managed to wrestle Strawberry around so he was facing the balcony. Then he attempted to heave the detective to his feet once more.

Strawberry's hands scrabbled on the stone columns. His fingers found cracks in the stone and he held on. The man beat his hands prizing his fingers from the cracks. Then he was punching him in the kidneys and hauling him upright again.

Strawberry found himself above the parapet staring at the vertiginous drop and the car roofs far below. Then he felt the man beneath him gripping his legs for the final upward thrust.

How instant would death be, Strawberry wondered? Would it be lights out, instant oblivion with no sentient knowledge of the body – his body – lying broken 200 feet below? Or would there be a much slower, agonising death impaled on a railing – or paralysed on the bonnet of a car? He closed his eyes and prayed for blackness.

Then the grip on his legs disappeared. There was no final heave pitching Strawberry headfirst over Arabella Pettygrew's balcony. Gentle hands guided him from the balcony – past the twitching body of his assailant – back into the apartment. Strawberry looked uncomprehendingly into the eyes of Brenda Gunn.

"Never used one before, but they can come in handy," she said, showing Strawberry the gun-like object in her hand.

"Tazer," Strawberry said weakly. "How did you…?"

"I was trying to clear up some loose ends on the main suspects, sir. Couldn't get you on your mobile, or at home and thought you might be somewhere around Balmoral Square Mansions. Saw your bicycle chained to the railings and came up here first. I heard movement inside – presumably you falling and him dragging you across the floor. Afraid I had to break the door down."

Strawberry waved his arm in dismissal. "Saved my life, Brenda." It was too dark to see her blush. "Who…?"

"Davie Affyer. Homeless guy. Glum Sue's flatmate." Strawberry nodded. Then he remembered where he had seen the man. "Bastard stole my bike."

"Sir?"

"I stopped at a newsagent a few days ago to get a Mivvi."

"A Mivvi?"

"Sorry, I forgot how young you are. Anyway, never mind the Mivvi. I left my bike outside and this guy Davie Affyer stole it. But he was so stoned he fell off and was arrested. I remember now: his real name is David Leithhead."

Brenda Gunn remained dumbfounded. "Your face, sir. You look terrible. I've rustled up another car to take you home."

"After this, I think you should call me Richard – or Strawberry if you prefer – at least when we're alone."

He could see she was uncomfortable. "For my sake. I would appreciate it, Brenda."

She nodded slowly.

"I prefer Strawberry, it sounds better than Richard."

In spite of the onset of a thumping headache, Strawberry broke into a wide smile. "There are too many Dicks around. And Brenda, put my bike in the car. I'll get by on a couple of paracetamol. We'll interview this Davie together."

TWO of the burliest coppers at St Leonard's brought Davie up from the cells to the interview room.

Strawberry was pleased to see the man looked the worse for wear as though he had 'fallen and bashed his face' a couple of times, either in the van or going down the stairs to the cells. He was rubbing his wrists where the handcuffs had made a deep and painful imprint.

Whether or not Strawberry was a favourite with the rank and file, no police officer liked to see one of their own injured in the course of his duties. It brought out the siege mentality. They banded together and targeted the perpetrator with a zeal disproportionate to any other crime – apart perhaps from those involving children.

The escort placed Davie in the chair opposite Gunn, and Strawberry signalled for them to withdraw. Introductions and formalities completed for the tape, Strawberry assessed his assailant.

The sores remained around his mouth and nose and – his swollen face aside – the detective wondered if the man was in a fit mental state to be interviewed. His eyes looked rheumy and unfocused as they wandered the room as though he had never seen the inside of a nick before.

"Mr Leithhead. Are you aware of where you are and why?"

Davie sighed deeply, but nodded. He then said something completely unexpected. "I'm sorry I attacked you. I've been trying to stay clean – out of respect for her. It was the sweats and the shivers. They hit me bad. I saw your shadow in the flat and I got muddled. I thought you were there to hurt her. I couldnie abide that, you understand – not efter what she'd done for me."

The man was blinking rapidly. He swiped a hand across his eyes and snorted disgustingly, swallowing snot. Gunn handed him a tissue. He blew his nose hard and noisily before trying to hand it back. She picked up a wastepaper basket indicating its use.

"Let's start at the beginning, Mr Leithhead. Why were you in Arabella Pettygrew's apartment?"

"She let us stay there. Gav an' Four-Fingers an' me. Never Glum Sue, mind." Davie stressed her exclusion. "She liked Glum Sue well enough, helped her like she helped us, but she didnae trust her. Thought she would use drugs in her home. She couldnie abide that idea."

"You do know that Miss Pettygrew is dead?" asked Gunn.

The tears began streaming down his face and he motioned for another tissue. "A terrible, terrible thing. I dunno how anybody could hurt that woman."

"We think you did, Davie. We think you killed her," said Strawberry.

Davie appeared bewildered, speechless for a moment. "A dunno how you could think that. She was nothing but good to me. Helped me with ma letters. Helped me learning to read. Telt me I had a future if I could get aff the drugs an' learn to read an' write. She wiz a marvellous person. I wouldnie harm a hair on her heid."

"How did you get into the flat, Davie?" asked Gunn.

Davie avoided her eyes, looking sheepishly instead at Strawberry. "She gave Gav a key. I stole it off him when he was sleeping. Let myself in. Dossed down in the back room wi' the glass flair."

"So you were there overnight and during the early hours of the morning when Miss Pettygrew was killed," said Strawberry.

"No, no, I wisnie, Inspector. That wiz the first of me back there when you came in last night. I'm trying to sort masel out. Stayin away fae Glum Sue's place. It's dangerous. The dark-haired men slaughtered her dogs. For aw I know they could be efter me."

Strawberry nodded to Gunn.

She cleared her throat. "David Leithhead, you are charged with the murder of Miss Arabella Pettygrew and the attempted murder of Detective Inspector Richard Strawberry. You have the right to remain silent. Anything you say can and will be used against you in a court of law."

STRAWBERRY and Gunn had adjourned to the police canteen.

She was drinking the sump oil canteen coffee, while Strawberry pondered the interview with Davie Affyer. His reflective mood was puzzling.

"I thought you would be delighted. Arabella Pettygrew's murderer in the bag. It's a great result, sir – sorry – Strawberry."

"I suppose so. A habitual addict involved in the supply of drugs. We know he has been a runner for the drugs gang the Real Apaches operating out of Saltire Court for a long time. Caught red-handed in her flat with complete access to the crime scene. It all adds up, Brenda, but…"

"But what, Strawberry? He's caught literally red-handed in her flat, then does his best to kill you. Through his own admission we know he slept there and that he had stolen her key giving him complete access at any time. What more do you need?"

"You're right, Brenda. He's a criminal. But up to now it's been thieving and burglary. Never violence. Then there's the help she gave him in learning to read and write. His gratitude seemed genuine."

"Or he's a great actor. The criminal world is full of people who could walk straight into RADA. Instead of moping you should be celebrating. I bet Bert Rothesay is dancing around his office right now."

"Probably singing as well," laughed Strawberry, "though we've yet to actually hear the 'Singing Detective' sing."

Strawberry rose, taking Brenda's paper cup to the bin. "What about these dark-haired men we keep hearing about? Who are they?"

Brenda Gunn shrugged. "Search me."

NOBODY knew who the dark-haired men were. Glum Sue was wrong about them being Romanians. It was much worse. They were Albanians. In the international league of global criminality Albania was up there with tinpot South American dictatorships and pariah African states like Somalia and the Congo.

The dark-haired men had been among the most vicious of their brethren during the nineties and Albania's descent into lawlessness. They were lethal exports.

Cousins, they had grown up together in a city ironically called Fier. Fier was the centre of the country's criminal network where the first heroin and cocaine laboratories had been established.

But their specialist interest was not drugs. They merely used mind-altering substances as a weapon to ensnare and then enslave women, before smuggling them abroad into prostitution.

Like many young men in their country, they relied on family and clan relationships. Their blood ties led to membership of a gang called the Kosovars.

Their lethal skills were learned initially in the internecine warfare between competing gangs for the turf rights on local territory.

Later they joined the military. But as officers of the Republican Guard they lost their jobs because of the inherent corruption within that section of the armed services.

They had blown up people in cars. Murdered people with guns and tortured people with knives. Like a number of Eastern European states the country was awash with armaments looted from military depots. Criminals could lay hands on anything they wanted from Kalashnikovs and hand grenades to anti-tank rocket launchers.

Following the break-up of Yugoslavia, Albania became a lawless state.

Copying the example of other career criminals they adopted bogus identities from neighbouring Kosova – claiming persecution during the conflict eighteen years before. Always on the lookout for more lucrative pastures they became involved in organised crime beyond the borders of their own country: first in Italy – after escaping Albania under cover of darkness by rubber speedboat. Then their horizons expanded and they were later smuggled into the UK in the back of a truck with genuine refugees.

They took along their knives as the weapons of choice they had used in Albania. Even on the streets of the UK they had no compunction in using them. Their criminal career in London started through the smuggling of women – Albanian and Italian – into squats throughout the city as bases for prostitution. The small dark-haired man was an expert with knives. He was the torturer, while the taller dark-haired man used his fists.

When it got too hot in London they moved north, first to Manchester and then Edinburgh, where they changed their modus operandi from people smuggling to drugs. They were now on the streets of Edinburgh as hired enforcers working out of Apache territory for the kingpin.

SUPERINTENDENT Bert Rothesay was in a bowling alley. He was wearing what looked like an American baseball shirt and jeans! It was an extraordinary sight, coupled with the fact that two small children were dancing around his legs tugging at his hands and pleading for 'Chips and juice, Granddad'.

"Apologies for this," he said, waving his arms at the surroundings. Strawberry and Gunn had to move in closer to hear their boss over the clatter of crashing skittles and chattering youngsters.

Gunn felt completely out of place in her uniform – as if she should be there to make an arrest. That was certainly the expectation of the line of parents and children staring at the police as they queued for bowling shoes.

"Half term," shouted Rothesay, "so I thought I would spend the day with the kids." He caught the quizzical look between the officers and pointed to the café on the other side of the hall. They moved to a table and Rothesay gave the children money and their instructions. Gunn watched, smiling as the pair tried to outsprint each other to the counter.

Rothesay apologised again for the choice of venue. In all the years Strawberry had known him, he had never heard his irascible boss ever say sorry and now the man had uttered the word twice in the space of as many minutes. It worried him.

Rothesay sat composing himself for a few seconds. "I'm suspended from duty as from next week pending an internal investigation into the seagull-killer case."

Strawberry and Gunn stared at their boss in disbelief. Strawberry began to protest, but Rothesay raised a placatory hand.

"They're pretending it's temporary. Calling it gardening leave. I know better. After the chief resigned I knew my hat was on a shaky peg. Apparently the First Minister's still livid at the cock-up. She fired that PA of hers, but she is holding the police to account and as lead on that operation I guess I'm next."

He shrugged, spreading his hands on the table. "It's not so bad. I only had a year until retirement and the fed rep has already assured me there will be no problems over my pension. Which means, if I go quietly, everything will be fine."

"It's a travesty," broke in Gunn. "None of it was your fault, sir. You just followed orders."

Rothesay gave a wry grin. "If I recall that's what the Germans said as well. Anyway, thank you for your indignation, Gunn. But I called you here because I wanted to congratulate you both personally on the arrest of Arabella Pettygrew's killer before I disappear from the scene. A great job – you're quite the double act – though you look as though you've been through a combine harvester, Strawberry."

It was true. Much of Strawberry's face had swollen to the size of a small pumpkin during the past twenty-four hours though the initial bruising was already changing from purple to a jaundiced yellow. He knew better than to laugh. His kidneys were in the same condition.

"However, I'm not gone yet. What's the latest on Operation Treetops?"

"Movement, sir," said Strawberry. "PC Dreever spotted a woman going into the premises. No further developments yet, but 'Happy Trails' has been initiated."

"It would be good to get a result before I leave," said Rothesay.

His grandchildren swarmed the table with their chips and juice pre-empting any further discussion. "Forgot the tomato sauce, Granddad," they trilled. "Can you get it?"

Strawberry and Gunn watched Rothesay's retreating back as the children pulled him to the café.

"Never had him down as a doting Granddad," said Gunn.

"No, doting is the last word I would ever use to describe him," agreed Strawberry. "Let's hope Dougie Nichols can give him a good send-off with Operation Treetops."

THE sun was setting and Blackford Hill was a golden blaze of whins by the time Strawberry arrived home.

The ache in his face and body had intensified. The little bastard had given him a proper beating, he mused, as he swallowed another couple of painkillers.

His bicycle had been dropped off in the front garden earlier and he was going back through the hall to retrieve it when he spotted the envelope lying upright by the door at the side of the mat. He recognised the handwriting on the front immediately.

He opened it tentatively as one might a letter bomb. He could smell her perfume on the notepaper. He read the words twice through sore, wounded eyes. His injuries suddenly felt worse.

He made to tear the letter up. Instead, he put it back in the envelope and placed it in a drawer. That way, like every jilted fool there ever was, he could torture himself again later by poring over each heart-stabbing word.

He hurried from the flat and got on the bicycle. He left it in manual during the entire ride over the Braids and out towards Swanston. By the time he got back it was dark and he was exhausted. That had been the idea.

He flopped onto the bed without removing his clothes and fell into a troubled sleep tortured by the ghosts of the past. He was standing above Princes Street on the Mound on a sharp spring morning. He glanced to his left and through the green railings glimpsed a sea of daffodils nestled on the slope leading down to the gardens. The tourists were out already, swarming over the steps as they jostled for position to take snapshots of the famous floral clock. As he looked, the large hand, covered in small red flowers he could not distinguish, suddenly moved to ten thirty. The tourists hummed their appreciation, but he was looking beyond them and away from the gardens – down the hill to the record shop on the main street. She would be coming out of the shop now. He narrowed his eyes, squinting through the watery sunshine. But all he could make out was an amorphous jumble of humanity. If she was there, try as he might, he could not see her. He jerked awake to the commanding ringtone of his mobile. He swore. Why couldn't the bugger just go quietly?

"There's been another murder, Strawberry," growled Rothesay, not sounding remotely like a granddad. "You'd better get on your bike, laddie."

THE bum was in the air above the sheets. No muscle. No tone. Flaccid alabaster haunches devoid of hair: flesh starting to mottle post-mortem livid purple. A small brown birthmark – or perhaps shite – shaped like Madagascar sitting high on the left cheek. Into the undergrowth a tussock of hair dark in the crack skewered by a knitting needle – the only pert object in view.

The uniforms were stifling sniggers as Strawberry and Gunn arrived. "Make a good bike rack," joked one PC to his mate, his arms miming the motion of docking a front wheel into a slot.

"I hear one more reference like that and you're on a disciplinary charge, Constable," said Strawberry. "This isn't the comedy club. This is a homicide investigation. Either behave in an appropriately serious manner or get out!"

Strawberry moved to the end of the bed as the police photographer captured the crime-scene images. Subconsciously he stepped in front of Gunn trying to shield her from the macabre tableau. She moved around him.

"Rectal temperature should give the approximate time of death," she said. The matter-of-fact nature of her statement both shocked and filled Strawberry with admiration. He was beginning to appreciate that Brenda Gunn was a police officer from the tips of her occasionally varnished fingernails to the toecaps of her black combat boots.

"It might," said Strawberry, hypnotised by the metal appendage sticking out of Nigel Smail's ample derriere.

"It looks like one of his, sir," said Gunn. "I remember seeing the button top as he was knitting that cardigan for the Garden Association secretary when we interviewed him. It was ornate with an intricate pattern of flowers. That one looks the same. Imagine being murdered with your own knitting needle."

Strawberry couldn't. For him the manner of death could barely be more undignified without worrying about ownership of the implement.

"Who found him?" he asked, addressing the joker.

"A neighbour, sir," he said. Strawberry noted with satisfaction the humour had been replaced by an embarrassed air. "The front door to the flat was slightly open and the neighbour, an elderly man, came in to investigate."

"Make sure you get a full statement," said Strawberry. "Now we need to locate Mr Smail's partner."

"I think he's done a runner, sir," said a second PC emerging from the hall. "We found a couple of drawers open in their dressing room. Clothes scattered on the floor – and the door- knob was off. Looks like someone took off in a hurry."

"All right, we need a photograph of Jeremy Sheldrake, pronto," said Strawberry. "He's a young man. Let's get looking for a picture, everyone."

Strawberry checked the cloakroom toilet. The miniature print of Hamish Agincourt still gazed out sternly from above the WC, but there were no other photographs. A PC found one in a frame in the drawing room.

"Okay, let's circulate this to the force," said Strawberry.

"What about the press, sir?"

"Not yet, Constable. He's our chief suspect, but we'll keep it internal for the moment."

They left as the body was being carried out by the forensics team. Gunn caught a glint of silver on the floor under the bed. Pulling on a pair of surgical gloves she crawled under. No woof or dust mites. The floor was immaculately clean. The image of Jeremy Sheldrake with his feather duster came back to her. She retrieved the object and showed it to Strawberry who gave a low whistle of surprise.

"What in the hell goes on in this street, Brenda?"

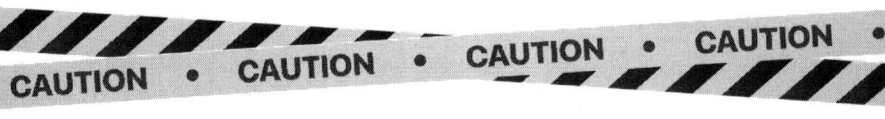

WAVERLEY Station was crawling with police officers. They were on the main concourse, the platforms and every entrance and exit.

Jeremy had never seen so many since he made the mistake of trying to take a train on the day of a Hearts-Rangers match at Tynecastle. And now he was about to make another mistake. He had to assume that Nigel had been found and the reception committee was for him. So taking a train was out of the question. His plan would have to change.

He slid from behind the newspaper rack and – pulling the cap lower – slung the haversack over his shoulders and, head down, threaded his way across the concourse to the left-luggage lockers.

An hour later he was on the bridge. It was mid-morning and there had been few people on the bus – a gaggle of pensioners and a couple of young mothers with buggies. He was too wrapped up in his own thoughts to pay attention. The fear and alarm he felt made it impossible to think logically.

Psychiatrists describe a 'red mist' descending upon the mind in moments of extreme distress. That mist can render the person temporarily insane, or at least incapable of rational thought. During this period the person is in dire peril of self-harm. A cacophony of emotions thrummed in Jeremy Sheldrake's mind on the journey. But the overriding emotion was one of hopeless despair. The scene replaying in his head was beyond comprehension. How had it happened? How could it have happened? Right now though, those questions were academic. They formed a constantly repeating tableau of horrifying images, but they had to be pushed away: banished if he was to survive. The problem was that no matter how hard he tried he could not expunge the violent images tumbling through his brain on a speed cycle that threatened madness.

Now he was standing on the footpath on the middle of the bridge. He had no awareness of reaching this point. Just as he had no awareness of the strong wind coming off the Forth tugging at his clothes, or the occasional cyclist cursing him – "Watch out. Are you fucking drunk, mate?" – as he meandered into their lane forcing them to take emergency avoiding action. At the Edinburgh end of the bridge, one such irate cyclist pulled out his mobile and reported the 'nutter' on the bridge to the police.

Budget cuts had decimated the service. The nearest police stations to the bridge – in South Queensferry and Dunfermline – were unmanned and a car was finally despatched from Edinburgh Airport Police Office.

Strawberry and Gunn got the call from the patrol car when the officers arrived on the bridge.

"A man fitting the photograph is on the Forth Road Bridge, sir."

"Where exactly, Officer?" asked Strawberry.

"Midway across on the pedestrian footpath. He's just standing there motionless like he's in a trance."

"All right. Keep your distance. Don't attempt to make contact unless something dramatic happens. We're on our way."

Strawberry was not a good driver. In fact he found great difficulty in reverse parking as testified by the number of bumps he had had and the monstrous amount on his car insurance. Besides the health benefits, his unerring ability to hit stationary objects was part of the reason he had switched to bicycles.

Fortunately – excepting the slalom of roadwork cones clogging the motorway – he only had to drive forward in a relatively straight line to the bridge. Siren wailing, he made it in thirty minutes with Gunn forcing a smile as, white-knuckled, she clutched the chicken handle.

Strawberry killed the siren as he approached the bridge and parked alongside the patrol car in a lay-by at the southern approach.

"Any new developments, Officer?"

"He's still staring out over the Forth, sir, but he has moved closer to the parapet."

Strawberry borrowed the officer's binoculars and scanned the bridge until he zeroed in on the solitary figure. He passed the glasses to Gunn. "That's Sheldrake, all right," he said as she focused on the target. "The thing is what to do now? We could close the bridge off. Make contact with a loud hailer, but that could spook him; turn the thing into a circus with a greater risk of escalation. What do you think, Brenda?"

"I think you're right. I think right now he's in turmoil. He doesn't know what to do, so we don't want to precipitate any dramatic action on his part."

Strawberry nodded agreement. Gunn got out of the car. "What are you doing, Brenda?"

"I'll approach him on foot. Negotiate."

"Wait a minute. This man is a prime suspect in a murder, Brenda. We have no idea whether he's armed or not."

"From what we found at Smail's apartment I'm willing to bet he has nothing to do with it, Strawberry."

She started walking onto the bridge. Strawberry cursed and followed her. They walked slowly along the footpath high above the Firth of Forth. A group of racing cyclists passed them struggling into the headwind. A couple with cameras were on the path coming towards them from the Fife end. In the distance they could see a woman with a buggy also approaching them.

"I'm not happy about this, Brenda. Us taking a chance is one thing, but look at these people. One civilian on the bridge right now is one too many. I should have closed it."

Gunn's response was carried away by the wind. She had to repeat it to be heard. "It's too late now. You can blame me, Strawberry."

They were thirty yards away from Sheldrake when he suddenly moved to the barrier and started to climb. Before Strawberry could react Gunn was running. She tackled Sheldrake round the legs as he was reaching for the top of the railings bringing him down on his back with an unceremonious thump onto the footpath. Twisting his arms behind him she had the handcuffs on as Strawberry reached the pair.

"**WHY** would you want to do something as stupid as that?"

Jeremy Sheldrake merely shook his head at Strawberry's question, the tears streaming down his face as he sat in the interview room at St Leonard's.

"Surely nothing is ever bad enough to warrant suicide, Jeremy?" asked Gunn.

"What is there left to live for? Nigel is dead. I found him lying there. It was the most terrible thing I have ever seen."

"So what are you saying exactly, Mr Sheldrake?" said Strawberry. "Are you claiming you didn't murder Nigel Smail?"

"Of course! I would never harm Nigel. We were partners. Lovers. It's not conceivable."

"It's for that very reason, that you were partners – lovers – that you are under suspicion, Jeremy," said Gunn. "Start at the beginning. Describe what happened."

"Nothing happened. I returned to the apartment and found Nigel in bed in that awful state. I didn't know what to do. I knew the authorities would never believe me. I knew I would be accused of his murder. So I panicked. I ran."

"And you saw no one on the stair or outside as you came back to the apartment?" asked Strawberry.

Sheldrake shook his head. "No one."

"Can anyone vouch for your whereabouts?" asked Strawberry.

"I was at Top Man in Princes Street."

"What did you buy? Can you show us receipts?" asked Gunn.

"I had no money. Nigel kept me on a tight budget." The tears came again. "Sorry, that was cruel. I shouldn't have said that." Jeremy looked heavenwards mouthing a silent apology. "I was just window-shopping. But hundreds of people must have seen me." Sheldrake was moaning like an animal in his despair.

"Was it your immediate plan to kill yourself?" asked Strawberry.

"My first thought was to escape. I aimed to catch a train at Waverley. Go north. My parents live up north. I needed to get out of Edinburgh."

"And then what?" asked Gunn.

"I don't really know. I wasn't thinking straight. There's a ruined castle on a cliff overlooking Stonehaven. It's called Dunnotar. I remember going there as a child with my parents on a picnic. While we were there a black 4x4 drew up on the grass. There was a family inside. They had a small dog. The little girl opened the back door and the dog jumped out. It didn't know any better. It ran straight off the cliff. Perhaps that would have been a good way to go." Sheldrake paused, staring into space. "But there were so many police at the station. I knew I would be caught. So I changed my plans and caught a bus to the bridge."

"It's just as well Gunn stopped you in time, Mr Sheldrake," said Strawberry. "That drop is 180 feet. Twenty people a year do it. That's 800 since the bridge opened – and only three have ever survived. The odds were stacked against you."

"That depends on how you look at the odds," said Jeremy Sheldrake. "Right now they look pretty good to me."

"**SEX** game gone wrong? What do you think, Strawberry?" Despite his antediluvian views on the gay community, Strawberry was glad to see Superintendent Bert Rothesay out of civvies, back in uniform and at his desk.

It was somehow reassuring, as if the small, incestuous world of Gayfield Square had returned to normal – albeit temporarily. It was inconceivable to think the Singing Detective would be gone within a week.

"This was definitely not a sex game gone too far, sir," said Strawberry. "The pathologist has come to the conclusion that Nigel Smail was murdered. Based on the autopsy, his report states that the temperature of the knitting needle was between 500 to 1,000 degrees centigrade when it was inserted, and I quote here 'with great force' up the victim's rectum."

"Pah! You know that bugger McNiven likes the booze a bit too much, don't you, Strawberry? Anyway, what's this 500/1,000 malarkey actually mean?"

"In layman's terms it means the needle was red-hot and literally exploded, chargrilling Smail's internal organs."

Rothesay grimaced. "Christ. What a way to go. Someone really hated this guy."

"It's little consolation to Mr Smail," said Strawberry, "but Dr McNiven's report says that there was evidence of a number of sleeping pills along with traces of alcohol in the deceased's system. Also the internal injuries were so severe and the shock so profound that death would have been instantaneous."

"It's the MO that's so cruel and bizarre," said Rothesay. "In my thirty years of policing I've never heard anything like it."

"You have to go back in history to find any precedents," said Gunn. "Though there's some debate over the exact nature of his death, it's claimed that Edward II died as a result of a red-hot poker being stuck up his back passage. The claim is his wife ordered the killing after deposing him and taking the throne. That was in the fourteenth century. Around a hundred years later Vlad the Impaler, the ruler of Wallachia – present-day Romania – is reputed to have murdered his enemies by driving wooden stakes up through their bodies."

"Thank you, Gunn. I think that's enough dodgy history to be going on with. Returning to the here and now, we've got a bad bastard on our hands. Is this Jeremy Sheldrake character capable of such a thing, Strawberry?"

Strawberry pondered the question. "It's possible, sir. Anything's possible as we've seen from the last couple of weeks. We're sweating him in the cells at the moment. He's been in twenty-four hours, but I'm not sure about holding him much longer without charge."

"Why not, Strawberry? You don't need me to tell you this is a murder investigation. He can be held for up to four days. If you think the bugger did it, considering the crime, he's getting off lightly."

"Yes. But taking into account his antics on the bridge,

he's on suicide watch. The longer we've got him in the cells the greater the risk he'll do something stupid to himself. If that was to happen in our custody…"

"Point taken. I think we've had enough bad press in the past few weeks to last us."

Strawberry nodded to Gunn. "There is one thing that could be a game-changer," he said.

She produced a small transparent evidence bag from her pocket placing it on Rothesay's desk. It contained a silver brooch engraved with an elephant, beneath which lay two crossed swords.

"Gunn found this brooch in Nigel Smail's apartment under his bed. The last time we saw it, it was attached to a pink turban worn by one of his septuagenarian neighbours named Marjorie Agincourt."

THE first thing they saw was the large, framed canvas of Hamish Agincourt smashed to pieces on the floor.

They found Marjorie Agincourt against the plumped-up cushions in her favourite spot in the bay window. She was wearing the same eccentric outfit Strawberry had witnessed upon their first encounter including the exotic headgear. A small bright patch on the otherwise faded pink turban betrayed the space for the missing silver brooch. Her husband's field glasses sat in their usual place within easy reach on the coffee table alongside the small brown bottle of pills. Marjorie's days of curiosity were finally over.

"Mogadon," said Strawberry picking up the bottle for closer inspection. "I had it once for pain relief when I was in hospital," he explained to Gunn. "Very pleasant. There was the sensation of my head sinking into the pillow and a kind of warm deep-red glow. Never experienced a sleep like it. That was on one pill."

He shook the bottle. "She took half the bottle – a better way to go than she deserved."

"A bit harsh, Strawberry," said Gunn.

"Try telling that to Nigel Smail," he said.

THE note was in her bedroom on top of an antiquated writing bureau. It was addressed to the bishop now universally known as Holy Smokes. The twenty-page epistle was both a confession and an eleventh-hour plea for forgiveness and redemption in the hereafter.

"Hedging her bets against fire and brimstone," said Strawberry. "A bit late coming from a life-long agnostic, but worth a punt I suppose. It's amazing how imminent death suddenly converts so many people to religion."

"You should try not to be so cynical. It's bad for your health – leads to acute indigestion," said Gunn.

Strawberry gave a jaundiced smile. As he read the pages, the seething intrigue – the smothering, claustrophobic intensity of hatred and passions – residing behind the net curtains of Balmoral Square Mansions became poisonously evident.

EXTRACTS FROM THE WRITTEN CONFESSION CONTAINED IN THE FINAL TESTAMENT OF MARJORIE AGINCOURT, DECEASED.

I never wanted to return to Scotland. But Hamish had a love-hate relationship with the place. While the French side of his ancestry were content to live their lives in the rural backwaters of France, Hamish, like many Scots before him, had the wanderlust. The pages of history are full of famous pioneering Scots – Livingstone, Carnegie, Alexander Graham Bell, America's founding fathers – and great military men like Gordon of Cartoon. You will not find Major Hamish Agincourt in any history book, but he was a great Scot who spent his military career fighting for Queen and country – and ultimately gave his life for the cause.

The breakdown in his health was the main reason Hamish wished to return to Auld Reekie. It began while he was serving with Monty at El Alamein. Egypt is a particularly filthy country cursed by all kinds of disease and pestilence. Hamish caught something contagious – a worm of some kind – that caused him extreme distress in his ablutions. He had to endure that curse for the rest of his life.

But what finally put the tin hat on it – as they say in military circles – was the Malaysian Emergency where he was badly wounded in his heroic action defending the British Embassy against a mob of filthy commies. God transport them to wherever their barbarian hell is.

After that he could no longer stand what he called the beastly steaming jungles. Of course his health was further affected by the shocking treatment he received at the hands of the top brass. They virtually made him resign his commission. Never mind the worm or his war wounds. To this day I think the army's callous treatment is what killed my Hamish. They might as well have put a loaded gun to his head and blown his brains out.

At any rate, we found passage back to the homeland where – although he never recovered from being virtually sacked by the army – he found some sort of contentment.

Gardening had been an interest in the tropics. But it became a passion for Hamish on his return to Edinburgh. He threw himself into the Garden Association and all its doings. They were very enthusiastic about his knowledge of tropical plants and he even tried to nurture the development of a stand of palm trees – although the rain and awful dampness of the climate killed them off. A bit like what happened to Hamish really. The association was where he met that loathsome blackmailer Nigel Smail.

Strawberry looked up from the note. "So far most of it's all our yesterdays – a rehash of their personal history and his record as an injured war hero. But she calls Smail a 'loathsome blackmailer.'"

"The plot thickens," said Gunn, who had decided they were in for a long haul and was sitting on the bed. "Read on, MacDuff."

Smail encouraged Hamish in his efforts and they became friends, with Hamish regularly attending association meetings and staying late to discuss what he called other business with Smail. I did not KNOW what that OTHER BUSINESS was or how FRIENDLY they had become until the photographs arrived.

You might say it was all my fault. That through my curiosity – and at this final stage in my life I can now admit that I have been too nosey for my own good – plaguing the council with complaints about neighbours' bin bags was a step too far. In the end my curiosity opened a Pandora's Box.

A couple of days after Bella's death – and following an extraordinary meeting of the Garden Association – I received an anonymous unsigned note. All it said was 'Here is the evidence of Nigel Smail's fraud. As guardian of the morals of Balmoral Square Mansions you will know what to do with it'. Along with the note came a receipt from a wine shop for 150 bottles of pinot noir.

I phoned Smail confronting him with this information. He denied it, but there was an awkward delay on the line. I knew he was lying and was about to raise my concerns with other residents and members of the Garden Association when the photographs came through my door.

They showed Smail and Hamish, MY BELOVED HUSBAND, in flagrante delicto behind a rhododendron bush in the communal gardens. It was clearly late at night but Smail must have used one of these phone camera things to record the whole filthy affair with them naked and going about the dreadful business like dogs in heat.

He enclosed a note saying that he had the original photographs and that if I breathed a word about his accounting or his wine cellar he would post the photographs through every door in Balmoral Square Mansions. He would expose Hamish as a camp. I couldn't stand by and let that happen.

Strawberry paused in his reading and looked across the room at Gunn.

"What?"

"Apparently Smail and Marjorie's husband were lovers. Smail had images of them having carnal relations in the communal gardens behind a rhododendron bush. He sent them to her because she had discovered that he was cooking the books of the Garden Association. He was blackmailing her with the photographs in order to ensure her silence."

Gunn shook her head in amazement. "Edinburgh's upper classes at play, Strawberry. Keep going."

Smail had boxed me into a corner. I dearly wanted to expose him for the scoundrel he was, but I could not contemplate the thought of those terrible pictures being revealed to the world.

Worst of all, I was heartbroken about the destruction of Hamish's memory. Smail had destroyed the image of my husband in my eyes. I felt my love for him gradually curdle to contempt and then disgust. How could the man I had devoted my life to betray me in such a manner? Smail had succeeded in making me hate my husband and I could never forgive him for that. In reality I knew he had already won by exposing the sham that had been my marriage. And for that unforgiveable sin I vowed revenge.

Smail would never know, but his act of blackmail showed me exactly what I had to do. The idea was triggered by Bella's death. I began to think about her brother again for the first time in years. The plan formed slowly because it was so extreme, but once the idea had taken root I knew I would go through with it.

Freddie Pettygrew and I had had a brief affair: I hasten to say two years after Hamish was gone. I don't really know why. Perhaps I was lonely. Maybe I liked his American burr. Or perhaps I simply liked the idea of spiting Bella – taking one of the few things she could call her own away from her.

Anyway, the important thing is that post-coitus one evening he was stupid enough to confide that he was helping himself to Bella's savings. He laughed as we canoodled saying he had duped his sister into signing a document giving him access to her bank account. And that for several years he had been withdrawing regular amounts.

Perhaps he realised he had said too much, or my face betrayed my shock, as he suddenly became serious justifying his action by declaring he deserved some reward for the dismal duty of having to visit her every year.

So when I saw him again at Bella's funeral I took my opportunity. I told him that I would expose his fraud to the police, which would undoubtedly lead to a prison sentence and possible disinheritance, unless he helped me dispose of Nigel Smail. Of course he didn't believe me at first. When he finally did he squealed like a sticking pig and continued to plead for a way out.

But Double Indemnity was my favourite film. I remembered the way Barbara Stanwyck twisted Fred MacMurray round her little finger to get her way. Only I had more than Barbara Stanwyck. I knew that if I pointed the authorities in the right direction there would be evidence of a crime that could be pinned on Freddie Pettygrew.

I phoned Smail and told him that he had won on condition that I could see the original photographs for myself. He giggled on the other end of the line and agreed. I pleaded for privacy in our meeting. He agreed to that too, saying he would have me round on an evening when Jeremy was out. I was a doddery old woman. He saw me as no threat.

When I arrived with Freddie Pettygrew he was mildly surprised, but unfazed. I always knew that Nigel Smail's self-conceit would be his downfall. He even insisted that we all have a drink to close the deal and produced a very tolerable brandy.

When he went to fetch the photographs I slipped the sleeping pills in his drink. He went out like a light. I was going to make Freddie smother him with a pillow. Then I had my brainwave.

I saw the appalling cardigan he was knitting for Dorothea Hislop. I took a knitting needle from the cardigan then told Freddie to get Smail undressed and into bed. I could hear him grunting with the effort and still protesting his objections as I was in the kitchen heating the needle on the gas ring. When I thought it was hot enough I put on Smail's oven gloves and took the needle through to the bedroom.

I thought Freddie was going to faint when he saw the needle. But I ordered him to turn that bastard over with his buttocks in the air. Then I shoved the thing up as hard as I could. It's amazing the strength a doddery old woman can have if she hates someone enough.

Strawberry skimmed the last few paragraphs. Marjorie Agincourt had believed that she would be in the clear with Jeremy Sheldrake targeted by the police as the prime suspect for Nigel Smail's murder – until she discovered the loss of her brooch. Her confession to the bishop as her *dearest friend* with the plea for forgiveness in the afterlife (if there was one) and the admission that Freddie Pettygrew had helped her carry out the crime: *But only because I blackmailed him into doing so.*

He stopped reading. His eyes made contact with Gunn. "We need to put out an urgent alert for the arrest of Freddie Pettygrew as an accomplice to murder."

DOUGIE Nichols had decamped from the communal garden to the church bell tower. As the officer in charge of executing Operation Treetops it would be his call on precisely when Happy Trails should be triggered.

From his vantage point high above Balmoral Square Mansions he could see a steady stream of people arriving at the target address. Most of them were moving furtively along the street, but a series of taxis had started arriving disgorging a great variety of individuals representing all ages and a cross-section of society from middle-aged men in suits to hippy students and male pensioners with ponytails and leather jackets. He had seen the same kind of audience at a recent Rolling Stones concert along the road at Murrayfield.

He focused his binoculars on a young woman pushing a buggy in the hope that she was simply out for an innocent stroll with her infant and would walk past the house. She parked the buggy outside the address and – leaving her child in it – joined the queue filing up the steps. It was that single selfish action – devoid of parental care for the welfare of her child in the overwhelming need for her fix – that decided Nichols.

Picking up the walkie-talkie, he went through the final checks. The entire surveillance team – still in their gardening overalls – were on standby. Instead of garden shears they were now armed with tasers. The team of officers in the bell tower were similarly equipped.

Three Black Marias, engines running, were stationed in a street adjacent to Balmoral Square Mansions. Looking at the stream of punters heading for the target address, he reckoned he would need more vans. In the event of an extreme event there were two ARVs containing specialist firearms officers. A secure safe between the seats in each car held a semi-automatic Glock 17 handgun for each officer, while 9mm Heckler and Koch semi-automatic carbines lay secured in each boot.

Inside the target house Dorothea Hislop was doing a roaring trade. She was standing behind a long trestle table stacked with small bags in a bare room at the rear of the house. On each side of her, two large men – heavies she had known for years – were stationed to ensure there were no thefts and everyone paid up. The need for security was simple. The bags – no bigger than doggie bags – contained cocaine. What lay on the table in utilitarian wrapping was worth £200,000. Dorothea had no idea what had happened to the anonymous drugs kingpin who had originally hired her. But this was the biggest pay-day of her life. No 'I owe you' notes, cheques, or credit cards accepted here. This was strictly cash on the barrel-head, a one-off transaction. There would be no repeat performance.

The large leather satchel strapped across her chest was already half full of notes. She could retire with this kind of money into comfortable obscurity back in her beloved County Donegal.

Yet she was beginning to get worried. The punters

seemed to have ignored her carefully calibrated instructions aimed at staggering the times. In their desperation they were turning up en masse. The queue remained reasonably orderly and moving relatively quietly. But it would only take one loose cannon to ignite a stampede and heaven knew there were enough of them in the drugs community.

As if to mirror her foreboding, she saw Westport Mary in the line. 'A character' was the polite description often assigned to difficult people. It fitted Westport Mary like a glove. It was hard to know her age as she had long, dark hair down past her shoulders and was covered in tattoos and piercings which included her face. She wore a nose ring and right now she appeared to be snorting through it like an enraged bull.

The subject of her ire was a younger woman in front of her who she was accusing loudly of jumping the queue. "Who does she fucking think she is? We're aw here waitin' oor turn but this yin here thinks she's special."

"I was only asking if I could move up because my child's outside on her own and I have to get back to her," pleaded the younger woman.

"Whit's that got to do with onything? Dinnae have kids if ye're takin' drugs. It's one or t'other. Ye dinnae see me wi' any bairns. It's that simple. Keep yer legs shut an' ye wouldnie have tae snipe aboot jumpin' any queues."

One of Dorothea's heavies had started moving towards the altercation. Dorothea held his arm in a staying gesture. "Look, you come through and get your stuff, Westport Mary, and then we'll keep the line moving with this young woman directly after you. That's fair, right. We don't need any trouble. Okay?"

A piercing whistle silenced the argument and any other rumblings of discontent. For a second the sound reminded Dorothea of old black and white footage she had seen on television of the signal for troops to go over the top in the First World War. The whistle was followed by a bellowing command. "Police. Open up immediately!"

The drugs line disintegrated, charging in all directions. Someone overturned the trestle table in the stampede with the baggies bursting open in a mist of white powder. The garden surveillance officers led the first wave, charging through the drug cloud to collar the addicts as they tried to flee.

Some addicts already under the influence perhaps thought they were having a hallucinatory experience; that Christmas had arrived early. The men in the green overalls were oversized elves gate-crashing the party bearing gifts of more drugs. If so, they were quickly disillusioned.

One punter who attempted to fight his way out was promptly tasered and fell spasming on the white-dusted floor. Westport Mary and the young mother she had been arguing with were seized. Mary resisted, yelling abuse and attempting to knee a policeman in the groin. The officer hauled her from the room by her hair. The young woman's arms were pinned behind her and she was frogmarched out of the front door sobbing.

A second wave of officers, unmistakable in their uniforms, crowded into the room. Linking arms, they moved towards the centre corralling the punters into an ever-decreasing space.

Dorothea watched the move as she hid behind the overturned table hugging the satchel. In a matter of seconds the pincer movement would be completed and she would be trapped in the circle. Keeping low and using the melee of dazed punters as cover she ran for the back door leading to the stairs and the basement. Somehow she made it through the door and down the steps.

She was at the door leading to the back garden when she remembered the young woman. Dorothea looked over her shoulder back up the stairs. No sign of pursuit. All right, a fast check and then out. Veering away from the garden exit she went straight into the basement room and crossed to the bed. The young woman was fast asleep. Dorothea placed a hand on her forehead. It was clammy, but not fever hot. She felt for the pulse in the young woman's wrist and counted for a minute. It was faster than she would have expected, but not galloping. The police would do a complete search of the property and find her alive and as well as could be expected for a junkie. She had discharged her part of the bargain to her anonymous boss. It was now time to get out!

She ran along the weed-strewn path glancing at the shed. No time for that check. The old man would have to take his chances. Lifting the latch on the back gate she moved slowly to the street and peered round the corner in both directions. The throng of police and punters was thirty yards away being processed at the front door of the property.

She strolled casually towards the cathedral. No time for feckin' prayers today, she thought, smiling to herself. Instead, home free to beautiful Donegal with a potful of cash at the end of the rainbow just like the leprechauns. Only this wasn't a fairy story with wee green men. This was the luckiest day of Dorothea Hislop's life.

She didn't notice the man in the cheap grey suit emerge from the church and cross the road. She wasn't aware of his presence until he was barring her progress on the pavement.

"It's a great view from the cathedral. You can see everything that's going on," said Dougie Nichols holding up his warrant card.

The elderly residents of Balmoral Square Mansions had a grandstand view. They had never witnessed anything so dramatic in their lives. The street was full of police vans. The back doors were thrown open and lines of people – men and women of all ages and classes – were being loaded into them by police officers with handguns on their hips.

Meanwhile, several taxi drivers had been removed from their cabs to be handcuffed to the railings of the communal gardens. A woman in a hippy skirt with tattoos all over her face had been carried bodily, kicking and screaming, to a patrol car, while another young woman was forcibly wrenched away from a baby buggy and placed in another patrol car.

The Tweedies, who were enjoying a fine Beaujolais as they watched from their bay window, were flabbergasted. "It looks just like New York," said Marcy. "What's the name of that programme? It's your favourite, Peter."

"*Blue Bloods*," said Peter. "But that's fiction, dear. This is real life. I can't believe it's happening in Edinburgh. Perhaps on one of those awful housing estates on the outer limits of the city, but in our street – Balmoral Square Mansions – it's unbelievable."

Indeed, things were happening so fast it was difficult

to keep up or know where to look. The Tweedies were beginning to do a good impression of meerkats as their necks swivelled right and left on the unfolding action.

From the direction of the church a vaguely familiar figure suddenly appeared between two police officers. Marcy and Peter gawped. It looked like... No, it couldn't be! It was! It was the secretary of the Garden Association – Dorothea Hislop – and she was in handcuffs. As they reached the police car, an officer placed his hand on her head and she bobbed down into the back seat. The door closed and she disappeared from view.

Then an ambulance sped into the street stopping outside the drugs house. The paramedics disappeared inside and minutes later the figure of what appeared to be a young black woman emerged on a stretcher. As if on cue, a large, expensive car pulled into the street under a police motorcycle escort and a tall, distinguished-looking black woman ran from the vehicle to the ambulance climbing inside beside the patient. Emergency light flashing, the ambulance sped away.

Peter and Marcy looked at each other in astonishment. "I've never seen anything like it," said Marcy. "The Garden Association secretary in handcuffs. Whatever next? I think I'll have to go and lie down, Peter."

He nodded in sympathy as he drained the remaining soupçon of wine from his glass.

There was only one notable absentee from the spectacle. Marjorie Agincourt would have been in her element sitting in her bay window riveted to the extraordinary goings-on through Hamish's field glasses.

DOROTHEA Hislop: so mundane, so correct in her presentation at the Garden Association, or her nightly peregrinations with her dogs, Ebony and Ivory, that Strawberry had completely overlooked her.

Dougie Nichols felt a sense of smug satisfaction as he sat beside Strawberry in the interview room at Gayfield Square. Here was a wee smelly Irish woman, sitting in a rattie, moth-eaten cardigan, who had successfully pulled the wool over his smart-arse rival's eyes. Some days were infinitely superior to others, Nichols decided, as he continued the interrogation.

"Now before our break, you were telling DI Strawberry and myself that you had no knowledge of the identity of – in your words – the 'Mr Big' of the drugs operation. Is that correct, Ms Hislop?"

Dorothea managed a sullen nod.

"Forgive me if I find that hard to believe," said Nichols. "For the past year you have been running a highly lucrative cocaine operation from a house in Balmoral Square Mansions yet you have no idea who your boss is? The individual who was masterminding your instructions on this illegal trade?"

"I have no idea, Mister Policeman, because I never met Mr Big. As I've already told you, my instructions came through phone calls – a robotic voice on the end of the line telling me when the next deal should happen."

"When you say a robotic voice, do you mean a voice that was altered in some way through technology?" asked Strawberry.

"A metallic-sounding voice. Yes. Like the ones you hear on crime films like that one with that black detective – eh, *Along Came a Spider* – where the serial killer needs to disguise his voice to give his ransom demands."

"But that doesn't explain how you became involved with this mystery person in the first place," said Nichols.

"It was two dark-haired men – Eastern European, Romanian, I think they were. I was walking my dogs one night and they spoke to me in the street."

"Do you normally speak to complete strangers outside at night?"

Dorothea ignored Nichols's question. "They appeared out of nowhere, but they seemed pleasant enough at first, petting the dogs and making bland remarks about the weather. I didn't feel threatened if that's what you mean. Anyway, the conversation gradually changed."

"In what way?" asked Strawberry.

"They began saying things that indicated they knew personal details about me." Dorothea paused at the uncomfortable recollection. "They knew I was from Ireland. Well, I suppose that was obvious as I still have a trace of the blarney. But they were also aware I had been a drug user – and they indicated that they knew I had money problems. All of which was true. I was piss-poor and struggling with my rent. But it was also true that I was getting very alarmed and I started thinking that they were maybe debt collectors about to slap a summons on me. Only, I seem to think that only happens when they come to your door. Anyway, I was about to call the dogs and make a rapid exit when the taller man put his finger to his lips.

"'Shush,' he said. 'Be calm.' That was when he made me what he called 'a golden opportunity' on behalf of a client."

"And that golden opportunity was to run a drugs house for financial reward? Enough to clear your debts and your money worries?" asked Nichols.

Dorothea nodded ruefully. "More than enough. It was a deal that no one in their right mind could refuse."

"Or at least no one with a criminal record and no conscience about their fellow human beings," said Strawberry.

Dorothea remained silent.

"How were the drug deliveries arranged?" asked Nichols.

"The robot phone voice would simply tell me the day and time of the next delivery – late at night or in the early hours, of course – and it happened like clockwork. My dogs were the perfect cover for my late-night walks. So I would always be in the drugs house at that time. There would be a knock on the door and I would go out and pick up the package on the step."

"Who delivered?" asked Nichols.

"I never saw anyone."

Nichols looked sceptical. "You mean to tell us you were never tempted to take a peek, Dorothea?"

She shook her head. "You never met the dark-haired men, Mister Policeman. The way he put his finger to his lips to keep me quiet. It put the wind up me, I'll tell you."

"Did you ever see the dark-haired men again?" asked Strawberry.

"Only the once. The robot voice contacted me and told me to expect a delivery. I expected the usual package on the doorstep but instead there was this girl propped up by the two men. She looked drugged."

Strawberry stared contemptuously at the Irish woman.

"What did the client tell you to do with the girl?"

"Nothing. The message was relayed by the men. It was simply to keep her safe in the basement."

"That's called kidnapping," said Strawberry. "Apart from the charge of dealing drugs, holding a person against their will is a very serious charge. If convicted on either or both of those charges you won't be seeing Donegal for a very long time."

DOUGIE Nichols stretched out in the uncomfortable plastic chair clasping his hands behind his head. If he had had a big cigar he would have smoked it. Dorothea Hislop had been taken down to the cells to consider her position and now he was alone with Strawberry.

"I have to congratulate you, Dougie, on a first-class piece of police work. You've given Rothesay a great send-off."

Nichols acknowledged the compliment, while silently considering the framing of Strawberry's congratulations: 'have to congratulate you, Dougie'. *I bet that sentence stuck in your craw, you wee baw-bag*, thought Nichols. To the victor the spoils.

"Then again," said Strawberry, "there is a glitch."

"What's that?" asked Nichols, sitting up.

"Well, we're no nearer finding this Mr Big – the drugs kingpin. A number of different sources have pointed the finger at the bishop – Holy Smokes. But there's no solid evidence linking him to the drugs network and he's still in a coma. Until we find the culprit the crime remains unsolved."

Nichols had to admit Strawberry was right. Maybe he should have waited slightly longer before giving the go on Happy Trails. Perhaps the kingpin would have made an appearance if he had shown more patience. Of course Dougie Nichols disclosed none of those misgivings to Strawberry.

"What do you think of her story about the girl?" asked Strawberry.

"Keeping her 'safe in the basement' sounds like a euphemism for something far more sinister," said Nichols. "How is the girl now?"

"She's coming round in hospital, but the latest is that she is dazed and confused. We'll have to give her a bit of space, tread carefully.

"Then there's the dark-haired men Hislop referred to as Eastern Europeans – Romanians. They're popping up everywhere and we know nothing about them, Dougie, apart from the fact that they are seriously involved in this drugs caper. Glum Sue claimed the same men forced their way into her flat and killed her dogs as punishment for a missing drugs consignment." Strawberry got up. "We're going to have to split our resources. Right now, I have to concentrate on the Pettygrew and Smail murders and finding Marek Wójcik and Freddie Pettygrew. Dougie, you get along to the hospital and see what you can find out from this girl. Who knows, she might give us a lead on the dark-haired men."

THE young woman had been transferred to a private room in the hospital. Dougie Nichols got a surprise when he entered.

A tall, slender African woman with piercing green eyes was sitting at the bedside. Her high cheekbones bore the markings of her tribe: two vertical stripes on each side burned into the skin in a childhood ritual. Rather than defacement, they appeared an adornment on her serene countenance. A tribute to a proud ancient heritage – though there was nothing old-fashioned or backward-looking about this woman. Her cropped hair was highlighted by gold earrings and a simple gold band at her throat. A closely fitting emerald-green suit complemented her skin tone perfectly. The ensemble was completed with a pair of Jimmy Choo heels.

Dougie Nichols recollected seeing a black woman running towards the ambulance just after he arrested Dorothea Hislop. But it was at distance and he couldn't be sure.

The woman looked quizzically at Nichols. "Can I help you?"

The kind of voice you would hear coming from a national news anchor: university educated, an even timbre with the hint of a transatlantic accent. An assured tone redolent of authority: at ease with command.

Then Nichols remembered the appearance of the expensive car with the tinted windows and the foreign registration. The woman with diplomatic immunity. What was her name again? Something to do with money?

She supplied the answer before he could get there. "My name is Savannah Bullion. And you are?"

"Detective Inspector Douglas Nichols. Apologies for the intrusion, madam. I wanted to ask the young lady (he indicated the woman in the bed) a few questions if she is up to it."

"The young woman is my daughter, Inspector. As you can see, Orisa is asleep. I would prefer that she wasn't disturbed. She has been through a traumatic time. Perhaps I can help you?"

Nichols considered. Careful here. Softly, softly, was the game when confronted by a foreign national with unknown influence.

"That would be good of you, Ms Bullion."

He waited. The woman seemed to come to a decision, rose and indicated the door. "I want to let her sleep. Let's speak somewhere else."

She led Nichols to a visitors' lounge unlike anything he had seen before. The usual mayhem of fractious infants and serried ranks of truculent patients in varying degrees of discomfort was entirely absent. In fact, it looked like an airport lounge for first-class passengers. The room was empty. It was tastefully decorated with lounge chairs, which were not broken or stained. Soothing classical music played quietly in the background. A vase of flowers decorated the unmarked coffee table alongside a glossy selection of upmarket magazines.

The woman smiled as if reading his thoughts. "The benefits of private healthcare, Inspector." She sat down, crossing a pair of elegant legs. "We have to begin at the beginning. This story goes back to my childhood in Nigeria."

Savannah Bullion explained how she was a member of the Yuruba tribe with a complicated family life. Her mother had been unfaithful to her father – an act that brought great shame upon them and opprobrium from the ultra-conservative rural community. As a result she had a half-sister. Her half-sister's father had been a cattle thief who had received summary justice when he was hanged for his crimes. Meanwhile, her own father was an educated man – an engineer – who had been highly respected in the village until his wife's betrayal.

Although Savannah's father remained loyal to his wife, the shame drove the family from Nigeria to the Congo where he had secured a position as manager of a gold mine. However, the country was wracked by lawlessness. The mine was attacked by bandits and her father was tortured and murdered when he refused to give the combination to the safe containing the staff wages. The mother and girls fled for their lives, but the woman died on the journey back to Nigeria.

"Given the stigma associated with our family, our cousins would not take us in. So my sister and I were placed in an orphanage in the care of nuns."

At this point Savannah Bullion paused, staring beyond the detective into a space filled with painful memories. Nichols waited her out. Filling difficult silences with meaningless platitudes rarely worked. They rang a false note, especially with sophisticated and intelligent individuals like the woman before him. His girlfriend had taught him that.

When she resumed it was with a steely focus that Nichols was certain had propelled her to the status in her country warranting diplomatic protection.

"Care is probably the wrong word when used in conjunction with the orphanage. The nuns were… what would be fairest way of describing them? God-fearing zealots of the Old Testament variety. They had plenty of religion – with fire and brimstone sermons about the appalling nature of sin and the consequences. But they had no love, Inspector. They were flint-eyed fundamentalists.

"Of course, they knew about our backgrounds and that made life very hard for both of us. Like many fanatics before them, they believed the only way to save our souls was to scourge the evil through beatings and confinement.

"Initially I was with my sister and tried my best to comfort and protect her. We had been inseparable as infants and, if anything, the bond was strengthened by the trauma we had experienced in the Congo. But then we were suddenly separated for no reason I could understand at the time.

"A wealthy childless couple, who had known my father and admired him, learned of my situation. They adopted me. In my childish naivety, I expected that they would want my sister too. But adopting the daughter of a hanged cattle thief might have been a stretch too far for the prestigious circles they mixed in.

"By the time I understood that my sister would not be coming it was too late. I begged my new parents to allow me to make contact with her. But – though they were generous to me in every way – they were adamant in their refusal. I smuggled letters out of the house – fifty, a hundred, I can't remember the number – pledging my continued love and support to her. But they had already thought of that ruse and warned the nuns to intercept them."

"Did you make contact in later years?"

Savannah Bullion shook her head, the movement of the gold earrings barely perceptible. "I tried but she had disappeared from the orphanage. Later, when I achieved a position of some authority, I made further inquiries. I discovered that she had run away from the orphanage and become involved in street gangs and drugs. Then she vanished off the scene entirely – until now."

"Meaning?"

"Look, Inspector. You must understand that this is a very delicate matter for me. I am an ambassador for my country and any bad publicity would not only reflect on me; more importantly it would be embarrassing for my country. Nigeria has many problems which are well documented. But it is also a very proud developing nation, so I must ask you to show utmost discretion."

Nichols was uncertain about where the conversation was going. One thing he was sure about was his duty as a guardian of the law. Powerful or not, if this woman was seeking some agreement for his complicity in overlooking a crime he would never be party to such a pact.

"You have diplomatic immunity, Ms Bullion, which means that you are immune from prosecution. So I don't know quite what you are asking."

Savannah Bullion's eyes glistened with tears. "My daughter, Orisa, is everything to me, Inspector. Orisa means 'an angelic manifestation' in our culture. I will do everything I can to protect her. She was kidnapped in your country – in your city – by unscrupulous men at the instruction of a woman seeking personal revenge on me. That woman is my sister. She is known here as Blessings McKenzie."

BLESSINGS McKenzie had discharged herself from hospital as early as possible. But it was still too late to stop Dorothea Hislop 'letting the dogs out'. The result had been disastrous.

In another part of Edinburgh, some distance from Balmoral Square Mansions, in a fashionable café in the student district of Marchmont, she had read a thrilling version of the police raid on the drugs house in the *Hoots Mon*. Throwing the rag down and leaving the cash for her coffee on the outside table, she struggled to get up on her crutches, cursing the impediment of a broken leg.

One fact was critically clear. She had to get out of Edinburgh quickly. Even for the Scottish plods it was only a matter of time before they figured out her part in the drugs network – or her bitch of a sister betrayed her – again. But there was one perilous though vitally important thing she had to do first and she knew she would need the help of the last people she wanted to call.

Reluctantly, she jabbed the number into her mobile. It was picked up on the second ring and she outlined her requirements in staccato commands in a bid to control the fear she felt at seeking their assistance.

The voice on the other end said three non-negotiable words. "One hundred thousand." She said, "Yes," and the line went dead.

Blessings McKenzie hurled the mobile to the ground and – even though the pain juddered through her to her gritted teeth – stamped the phone to smithereens under her plaster cast.

SHE was gritting her teeth again. There were ninety narrow, winding steps – including a hobble across a slippery moss-covered rooftop – to the bell room and every inch of the journey was a lightning stab of pain.

Though it was almost midnight with a cool wind coming off the Forth, her face was covered in a sheen of unhealthy sweat and her blouse was plastered to her body. Part of it was the agony induced by mountaineering up a vertiginous cathedral staircase on a broken leg, but another substantial part came from her fear of the men waiting below.

The two dark-haired Albanians were like attack dogs. Blessings McKenzie had bought and paid for their services during the past months and as long as the money was forthcoming they came to heel. Essentially though, they were feral mercenaries owing allegiance to no one. One slip of the chain and they were off the leash. Then the deadly weapons you thought you controlled could turn and rip your throat out.

She had already paid them £50,000 for the first part of the plan. They didn't like that. They wanted it all up front. The tall man had given her the jaundiced eye, but said nothing. He didn't need to. Heart thumping in her chest, she screwed up her courage insisting that the balance would only be paid on completion of the plan. Then she hobbled quickly inside before they could see her trembling and began the ascent.

Halfway up she saw the cupboard where she had hidden only a week before, but which felt a lifetime away. The scene came flooding back. The sound of the plodding steps and the laboured breathing as the bishop drew ever closer to her hiding place. Her panic as she dropped the Thermos to smash on the concrete floor. The mutual shock as the door opened and she and Holy Smokes confronted each other.

He was a transparently honest man. She had seen the confusion and then the dawning realisation cross his features as obviously as a clear blue sky turns to dark thunderclouds. He knew why she was there. Probably not the reason behind her clandestine activity, but he understood that she was spying on the police surveillance team. She could not allow him to pass on that information.

They had wrestled on the narrow stairs. Perhaps she had pushed him, perhaps he had lost his footing. In the ensuing struggle she couldn't exactly remember what had happened. But they had fallen together down the steps in a desperate tangle of arms and limbs. She had seen his head hit the wall and then there was the searing pain in her leg and she had passed out.

Vision swimming, she regained consciousness slowly to see Holy Smokes lying in a contorted, motionless sprawl at the foot of the stairs. The physical agony and alarm on that night had threatened to overwhelm her, but the clinical reasoning of a survivor kicked in.

It would be the same tonight she vowed as she finally dragged herself through the door of the bell tower.

All signs of the police surveillance team had disappeared. The bell room looked exactly as Blessings McKenzie remembered it. She moved over to the curtained far wall. Drawing the curtain aside, a small alcove was revealed containing a series of very large bells standing on a low bench. They had been collected over the years from other churches throughout the country. The hiding place lay behind them.

Removing the knife from her coat pocket, Blessings bent down to the base of the wall and began to prize the brick out. It was a slow process as she had used a plastic sealant to hold the brick in place before applying a paint to simulate the render. Afraid that one of the dark-haired men might grow impatient and enter the bell room at any minute, she sped up her efforts.

Finally, the brick came clear and she felt in the space behind – her hand emerging with a large polythene bag. It was stacked with tight bundles of £50 notes secured with rubber bands. Her plan would only allow her to take a small percentage of the money she had garnered over the years as a result of her illicit activities. But it would be more than enough to tide her over until the commotion died down and she could return to collect the rest. Then she returned the bag to its hiding place and replaced the brick. It was still a good fit without the sealant. She stood back and appraised it. Not perfect, but a person would have to look very closely to see any signs of disturbance. And she had never seen anyone draw back the curtain to look at a few dusty old bells in the alcove. It would have to do. Pushing the sealant scrapings under the bench with her good foot, she placed the bundles in her coat pockets and began the painful descent to the waiting Albanians.

BLESSINGS McKenzie was in a wheelchair being pushed through the throng at Edinburgh Airport by the small, dark-haired Albanian. He was wearing dark shades which she thought ironically theatrical. After all, she was the one about to risk everything. So she was the one who needed the sunglasses to conceal the panic in her eyes.

It was 6 a.m., but even at such an early hour the place was crowded with long queues of people pushing trolleys piled so high with luggage they were having difficulty steering or seeing where they were going. The coffee shops and bars were similarly packed and many were starting their holiday celebrations early.

Blessings McKenzie wasn't prissy – how could she be in her line of business – but she had never understood how Scots could get slaughtered on alcohol at breakfast time.

The small man pushed her across the main concourse to the lifts and they ascended to the departures level. This was the part where the plan became increasingly hazardous. She had already been pressured into paying them the balance of their extortionate fee in the car park. It was either that, they said, or they would abandon her to her own devices. She had had no choice. It was an ultimatum she had expected.

She signalled a disabled toilet and the man wheeled

her in. "Ten minutes," she said, locking the door on the dark, inscrutable features. She took the knife from her coat pocket and worked as quickly as possible given her handicap.

A record-breaking six minutes later – after depositing the debris in the waste bin – she opened the door.

He was gone. He had probably left the instant she closed the toilet door. She had known that in her heart, but she would not fail now. She was disabled, after all, and she would use that as her trump card. She locked the door again and pulled the emergency cord. The airport assistant arrived within minutes urgently knocking on the door. "Are you able to open up?"

Blessings McKenzie unlocked the toilet to see a large, overweight man with a turkey neck. He was breathing heavily from the exertion of moving too fast for his physical condition. But he had sympathetic eyes. This would be fine.

"I'm so sorry, but my brother-in-law seems to have gone walkabout." She raised a conspiratorial cup-shaped hand to her lips. "I'm afraid he likes a snifter in the morning. But now I'm stuck in this chariot and my flight to Nigeria is in an hour."

The man shook his head in disgust and the fleshy neck fillets wobbled disgustingly. "Selfish bugger. Don't you worry, darling. We'll get you on that flight. Top of the queue." With that, he levered his large frame into the toilet behind Blessings McKenzie and wheeled her out.

The assistant passed her ticket over the electronic gate and her carry-on bag onto the scan. Now came the moment of truth.

"Can you manage to stand, dear?" he asked. Blessings shook her head.

"It comes in spasms. It's very painful at the moment." The tears were genuine and came easily. They had nothing to do with pain – and everything to do with terror.

The assistant shook his head at the female on the far side of the full-body scanner. She waved the wheelchair around the gate and produced a hand-held scanner. She ran the device up and down Blessings McKenzie's body as she sat immobile in the chair not daring to make eye contact with the young woman lest she betray herself. This was the moment of truth. If the machine detected, the game would be over. She would be taken to a room, searched and then arrested.

"I hope you have a comfortable journey." Blessings only registered what the young security woman said as her chauffeur steered her to reclaim her scanned luggage from the roller. She had to force herself not to turn around and thank the woman.

True to his word, the assistant sailed Blessings past the queue of boarding passengers and down the corridor leading to the plane.

She looked out of the window at the grey Edinburgh morning and the hills in the background. She watched the frantic last-minute activity below on the tarmac as the baggage handlers stowed the luggage and the ground crew made their final checks before gliding back to the terminal in their electric buggies. She could see the bulk-head door and the smiling stewards inside waiting to welcome her.

The assistant ferried her up to the entrance and helped her up. "I can help you get to your seat, dear."

She wished she had money to give him a tip – and almost laughed hysterically at the thought.

"Thank you very much, but I'll be fine. The pain has eased a lot." Blessings smiled at him and smiled at the stewards. If she could, she would have danced up the aisle. She was moving to her seat and sanctuary when she felt rather than heard the barely discernible crack.

The first wad fell with a muffled slap onto the aisle. Then the plaster cast split down its length spewing the money in a heap at the feet of a bewildered stewardess, while the following passengers concertinaed into each other in stunned disbelief.

"**SHE** was within minutes of take-off. She had stuffed £100,000 in her stookie. Can you believe it?" Dougie Nichols was punching the air as he relayed the news to Strawberry on his mobile.

"That's brilliant, Dougie. It's the best leaving present Rothesay could have. What's she saying?"

"Very little, but enough to put her away for a very long time. She hasn't admitted to being the drugs kingpin, but all the evidence is pointing that way. She's also facing the very serious charge of abduction."

"How's that?" asked Strawberry.

"I spoke to Savannah Bullion yesterday. You remember the high heid yin with diplomatic protection."

Strawberry recalled the briefing about the regular sighting in Balmoral Square Mansions of an expensive mystery car with a foreign registration.

"How does she tie in?"

"Turns out Bullion and McKenzie were sisters brought up together in Nigeria. It's a long story, but they were sent to an orphanage and then separated. Bullion was adopted by a wealthy family, while McKenzie stayed put. McKenzie thought her sister had betrayed her and vowed revenge. The upshot is she somehow discovered that Bullion's daughter was a student in Edinburgh. She had her kidnapped and held by Dorothea Hislop – we're pretty sure with the intention of turning the girl into a drug addict."

"Charming," said Strawberry. "Keep sweating her, Dougie. I'm pretty certain she was responsible for manipulating the finger of suspicion to point at the bishop as the drugs kingpin. I would bet my pension she came up with the Holy Smokes nickname and fed it through Hislop to the addicts on the street."

"Sounds logical," said Nichols. "Which makes me wonder about what exactly happened when they had their alleged accident in the cathedral."

"Only she can answer that now," said Strawberry. "The bishop died an hour ago without recovering consciousness."

STRAWBERRY and Gunn had returned to Arabella Pettygrew's flat. The trail had gone cold on Marek with his girlfriend Sandra – despite the threat of misleading the police and the course of justice – staunchly maintaining she had no idea where he was. So now they were looking for clues that might indicate the whereabouts of Freddie Pettygrew.

The deceased's brother had not been seen since Angus Robertson witnessed him throwing a black bag over the sea wall and then disappearing in a taxi. Though the driver had been traced, all he knew was that he had taken his passenger back to his Leith flat.

Marjorie Agincourt's final confession had triggered a nationwide police hunt covering airports, ferries, train and bus stations. But at least forty-eight hours had elapsed between the last sighting of Freddie and the discovery of Marjorie's letter. Two days was an eternity in a world of instant global travel.

Strawberry knew their fugitive could now be anywhere. Contact with the police department in Boca Raton had established that Freddie Pettygrew had not returned to his home in Florida. The trail was cold. It was as if Freddie Pettygrew had vanished from the face of the earth.

The officers moved through the chaotic flat respectfully.

A patina of dust had already settled over the careworn furniture. The only sound was the constant drip of a faulty tap somewhere at the back of the house. An abandoned property neglected in death as in life – just like the owner, Strawberry thought dismally.

They went through the whole search routine again working silently as they opened drawers, looked inside cupboards, checked kitchen cabinets and upended jars and boxes containing worthless old coins and aged bric-a-brac. They went through her meagre book collection shaking the spines in a bid to unearth any scribbled note that might conceivably assist them in their investigation. They did the same intricate examination of her small collection of classical LPs in the bedroom. No glimmer of a lead. Nothing.

"Well, it was worth a try," said Strawberry trying, but failing, to sound upbeat. "I guess we recalibrate, go back to square one and relaunch the TV appeal with his mug shot. Who knows, he might be hiding out on Skye or the Outer Hebrides."

"I doubt it, Strawberry. Those are the last places I would go. He'd stick out like a sore thumb. And you know how nosey locals are in small communities. Want to know everything about the incomer. Big, impersonal centres of population – London, Birmingham – that's where I'd head."

Strawberry nodded solemnly. He had seen too much of this depressing flat and this depressing street. He had to get out.

"Oh look, my favourite." Gunn picked up the Debussy LP. She moved over to the ancient record player on the dresser, put the disc on and the stylus moved geriatrically onto the black vinyl. The haunting strains of *Clair de Lune* filled the room.

"My primary-school teacher used to put this on every Friday afternoon. She got the class to close our eyes and think of something peaceful. It was her idea of re-establishing calm and order after a boisterous week. Of course it didn't really work. Half the boys would snort like pigs or make farting noises," she laughed. "But for some reason I liked it."

The record suddenly stuck repeating the same bars over and over again. Gunn moved to the turntable to rectify the situation. Strawberry saw her frown.

"I don't think it's the record. The turntable seems to be out of true as if it's not sitting properly."

She opened the small drawer underneath that formed part of the player. She brought out an old leather-bound photograph album and re-crossed the room to Strawberry. She opened the album to reveal the black and white images of a very young Arabella Pettygrew with her father.

Strawberry flicked through them. Most had been taken in the hills, or by the side of lochs on isolated tracks. A few showed the decaying relics of a forgotten existence – an isolated roofless highland croft or a rusting tractor in the middle of a barren field. And some were mementos of death and war – the burned-out wreckage of planes often lying alongside a small cairn of stones left by anonymous hikers.

"That's what must have caused the problem," said Gunn as she went to put the album back.

"Just a second," said Strawberry. "Why would she put

it there? Was she hiding it?" He took the album spine, turned it upside down and shook it. A smaller, newer-looking photograph fell on the floor face down. He turned it over and gave a low whistle. It looked as though it had been taken from above and in haste as it was out of focus. But there was no mistaking the image of Agnes Blunt on the landing kissing a man who was definitely not her husband.

"We came here searching for clues on one killer. It's possible we have found another," said Strawberry.

SHE had been given no warning. They simply arrived first thing with a perfunctory rap on the door, a search warrant and faces appropriate to the investigation of a grave crime.

There was no sign of Agnes Blunt's partner, the businessman Jim Ross, or her children, 'the poppets' Gwennie and Daniel. Was that simply luck on her part, or did she possess a kind of sixth sense intuiting danger? Strawberry did not discount the latter.

He was a severely pragmatic man, not given to superstition. But there had been occasions in his police career when he had encountered serious criminals and sensed – how would he describe it? – a difference in the air surrounding them. An invisible malignance that transmitted itself causing the hair at the back of his neck to prickle.

There had been no hint of that sensation on his first encounter with Agnes Blunt, but the situation had changed and the atmosphere was now very different. The shockingly white face behind the large black frames, the eyes still and unblinking, looked the way a cat might before tearing its prey apart. She knew that he knew.

There would be no sympatico – no surrender – in this interview. But Gunn had found the evidence and he let her lead. She went straight for the jugular.

"Miss Blunt, some very disturbing evidence has come to light during the course of our investigations which makes you a person of interest in the death of Arabella Pettygrew."

Brenda Gunn might just as well have been congratulating her on the shine of her counter tops. Not a twitch of emotion flickered across Agnes Blunt's Halloween face. Hands crossed on her lap she sat immobile, patiently waiting. How different from the first meeting with the nonplussed looks and alarmed protestations about being 'law-abiding citizens'.

Like a lizard shedding its skin, this was the real Agnes Blunt showing her true character.

Brenda produced the photograph and laid it on the expensive coffee table. "We found this in a photograph album in Miss Pettygrew's flat. It clearly shows you kissing a man other than your husband."

Agnes Blunt could not disguise the shock that flitted across her features. "Where…?" But she recovered quickly. "So what?"

"Why would the private person you acknowledged Miss Pettygrew to be, a person who minded her own business, take a photograph like this?"

"I have absolutely no idea. Anyway, I have no idea what you think this proves. He's my brother."

"We will get to what it proves, Miss Blunt. But the man in the photograph is not your brother. For one thing, brothers and sisters don't normally kiss like that! Secondly, we have traced the man in the photograph. He is a car mechanic from Coaltown of Wemyss named Billy Thain."

"So you are having an affair with this Billy Thain," said

Strawberry. "Slightly immoral perhaps since you have a partner with whom you have had two young children, but no law against it."

Agnes Blunt's eyes smouldered behind her large spectacles. If looks could kill, thought Strawberry, he would be flat on his back in need of a defibrillator.

"And now I suppose you are going to reveal my secret to my partner."

"Nothing so trivial," said Strawberry. "We are here to arrest you on suspicion of the murder of Arabella Pettygrew."

Agnes Blunt rose stiffly. "I did not kill her. I want to see a lawyer."

AGNES Blunt had been in police custody for four hours and her partner, the businessman Jim Ross, had yet to make an appearance. Strawberry and Gunn found that strange and – though they harboured their own suspicions about his absence – refused to jump to conclusions.

By contrast, her lawyer – a snappy little man named Reginald Hook – arrived at the station on their heels. He was currently sitting with his client in the interview room opposite the officers, sniffing and sneezing like a dog detecting a bad smell.

"I am finding it difficult to comprehend why my client has been arrested in the first place. What possible grounds do you have for charging her – a respected law-abiding person from the upper echelons of Edinburgh society, and in addition with the responsibility of caring for two very young children – with MURDER?" He snuffled the air in indignation. "You must release her immediately, or suffer the consequences of a civil action."

Strawberry was accustomed to the tactic. Unlike poor malefactors, who were financially incapable of fighting the system and therefore accepted their situation in a state of doleful indolence, the rich had an air of self-entitlement. Many regarded themselves as above the law employing every threat and device to avoid prosecution.

"We have strong circumstantial evidence to suggest that your client Agnes Blunt was at least complicit in the murder of Arabella Pettygrew," said Strawberry.

"And what is that?" asked the lawyer.

"We have the sworn statement of three witnesses testifying to the fact that Ms Blunt and her partner, Mr Jim Ross, carried out a campaign of bullying and harassment against the deceased which ultimately led to her feeling imprisoned in her own home."

"Who are these witnesses?" asked the lawyer.

"Individuals whom Miss Pettygrew invited as guests to her flat," said Gunn.

The eyes behind Agnes Blunt's large spectacles rolled dramatically as she sneered.

"You mean these homeless, good-for-nothing drug addicts she smuggled into the building. How could anyone believe a word of what such people say? They'll say anything for money to buy drugs. I was the victim here. I was in fear of what these people might do to us in the middle of the night. Do to me or my partner, but more importantly, my poppets. I had to protect my poppets."

"So you're saying you didn't harass Arabella Pettygrew?" said Gunn.

"We did not. We simply requested that she keep the noise down so my poppets could sleep."

Strawberry slid the compromising photograph across the table. "We believe you bullied her to such a degree that she was forced into trying to stop you by threatening to send a photograph of you and your lover to your partner, Jim Ross. Consequently, you were so outraged by this that you murdered Arabella Pettygrew."

"You believe?" said Reginald Hook. "You will have to do a lot better than that, officers." He put his hand on her arm. "Don't say another word, Ms Blunt."

She pushed his hand away as if he was contagious. "I didn't kill the woman. It was Billy Thain."

THE car mechanic from Coaltown of Wemyss looked as though he had been zapped by a taser.

He had been on his back under a car fitting a new exhaust when the police arrived. The first indication he got was when a black shoe tapped his foot and he slid out on the car trolley to see two policemen standing above him. They arrested him in the garage in full view of his workmates and he was still in his overalls with oil smeared on his face when confronted by Strawberry and Gunn in the interview room.

"You are facing a grave charge," said Gunn, feeling almost sorry for the smudged specimen in front of her.

Billy Thain was average height with black curly hair and regular if unremarkable features. He had the bony, underfed look of an amateur footballer – an appearance Agnes Blunt clearly favoured over the quaggy plumpness of her partner, the businessman Jim Ross.

For a moment he simply sat in stunned silence. Then as the seriousness of the accusation sank in, he stuttered into the broad dialect of Fife. "Whit charge?"

"Agnes Blunt, who I think you know, claims you are responsible for the murder of Arabella Pettygrew."

Billy Thain drew his hand across his face, subconsciously spreading the oil even further. "Whoa.

Whoa there now. I've no idea aboot that. She's sayin' I kilt that auld wifey she wiz havin' a fight wi'?"

"That's correct, Mr Thain," said Strawberry.

"Well, I know Agnes. That's right enough. We've been the gither since we met at the Miners' Welfare Club in Buckie. But that's the extent o' it. I never kilt onybody."

"But you were aware that she was in conflict with her neighbour Arabella Pettygrew," said Gunn. "You were also aware that Miss Pettygrew took a compromising photograph of you and Ms Blunt on the stair landing? We believe she intended to send it to Jim Ross if Agnes Blunt did not stop harassing her?"

"All o' that is true, right enough," said Thain. "Agnes telt me that. But I wisnie too worried. I could handle that bawheid Ross wi' one hand. An' I wisnie too concerned aboot it gettin' out. It wiz a fling wi' Agnes, that wiz all. Oh, she was bilin' mad at that woman. Cursing her upside down an' all sorts. Screaming she wid put her in her box. Agnes could be a bit peculiar – though she was a passable shag. But I wid never kill for her or anyone else."

THE post-mortem on the interviews was a bleak affair for the officers.

"I believe Thain's version of events, but we're no further forward," said Strawberry as they sat in the office at Gayfield Square. "It's still 'he said/she said'. And her lawyer is correct. So far all we have is conjecture. Even if the procurator fiscal thought there was a case to answer – and that's highly doubtful – it would never stand up in court. All we have so far is circumstantial. I'm convinced she did it, but we need solid, incontrovertible proof."

Strawberry's fist pounded the table in frustration. "We're missing something, Brenda. It's hiding in plain sight. Let's review what we know so far."

"Her first word was 'where'," said Gunn. Strawberry looked askance at her. "It was her first response when she saw the photograph. Then she paused and went on the offensive with 'so what?'. I'm thinking about that pause, Strawberry. What if she was about to add to that one-word answer, but then thought better of it? Thought it might incriminate her if she said any more. Let's try filling in the blanks."

Strawberry mulled the question over. "Okay, as in, 'Where are you going with this?'?"

"That's possible," said Gunn. "Or how about 'Where

did you get this?'? If we suppose for a moment that my interpretation is what she was going to say, what could be deduced from that?"

Strawberry's brow furrowed as he pondered the question. "I would say that she was possibly surprised – not at what the photograph showed – but that it was in our possession in the first place."

Gunn nodded. "Meaning that she had already seen the photograph. The content was no surprise to her but the fact that we had it was."

Strawberry snapped his fingers. "Arabella gave Blunt the original. But Blunt was so arrogant and dismissive of her pathetic old neighbour that it would never have occurred to her that Arabella might have had the nous to make a copy. If we are correct, the question must be where is the original?"

"And where is the camera?" said Gunn.

THE crew were late. Two weeks late. Nothing novel in that, especially in Scotland's capital where the historical epithet Auld Reekie was proudly upheld by the city's waste-collection service.

Communal bins all over Edinburgh were overflowing with the detritus of everyday life and Balmoral Square Mansions was no exception. The West End had been their last call that day and the square was at the end of the line before the journey to the tip. True to habit – and already late – the bin men were jogging beside the truck hurling wayside bags into the vehicle and ignoring 'street spillage' which was left to rot and stink.

The screeching arrival of a police car halted progress. A constable moved smartly towards the crew. At least one of the men noticed her lazy eye, but like Strawberry, thought the flaw rather attractive. What the officer next said made little sense to them, but they were happy to go along with it as it meant a premature end to their long shift. "Sorry but I'm afraid this truck is impounded. Please take your belongings and go home."

A team of five officers arrived in a police van. They were clad in white protective overalls, plastic boots and surgical gloves. They started sifting through the contents of the bin lorry. The filthy job took them three hours, but they found the bag they were looking for and Gunn hit the speed dial on her mobile.

"We have it, Strawberry. It's en route to the lab. I'm going with them. I'll let you know as soon as we have more information."

STRAWBERRY and Gunn were once more in Superintendent Bert Rothesay's office. It was their boss's final day and this would be the last time he would receive their report.

Once again they had things to show him. This time two items in transparent bags sat on his desk. The first was an ancient Box Brownie camera. The second was a simple flyer for an upmarket furniture store, but the name and address on the envelope were the crucial evidential elements.

"We knew we were running out of time to hold Agnes Blunt," said Strawberry. "So we went over all our case notes last night. During my initial interview with Marjorie Agincourt she referred to Arabella Pettygrew's ancient Box Brownie camera going everywhere with her when she was a child roaming the Scottish hills with her father. There was plenty of evidence of that in the album we…"

"Yes, yes, Strawberry. For heaven's sake, get on with it, man."

"Of course, sir," said Strawberry. It was somehow reassuring to see the boss bad-tempered to the last. "After discovering the incriminating photograph of Blunt and her lover we naturally started to wonder about the whereabouts of the camera. We contacted Arabella Pettygrew's solicitor, J. B. Grimwood, and he said the camera had been left in her will to her brother. However, he told us that although he managed to hand over the deceased's cat, Noodles, to Freddie Pettygrew, the camera had never come into his possession. Grimwood assumed that the camera was still at the crime scene and the police had kept it for evidential reasons."

"Assumptions. They make an ass out of you and me," growled Rothesay.

Strawberry had no idea what his boss meant. He decided to move on. "Anyway, it was in Marjorie Agincourt's letter, sir. Brenda, sorry, Gunn spotted it."

"Spotted what, man? If you don't spit it out soon, I'll be retired."

"In her confession to the murder of Nigel Smail, Marjorie admitted to being too nosey for her own good. She then referred to 'plaguing the council with complaints about neighbours' bin bags'.

"Gunn phoned the council waste-services department and they confirmed that they had received many complaints from Marjorie about neighbours simply dumping their black bags on the street when the communal bins were full. Her latest complaint had been two days after the murder of Arabella Pettygrew when she named Agnes Blunt as the guilty litter-lout.

"Thanks to the council's terrible service in finally picking up the rubbish two weeks later we managed to find the bag containing the Box Brownie in the nick of time. A day later and it would have been on a city tip along with thousands of tonnes of garbage. Anyway, Agnes Blunt's fingerprints are all over it, sir. As confirmation that the bin bag belonged to her we also found a furniture flyer addressed to Agnes Blunt. She likes very expensive furniture, which along with a few other things has been her undoing."

"Strange to think that one killer from beyond the grave has been responsible for bringing another killer to justice," said Gunn.

TWO WEEKS EARLIER

ARABELLA Pettygrew adopted Marjorie Agincourt's tactic. She stood behind her door patiently waiting for the front door in the apartment below to open and close. At 8.15 a.m. she heard the heavy footfall of Jim Ross descend the stairs. To ensure he really was leaving, she hurried through to her lounge and looked out of the front window. She arrived just in time to see his bald pate duck into his large silver car and drive off.

It was now or never, she told herself. She had mulled over her plan the entire day and then spent a sleepless night wrestling with the ramifications of the course of action she was about to take. Witnessing the clandestine tryst and then taking the photograph had been a moment of triumph for her. The thought of having something that would exert a hold over her awful neighbours and stop their bullying filled her with joy and hope when up until that moment of discovery she had only imagined a bleak and fearful existence.

She knew she had no option but to carry it through. To, in the paraphrased words of Shakespeare's Lady Macbeth, screw her courage to the sticking place. Even so, she descended the stairs with trepidation.

Her faint knock on the door was greeted by such a prolonged silence that she raised her fist to try again. She was in mid-motion when the door opened and Agnes Blunt stared out at her. There was no sign of the children, not that it would have mattered. They were too young to comprehend their mother's duplicity, far less report it.

Blunt said nothing: simply kept staring. Arabella's mouth felt incredibly dry and her throat constricted. She forced the words out in a voice she barely recognised. "I saw you kissing that man early yesterday morning. I have the proof and I will send it to your partner if you do not leave me alone."

Two red heat spots appeared high on the cheeks of the white mask that was Agnes Blunt's complexion. Arabella had expected the screaming foul-mouthed invective of the banshee she knew this woman to be. Instead, Blunt's voice was low and measured. "What proof?"

"I saw you both on the landing through my glass floor and I took a photograph. You can have the photograph on condition that you write a statement declaring that you will never harass me again. I will give that statement to my lawyer and, providing you honour our agreement, your partner will never know."

"Where's the photograph?" Blunt maintained the same slow monotone. It did not fool Arabella for one minute. Apart from the pinpoints of colour, her features were immobile and the eyes behind the large black frames unblinking in their study. It reminded Arabella of the reptile head on the wall of Emile and Fanny Cruducker's apartment. She prayed that Blunt had not detected her shudder.

"In a safe place. I will exchange it when you give me the letter."

Blunt closed the door without a word. As Arabella went shakily back up the stair she thought she heard a scream of rage. It could have been her imagination; the walls were so thick it was impossible to tell.

Thirty minutes later Blunt was on Arabella's doorstep. She handed over the letter. Arabella made herself study it, despite the hatred she felt emanating from her neighbour. Satisfied, she handed over the photograph, which Blunt – never breaking eye contact – tore into tiny fragments before picking them up and putting them in her pocket.

IT had been a terrifying, nerve-wracking experience, but Arabella had done it. She had come through the ordeal of facing up to the despicable woman and emerged victorious.

She celebrated that evening by playing Debussy's *Clair de Lune* at *her* normal volume. Not a peep disturbed her entertainment. Afterwards she hid the album – containing a copy of the photograph she had had processed in the camera shop two days previously – in the drawer beneath her record player. Then she lay in bed reading the letter several times before falling into an exhausted, dreamless sleep.

She woke early the next morning revitalised in body and spirit. For the first time in several months she felt optimistic and hopeful for the future.

She rose and dressed and listened as the cathedral bells proclaimed a saint's day, a bereavement, a celebration – she knew not what – but was happy all the same. She placed the letter alongside her faithful Box Brownie on the hall table. She would take Agnes Blunt's signed statement to her lawyer two days from now when she visited to change her will.

The thought came spontaneously. Why not enjoy the bells and the fresh morning air in her favourite place? The place she had escaped to so often in the past when beset by doubt and troubles. Leaving her front door ajar as she would be no time, she unlocked the trapdoor and climbed the ladder to the roof. Heights had never bothered her. She had grown up a roamer and a climber of hills with her father.

She went to the parapet and looked out across the magnificent panorama of Edinburgh's rooftops. The legendary fictional character of Sherlock Holmes was born in this city. Down there somewhere among the Georgian grandeur of the New Town, the sulphurous evil of Dr Jekyll and Mr Hyde had been spawned from the fertile imagination of Robert Louis Stevenson. And the real-life body-snatchers Burke and Hare had carried out their diabolical trade in the cobbled vennels of the old town. And now 130 years later here she was, Arabella Pettygrew, enjoying the same view as famous authors and notorious criminals. A view to die for, she thought.

The clamour of bells obscured the sound of Agnes Blunt's approach. Like Arabella the previous day, she had waited patiently behind her own door listening for her neighbour's door to open. She couldn't believe her luck when she heard the old woman climbing the ladder.

An implement. She needed a weapon. She looked at her daughter's wigwam and the idea came fully formed. She removed one of the steel poles from the frame and hefted it in her hand. It was light, but the element of surprise was on her side and it would do for what she had in mind.

Going up the stairs she saw Arabella Pettygrew's open front door. She could hear the woman on the roof. She had time.

She went into the apartment and saw the Box Brownie and the letter on the hall table. Perfect.

She climbed the ladder leading to the roof and saw her victim staring out from the parapet across the city. Agnes Blunt did not hesitate. Metal pole in hand she covered the intervening space soundlessly in her trainers and smacked the woman as hard as she could on the back of her legs just behind her knees. Arabella Pettygrew's legs buckled and Agnes Blunt pushed her over the parapet.

She heard a muted thump and then a faint punctured sound like air escaping a tyre. Then the transcendent bells once more.

She didn't look over the parapet, but went back down the ladder and took her letter and the Box Brownie from the hall table.

Back in her own apartment she replaced the metal pole in the wigwam frame before tearing the letter into tiny pieces and placing the camera among rubbish in a black bin bag. She couldn't get rid of it yet. She couldn't be out on the street at this time of the morning. Heaven knows what she might find.

She went to the bathroom where she sprinted on the spot pumping her legs and laughing hysterically until the adrenaline dissipated. Then she went back to bed. Her partner, the businessman Jim Ross, was away on business and her poppets wouldn't wake for another two hours. She fell asleep.

THE prison van arrived at the back of the courthouse, its high windows blacked out to block snatched photographs of the inmates. It had no effect on the waiting paparazzi who charged the moving vehicle in a chaotic melee running alongside and jumping like geriatric basketball players as they blindly triggered their cameras at the windows in a bid for that one shot. The image that would be splashed across newspaper front pages. *Blunt Force: roof-top murder trial begins.*

Jim Ross watched the television images from a hotel room in the Western Isles as his partner, Agnes Blunt – her head covered by a blanket – was escorted from the van handcuffed to an officer. He hit the off button as she disappeared into the court building. He needed air and time to think. He walked down to the tiny harbour and ferry point so consumed by his own misery that he had passed the man before a glimmer of recognition dawned. He turned to double-check and picked out the spot of colour, the red rucksack in the midst of the boarding passengers before the figure disappeared onto the ferry.

In the days leading up to the trial, the press had indulged in a feeding frenzy offering their readers any titbit they could get away with given that Agnes Blunt had been charged with murder.

Wary of contempt, the newspapers majored on what they could safely report – the tragic death of the elderly spinster Arabella Pettygrew. Somehow obtaining the poignant photographs of her as a child walking in Scotland's wild places with her father, their feature writers, milked the nostalgic and human-interest elements of her solitary life down to Noodles: her only companion in a selfish, indifferent world.

The *Hoots Mon* even launched a readers' campaign offering a reward for anyone with information leading to the successful recovery of her cat.

The readers loved it. Arabella Pettygrew would have hated it. The last thing she had wanted in life was the invasion of her cherished privacy. Now, in death, every aspect of her existence was being forensically trawled with the inescapable epitaph that here was a sad, pathetic, victimised soul: the very thing she had fought against so valiantly right up to the end.

In their insatiable hunger for copy, the papers targeted Balmoral Square Mansions sending their reporters to doorstep the residents.

Naturally, cuttings libraries were raided and the macabre murder of Nigel Smail, the suicide of Marjorie Agincourt, and the spectacular drug-house raid were all rehashed across double pages under the banner of *Special In-depth Report*. This microscopic examination did not go down well, especially when the *Hoots Mon* posed the question in a twelve-point headline: *Is this the most criminally heartless street in Scotland?* It didn't need a special meeting of the Garden Association to conclude that the hitherto eye-watering property prices in Balmoral

Square Mansions would dive-bomb as a consequence of such adverse publicity.

The public gallery was packed. Even some of the residents, Peter and Marcy Tweedie, Emile and Fanny Cruducker, the Russian lecturer minus his large dog, had sneaked in to hear proceedings. Everyone who didn't really matter was there: the gawpers, the hawkers, the rubbernecks – a gallimaufry of curious busybodies with nothing better to do.

No relatives were present to see justice done for Arabella Pettygrew. Her brother, Freddie, was still on the run as an accomplice to murder. The only people who cared were the professionals and the homeless men she had helped.

Strawberry and Gunn sat quietly at the back of the gallery surveying the fifteen members of the jury while trying to guess how many would return a guilty verdict. There were eight women and seven men representing a wide range of ages and classes judging from the way they were dressed. At least four of the younger jurors had turned up in jeans and one was wearing tracksuit bottoms. There was one suit on view. He was one of the more elderly jurors with a *Daily Telegraph* under his arm. One guilty vote in the bag, reckoned Strawberry.

Contrary to popular perception, women jurors were often tougher than men in their judgements, but this was skewed by the fact that the accused had two small children – a telling factor if the count was close. Evidence pointing to her guilt was there, but neither Strawberry nor Gunn knew if it would be enough. The decision was impossible to call. Meanwhile, Agnes Blunt sat dwarfed between two sturdy warders as still and unfathomable as an Easter Island statue.

Four days of claim and counter claim went by with the jury becoming increasingly bored by the repetition of laborious minute detail offered by both defence and prosecution counsels.

The graphic photographs they had received – that had initially drawn gasps of horror (one female jury member had actually fainted) – showing Arabella Pettygrew skewered on the wrought-iron railings had been consigned to the bottom of their folders. Even the most assiduous jurors had stopped taking notes on the large A4 sheets of paper provided by the clerk.

Then on the fifth day a woman described as a life-long friend of the accused appeared as a character witness. She said she had known Agnes Blunt both professionally and socially and she expressed the opinion that it would be impossible for such a loving mother to harm anyone, far less murder a defenceless pensioner. The woman was attractive and articulate. Her performance impressed the jury. Some had started taking notes again.

Then the soldiers were called. Four-Fingers Bob and Gav appeared as witnesses for the prosecution the following day. They both wore suits and ties and shoes that shone in the reflection of the overhead lights as they walked to the witness box. The men described the support they had been given by Arabella Pettygrew when they were homeless. They said that she had told them she had been disturbed by the bullying behaviour of her neighbours, particularly Agnes Blunt – although she had not sought their assistance.

The defence counsel made much of their drug problems and 'feckless' lives on the streets. Could such men be reliable witnesses in such a serious case, he asked, searching the faces of each juror as he posed the question.

The prosecution counsel highlighted the men's outstanding army records in Afghanistan citing Gav's courageous action during the ambush and the subsequent award of a medal.

Close. Maybe a draw, thought Strawberry. The judge intimated that the closing statements would be made the next day, the sixth day of the trial. Then the jury would retire to deliberate.

THEY were in the pub. "Fancy a drink?" Strawberry had thrown out the invitation casually, covering up quickly with: "Big day tomorrow. Give us a chance to chew over the trial."

As it happened they didn't speak about the trial at all. On his second pint Strawberry told Gunn what she had already guessed. That he and the rising Scottish curling star Fiona McLuckie were no longer an item.

"She met some banker on the Hong Kong team during the competition," he said, keeping his voice as matter-of-fact as possible. "Sent me a Dear John letter saying she intended to stay over there for a while – see how things panned out." He refrained from saying he had bought an engagement ring intending to propose when she returned. In reality, it was all water under the bridge anyway. He was moving on.

This was clearly the time to exchange confidences. Gunn didn't mind. Remaining sympathetic, but carefully neutral about his break-up, she told him she had been seeing Dougie Nichols.

Strawberry nearly choked on his beer at the revelation. "I had no idea, Brenda."

"I know you didn't, Strawberry. That's the reason I'm sitting here with you." She smiled warmly, her lazy eye twinkling mischievously. Then laughed when Strawberry blushed the colour of his name. "Got you back. I'm the one who usually goes crimson."

"Touché," he said. "I've got a surprise that might have you blushing again. Before he rode off into the sunset, the Singing Detective recommended your promotion to detective."

"And you had nothing to do with that decision, Strawberry?"

"Hand on heart," he mimed theatrically, "I can honestly say that is the case. Rothesay witnessed your investigative skills and dedication to duty at first hand. There was no need for me to point out the blindingly obvious."

Strawberry raised his glass and was gratified to see Gunn blushing furiously.

IT transpired that the sixth day of the trial was not to be the last. As usual, the jury had been lined up in the corridor like school children by the clerk, led into the court in single file, and taken their places, eagerly anticipating their own freedom from judicial sequestration and the imposition of dreadful lunches, when the bombshell exploded.

The judge had barely taken his seat when the prosecution counsel was bobbing to his feet. Adjusting his wig, thumbs gathering his robes self-importantly, he drew himself up to his full imperious height of five-foot three inches.

"M'lud, I must crave your indulgence. Vital forensic evidence has come to light. I realise it is late in proceedings, but I would ask that this evidence be admitted."

The defence counsel was on his feet before his opponent could sit down.

"Your Lordship, I must protest in the strongest possible terms. This is extraordinary behaviour on the part of the Crown. Claiming new evidence at the eleventh hour has the taint of non-disclosure. What is this so-called new evidence? This is the first we have heard of it. I would ask Your Lordship to refuse the prosecution request and proceed directly to the summing-up as scheduled."

The judge sat seemingly contemplating nothing in

particular for a full minute before speaking. "The court will adjourn for one hour. I will see you both in my chambers."

When the court reconvened the body language of the defence counsel was there for all to see. There had clearly been a tectonic shift in the weight of evidence in support of the prosecution case. The judge dismissed the jury until the following morning to allow the defence 'sight of the new evidence' and the opportunity to review its own position.

Strawberry and Gunn hurried back to Gayfield Square where he was called into Bert Rothesay's old office. A new man transferred from England was in charge. Taciturn where Rothesay had been volcanic, his tall rail-thin successor spelled out the information in a thick Brummie accent.

Strawberry emerged triumphant. "It's a complete game-changer," he told Gunn. "You remember the faint print I found on the roof? The one I bollocked forensics for missing?" She nodded.

"Well, it seems they woke up just in time. During a search of Blunt's apartment they found a pair of Blunt's trainers in the back of a cupboard. A section of tread was worn off the sole at the front of the right shoe. When they compared that print to the one from the roof the match was perfect. It puts Agnes Blunt on the roof near the parapet. If the slipper fits, as they say. We got her stone cold, Brenda."

That night Strawberry enjoyed a deep and untroubled sleep, the best he had experienced since the beginning of the investigation into Arabella Pettygrew's cruel and unusual death.

He awoke refreshed to the sound of rain pattering on his bedroom window, but even the end of the long, hot summer and the return to normal Edinburgh weather could not dampen his spirits. In a voice exclusively reserved for the shower, he was singing 'Things Can Only Get Better' at full cat-strangling volume as the hot water washed away the stress and exhaustion of the past weeks. Exiting the cubicle, he dried himself briskly with the towel before towelling down the steamed-up mirror in order to shave. He had applied the shaving cream and was cutting a swathe through the stubble when his razor-hand slipped. It was a nasty cut, but as the white foam turned crimson, Strawberry, oblivious of the blood, dropped the razor through nerveless fingers. For the face in the mirror was no longer his. He hadn't seen her for more than twenty-five years. She had been eight years old then and the face he was staring at now was that of a thirty-five-year-old woman. But he knew her immediately and her harrowed features needed no words – though the voice in his head was hers repeating the same beseeching plea: 'Where are you? I tried to wait. I'm still waiting. Please. Please find me.'

THERE was no hissing, spitting or cursing from the accused when the judge passed sentence. According to time-honoured custom he thanked the jury before taking the extraordinary step of commending Four-Fingers Bob and Gav for their character and military service to their country. "It is an abomination in twenty-first-century Britain that men like you are homeless," he said.

Agnes Blunt went quietly between her turnkeys. There was no sign of her partner, Jim Ross, or the woman who had put in such an impressive performance as her character witness. It later transpired the woman was a complete stranger to Agnes Blunt. She was an unemployed actress who had been paid a thousand pounds by an unknown source to perjure herself.

Strawberry watched Blunt disappear from view as she was taken down to the cells. Ordinary, unremarkable, simply a very nasty piece of work, he thought. But a flutter of apprehension remained. Put the viper in its basket. Nail the lid down. Banish the turbaned shaman and his hypnotic charm. Whip-crack its back. Cut off its head. The snake is dead.

ROMMEL saved 'The Lieutenant's' life. After inadvertently leading Jock Witherspoon into an ambush and near destruction, the rescue dog became the old soldier's salvation.

Witherspoon had eventually recovered consciousness and attempted to break out of the locked shed. But he had been incarcerated for two days and was badly dehydrated. The hospital doctors would later tell him that he was within a few hours of death. As he attempted to kick down the door he was overtaken by a bout of dizziness and fell to the ground.

Fading in and out of consciousness he imagined he heard a scraping sound near at hand. Then the scraping became barking and the very real sound of tunnelling. He raised his head, looked at the door and saw the small chink of daylight at the bottom grow bigger as the earth flew backwards.

Then came the voice: a distinctive Home Counties accent demanding an explanation. "Rommel. What in heaven's name is wrong with you, boy?"

Daylight suddenly flooded in causing Jock to cover his eyes and squint after his long imprisonment. He saw a woman: an attractive blonde. He noticed her hair at the back was held up in a kind of bun with a large comb securing it as she turned to grab her dog.

"What are you doing here?" she asked in the patrician interrogatory tone uniquely employed by a certain class of the southern English.

Christ! She must be strong to force that door, he thought, as he passed out with a weak smile on his face.

TOWARDS the end of that Mediterranean Edinburgh summer, on a morning sharp with the first tang of autumn but glorious nonetheless, the cathedral bells rang out once more.

This time the tolling of the bells was a more sombre affair in tribute to the passing of Holy Smokes.

Justice. Fortitude. Humility. Faith. Temperance. Patience. Holy Fear. Devotion. Hope. Peace. Charity.

The heavenly virtues might also have been invoked for the departure of other souls – good or evil – from Balmoral Square Mansions. Arabella Pettygrew, Marjorie Agincourt, Nigel Smail, Dorothea Hislop, Blessings McKenzie, Freddie Pettygrew, The Glaikit Twin Ginger Duncan, Jeremy Sheldrake, Agnes Blunt, Jim Ross and the poppets. In the case of the above named, the absence of prudence was entirely appropriate.

STRAWBERRY never heard the bells. The cycling detective was off duty and on his bike again. Only this time he had company. Brenda Gunn was with him on his ride around Gladhouse Reservoir on another electric bicycle he had hired for her especially for the trip.

They stopped halfway round looking across the water and the stern countryside to the Moorfoot Hills.

"What's wrong?" asked Gunn as she saw the inexpressibly sad expression on Strawberry's face.

"She's speaking to me again. She speaks to me all the time. It's getting scarier, Brenda. When I was shaving yesterday the face I saw in the mirror wasn't mine. It was hers."

"Who, Strawberry?"

"You'll think I'm mad. Maybe I am. I've never told anyone. I shouldn't burden you with my craziness, Brenda."

"Maybe not, but you can't begin a story and then leave it dangling. I already know you're pretty damned strange, so you might as well go on. I'm a good listener, Strawberry."

He nodded in affirmation and a wordless thank you. "I have a twin. Her name is Charlie. I'm her big brother by seven minutes. She disappeared when we were eight. It was midday on a bright April morning in Princes Street. It was the Easter school holidays and we were looking round the shops. We were in a record store. Those were the days when they still had LPs. I remember the Hibs anthem "Sunshine on Leith" was playing. I was rifling through the U2 albums on one side and she was on the other side looking for the Carpenters' latest. Then she wasn't there."

"What do you mean?"

"Exactly that. One minute she was there and the next she wasn't. I can't be certain, but I think I got a glimpse of her in the middle of a throng of people heading towards the exit. I have never seen her again from that day in 1991. It's as though she disappeared off the face of the earth twenty-seven years ago."

"What about the police? They must have searched for her?"

Strawberry nodded slowly, his complexion suddenly grey in the morning light. "Extensive hunt throughout Scotland and the UK. There was a media blitz for a week or so, but you know how it is. Every day is a new news day. She slipped from the headlines. Just another anonymous missing child, one of hundreds. Revisited after six months and again on the first anniversary – a big splash in the papers. But then, like an old photograph, she simply faded away as though she had never existed.

Strawberry punched his thigh in exasperation. "Only I know, I am absolutely certain she is still alive. In my last dream I saw her face turning towards me for the first time as she was bustled out of the exit. I am her twin. Our connection is telepathic. As children we often didn't have to say a word. We knew what the other was thinking. I know it sounds crazy but I am convinced she is psychically trying to communicate with me. And it's getting spookier.

On the last morning of the trial I was shaving and it was her face I saw in the mirror. Not that of the eight-year-old, but the woman she would be now. It was anguished and desperate, but I know without doubt it was my sister, Charlie, pleading for help. And I intend to find her and the person who took her because that's what we are talking about here – abduction."

Gunn placed her hand on his shoulder. "We will find her."

Strawberry remounted his bicycle. "I made sure your battery was fully charged. We should make it home without any mishaps," he said.

"Thank you, Strawberry," she said. Brenda was listening to music on her mobile. She removed one earbud, leaned over and plugged him in, their heads almost touching. She led the chorus and, despite his pain, Strawberry found himself singing along to 'Together in Electric Dreams'.

POSTSCRIPT

- Rommel vanished and was never seen in Balmoral Square Mansions again. The blonde woman with the chignon adopted another rescue dog – a snappy Pomeranian – she named Himmler.
- 'The Lieutenant' Jock Witherspoon made a full recovery and continues to lead the nightly dog-dirt patrol.
- The surviving Glaikit Twin, Bob Duncan, never managed to get over the death of his brother, but went 'straight' working as a hod-carrier for a local building firm.
- The Tweedies, Peter and Marcy, still enjoy annual vacations in Barbados in order to top up their tans.
- The Cruduckers, Emile and Fanny, remain wedded to exotic 'heads' and live in the same chaotic emporium.
- The Russian university academic still lives in the street and continues to walk St Beaufort Le Grand every evening.
- Agnes Blunt is serving a life term in Cornton Vale Women's Prison near Stirling for the murder of Arabella Pettygrew. Her partner, Jim Ross, has filed for divorce and custody of their children. He sold the

apartment in Balmoral Square Mansions and now lives at an undisclosed address somewhere in the Highlands.
- David Leithhead (aka Davie Affyer) is serving an eight-year prison sentence for the attempted murder of a police officer.
- Freddie Pettygrew's whereabouts are unknown.
- The dark-haired Albanians' whereabouts are unknown.
- Glum Sue's whereabouts are unknown.
- Westport Mary can be seen most days in the Royal Mile advertising a local tattoo parlour.
- Commando continues to be a regular on the buses. Thanks to the intervention of Brenda Gunn he was given a special free bus pass.
- Four-Fingers Bob and Gav are off the streets. They have gone into partnership and – with the aid of a government grant – are in the process of setting up a residential centre to accommodate homeless service veterans.
- DI Dougie Nichols is looking for a new girlfriend.
- Fiona McLuckie did not return to Scotland following the curling championships in Hong Kong. She is currently engaged to a banker and lives on the island.
- Jeremy Sheldrake is living with his parents in Stonehaven. He is a part-time dog walker, but does not include the cliff-top area surrounding Dunnotar Castle in his daily perambulations.
- Marek Wójcik has not been seen in Scotland since his arrest for public disorder and subsequent release. The other Polish workers still enjoy drinking outside

in public places, but they have tempered their exuberance.
- Sandra McGinty still lives in the same flat in Constitution Street.
- Blessings McKenzie is serving a fifteen-year prison sentence for the distribution of drugs and the abduction of Orisa Bullion.
- Dorothea Hislop is serving an eight-year prison sentence for the distribution of drugs and aiding and abetting the kidnap of Orisa Bullion.
- Savannah Bullion returned to her high-powered position in London's Nigerian Embassy.
- Orisa Bullion is recovering from her abduction and forced addiction in the care of her mother.
- J. B. Grimwood is still practising law from his antiquated offices in Leith assisted by his antiquated secretary.
- PC Derek Murch has given up his dream of joining the firearms unit – though he still produces very sweet tomatoes from his allotment.
- PCs Meikle and Dreever remain in the force.
- Laundry is out there somewhere.
- *Furst Meanister's* assistant Kezia's whereabouts are unknown.
- *Furst Meanister* Nicola Sturgeon has left the building.
- Billy Thain is still working as a car mechanic in Coaltown of Wemyss and seeing a new woman who works behind the bar at the Miners' Welfare Club in Buckhaven.
- A black bag washed up on the beach off the coast of France. It had tears on it reminiscent of the type of

marks a cat's claws might make. To this day no one knows whether Noodles used up all of his nine lives, or somehow miraculously survived.
- Strawberry and Gunn will be cycling onto another case in the near future.

ABOUT THE AUTHOR

Born in Edinburgh, A. Gill-Gray is an award-winning journalist who has written for British national and regional newspapers such as the Yorkshire Post and the London Evening Standard. He has earned accolades, including being named National Feature Writer of the Year. Gill-Gray is now pursuing his passion for fiction and is in the final stages of completing a dystopian novel. He lives in Edinburgh with his wife and their Westie, Conrad.